summer snow

Amy Warwick
July 4, 2009
Oakesdale, WA

www.amywarwick.com

summer snow

a novel by amy warwick

Budding Rose Press
Oakesdale, WA

Summer Snow © 2009 Amy Warwick

ISBN: 978-0-615268934

Book packaged by Ink & Paper Group, LLC
Photograph by Greg Hahner
Design by Dorothy Anne Mix
Typeset by Bo Björn Johnson
Editing and proofreading by Lynn Lamb,
    Erin Murray, Robyn Crummer-Olson,
    Katie Mitchell, Linda M. Meyer

Set in 10/14.4 Constantia

First Edition
March 2009

Budding Rose Press
PO Box 379
Oakesdale, WA 99158
amywarwick.com

To Denise

Acknowledgments

Since this is my first published book, I would like to thank everyone who has contributed—even unwittingly contributed—something that helped me achieve that goal.

To the authors of my first reads: Julie Campbell, John Saul, Dean R. Koontz, and Alice Hoffmann. Thank you for creating friends and allies for me during my growing-up years. I only hope that someday my books will have that same effect on even one person.

To Lori, for graciously loaning me your collection of Trixie Belden books. They opened a door in my imagination that I will probably never be able to shut. I could only wish that for all kids today. I'm sorry if you didn't get all of your books back.

To my parents, Lon and Denise Ottosen, and my sister Erika. Thank you for the years on "the farm." It must have been difficult raising two teenage girls, but you didn't let it show. I think I can speak for Erika and I both when I say that those were some of the best years of our lives. I hope they were for you as well; if not, well, now we are raising our children on farms, and you know what they say about paybacks...

To my first reader and every woman's best friend, Mary. My life is richer because of you.

To my first editor, Lynn Lamb of Black Sheep Consulting. Without your care, guidance, patience, and teachings, I never would have done this.

To Lake Boggan, Linda Meyer, Erin Murray, and Dick Warwick. To Lake for her brilliant rainbow-colored aura that called me in. To Linda for never getting irritated with my constant questions. To Erin for having such great insight and not being afraid to tell me what she thought. To Dick for taking me to my first writer's conference. Thanks for helping me in the final steps of this journey.

To my children. Thanks for trying to be quiet. I know it wasn't easy, but it was appreciated.

Last, and definitely the most, to my best friend, soul mate, and husband, Waverly. Thanks for your unwavering faith, honesty, and love. This one is for you.

chapter one

Mystery Abbott

jagged blue-white blade of lightning sliced through the late-night Glendale sky signaling another torrent of rain that pounded the already saturated wheat and barley fields around the little Eastern Washington town. As the latest in a long series of storms moved in over Cemetery Ridge, a seven-acre marble-and-granite-topped plateau just south of town, rivulets of water formed like well-nourished veins, cutting through the morning glory and blooming sage growing up the clay bank in record patches this year. The lightning struck somewhere among the gravestones and the deep sound of thunder reverberated off the hundred-and-fifty-foot walls of the crescent-shaped canyon in which the town was founded. Secretly, townspeople had forever feared that Cemetery Ridge might give way someday and tumble headstones and caskets alike onto the houses below, but in public they bragged that everything in their town was stable and solid.

Just two blocks north, on Carlisle Street, Mystery Abbott unconsciously rolled away from the flashing light and buried her face in John Spencer's back. As with most other nights, she was exhausted from her long day at work, but she awakened a bit when she inhaled the light scent of his Stetson cologne. The enticing smell summoned the realization that she really should wake up and make John leave. Each Monday and Wednesday for the past few months, Mystery allowed him to stay on the condition that he'd leave as quietly as possible by two o'clock. She did not want to alert her children, seventeen-year-old fraternal twins Dana and Janie and four-year-old son Bennie, to his presence in the house.

However, that was not the only reason Mystery forced him to leave under the cover of darkness. She didn't want anyone else in Glendale knowing about their relationship either, least of all her neighbor Olivia Randall, head of the PTA and the biggest gossip in town, or Mystery's mother Maude. The damage either of them could do with that information terrified Mystery and caused her to regress to her younger days of sneaking her beau in and out through her bedroom window.

John knew about Olivia — Liv, as she was called — and Maude, too. After a glass of wine one night, Mystery had confided to John that her neighbor not only hated her, but at one time had suggested Mystery give up her children to a *married* couple who might better be able to provide for them. She also told him of her mother's disdain toward her, and how difficult it was to live just two blocks from a parent who loathed her.

When John pressed for a reason, his deep brown eyes intent on hers, Mystery said only that Maude had felt that way since giving birth to her, when Mystery's father Peter insisted on naming her after his grandmother. Had Mystery accepted one more glass of wine she might have told John the rest of the truth about the origin of her name, but so early in their relationship she was reluctant to label herself. He would find out eventually should their relationship ever come to light. She hoped it never would.

Lately, however, John had been staying later and later, and Mystery couldn't tell if that was her fault or his. She hadn't exactly pushed him out of bed when the alarm clock sounded, and he had been quick to smack the snooze button as well. Here in his arms, it was way too easy to ignore the problems that gnawed at her in her daily life: the kids, her parents, her neighbors, and her overdue bills. She spooned him closer, blocking out the thoughts and wrapping herself around his solid center — at least for a few moments longer.

The storm hit harder, as if it were determined *not* to let her fall back to sleep. Mystery opened one tired eye to read the green lights of the alarm clock, but one of them must have turned it around to face the headboard during their lovemaking a few hours before. *Five more minutes*, she pleaded silently.

But, the wind and rain slammed the house again, as if trying to force their way in. If the wind were persistent enough, she knew it would finally break through. There wasn't much holding it at bay. The house was beginning to cool internally now, and she could no longer ignore reality in favor of fantasy. She could practically hear the roof sagging above and feel the cold air pulling her from the comfort of her warm sheets. Like it or not, she was waking up and John would have to leave.

She turned onto her back, eyes closed, as she listened to the house groan. She had always thought of her house as an old man. It did its best to protect them all, but it was getting weaker and more fragile by the day. The windows were brittle with age and had little caulking around the wooden trim. The fake brick siding had broken off in so many places she could scarcely plant enough climbing rose bushes to hide the foundation. The west corner of the old wood porch sank so far into the ground that Bennie could sit with his legs apart at the eastern corner, roll a ball to the west, and have it return to the same spot between his legs every time.

But worst of all was the roof.

Two years ago, the first leak had appeared above her dresser with a second soon to follow in Dana's room on the other side of the wall. Her mother had told her in no uncertain terms to have the house reroofed, but with few financial options available, Mystery had been forced to nail up a tarp inside the attic and place pans just below the yellowing water rings on the ceilings to catch whatever drips found their way through.

Mystery knew she was tempting fate by not doing more about the roof. Her father had offered to help, as had her boss, Walt Smith. Mystery had been working as Walt's secretary at the local John Deere store for over five years now, and she knew he would help her with anything, but she had paid too high a price for a man's help in the past, and frankly she would rather take her chances on fate.

Thump! Something smacked the house outside. With the storm raging, she knew it was probably a branch from the old willow out back breaking loose and blowing up against the window. It did it again, so she roused herself and lifted her head, looking around in the dark room to see where the noise was coming from.

She brushed something off her cheek and reached over John to turn the alarm clock around. Her fingers came away from her face covered with some kind of gritty substance. She shook her head, which seemed oddly damp. "Oh no," she said, pushing the covers back and jumping out of bed.

As lightning filled the room once again and thunder gurgled an angry response in the distance, Mystery saw the full reality of what was happening. The rain had finally been too much for the roof. Her ceiling was saturated and was plopping bit by bit onto the green wool carpet in her room. For a moment, everything fell away: John, the kids, what her parents would say. She had just failed the only thing that was truly hers and hers alone. Her house. Her protector from storms and her shield from the outside world. Through her neglect she had let it down just like she had done with everything else she held dear.

Her shocked stasis was broken by the sound of someone knocking.

"Mom," she heard Janie say. "Mom, are you okay?"

She looked to John who had awakened from the knock at the door.

"John," she said, "Get up, please."

John was under the covers, looking back and forth from her to the door. She could tell he was confused, not quite awake, but taking it all in. Had she only made him leave an hour ago, he would not be in this situation. As the knocking commenced again, Mystery felt herself move into damage control mode, something she had become accustomed to as a result of being raised by Maude Abbott.

"Get in the closet and stay there. Please," she whispered to John.

"No way." John flipped back the covers and stood tall. Mystery stole a moment to appreciate his body. As a rancher, he was thick and strong around the middle, and although others might call him rugged,

Mystery found his appearance not only appealing, but comforting as well. He stood well over six feet tall, legs apart as if ready to defend them both against some unforeseen attack, and was bald on top apart from a closely shaved ring of black stubbly hair that covered the lower half of his head from ear to ear. On his face was a matching five o'clock shadow and under his left eye was a small scar earned in a battle with a calf and a barbed wire fence when he was fifteen. His body told the tale of a man in tune with nature and in his starkness, Mystery could not help but admire him, despite the situation.

"John, please," she implored, finally turning away.

Another knock sounded, and Mystery rushed around the other side of the bed just in time to hear her doorknob begin to rattle.

"Mommy?" It was Bennie. He sounded sleepy and worried, and Mystery longed to comfort him and put him safely back to bed.

She pushed John and his clothes into the closet before he could protest any further, grabbed her terrycloth bathrobe off the hook, slung it on, and opened the bedroom door. Bennie ran to her, grabbing her around the thighs and burying his mop of curly blond hair into her stomach. On the other side of the threshold, her twin daughters stared at her. Since birth they had been as different as night and day. Dana was taller than her sister by a head, with auburn hair and peach-colored skin painted over with so many colors that it betrayed the loss of innocence Mystery knew had happened long ago. Janie, on the other hand, was fair with tight blond curls that had been twisted into a ponytail before bed, naturally bright red lips, and not a trace of make-up on her sweet face.

"Mother—" Janie started, but Dana quickly interrupted her.

"My pink canopy, Mystery," Dana complained, wiping a smudge of black eyeliner from beneath her eye. "The ceiling is raining crap all over it. You should have fixed it a long time ago. Now everything's ruined."

"Mother," Janie resumed as she stepped between Dana and Mystery to pick up Bennie, "are you okay?"

"Yes, are you?"

Dana threw her arms up in the air and turned from the rest of the family to survey her face in the bathroom mirror next door. Mystery was about to speak to her when she noticed flashing lights swirling through the living room windows. "What's that?" she asked.

"It's the fire department," Dana said, running a brush through her hair. "I called them."

"*What*? Why would you call them?" Mystery nearly shouted. Keeping her cool with Dana was a constant struggle, and under this pressure Mystery wasn't certain she would be able to control herself.

"I called them because I didn't know what else to do," Dana said. She threw the brush at the back of the sink. It clanked against the porcelain and dropped to the floor. Mystery would have to pick it up later. "The whole roof caved in and you wouldn't get up. I knocked. Janie knocked. You went to bed at nine. You shouldn't be so tired that you didn't hear the ceiling fall in and your children knocking!"

"You have no idea how tired I am!" Mystery snapped, momentarily forgetting that she had just stashed John in the closet like an unwanted old coat.

"Well, what did you expect me to do then, *Moth-er*?"

"I expected you to let me handle it!" Mystery retorted. She felt a vicious headache coming on.

She thought about turning to grab some clothes, and apologizing to John, but it was too late. Naked, save for her bathrobe, was not how she wanted to greet the Glendale Volunteer Fire Department now galloping to the rescue, but she had no choice. She cinched the belt around her waist and glared at Dana as she pushed past her to get the door. The lights of the fire engines twirled wildly through the living room.

Dana threw out a sarcastic "*What?*" but Mystery ignored her. It was either that or slap her silly. Ignoring her seemed like the more responsible option.

Knock! Knock! Knock!

"Glendale Fire Department, Ma'am," she heard.

She gave a nervous laugh in spite of herself. Walt Smith. Why was he putting on airs now? He knew who she was and where she lived. She opened the door halfway and peeked out at her boss.

"Hi there, Walt." Mystery attempted a nonchalant grin as if Walt were just dropping over for a cup of tea, but her hands were shaking and she wondered how she was going to convince him that everything was fine without an inspection. Mystery had been Walt's secretary long enough to know how seriously he took his "job." Every time his pager went off, he confided in her how much he loved being the fire chief. "Protecting my friends and neighbors is what part of living in a small town is all about," he would say proudly as he left the store in her charge.

A night like tonight was what Walt Smith lived for. Mystery had yet to get used to seeing Walt in his "yellow space uniform," as she liked to call it. He was a stout man in normal clothes, but in his uniform, he was downright robust. Had it not been for one of his customers hiding out in her closet, Mystery might have welcomed him and his opinion.

"We're fine, really. Dana shouldn't have called."

"Yes, I should have," Dana said, stepping up to the open door. "This whole roof caved in."

Mystery was about to protest again when she heard someone interrupt from behind the men. "Mystery, let us in," Maude said, pushing past Walt.

Mystery felt her heart sink. While other women might be able to run to their mothers for support and advice at a time like this, Mystery had never been so lucky. When Maude Abbott arrived on her daughter's doorstep, it was to gain a confession or explanation only.

"Mother, what are you doing here?" Mystery protested.

"Dana called us, and we called Carl," she said, pointing to Mystery's neighbor who was also fighting his way through the storm to huddle in with the rest of the crew. Behind him Mystery could see his wife Liv and their son Taylor racing to catch up. The Randalls lived kitty-corner from the Abbotts in such close proximity that Mystery felt monitored by the Randalls on a daily basis and dreaded the thought of them coming into her house uninvited now.

"Mother," Mystery cringed. "Why would you call Carl?"

"He was the closest man to you," Maude snapped. "What did you expect me to do?"

The fact that her words and her tone echoed what Dana had said only moments before sent a shiver up Mystery's spine. The fact that they were wrong, sent another. There was a reason that Mystery had a harder time getting along with Dana than Janie, and her mother was it.

"Mother, no," Mystery said, but as usual, Maude Abbott forced her way in and threw Mystery off balance. Before she could regain her composure, Maude and Peter Abbott, Walt, two other men in full yellow turnouts, and the Randall family crowded into her living room leaving muddy footprints all over her wooden floor. Mystery closed her eyes against the invasion, willing John to stay quiet and the rest of the roof to stay intact. *Oh, God,* she thought, *what John must be thinking!*

At that moment Taylor pushed angrily through the entourage, not stopping to speak to Mystery, until he reached Janie, who hurried into his open arms. Mystery's hackles rose as she watched Taylor Randall comfort her daughter.

"Walt," Carl said as he stepped in front of everyone else, "what's going on? Maude said something about a fire."

"No, no, Carl," Maude interjected. "I said *fire department.*"

"I called them," Dana added with smug satisfaction.

"Mystery, is everyone okay?" Carl asked.

Mystery gave an exhausted nod. She couldn't tell if Carl's concern was neighborly or more to do with the fact that he was the only lawyer in town. She thought for a moment he might instruct her not to say anything to these men before talking with him first.

"No fire," Walt said. "Something about the roof falling in. We're just about to check it out if you want to join us."

"No," Mystery said. "That won't be necessary."

"Yes it is," Dana protested.

"Where's the problem, miss?" Walt asked.

Dana was about to get up and show him when Mystery stepped in. "Dana, sit down!" she commanded. "Walt, it's not necessary."

"I can't leave without checking it out, Ma'am," Walt said. "Where's the problem?"

"Walt, for goodness' sake, stop calling me *ma'am,*" she said. "And there isn't anything to worry about. It happened in my bedroom, not in here." She regretted saying so the moment it escaped her lips.

"And mine!" Dana yelled.

"We better take a look," he said, snapping his fingers for the others to follow. Without asking permission, or removing their boots, Walt and his crew, followed by Carl, tramped through the living room and into her bedroom where they clustered in a tight knot just inside the doorway.

Strips of sheetrock and newspaper swayed back and forth from the gaping maw in the ceiling. The swag of dried roses Mystery had bought last year at a yard sale in Kennedy no longer hung above the window, but laid in a mucky clump on the floor. She should have known better. It was a stupid impulse purchase in the first place. She had paid a whopping five dollars for it, but even that small amount could have been better spent on the water bill or lunches for the kids. She deserved to lose it.

She tried to look away from the mess on the bed. Brown and gray water-stained rumpled bedding that only moments before had been covering her and John's naked bodies. No one said a word; they just stared at the mess that was her bedroom. She wished she had thought to pull the covers up. Contrary to popular belief, not one of these men, aside from her father, had ever been in her bedroom before. At least the closet door was still shut.

"Wow," Walt said. "Does that hole go through to Dana's room?"

"I don't know," Mystery sighed. "I haven't had a chance to check it out yet."

"Yeah, she slept right through it," Dana added taking up the rear with the rest of the onlookers.

"This isn't good, Mystery," he said. "Frank, get me an ax." Obedient as a lapdog, Frank Ingram, the science teacher at the high school, was out the door to fetch the fire ax.

"A what? Oh no," she said, stepping between Walt and the dresser.

"Mystery, see that bulge up there?" Walt pointed his finger toward a grapefruit-sized bubble that had a single drip of brownish water dangling from its middle. To Mystery it looked like a woman's breast, but she didn't think that now was the time to share that observation with Walt.

Mystery tucked her damp hair behind her ears and looked up at the slight bulge in the corner of her room. It was nothing. She could handle that in the morning with a butter knife.

"I can deal with it, Walt," she said.

"Not on my dime," he said. "I can't leave until I know you and the kids are safe. I could be liable."

"Walt, I'm not going to sue you for what happens in my home. You know that."

"No, no," he agreed. "But it's my job."

"It's not your *job*. Your job is managing the office at John Deere. You're a *volunteer* firefighter." Mystery gulped hard as she saw the hurt look in Walt's eyes at her accusation of him being *just a volunteer*.

"I'm sorry, Walt," she whispered.

Frank returned just then and handed the ax to Walt with a simple head bob. Walt responded in kind and then pointed at the hole with the business end of the ax to punctuate his next sentence.

"Either way, I can't leave here until I know that ceiling is secure. That bubble will pop, with or without my help, but I would sure sleep better tonight if you would let me take care of it before I go."

She thought about how long John had been stuck in the closet listening to her neighbors talk about her and her house and it made her want to crawl under the bed and hide, but she couldn't bring him out. Not with these people here and not under these circumstances. What would they think of her if they found out she had a lover that none of them — aside from Walt — had ever seen before?

"Okay," she said. "But only that. Nothing more."

Walt took two more muddy steps on her carpet, and then reached up with the pick end of the ax to poke the bubble. It popped easily and wet newspaper, once used to insulate the ceiling, splattered down onto the already soggy carpet. The hole now seemed large enough to drive a Volkswagen Beetle through it. Wind swirled through the shingles and boards on the roof and tangled Mystery's hair. Goosebumps rose on her bare flesh beneath her bathrobe as an oblivious Walt sized up his work with apparent satisfaction.

"Are you done now, Walt?" she nearly whispered.

Walt came back to reality and placed a gloved hand on her shoulder while calling into his chest-mounted radio. "This is Unit 220," he said. "No injuries. No need for backup. Current resident will follow up with repairman in the morning."

"Canceling backup, 220," a man called back. He almost sounded disappointed.

Mystery turned around to see Liv surveying the damage in her bedroom. Walt put his arm around Mystery, giving her a reassuring squeeze, and Liv quickly looked to the floor. Her thin arms were visibly shaking in the cool air, and Mystery was certain this wasn't the kind of situation Liv Randall had ever been in before.

"Some people never learn," Maude informed Liv, as they turned to follow the men out of the room. "I told Mystery not to buy this house, but she didn't listen any better about that than she did about anything else I ever told her as a child."

Mystery ignored her. Everyone was just about out of the room and on their way to check out Dana's, when Mystery heard a series of muffled sneezes from the closet. She closed her eyes and prayed that Maude's snide commentary had been loud enough to block out the noise. No such luck. Alert as a fox, Maude spun around to scan the room. Liv stopped too, but thankfully the others had moved on.

"What was that?" Liv asked.

"What?" Mystery said, feigning innocence.

For the first time all night, the house was silent, as if it too were awaiting an explanation. Thunder grumbled just north of them as the storm swept through to the other side of town.

Maude looked toward Liv and then back into the room, ears perked. "Yes," her mother said, moving past Liv. "I heard it, too." Before she could stop them, Maude and Liv were back in her bedroom. They stood there as if hoping to catch a rat in a trap.

"Someone sneezed," her mother insisted. "Is there someone else in here?"

"Good God, Mother, it could have been anything with that hole up there."

The wind and rain were now cascading into the room. Mystery

looked at the bed and cringed. Both sides of the covers were flung back. The men might not have noticed, but a woman would not overlook a detail like that. Her mother turned to her.

"Where is he?" Maude demanded.

"Who?"

"There's a man in here," she said, pointing to the bed, "I can smell him."

Mystery stiffened at her mother's outright accusation.

"You can *smell* him?" she scoffed.

"Don't get smart with me," Maude uttered behind clenched teeth. "There's a man here and I know it."

"There's no one here," Mystery lied, watching Liv's gaze dart around the room.

"Good god, *Mystery*," Maude mocked, accenting her name as though this were a fitting opportunity to remind her of what her name really meant. "Will you ever learn? You can't have random men staying the night while the children are here. It's no wonder Dana is the way she is."

"*What did you just say?*"

Thankfully, Dana was too busy giving Walt and crew a tour of her bedroom to hear what her grandmother had just said.

"Come out," Maude demanded, ignoring Mystery's outrage and addressing the room. "We know you're in here!"

"Mother, stop it, and get out of my bedroom."

"Who is he?"

"Well, he's not Carl or Walt or Frank," said Liv behind a hand raised to her mouth. "Thank goodness they're accounted for."

"Jesus Christ, you two," Mystery exploded. "I don't have random men sleep over — married or single."

"He's in there, isn't he?" Maude accused, pointing a bony finger toward the closet door.

"It's really none of your business what *or who* is in my closet," Mystery said. "Now get the hell out, both of you."

Beneath her anger, Mystery trembled with fear — of her mother, of John's discovery, of being caught in a lie — but she was not about to show that in front of Liv and Maude.

"Not until I see who it is this time," Maude said.

"*This time?*" Mystery barked. "When was the last time?"

"I'm sure I don't know," Maude said, "but from what I gather this isn't the first."

Maude started for the closet door, but Mystery stepped in front of her. She was taller than her mother by at least a foot so she glowered down at her in an attempt to make her back down.

"Move," Maude ordered.

"No."

"Mystery, let's not make this any more awkward for our family than we have to," Maude said glancing at Liv. "Now move." Maude stood on her toes to emphasize the command.

"Not on your life," Mystery replied.

With that, the door behind Mystery flew open, smacking her in the head. John, now fully dressed, cowboy hat in hand, stepped out of the closet.

"Mystery," he said, "thanks for trying to protect me, but this is ridiculous. Are you okay?"

She nodded at him as she rubbed the back of her head. He was taking the blame for her and he didn't even know what he was getting into.

"See?" Maude said to Liv, dabbing at the corner of her eye as if emotion was about to overwhelm her. Mystery wanted to laugh at her dramatics but knew better.

Maude turned back to John. "Who in the world are you?"

"I'm John Spencer," he said, "and I'll be damned if I'm going to stay in that closet while you are out here berating your daughter this way. You two ladies *must* be Maude Abbott and Olivia Randall."

Maude scowled at Mystery before turning back to John. "That's right," she said, hitching her chin up a notch.

"Well, *Maude*," he said with quiet intensity, "it's no wonder Mystery wanted to hide me in the closet and away from her family."

"I beg your pardon?" Maude gasped.

"And you," he said, turning to Liv. "Didn't your mother teach you any manners?"

"Wh-what?" she said. Liv's eyes were like saucers now.

"You need to leave. This isn't your house."

Liv's lower lip quivered and the veins in her skinny neck bulged as if she were about to choke. She looked to Maude, but Maude was too busy staring John down to notice the tag-team request. Mystery was about to reiterate John's words when Dana appeared at the door.

"Mother!"

Janie plowed into the back of her sister as Dana stopped short just inside the threshold. Behind them, Taylor, Walt, Carl, and Frank practically tripped over themselves in Mystery's tiny hallway. Mystery tried to find her father, but he was nowhere to be seen. Scanning the room, she saw the painful truth on the faces of everyone in the group, the kind of truth that only surfaces in the most shocking of circumstances when you have no time to regain your composure. Mouths agape with scornful looks told Mystery she had once again screwed up royally.

"Hi." John's deep voice broke the silence as he nodded to Dana and Janie. It seemed soothing in comparison to Maude's shrill squawks of disapproval. "I'm John Spencer. I'm your mom's boyfriend." He extended a hand to Dana and waited. Janie reached around to shake it and then turned to pick up Bennie.

"I'm Janie and this is Bennie," she said.

"Nice, Mystery," Dana snarled. "Really nice."

"Well, I never," said Maude.

"Maude." They all turned to see Peter moving purposefully through the crowd. "Let's go."

"But Peter..." she protested.

"Let's go, dear," he repeated calmly. "We can talk to Mystery in the morning. John, nice to meet you."

"Sir," John said, nodding his head to Peter.

With his fur-lined cap in hand, Peter gave a quick wave to Mystery and John, collected his still-protesting wife, and wound his way back through the crowd.

"Mystery," Walt said, stepping forward. "If there is anything I can do. If you need a place to stay..."

"No thank you, Walt," she said sheepishly. "I think we'll stay here."

"Okay then. John, good to see you."

Walt flashed a sympathetic smile at Mystery, nodded, and left. She didn't want to have to explain this to him tomorrow.

"That goes for us, too," Carl interjected. "Liv, it's time to go. If you need anything, Mystery, remember you are always welcome to stay in our guest room." Mystery nodded and moved closer to John as Liv brushed by.

"I'm going to Grandma's," Dana announced, turning to leave without waiting for a response.

"Mom," Janie added. "Taylor wants me to come over there tonight."

"That's fine, Janie," Mystery answered, trying to quickly compartmentalize the litany of comments and barrage of condescending gazes that she and John had received from the group.

"Nice to finally meet you, John," Janie added.

"You too, Janie," John said. He stood his ground, solid and fearless as Mystery's family and neighbors filed out amongst whispers. The gossip mill would be abuzz in Glendale tomorrow, and once again, Mystery Abbott would find herself smack dab in the middle of it.

chapter two

Liv Randall

As Liv drove down Main Street just after noon to head up the first PTA meeting of the summer, she thought the town looked like it had been hit by a tornado. The streets were covered with clumps of wet cotton that the storm had stripped from the old trees in the cemetery and rained down upon the town. Branches covered roadways and made it difficult to drive. A month ago, Liv would have welcomed a frog-striper like the one that came through last night, but this late in June with a forecast calling for at least another week of the same kind of weather, not a single person in Glendale was smiling about it, least of all Olivia Randall.

This was the sort of climate that irritated her most. She had grown up in the rain — real rain that came in off the ocean. These short interludes of precipitation that the locals referred to as "real gully-washers" were mere sprinkles compared to the sky-rolling monsoons of the Pacific Coast, yet the people of Glendale still acted like they had a clue as to what a real storm was. It was a joke. When Liv was a little girl, she swore the sky had the power to suck up the entire ocean and pour it out on the sand dollar beaches and planked houses lining the gentle curves of the coastline. She hadn't seen that kind of rain in five years now, ever since Carl had dragged her to this dryland farming community.

Sometimes she felt like ditching her briefcase full of info about PTA dances and bake sales, running full tilt to her car, and driving as fast as she could back to the ocean and the love of her grandparents.

Liv had grown up in Seattle, but her fondest memories were of summers spent at her grandparents' beach house in Ocean Shores. Those were the times that had shaped her. While her friends were sweating it out in the city, Liv was reveling in sandy warm days and cool coastal nights in front of the fireplace at her grandparents' cottage. She had never seen a love like her grandparents', and as far as she could tell, she never would again. Her grandfather had been a lawyer, a hard worker who had little time for anything other than work and his family. For her and her grandmother, he would stop anything.

During the summer, he had moved his practice to their beach home. If a client had to be seen, it would be at the house, and discussions would be conducted during long walks on the beach while Liv and her grandmother dug for clams or played in the surf. Carl had been a paralegal in her grandfather's firm, and just as her grandfather had planned, Liv and Carl fell in love — or at least Liv thought it was love at the time.

She hadn't dreamed that Carl would want to move to the other side of the state and set up his own law practice in a town with only a handful of potential clients. When his Aunt Ilsa died and Carl inherited her house in Glendale, he put down the first month's rent on his Main Street office before he even told Liv they were moving. It was only afterward that Carl informed Liv and her grandfather that he had always planned on moving back to his hometown instead of continuing at the firm.

Liv swallowed hard to try and block out the memory as she walked through the double glass doors of Glendale High School. Tall and thin, Liv was dressed in a knee-length black skirt and a short-sleeved paisley blouse. Being summertime, she opted for diamond accents instead of pearls and pulled her blonde hair into a perfectly tied French knot.

Since becoming president, she had instructed the women of Ma Bell to dress in semiprofessional attire for the meetings in order to set a standard for the rest of the women in the community.

From inside, she could feel the eyes of her peers staring out at her. They had to wait for her to start the meeting—after all, she was the president. Though Taylor was no longer in school, she had agreed to stay on for one more term. It was unofficial of course, a vote obtained simply from the six women of Ma Bell, the local gossip chain that Liv had unintentionally joined after moving to Glendale. Carl wanted her to be friends with them, but Liv hadn't meant to become their leader.

Over the years, Ma Bell had become something akin to a secret city council. From the privacy of their own homes, with their husbands at work and children at school, the women of Ma Bell could change people's lives. With their joined voices, votes for mayor and council members were swayed, committee meetings held or cancelled, fundraisers arranged, surprise parties planned, mischievous husbands punished, and children controlled.

As Liv entered the room that served as both cafeteria and high school auditorium, the women of Ma Bell stood to greet her. They all had curious looks on their faces and Liv wasn't certain if it was due to her tardiness or to their unquenched thirst for firsthand knowledge of what had happened at the Abbott house last night. Liv stepped back as they approached. Although she was used to them acting like paparazzi whenever there was potential gossip to be shared, Liv was still trying to decide what to tell them. Gossiping was a mixed bag for her; she liked being a member of the "in crowd," even if that crowd was in Glendale, but she had always fancied herself a better person than that as well. Today, she had placed a rubber band around her wrist to snap if she gossiped.

The mayor's wife, Jane Caldwell, whom Liv considered her best friend in Glendale, held the door open. Next to her were Dora Sievers, the realtor who worked next door to Carl; Melinda Smith, whose only claim to fame was that her brother, Walt, owned the local John Deere; Faye Gordon, the town clerk; and, of course, Emily Cardinal, the hairdresser and goody two-shoes who was only allowed to be involved because she had gone to school with the other women. Liv tried not to show her disapproval at their jeans and tennis shoes. Emily was even dressed in shorts. She took what solace she could in the fact that they at least remembered to wear blouses and immediately went to the coatrack to stow her jacket and umbrella.

As her friends began to approach, Liv looked toward the other women in the auditorium in an attempt to carefully remind the gossipers that here was not the time nor place for gossip, but before she knew it, they had swooped around her like a group of starving crows and she was forced to face their questions. At first there were "innocent" inquiries about the welfare of Liv's troubled neighbors — the probing ones that gauged how far they could safely go in front of the other women in town.

"Are the kids okay?" Faye asked.

"They're fine," Liv whispered. "Janie, of course, had to come and sleep at our house last night." At this first deviation from her intended course, she reached carefully beneath the cuff of her sweater and gave herself a quick snap.

"Anything to get close to Taylor," Melinda cackled.

Emily asked if Mystery was okay. She always rooted for the underdog and Liv abhorred her tactic of oh-so-innocently fueling the fire. Even without the aid of the rubber band, Liv kept the information she gave to Emily limited at best.

Liv nodded her head and moved the entourage to the coffeepot, far away from the ears of the other PTA members. She helped herself to coffee and a couple of the chocolate chip cookies that Melinda always brought. She knew she would pay later for eating them, but she thought they might help her to keep her mouth shut. About twenty other women waited in the auditorium for Liv to finish gossiping and start the meeting. She knew they really didn't mind the wait; it wasn't like they had much else to do.

"What about the others?" Jane asked.

"Well," Liv said, rubbing her wrist instead of snapping it. "Dana hightailed it off to her grandmother's house, but Mystery insisted that she and that little boy stay at their home for the night."

"After the roof fell in?" Dora Sievers asked. "Poor baby."

"I know," Liv said. "We even offered to let them stay in our guest room, but she flat out refused." She felt a twinge of guilt at the exaggeration. Carl had actually offered, not her.

"He's not really a baby," Emily said.

"He doesn't talk," Jane added. "Sounds like a baby to me."

Liv was silent as the women began to giggle. Though she would not admit it—nor would she tell them why—their making fun of innocent little Bennie made her want to cry. She thought about saying something, knowing full well the weight of her opinion on these women, but then decided against it. That would only create a new series of interrogations about Liv's inner feelings and personal inclinations, and the thought exhausted her.

Within ten minutes, the jury of Mystery's peers released the verdict. Guilty as charged. Guilty as usual. Liv felt her stomach eagerly digesting the cookies. She held fast to her wrist, practically cutting off the circulation. She had promised herself she wasn't going to stir the gossip stew with these women, and yet here she was not only participating but adding key ingredients to make the poisonous concoction complete. "Look ladies," she said under her breath, "it's really none of our business what happens at that house, is it?"

"It isn't?" Melinda looked startled.

Liv shook her head. She didn't want to take this any further. She felt guilty enough as it was.

"I heard there was a man there last night," Jane added before Liv could escape. The other women turned their heads toward Liv for confirmation, as if they had a right to this information.

"Look, honey," Jane said, smiling sweetly, "we know how you hate to gossip, but it's not really coming from you, is it? Melinda dug the truth out of Walt under the guise of concern for a fellow neighbor. That man is way too easy if you ask me."

Melinda rubbed her knuckles on her shirt as if she had just won a bet. All five heads swiveled toward Liv for an apparent confirmation, and the action caused the rest of the women in the crowd to turn their heads and watch. Liv said nothing. Something seemed to be lodged in her throat. She gave a single slow nod.

"Who was it?" Jane asked.

"I don't know." Liv tried not to sound exasperated as she moved out of the circle. "He's not from here. John something. Look, ladies, this is neither the time nor the place; you know that. I need to get this meeting started, okay?"

Melinda, Dora, Emily, and Faye took their seats as instructed, but Jane put her hand on Liv's arm.

"Wait, Liv," Jane whispered. "I need to speak to you."

"Not now, Jane," she said. With that, she motioned everyone to their seats and sounded the gavel. All faced forward in compliance.

"Let's start with old business, shall we?"

Heads bobbed in unison. Liv could see the women in the audience straightening their wrinkled tee-shirts as they stared at her. They sat on tan metal folding chairs that Melinda had arranged before the meeting. Liv leaned forward into the microphone. With only twenty-five women in attendance, she really didn't need the thing, but it helped to keep them in line. "Ladies, is there any old business?"

The members looked at each other and back at Liv shaking their heads. Liv watched the five women of Ma Bell, in particular. They too looked back and forth at each other, but no one said a word.

"Well, we can all agree that it was a successful year. With our fund-raisers, we were able to sponsor two dances and a talent show. There was some controversy over having a woman oversee the boys' locker room after P.E., but as we have seen, Jane has done a fabulous job, and I'm sure we all concur that the young men have acted with a little more decorum since having a mother just outside the door. These are just a few of the successes that we were involved in last year. The list goes on and on."

The women congratulated themselves and each other. Liv rapped the gavel on the table and motioned everyone to silence. "Therefore, let's move on to next year." She looked down at the agenda she had typed the night before.

"As you can see, there are no student representatives in attendance. That is because it is time to elect three new student representatives for the upcoming school year, and as is traditional, they are not allowed in the meeting during the election process. You should all have received a voting ballot from Secretary Melinda when you walked in the door. Yes? On it, you will see that I have compiled a list of reputable students to choose from. There are six on the list; please mark three and pass your ballot to your neighbor on the right. Melinda will collect the papers and have the tally by the end of the meeting. Are there any questions?"

Heads turned to each other as if waiting for someone to respond.

"Good," she said, again striking the gavel on the table. "Please take a minute to mark your ballot and hand it down."

"Excuse me."

Liv looked up to see Jolene Cartwright standing with her hand raised. Jolene was about twenty-five and had been hired the previous year as the high school history teacher. The PTA had voiced concern about hiring such a pretty girl to teach impressionable high school boys but the superintendent overrode them, and the women of Ma Bell had been less than supportive of her ever since. When the teachers were given mugs of Hershey's Kisses on Teacher Appreciation Day, Jolene was accidentally left out. When chaperones were requested for the history class's midterm field trip to the museum in Kennedy, nary a parent volunteered. However, instead of alienating the young teacher, it seemed to spur her on. She was the only teacher in attendance at the summer PTA meeting.

"Yes, Ms. Cartwright," Liv smiled, "what is it?"

"I just wondered about the elections for the upcoming year."

Liv held up her ballot. "Well, now is a great time to ask."

"I wondered why the parents' positions aren't posted on here."

Liv looked out at the audience and cleared her throat. A few women leaned over and whispered in their neighbors' ears. The women of Ma Bell watched Liv closely. She looked at Jane who mouthed, "That's what I wanted to tell you."

"Well, dear," Liv glowered, "I know you are new to this school, but we do things a little differently here than they do in bigger schools. There wasn't enough interest by other parents when we held elections, so we just stopped having them all together."

"Um," Jolene said, "I'm not trying to be rude, but since your son has graduated, it seems that maybe it's time to see if we can get some interest from other parents who still have children in school."

"Just because Taylor has graduated doesn't mean that I have no interest in what happens at this school," Liv replied. "It's a small town, Ms. Cartwright, and as they say, it does take a village, now doesn't it?"

Jolene smiled, and the women in the audience tittered nervously. Liv waited for the laughter to abate without striking the gavel this time. "I have no plans to abandon my post or the interests of the future generations of Glendale."

"Oh my," Jolene drawled, "I'm not talking about abandoning your post. I'm simply saying that maybe you should step down as President and let someone else give it a try."

There was a collective gasp from the audience. This time, Liv brought the gavel down hard on the table and the group fell silent. "Have you had any other parties interested in my position?" Liv asked sternly.

"Yes," Jolene said, "actually I talked to quite a few ladies who still have kids in school who would be quite interested in learning how to run the PTA."

"Really," she smiled. "Like who?"

Jolene was silent for a minute and glanced around the room. The women seemed to recoil into their seats. No one made eye contact. "Dora, for one."

"Really," Liv said, staring directly at her so-called friend.

"And Jane."

Liv gripped her gavel firmly, but her hands shook nonetheless. "Well," she said, "it seems there was a little meeting before the meeting today, now wasn't there, ladies?"

No one said a word. Liv straightened her papers. "Okay," she said coolly, attempting to maintain her professionalism. "In keeping with tradition, nominees are not allowed to be in attendance at the meeting while elections are being held. Melinda, I am going to leave, as are Jane and Dora. Please take over the meeting and hold the election in my stead."

"Actually," Jolene interrupted, holding up a pencil, "you don't need to go. No one has nominated you yet."

Liv felt the glob of chocolate chip cookies and coffee beginning to churn in her stomach. It had gotten to the point that she didn't have to stick her finger down her throat to throw up anymore; all it took was a little stress, and anything more than a cracker would come up within minutes. She carefully put down her gavel and picked up her purse. Without looking at Jolene or the ladies of Ma Bell, she exited the building and headed for her car.

A familiar gray cloud appeared in her peripheral vision; one that had haunted her on and off since she was a little girl. Every time she was scared or stressed, gray tentacles of darkness slithered around her temples and threatened to blind her. When she was younger, she had thought that everyone had a cloud, but as she grew older, she learned differently. She had no idea what would happen if the cloud ever did move in for good, and she didn't want to find out right here in front of all of her so-called friends.

"*No*," she crooned, rubbing her brow as her head began to ache. She closed her eyes to try blocking it out so that she could at least make it home.

As she got into the Jetta, she noticed a small yellow sticky note just above her windshield wiper.

"Just remember, the way you treat others has a way of coming back to you."

Liv crumpled the reminder and quickly drove way. It took only five minutes to get home, but in that time, the cloud had already reached her temples. She took a deep cleansing breath and dashed inside. Thank goodness, Taylor was not home. She dropped her purse on the bathroom floor and leaned heavily over the toilet, inhaling deeply and holding the rancid breath in her lungs. As she let it out, she purged the coffee and cookies. Her throat burned from the acid, and strings of liquid poured from her nose as she heaved again. She felt relieved as the last of it came up. The pain sent spasms through the muscles in her back, and her thin arms quivered, but it was over; her stomach felt empty. She stood up, flushed the toilet, and pulled the pink hand towel embroidered with the initials IR—Ilsa Randall—off the towel hook. Wiping her puke on those towels was always the best part of her day.

Liv took a deep breath and walked back to the kitchen. She couldn't smell anything except vomit. There was nothing cooking and no candle burning. She grabbed a bottle of Windex from beneath the kitchen sink and squirted a few random shots in midair, then sat down at the table to wait out the shaking in her forearms. Finally, she removed the rubber band and shot it at the wall. When she felt steady enough, she got up and went to the sink where she noticed that Taylor and Janie had left their crusted cereal bowls. She consoled herself a little with the fact that at least they had eaten Cheerios instead of one of those damned sugared cereals Taylor had convinced Carl to buy for him. There was even a browning banana peel on the counter. With any luck, Taylor hadn't been completely corrupted by the Abbott girl.

She forgave the dirty bowls, rinsed them, placed them in the dishwasher, dropped the banana peel in the trash, and then lit the apple pie–scented candle above the sink. It didn't smell exactly like homemade, but there was no time before Carl would be home to create the real effect, so the candle would have to do. She opened the east-facing window and scowled at the willow branches and leaves that covered her yard. She didn't have trees in her yard, simply because she hated the mess, but Mystery Abbott had one, so she suffered anyway. Liv turned away from the littered yard and took another deep breath. The wind and rain were still coming from the south, but maybe it would swirl around enough to force the smell of the candle through the house.

She looked over at the hole in Mystery's roof and shook her head. The willow in the back was flailing around like a flag in the wind and Liv could see a depression on the south side of the roof over Mystery and Dana's bedrooms. Still no repairman. Mystery Abbott was never going to take responsibility for her actions, and that was what irritated Liv about her the most. Liv turned to her to-do list on the stove. Every morning at six o'clock she made a list of tasks with the intent of finishing it by six at night. As she began to review it, she contemplated making one for Mystery and tacking it to her front door just to see what actually got done.

Liv's list was numbered one through fifteen. She had ten things crossed off in random order already today. She drew a thick line through number eleven: *PTA meeting*. She probably wouldn't have that on a list again. Anger swelled in her at the thought of what they must be discussing right now, and whom they had voted in to take her place. She closed her eyes and relaxed, opening them only to refocus on the tasks at hand. Below *PTA Meeting* was *laundry*. That was always the last thing she finished. It took so long to be able to cross that one off.

She threw another load in the washer, emptying the basket. She was tempted to reward herself by crossing it out, but she knew better. It wasn't done until the last load was folded and in the dressers, with Carl and Taylor's morning clothes laid out on top, just as she had done for the past eighteen years.

Number thirteen was dinner. She pulled the thawed hamburger from the fridge. Meatloaf. It was always meatloaf for them on Thursdays. For her it would be celery and pretzels. After devouring the cookies, it was all she deserved. When she turned back, she saw Carl pulling in the driveway earlier than expected — *the beauty of being self-employed,* Liv fretted, *and sometimes the curse.* It seemed she always had to be prepared for him. She surveyed the kitchen. Candle burning. House clean. She couldn't wait to tell him about that little witch at the school today.

Carl walked in through the sliding glass door, placed his briefcase on the dining room table, and stripped out of his shirt and slacks. Just like every other day, he left them on the floor right where he dropped them.

"How was your day?" Liv asked. She couldn't avert her eyes from the pile of dirty clothes. She wouldn't be crossing off number twelve today either.

"Awful. How was yours?"

Adrenalin surged through her at the thought of telling him about the betrayal of these women he so wanted her to be friends with, but she decided to be polite and ask about his day first.

"Well, I had a PTA meeting. Why was yours awful?"

"People are stupid. Other than that, it's privileged information, as per usual."

Liv hated that saying. Every night he came home and said how horrible it was at the office and every night it was privileged, "as per usual."

"Anyway," he said, "how are the gossips? Bet you all had a field day with Mystery after last night, didn't you?"

"Well," Liv said, slicing into a potato, "the woman brings it on herself."

Carl scratched himself as he walked to the bathroom to pee. He didn't even bother to close the door. "Why don't you gals just lighten up on her?"

"Huh?"

"You heard me." She could see him wagging his penis above the toilet. She would have to clean the bathroom again before she could call that one done as well. "I suppose you told everyone about John."

"Why would you say that?" she asked.

"Come on, Liv."

"They already knew. Melinda's husband told her, and she told Dora, and so on down the line." Liv was waving her knife around in the air for effect.

"What's with the smell in here? Are you sick?"

"Oh, well, just a little," she stammered. "Don't worry about it."

"Well," he retorted, "I worry about it when you're fixing our dinner. You know I can't afford to be sick right now."

The toilet flushed and blocked out the rest of what he said.

"Why not? What's the big deal at the office?"

He came out dressed in purple jogging shorts and a yellow Glendale Bobcats sweatshirt. "I already told you, it's privileged. I'm going for a jog to run this off, and after that I'm back at it."

"Back at what?"

"I have to go back to the office," he huffed. "Meeting a client, and don't wait dinner for me. I'll be late. I'll catch ya when I get back from my jog. Okay?"

With that, he was out the door. No *I love you*. No *Goodbye*. Not even a *Screw you*. Liv's hand clenched around the knife. The gray cloud rematerialized in her peripheral vision. She didn't get to tell him about Jolene Cartwright. She didn't get to tell anyone.

The blackening cloud nearly obscured her vision. She closed her eyes, carefully placing the knife on the cutting board, and tried to convince herself this wasn't happening again. It had taken almost six months to make the cloud disappear after Carl moved her to Glendale and forced her to live among Ilsa's things. She opened her eyes and looked out through the wet, splattered cotton on her kitchen window. Carl had always been the reason the cloud came back.

chapter three

Dana Abbott

regnant black clouds drooped over the town, and to Dana Abbott it seemed like this stormy spring might never end and the warmth of summer might never begin. On Main Street, hidden in the alley next to The Watering Trough, Dana's thoughts wandered as she studied the interior of the steamed-up Chevelle while Cord Galloway kissed her neck. Her eyes trailed the diamond pattern of the black velvet upholstery he and his brothers had recently installed on the ceiling. There wasn't a single pleat or seam showing. It looked nice. She moved her head so he could kiss the hollow between her neck and collarbone — exactly where she liked it.

Whenever Dana closed her eyes, she saw Mystery and John rolling around in the bed together, so she kept her eyes wide open. This morning, after crying out her misfortune to her sympathetic grandmother, she had reluctantly gone back home, back to a bedroom still drying out from the previous night's roof collapse. The sight of her mother disgusted her. Wide hips, bleached-blond hair, and sagging tits. She had sulked in her bedroom for most of the day, moving and throwing things strategically to keep Mystery aware of the fact that she hadn't forgotten about the unrepaired leak in her ceiling. It really hadn't been that bad—nowhere close to as bad as it had been in her mother's room. The hole above her bed was about the size of a lemon where the water had formed a bubble and eventually popped. Her canopy had sustained a few water stains and some flecks of white paint. All of it could have been handled with a vacuum cleaner, a little Spackle, and a washing machine, but she didn't tell Mystery that.

Finally, just after four, the phone rang and Mystery called to Dana to answer it. She had complied, but not without a well-placed glare and a proper door slamming. It was Cord; he wanted to meet downtown at six. Dana said nothing to Mystery until just before walking out the door, and then only: "Get me a new canopy." She hoped Mystery got the clue that her carelessness was going to cost her dearly.

Cord moved his hand up underneath the back of her shirt and effortlessly unsnapped her black bra. When she first spied him driving into town just over a month ago, he seemed like the type of guy who knew how to undo a bra, but after a few fumbled attempts, she concluded that—as with all the other boys—she would have to show him how.

This time, he moved his hands up to her bare breasts. She was warmed by the anticipation of what she and Cord finally might do.

She placed her hand on his head and guided him further down into her black tank top. His attention to detail was causing butterflies in her stomach, and for a moment she had a vision of being naked on top of him. He reached back down and pulled the tank over her head. She leaned her head back to help him continue the work on her neck when the tank got caught on her ponytail. She felt her hair pull up from the base of her neck as the black scrunchie pulled free. She gave an inadvertent yelp and Cord pulled back, as if he was afraid to hurt her.

"Sorry," he whispered.

The butterflies subsided as a result of his lame apology, but she wasn't ready to give up hope altogether. This was far better than he had ever done in the past month. This time only, she pulled the shirt and bra off for him and readjusted her ponytail. It wasn't a mistake she would let pass twice.

He reached his hand down to her shorts and fumbled with the button. When he tried to remove her shorts she decided to give him one final test. It was a test he had yet to overcome.

"Cord," she said breathlessly, "no."

Cord obediently rolled off of her and sat up in the back seat, running his hand through his hair and staring out the fogged window.

"I'm sorry, Dana," he smiled touching her arm. "Are you okay after last night?"

Dana studied him dispassionately. *What an idiot*, she thought.

Although he looked like a man on the outside, he was obviously nothing but a boy. For a moment, she thought about telling him where he went wrong. After all, he had finally gotten her far enough that she was almost past the point of maintaining her normal rules of conduct that had served her so well in the past.

Cord turned, smiled at her, and placed his arm around her. "Are you okay?" he asked again.

"Yeah," she said dryly, staring out the window across the street at Carl Randall's office. "I'm fine." She zipped her shorts back up and pulled on her shirt, leaving her bra off for the time being. With any luck, maybe this time he would get excited enough to just take what she knew he wanted. Instead, he sat there and stared out the window at the Bank of Glendale. Dana reached over him, grabbed her purse, and fumbled for her smokes. She knew how much he hated when she smoked in his car, so she reached up, rolled down the front window a crack, and lit one.

"Dana—" he said.

"Yes?" she snapped, rolling her eyes.

"Nothing."

Just last week she had decided to dump him. She was going to do it today, but then he had given her a beer and kissed her neck. She would at least have to wait until the beer was gone.

"I'm going away for the night," he said.

"Oh," she answered as she blew the smoke from the car. She watched a ring of it drift back and encircle his face. He waved it away.

"That's why I wanted to see you. I know you've been through a lot with your roof problem and everything. I just wondered if you would like to come with me?"

"It's not my problem, it's Mystery's. Where are you going?"

"To Idaho. My old house." He had asked her that three times in the short time they had been dating, and she had always found a reason to say no. She didn't know why Cord's family had moved to Glendale from the reservation in Idaho, and she hadn't asked.

"I can't go," Dana said, feigning regret. "I have a job."

"You do? Where?"

"Starting tomorrow night at The Trough."

"The restaurant?"

"The one and only."

Dana watched as the lights came on in Carl Randall's law office. She could barely make out who was in the window, but it looked like Carl and a woman. Maybe it was Liv. "Who's that?" Dana asked, letting another stream of smoke blow into him.

"Who?"

She rubbed the steam from the window and moved her head so he could see out.

"I don't know," he said. "Says *Carl Randall, Attorney at Law* on the window."

"I know *that*. Who's the woman with him?"

He looked again. "Maybe it's his secretary or something?"

"After five? I don't think so."

"I don't know," he said again. "It's none of my business."

She shook her head and rolled down the front window to get a better look. Just then a car flew by and splattered mud and rain in her face.

"You bitch!" Dana yelled.

She pulled her head back inside while Cord choked on a laugh.

"Are you okay?" he asked.

"Fine." She looked back out the window. One oblivious Liv Randall had just flipped a u-turn on Main Street and parked her red Jetta toward them on the other side of the street. Dana wiped her face with the edge of her shirt and waited for Liv to get out and head for Carl's office, but she didn't. Instead, Liv stayed in her car and stared straight ahead through the slapping windshield wipers. She was holding a cigarette to her pouty red lips, and it made Dana feel connected to her. The window was cracked open, and even through the rain, Dana could see the smoke winding its way up to the sky.

Though she and Liv rarely spoke, Dana knew the woman better

than she knew her own mother. Ever since Liv had moved to Glendale, Dana had spent numerous nights at her window ledge studying the nocturnal habits of her neighbor. To Dana, Liv Randall was everything that any girl would want to be. She was beautiful, skinny, and deeply mysterious. At night, Dana would open her window and smoke countless cigarettes while she watched Liv go back and forth between rooms turning on lights, cleaning windows, sweeping floors, washing dishes, dusting, and straightening pictures. It was like having her own private theater with an ever-changing movie of a single beautiful character.

On nights of the new moon, with the black sky accentuating the action in the lighted Randall house, Dana would see Liv fall asleep up against the wall with a glass of wine in hand. Other nights she would watch her slam stuff around in an apparent fit of rage until the wee hours of the morning. It was a wonder she didn't wake the whole household. Most nights, Liv would outlast her and Dana would fall asleep with her head resting on the window ledge breathing in the sweet scent of the roses Mystery had planted next to the house. Sometimes Dana made it long enough to watch Liv's final ritual. Just before retiring, Liv would walk outside in her flowing nightgown or bathrobe and remove a hidden pack of cigarettes from beneath the red Adirondack chair on the deck. In the last five years, that was the only time Dana had ever seen her smoke, until now. Dana was certain no one else knew about Liv's nightly habits, not even her own husband.

This evening, she didn't seem to want to hide it. Through the drizzle of the rain on the car window, Dana could see that Liv's wavy hair was tied back in a scarf that extended the length of her back. She reminded Dana of Grace Kelly in *To Catch a Thief*. It was one of the few old films that she had ever seen. Dana decided that with the first money from her new job she would have to buy a scarf. Liv slammed her hand into the steering wheel, inhaled deeply from the cigarette, turned off the ignition, and sat there staring at the lit window of her husband's office. Finally, she opened the door and got out.

"Well," said Cord. "Are you ready to go?"

"Shh!" Dana admonished. She threw her cigarette out and continued to watch.

Liv was wearing a short black skirt, similar to one of Dana's, and a free-flowing paisley blouse that opened just enough in the front to catch a glimpse of her black lingerie. She dropped her cigarette as she stepped out in the rain and opened a small black umbrella. Dana wondered why a woman like that didn't work. Any man would hire her right on the spot, even without the qualifying credentials. Liv walked into Carl's office and slammed the door.

Through the large fishbowl window that perfectly surrounded Carl's desk, Dana could see Carl talking with someone. Liv must have stormed in because they both stood quickly to their feet. Through the wind and rain, Dana could tell the other woman was tall, slender, and had long blond hair. Dana thought she looked like a hooker compared to Liv.

"Who are you watching?"

"Liv Randall. The attorney's wife."

"Who?"

She motioned him to look at the name on the window again. "Says *Carl Randall, Attorney at Law*," she mocked, as if he were incapable of reading or remembering it. "The lady who stormed in is his wife. They're our next-door neighbors."

"So what," he said. "Let's get out of here. Do you want to go to the cemetery and have a couple more beers?" He reached over and put his hand up her shirt. "Maybe we can try this again," he grinned.

She pulled his hand from her top and continued to watch the fishbowl.

Liv was standing between Carl and the lady, flailing her arms about something. She looked like she was flying into one of the rages Dana had witnessed late at night. Liv Randall was pissed. Dana wished she could figure out what they were yelling about, but Cord kept babbling in her ear.

"Do you want to get out of here?"

"No thanks," she snapped, brushing his hand away and shoving her bra and cigarettes in the front pocket of her bag. "Look, I think I'll just walk."

"It's pouring rain out there," he said. "I can't let you go home like that. What will your mother think?"

"She doesn't think anything, Cord," she said. "Let her be my problem, okay?" She got out and he rolled down the window.

"Are you sure?" Cord persisted.

"It's not that bad out here," she said. "Do you think I'm so sweet that I'll melt in the rain?"

He laughed and leaned up for a kiss goodbye. "I'll see you when I get back," he said.

"Sure," she said. "Call me when you're done up there." As he drove off, she sprinted across the street before Carl or Liv caught sight of her. As she stepped onto the sidewalk, head down to avoid the rain ruining her mascara, she nearly ran into Dylan Masters, the new cop in town.

"Careful there, young lady," he said, grabbing her arm to steady her.

She latched onto his forearm for balance. It was big and strong, and when she looked up into his deep hazel eyes, her heart skipped a beat and she imagined herself kissing him. She had seen him around a couple of times but hadn't taken the time to really check him out. Today, in his black uniform and black baseball hat embroidered with *Glendale P.D.*, she thought, *Now this is a serious man who would know how to take charge in the bedroom.*

"I'm fine," she muttered, standing up straight and brushing her hands down her shorts.

Heart beating out of her wet shirt, Dana said a quick goodbye to him and dashed off through the alleyway before steam began to rise from her skin. Spying on Liv would have to wait today. She had a new conquest on her mind.

chapter four

Janie Abbott

The evening after her family's roof caved in, the local weather station advised all farmers and gardeners to prepare for the worst. It looked like frost within a week. To Janie it didn't seem possible; to the gardeners, covering tomatoes or leaving a sprinkler on over their corn all night seemed like an admission of defeat. Janie's skin crawled as she wondered if this weird weather was Mother Nature's idea of a high school graduation present. It seemed like a portent of bad luck that might follow her forever.

As Janie walked to the treehouse that she and Taylor had built in the old willow in her backyard, she sighed at the thought of everything that was changing this summer. Her mother had a new boyfriend, her sister had a job, and no matter how she tried to avoid it, Taylor Randall was using their graduation as an excuse to push her into having sex with him.

Sometimes she wondered why she had dated Taylor for so long. He had lived kitty-corner from her for the past five years and in the beginning, unable to venture very far from their neighborhood without permission from a parent, they were all each other had. He had been fun back then, always smiling and paying attention only to her and the imaginary world inside their treehouse, but when they hit fifteen and Taylor got his driving permit, things began to change. That was when Taylor's beautiful blue eyes began to wander, and Janie saw Taylor putting his hand up Emmie Parkins' tee-shirt behind the bleachers during a football game. That was also around the same time that Taylor tried to have sex with her for the first time.

Ever since then, her relationship with Taylor had been dependent upon whether another girl was available or not. Many times Janie told him off and swore to herself she wouldn't believe his lies again. But he always found a way to get her alone in the treehouse where he would swear that "the other girl meant nothing." She was all he wanted; "best friends forever and always," until she promised to believe him, through the tears and kisses and uncharacteristic sexual patience. And every time, she wanted desperately to believe him because Janie knew something that Taylor didn't. She knew that once they let go of their imaginary world in the treehouse, childhood would be over for good, and Janie wasn't ready for that.

As she climbed the slick wood ladder at dusk, she wondered what Taylor wanted now. He had seemed content with her since graduation even though she had yet to fulfill his sexual desires. As far as she knew he didn't have another girlfriend, but his increasing sexual persistence was a mixed bag for Janie. There were times — when he held her face in his hands just right while kissing her deeply, or he hugged her tightly to him and whispered how much he adored her in her ear — that she wanted to be free and just tell him to do it. But something always stopped her, and to this day she couldn't define it. She stopped him every time he reached for the button on her pants. There was a voice from someplace deep in the back of her mind that screamed *No!* But then the voice faded and she couldn't tell what it said next. It was either *Not with him*, or *Not now*, but whatever it was, that little voice did the trick. She had finally decided it was all of those sex education classes at school, the ones that warn you about AIDS and pregnancy. The classes didn't seem to bother Taylor, but they sure had put the fear of hell into Janie's mind, and she hated them for it.

Wind and rain blew nonstop through the old wooden slat walls of the treehouse as Janie lifted the hinged trapdoor. Taylor sat in the beanbag chair as usual, sandals kicked off. He had propped his feet up on the green milk crate he had stolen from outside The Watering Trough last year. A lighted lantern had been placed in the middle of the crate and Janie noticed that Taylor had hair on his toes. She had always liked watching him grow up. Without a father in her life, Taylor was the closest male around to learn from.

"So, what was so urgent?" she asked as she stepped in and sat down on the blanket in the corner.

"You," he said. "I wanted to make sure you were okay after last night."

He didn't move directly to her as usual. Instead he watched her intently, twitching his feet back and forth.

"I'm f-fine," she stammered. She wasn't sure if he was referring to her roof falling in or how reluctant he had been to take no for an answer in the spare bedroom of his home while his parents slept just one door down, so she kept her answers brief.

"Janie," he said, "you don't have to hide things from me. You know that. I know you. You were quiet all morning."

Janie shrugged in apparent agreement. It was cold out, so she wrapped the blanket around her shoulders. Taylor reached into his jacket pocket and pulled out two cigarettes and the matches he had swiped from his mom's stash under the Adirondack chair on their deck. Janie reached out for one of the long cigarettes and let him light it for her. She wasn't going to continue smoking when she grew up, but life in their fort was a separate world. She leaned back against the semidry wall, and took a deep drag off the smoke.

"I'm fine Taylor, really," was all she could think to say.

"Janie, you're not okay." He peered out the porthole window he had cut out last year. His lips turned upward in an arrogant smirk and for a moment Janie had an urge to slap it off his face. She looked over his shoulder at a picture of their freshman homecoming dance and reminded herself not to be a bitch like her sister. He was obviously just trying to help.

"I know you better than you know yourself sometimes," he mused. "You are not okay with last night. I know you're embarrassed and afraid. You don't have to hide that from me."

She mulled over possible responses as she watched puffs of cigarette smoke rise and swirl into nothingness as the wind invaded their private hideaway. Finally, she decided to just ask him what he was referring to.

"Taylor, what are you talking about?"

"Come on, Janie. I'm talking about last night at your mother's. The roof and that man who looked like a pedophile hiding in her closet."

"Oh, that," she laughed. When she looked up, she saw the puzzled look on Taylor's face. In the yellow glow of the lamplight, he looked dark and angry.

"What the hell else would I have been talking about?"

"Nothing," she whispered. She thought about John and her mother in the bedroom last night. She supposed he was right. Maybe she should be embarrassed. After all, their roof had fallen in because Mystery didn't have the money to fix it properly when it needed it. Now everyone in town was probably talking about the fact that her mom was having sex with some guy while they were all sleeping in the other rooms. "Okay," she allowed, "I guess it's a little embarrassing."

"Jesus Christ, your mother! What the hell was she thinking hiding some man in the closet?"

"I don't know," Janie hedged. "Maybe she just didn't want us to know that she had a new boyfriend."

"Yeah," Taylor laughed, "and with good reason. Did you see that guy?"

"Who, John? I liked him. I thought he was kind of bold."

"Bold?" His condescending laugh lurched him forward and he practically spat the words in her face. "Janie, he was hiding like some kind of fugitive right after he gave it to your mom. What kind of man is that?"

"I don't know," she retorted, "why don't we ask *your* mom. It looked like she got a pretty close look at him."

"Janie," he said apologetically, "I'm sorry. I really am. You know how my mother is."

"She's a witch, Taylor," Janie snapped. She rarely defended herself against Taylor's accusations that she was too innocent to realize the true severity of any given situation—because she thought he might be right. However, when it came to comparing their families, Janie felt strong in her defense, and Taylor had learned years ago that she wasn't going to back down.

"I know," he said, "I know." He moved off the beanbag chair and sat next to her, careful not to upset the lantern. He lowered the wick leaving no more than a candle's light in the room, then he put one finger under her chin and moved her mouth toward him. She didn't stop him this time. Goosebumps rose on her cool flesh as he kissed her deeply.

"We are not them, you know."

"I know," she said.

He turned in front of her, gently moved the blanket off her shoulders, and pulled her down beneath him. "You know I love you, right?" he asked stroking her hair from her forehead.

"Yes."

As with most answers to Taylor's questions, Janie spit out the perceived correct one before she even thought it through. She had learned that with Taylor Randall it was often easier to give him what he wanted than to question what he believed. The wind began to howl as the rain spattered further into the treehouse.

Taylor began kissing her neck and Janie felt the pressure of his arousal against her thigh. His body was so heavy on top of her that she began to feel claustrophobic. She looked for the hatch, but his feet were sprawled out over the top of it. She wiggled to gain some breathing room as he put his hand down to her hips and pulled at her shorts.

"Taylor, wait a minute!" She tried to squirm from beneath him, but he persisted. She moved her leg up to stop the unzipping of her shorts and tried to move out to the side.

"Taylor!" She laughed in a feeble attempt to keep the situation light. "Wait just a minute."

"Why?" he asked between kisses.

"Because I don't want to, that's why!"

"Yes, you do," he whispered into her ear. "You just don't know it yet."

"No, I don't!" She pulled her leg up tight against his groin and pushed him hard to the side. He reluctantly moved and let her up. He looked down at the floor and ran his hand through his thick blond hair. She turned the light of the lantern back up. In the harshly illuminated room she could tell he was disappointed, so she sat down next to him and rubbed his arm for reassurance. He turned cold blue eyes on her.

When Taylor got mad his eyes reminded Janie of the blade of a knife, hard icy blue, with enough hate to slice right through if provoked. However, when he felt loving toward Janie his eyes were as inviting as the blue waters of the ocean, seemingly full of promises that almost any woman would spend a lifetime trying to believe.

"I think you should marry me," he blurted out.

"*What?*"

"You heard me."

Janie looked away from Taylor and tried to stifle the giggle bubbling up inside her. Marriage? Why would he say marriage? They had just graduated from high school. She figured Taylor would spend the next years sewing his wild oats while she stayed on with her mother in Glendale. Anything beyond that had not entered her mind. When she looked back she noticed the softness had returned to his eyes, and she absentmindedly released the pent up air she had been holding.

"I thought you were going away to college at Evergreen," she said. "That's what the superintendent told the whole town at graduation."

"I changed my mind," he said. "For you."

"For me?"

He beamed as if he had just given her an unexpected birthday present. "I've decided that instead of going to college, you and I are just going to leave. You can't stay here and live in a house full of holes with men coming in and out at all hours of the night, and I can't live without you."

"Taylor, you're insane. And my house isn't like that."

"That's not what I saw last night," he said, shaking his head for effect. "And, I'm not insane. I've thought this through very clearly. I've always wanted you Janie, and you know that. The only reason that we aren't together right now is because we're not married. I know you; that's why you won't have sex with me."

She felt a contraction in her groin. She wouldn't admit it to him, but what he said excited her more than anything he had said or done in the past.

"Let me ask you something," he said, "and be straight with me, please."

"Okay?"

He took their smokes, disposed of them in a beer bottle, and then sat across from her. "You're still a virgin, right?"

"What—? Taylor Randall, that is none of your business."

"It's something you'd tell your husband, isn't it?"

She thought about it for a few seconds. She hadn't considered having a husband before. Well, not really. He was right, but she didn't really want to let on that—besides him—she had only kissed one other boy.

"Yes. I guess I'd tell my husband."

"Well, tell me then."

"Why? You're not my husband," she laughed.

"I just want to know."

She hesitated, and then sighed. "Yes," she admitted, "I'm still a virgin."

She could see his muscles relax as he heard the answer. "I thought so. You are such a good girl, Janie. You are exactly what I want in a wife."

"A virgin? You want—"

"No. Yes. Well, someone who has waited for *me*." He placed his hand on her knee and smiled over at her.

"Okay," she said. "Let me get this straight, you want me to marry you so you can sleep with me?"

"Well," he laughed, pulling her to him again, "unless you're going to give it up right now."

"Taylor!" Janie pushed away and sat back down.

"I'm kidding," he said. "I think we would be great together. Both in bed and out."

"How would you know? Besides, if you want to sleep with someone you can have any girl in town. I'll call Dana right now."

"Dana," he laughed, "she's been used by every man in Glendale. It's the same with every other girl. We both know that I've made some mistakes in the past, but I've learned from them. I don't want any of those girls. They're way too easy."

"Is that supposed to convince me?"

"No." He gazed steadily at her. "Look, I don't want to keep any secrets from you. You know what I've done in the past. I just needed some time to try out a few things before I figured out exactly what I want."

"And *I'm* exactly what you want?"

"Yes," he smiled.

She thought about it for a minute. Her heart fluttered at the thought of marriage and a stable family life. Imagine, Janie Abbott marrying a Randall in Glendale. Her future would be set in stone, and maybe that was love—the security of knowing her future. Maybe Taylor was right and he just knew it before she did. After all, who would be better suited for each other than two people who had spent most of their teenage lives together in a treehouse? She wanted him right now more passionately than she ever had. She leaned forward and kissed him. She thought about just leaning on top of him and trying it out, but then she remembered what he had said. He liked that she was a virgin. It meant something to him.

"Okay," she agreed, "I'll marry you."

"Great!" He clapped his hands together as if they had just agreed to terms on a new car and then yanked her up into a hug on their knees. A sharp nailhead drove into her skin, but she didn't move.

"This will be best for you," he said, "you'll see. Now you won't end up poor and alone, like your mother. I'll always make sure of that."

chapter five

Mystery Abbott

I t was June 21—the first day of summer, the longest day of the year, and for Mystery, *two days after my damn roof collapsed.* The wind had blown cold off Cemetery Ridge all day, and from her perch on the ladder, Mystery shivered as she took a moment to look around. The temperature was barely into the sixties and was predicted to make a sharp fall by the end of the week. She knew that in 1897, city founders had carved out Smith Boulevard right beneath the canyon wall in order to avoid the persistent wind, but it was no use. Trees were strategically planted around houses, and lilac trees had been placed on the eyebrow of the ridge as a break, but no matter what the founding fathers did, stormy weather had found its way through then just as it did today.

The wind lost a little speed as it maneuvered in and out of back-yards, scaled fences, and stole between the privacy hedges on Oak Street. Mystery could see her parents' house from atop her own. The wind jangled the numerous wind chimes that ran the length of Maude and Peter Abbott's deck. She watched as her father trotted across the driveway from his shop to remove each one of them. He would have to rehang them when the wind subsided, she knew, as he had yesterday and the day before that. After being married to Maude for thirty plus years, he had a system. Just after their marriage, when the wind chimes were hung, he had hammered two nails into the end of a broom handle and placed it next to the porch so that he could reach each chime and pull it to safety without having to climb a ladder.

The broom had been sitting there all of Mystery's life, assisting her father like a faithful partner and friend. Many years ago, he had secretly named it "Kate" after his high school girlfriend—the one that got away. Mystery had overheard him talking to "Kate" one day, and teased him into confiding in her.

As the wind and scattered raindrops increased, a gust reached Carlisle Street and slithered indecently up Mystery's blue cotton pants. It was not a good day to climb a ladder to the roof. Not a good day at all. But she had told Walt she was taking one more day off to deal with this, so that was exactly what she was going to do. Walt had asked to help but she refused. Just because she was a woman didn't mean she couldn't fix her own roof, so wind or no wind, she had gone up. She did, however, agree to borrow a new ladder from the store. He had told her to keep it, but she refused and promised to return it when she came to work the next day.

As she clung to the ladder in the blustery wind, she recalled the realtor who had tried so hard to keep her from looking at this house. Fifteen years ago, both her mother and the realtor who had the shop where Dora Sievers now worked, had tried to sell her a doublewide mobile home on Oak Street that was in much better shape and quite a bit larger than the little house on Carlisle Street. The doublewide had a separate breakfast nook where she and the girls could watch the sunrise, and she'd be closer to her parents just in case she needed help with anything... but she couldn't do it and she knew better than to tell them why. The little house had one thing the doublewide did not—a fireplace. That was it; there was no other reason. Since she was a girl, she had loved the little house with the fireplace and the long porch on the front. She could see herself and her kids cozy in a big easy chair while she read a J.R.R. Tolkien book in front of the fire, and that was enough to seal the deal.

Though her mother cursed her for wanting to raise the girls in such small quarters, Mystery was determined to have the little house. There were three quaint bedrooms, one bathroom in which you would knock your knees against the bathtub when you sat down on the toilet, a living room with the wood stove, a kitchen, and of course, the porch. So, it leaned a little on one side. Someday she would have the money to fix it. *That someday is still looming out there like a carrot*, she thought, *leading me on like the hopeless dreamer that I am.*

Mystery surveyed her roof from the relative safety of the ladder, searching for any excuse not to have to mount the slippery asphalt shakes above. There were no visible holes in it from the front, thank goodness; that left just the large one in the back.

She stuck a foot out and carefully climbed the boards she had nailed down the last time she had been brave enough to check the roof: three one-foot-long boards to the top and a five-foot-long one just below the ridge. She hadn't been up here since then, but the boards still held strong. Heart thumping and palms sweating despite the chill wind and rain, Mystery perched on the roof peak and pulled hard on the rope dangling from her tool belt. Just below, the tarp swayed on the end of the rope as she pulled it up over the gutter. About a foot down on the backside of the roof, Mystery got her first close-up look at the hole that led to the damage sustained inside the house. The water had pooled for so long in the attic that the outside hole was not quite as large as the one in the house. As her eyes adjusted to the dark interior, she saw what looked like a gnarled old arm poking up from inside the hole. She tentatively reached in, wet asphalt shingles rubbing against her bare arm, and forced her hand to secure the clammy limb. She gave a strong yank and pulled it up. The branch was about three feet long and a good five inches in diameter. As it emerged, she saw fresh willow leaves still attached. She turned and glared at the old tree out back, thinking about just how much Liv would love this. Her fault again. She shouldn't have allowed her anger toward Liv to affect her decision when Carl offered to cut it down. *Pride goeth before the fall*, she recalled from Bible school. She should have listened better.

She discarded the branch and gazed deeper into the hole. Nothing. The vast space was as unrevealing as the night. She realized she should have turned a light on in her bedroom before she came up the ladder. For now, she would have to deal with the outside of the attic; the inside would come later. Unfortunately, probably much later. She had cleaned up the mess in her room as well as Dana's. She had washed the canopy and rehung it above Dana's bed. As far as Mystery could tell the canopy looked as good as new. Better in fact, considering it was the first time it had been washed in years, but that would not placate Dana. She would still demand a new one, but with Dana's attitude recently, Mystery wasn't about to cave in.

She grabbed the hammer and undid the plastic casing around the tarp she had allowed Walt to give her and inadvertently let the empty packaging fly in the wind. Just as Mystery knew it would, the plastic landed in Liv's yard. Mystery would have to get that later.

She folded the tarp in half to double its strength and spread it over the hole with her foot. She squeezed her thighs tight to the roof peak and hammered nails for all she was worth. Some went straight through the wet asphalt and rotted boards, others bent in half. By the time she was done, she had forced twenty nails through the tarp around the hole, and it looked secure. She looked up into the now driving wind and rain and smiled. Really, she hadn't felt this effective in a long time. She had turned toward the ladder to get down and retrieve the plastic packaging now smacked up against the rose bushes in Liv's front yard, when she heard John's truck rounding the corner on Carlisle.

She tried to straighten her snarled, wet hair and wipe the mascara from beneath her eyes, but it was pointless. Before she even had a chance to complete a quick cleanup, John hopped out of the truck and walked to the rear of it. She felt self-conscious in her rain-soaked shirt, now plastered to her skin. This wasn't a wet tee-shirt contest, and she wasn't twenty-five anymore. She felt like an idiot, perched on the peak of her caved-in roof. She figured that he would not be back until next Monday and loathed having him see her — or her house — in such a deplorable state. A man like John should know that no woman worth having would ever be caught dead in a situation like this. In fact, she was sure Ma Bell would be happy to tell him that very thing.

She thought about getting down, but she didn't want to get that up-close-and-personal with him right now. Maybe he would just yell a friendly hello and she could tell him that she would call him later.

No such luck. He grabbed a tool belt from the back of the truck and strode toward the ladder.

The situation was ludicrous. She was trapped now, and a mad little laugh escaped her as he climbed to the roof and mounted the makeshift wooden steps. She prayed they wouldn't give out beneath him.

"Hi," he smiled.

"Hi."

He straddled the roof in front of her. Mystery knew that if they sat any closer terrible things would happen. She might just lean in and kiss him right here on the rooftop. Rain dripped off the rim of his cowboy hat as if he had just rode in off the range to take her in his arms and make her live *happily ever after*. He looked from Oak to State Street.

"Wow," he said, "great view from up here. If you look at it from just the right angle, Glendale's not a bad looking little town."

Mystery looked around again. She saw the tar-black tops of the buildings on Main Street and the peaked asphalt roofs of the houses on State Street. The multicolored colonial style houses looked to Mystery like a block-long patchwork quilt. Smoke streamed nearly horizontally from a few chimneys. It didn't seem right this time of year. Glendale looked more like a depressed suburb of Seattle than an Eastern Washington farming community.

"Yeah, but you don't have to live in Glendale," she laughed.

"I would if you'd let me."

She ignored the comment for now. John lived alone on a ranch outside of Kennedy. He had no idea how stifling it could be living in a town the size of Glendale—beautiful or not.

"What are you doing here? It's not Monday."

"You didn't call me this morning like you *promised*," he goaded, but it was with a smile.

"Promised?" she repeated.

"Yes, you promised."

"I'm sorry," she laughed, "I guess I'm not very reliable."

"Well," he said, hoisting his tool belt in front of him, "I thought as much, so I decided not to wait. I'm here to help."

"John, I already told you, this is my roof and my problem." She placed a hand on his arm hoping her words were taken as gently as she intended.

"And I already told you that it doesn't have to be," he answered just as gently.

She looked away toward her parents' house to evade his understanding eyes. The lights in the living room had been shut off, but she swore she felt the cold, disapproving gaze of her mother boring down on them.

"John, please —"

"Mystery, I'm not leaving you to go home and let you handle this alone. I can't do that."

"Yes, you can."

"No, I can't and I won't. You're a strong woman but not strong enough to do this alone, and I don't see anyone rushing to help you."

"No," she laughed. "That is the truth of it." She looked off to the south again. She didn't want him to see the tears of embarrassment welling in the corners of her eyes. Thunderclouds rolled northward and there was no end in sight. "Don't you have some cows to tend to or something?"

"Already tended," he said. "I'll have to go back by tomorrow."

"Tomorrow?"

"Yep. My dad will feed them tonight and tomorrow morning, I'll have to go back around midday, but then I'll come back, and so on and so forth until we are finished."

"Until *we* are finished?"

"Look, I'm not taking no for an answer, so we can sit here and argue in the rain or we can get this roof fixed."

Mystery thought of Bennie and Janie inside the house, or the *half house* as she had come to call it. They didn't deserve this. "Okay," she finally agreed, "but please, no staying the night."

"We'll see," he said with a smile.

She let it go for now, but by five o'clock she would have to reinforce it. "So, what can I do to help?"

"Help?" he asked.

"Yes, help," she nodded. "It is my roof and my problem."

"Okay, okay," he allowed, "but first off, we have to make a deal. This is not just *your* problem anymore, got it?"

He was smiling at her. She loved it when he smiled. He reached up, pulled a gooey strand of hair from her cheek, and tucked it behind her ear. He failed to move his hand at that point, and out of habit, she leaned into it. It seemed so odd that they had only been seeing each other for six months and yet she felt more comfortable with him than she ever had with anyone else.

"Okay," she conceded, "so, where do we begin?"

John looked at her a moment longer, seeming to have something to say but then shaking his head with a rueful grin, he let her off the hook. The edges of the blue tarp flapped back and forth in front of them.

"Well," he said. "You did a fine job, but unfortunately, that is not going to hold in this wind."

Mystery grudgingly nodded her head.

"And," he continued, "there's no telling right now how bad it is underneath."

"That's what I was thinking," she agreed. "I looked in the hole, but I couldn't see anything."

"I'm going to have to tear into it, you know."

Dollar signs formed like sunspots in front of her eyes. He didn't seem to notice. "This is going to get expensive, isn't it?"

"Well, that depends," he said carefully. "If it's just on this side of the roof, I can take care of it easily, but if it's not, then it could get expensive. We'll have to cross that bridge when we get in there."

"John," she said reluctantly, "I..."

"Look," he interrupted, "let's get down, get the stuff that I brought, and take a look at what we're dealing with before we worry about the cost."

"I don't work like that, John. I don't have the luxury."

"Well, let's just get started then, and if you get worried about it at anytime after that, we'll talk about it then, okay?" John rubbed her arm and then climbed down the ladder without waiting for her to respond. Drained from too little sleep and too much worry, she reluctantly followed. From the back of the truck, he retrieved a crow-bar, a large piece of plywood, and a roll of asphalt roofing.

"Where'd you get that?" she asked.

"Kennedy," he teased. "After you kicked me out and *failed to call me,* I decided to bring you a present. It's not roses, I know, but I thought it might make you feel better."

"John," she breathed, "thanks. Really."

"You're welcome."

"Hi there!" Mystery turned around and saw her father approaching with her mother close at his heels. Her temporary relief instantly turned to dread at the sight of Maude. This time she wanted to crawl under the roofing and hide. This was not going to be good.

"Hi," John said without hesitation. He extended his hand to her father as if they were old buddies, and tipped his hat to Maude as if no angry words had been exchanged between them. Mystery waited for bloodred lasers to shoot from her mother's eyes, but it didn't happen. Maude Abbott said a simple hello. It was her mother's lack of visible hatred that worried Mystery the most. Maude had to be holding out for something. Mystery tried hard to avoid looking at her, but her eyes kept venturing curiously over to her mother's face. Her father was smiling broadly at John, though Mystery could see a nervous tick just at the edge of his right eye. He was stepping out on a limb here, and Mystery feared that somewhere under that coat her mother was hiding a chainsaw.

"I saw you and Mystery on the roof and thought I'd see if you need anything."

"Well," John nodded, "I was just about to rip into the old roofing and see how bad it is. There's another crowbar in the back of the truck if you want to help, Mr. Abbott."

"Peter," Maude interrupted, "I don't think that's a very good idea in this weather, do you?"

Mystery could practically hear the *vroom-vroom* as her mother revved up the saw.

John and Mystery waited for her father to agree with his wife and decline to help, but instead he turned and looked at Maude. There seemed to be some kind of silent conversation going on between the two of them. Eventually, Maude looked away and smiled sweetly at Mystery. Then Peter Abbott looked up to the sky and allowed the rain to fall directly into his eyes. He patted Maude's shoulder and replied, "This looks like the best day to work on the roof to me."

"It's okay, Dad," Mystery interjected, "I was going to help John."

"No, no, we got it. John, could you just point me in the direction of that crowbar."

"You bet, sir."

The two men walked off, leaving Mystery alone with her mother for the first time since the closet incident. Her heart pounded as it had when she was a young girl caught stealing a ten-dollar bill from her mother's purse. And Maude looked like she was contemplating whether to spank her or ground her.

"How are you this morning?" Maude offered.

"Good," Mystery replied. "How are you?"

"Fine. I've been worried about you."

"Oh, that's nice, Mom but really, I'm doing okay."

"Mystery, can we please step out of the rain?"

Mystery felt a twinge of guilt at her lack of manners. "Sure," she said, walking to the porch. "Where's your umbrella?"

"I didn't bring it. Your father thought that a walk in the rain might be nice."

"*Really?*" Mystery asked, "I'm shocked."

"We walk in the rain a lot. I'm not made of sugar, you know."

"I know," Mystery said carefully. She had a hard time holding her tone and suppressing a laugh.

"Mystery," Maude continued, "can we please sit down?"

"Sure," she said amicably, knowing this was going to be a long one. Maude Abbott wouldn't stand through a negative conversation. It was better to get a child at eye level to be sure they heard what a piece of crap they were. Mystery reluctantly took her seat at the far end of the porch swing from her mother. Maude grabbed the red and white checked throw blanket from the back and smoothed it out over her black pleated pants.

"I've always liked this swing," she said politely. "After you moved in here, I almost had your father make me one, but that would be a little crazy, wouldn't it? To copy your daughter, I mean."

"No," Mystery said. "That's how I get most of my best decorating ideas."

"I like that you keep a blanket here as well," Mande continued. "It makes it cozy."

"Th-thanks, Mom." The shock of being treated like an adult was scary and she was afraid she might lose her guard if she wasn't careful, so she changed the subject.

"I'm sorry. I'm being rude. Do you want some tea or something?" Mystery half rose from the swing and was ready to retreat to the kitchen.

"Goodness no," Maude said, again smoothing the already flat blanket. "You've just come off the roof. Now sit down."

"Okay."

Mystery slowly took her seat again as if any sudden movement might cause her mother to charge like a lion.

"I watched you as you covered that hole," Maude continued. "Very impressive. When did you learn to do that?"

"When there was a hole in the roof I couldn't afford to fix."

"Oh." Maude nodded as if the answer was enlightening instead of accusatory. "Well, that was what I wanted to talk to you about. Are you going to call a repairman?"

"I wanted to, but basically they are going to tell me that I need a new roof and trusses and everything. Or worse yet, they might just tell me to move out and burn the place."

"Well," Maude asked, "how about it?"

"How about what?" Though Mystery tried not to show it, the polite conversation was flustering her. This patient understanding was downright creepy. She wanted to tell her mother to just say it, whatever it was, instead of making Mystery drag it out of her.

"Mystery, you can't keep raising the kids in this environment."

Mystery felt a level of comfort return to the conversation. Ah the insults; she could take the insults. She was familiar with those. "Oh," Mystery nodded, "are we talking about the roof, or are we talking about John?"

"Both," Maude said flatly.

"Look, Mom, I don't know what you think has been going on, but I'll gladly tell you all the details."

Maude turned her head, and covered her mouth as if she was about to throw up. "Good lord, no, I don't want any details. I've heard *enough* about your sex life already."

"Oh really," Mystery laughed. "I don't remember us ever having a sex talk. If I remember right, the subject was taboo in our house while I was growing up."

"Well, I would have thought that after raising teenaged girls you would understand that, but clearly you still don't."

"Do you have sex with Dad?" Mystery prodded.

"Mystery! That is not an appropriate question, young lady."

"See that's the thing, Mom," she replied, raising her voice an octave. "I'm not a young lady *anymore*."

"Don't raise your voice to me, Mystery Abbott. I have put up with just about enough from you."

"I'm sorry," she conceded, knowing there was no point in continuing this conversation. She didn't even know why she tried, but something in her made her want to force Maude to understand what she was saying every time they fought. It had taken Mystery a long time to realize that no matter how hard she tried, that was not going to happen. Now, when they fought she had to remind herself that it didn't matter what Maude Abbott thought of her. All that mattered was what the kids thought of her, and today she knew that that probably wasn't much.

"Look, Mom, the only reason John was in the closet was so that the girls didn't know I was seeing someone until we knew if it was real or not."

"*Real?*" she asked. "Mystery, that is your problem. I don't mean to be rude, but at some point you need to wake up. You are a hopeless romantic just like your father. Look at your past."

"What about it?"

"Well," she said. "First there was Daniel, the girls' father. Goodness knows he was a loser no matter how hard his mother tried. I actually approved of you divorcing him. Then there was Walt Smith, and then Bennie's father, whoever that is—"

"*What?*"

"Oh," she nodded, "well, I'm sure that a mother doesn't know them all, but you get the point."

"*Walt Smith?*"

Maude nodded her head as she said, "I'm not stupid, Mystery."

"Who told you I slept with Walt Smith?"

"Everyone knows that."

"Everyone, who?"

"Everyone," she said again, as if there were an understood list of people posted somewhere — that Mystery had forgotten to read. "Look, I'm not judging you, I'm just pointing out that the men you are with aren't really the committing type."

"Mother," she said, standing up, "I have *never* slept with Walt Smith."

"Okay," she said. "Okay."

Mystery could tell that her mother didn't believe her, but it seemed that there was nothing she could do about it. "Mom," she stated, "I've never slept with Walt Smith or any other man in this town aside from the girls' father."

Maude gave her a crooked smile and lowered her eyes as if to say, *Makes no difference either way; I know you are lying.*

"Then where did Bennie come from?"

Mystery swallowed hard. She wanted to say that Bennie was created out of one night of passion that Mystery did not regret, but her mother would demand more information than that, like the man's name for one thing, and for everyone's sake, Mystery was not about to tell her that.

"What is it about me, Mother, that makes you always believe the worst about me?"

"Well," Maude huffed, "I don't *always* believe the worst."

"Then why don't you believe me now?"

"About what?" Mystery could tell her mother was playing dumb in order to buy time on her response.

"About Walt Smith?"

"I don't know," her mother said, looking away, "because everyone else in town says it."

"Again, Mother, everyone who?"

"Everyone. Dora Sievers, Faye Gordon..."

"Well, I don't know where they get their information, but it isn't true."

"Come on, Mystery," she chided, as if they were two girlfriends sitting down over tea to discuss their latest love interests, "you can tell me."

"I am telling you! See, this is just what I'm talking about. You would believe Dora and Faye over me. They are two of the biggest gossips in Glendale, aside from Liv, and they rarely have their information right. You know that."

"Yes," she said dryly, "but I also know you."

"Know what about me? You've never trusted me, *ever*!"

"You have always been beautiful," Maude said sadly. She looked away as if reflecting on a lost loved one. "People used to stop me in the street and look into your baby carriage simply because they had heard how beautiful you were." Her mother was still gone, eyes clouded over with memories.

"So what? Why is that a bad thing?"

"I knew it was going to be a problem from the time you were born and I saw those deep blue Abbott eyes. And then your father insisted on naming you after that horrid grandmother of yours. She always hated me, you know. I wasn't as beautiful as the rest of the Abbott women, but then again, I wasn't as loose either."

"Mother!"

"I believe a name has meaning from the time a child is born. 'Dana' is strong because it has both masculine and feminine ties, and 'Janie' and 'Bennie' are both sweet—I guess that is the feminine ending on the name that makes it so; but 'Mystery'? That name has been cast in sin since biblical times. 'Mystery, the whore of Babylon.' I could not believe your father wanted to carry on that legacy. Either way, I tried my hardest to steer you in a better direction, but sometimes the nature of the name takes over no matter how hard you try."

"What are you talking about?" Mystery asked, exasperated.

Maude woke from her reverie and fixed a familiar cold stare on her daughter. "Where did that little boy come from?"

"What little boy?" she asked, her anger rising at her mother's refusal to use Bennie's name.

"Don't get sly with me," Maude snapped. "You know who I'm talking about. *Bennie.*"

"Yes, I know who you are talking about, and *Bennie* is starting to know as well. Almost every time you talk about him, you call him 'that little boy.' His name is Bennie, and he's your grandson. Don't call him anything else ever again!"

"Fine! Bennie, whatever."

"No," Mystery snapped back, "not whatever! *Bennie!*"

"*Shh,*" Maude whispered, pointing a finger to the roof, "the men will hear us."

Lowering her voice only slightly, Mystery plowed on. "Well, he didn't come from Walt Smith, if that is what you are implying."

"It's been said that he looks a little like him. Has his eyes and all."

"*His eyes?*" Mystery bellowed.

"They are blue, just like Walt's."

"You seem to be forgetting something. Dad's eyes are blue as well, and so are mine. Maybe he gets his eyes from the Abbotts."

"Maybe," Maude shrugged.

Just then, Mystery spied Bennie and Janie shadowed behind the mesh of the screen door. They had obviously been listening. Mystery turned and shot a look at her mother. Maude rose and straightened the pleats on her pants.

"Hello, Bennie, Janie," she said happily.

"Hi," Janie replied. Bennie walked through the door and stood between Mystery's legs. Janie followed and stood next to her mother. Maude leaned down and touched Bennie's arm.

"Can you say, *Grandma*?"

Bennie shook his head and looked up at Mystery.

"He can't say it, Mom," Mystery said, "you know that. Sometimes he says Mommy, Janie, and Dana. But, that is all and you know it."

"Well, you've got to keep trying. He's going to be in kindergarten next year. He'll have to talk by then." Maude stood up, refolded the blanket, and placed it on the back of the swing. "Mystery," she said, "we will have to talk again later."

"Anytime, Mother," Mystery gritted her teeth against calling her *bitch* instead of *Mother*, but then she thought of the kids. "My door is always open. Heck, for that matter, so is my roof. Maybe you could just shoot me a note in a paper airplane."

Maude glanced at the kids. "That's not funny, Mystery. You have to do something about this situation before someone else does. It is not safe for the kids to live here."

"Do you mean because of the roof or because of John?" Janie quietly asked her grandmother. Mystery instantly feared for her daughter.

"Janie," Mystery said, placing a hand on her shoulder. For a moment, she wasn't sure if she was trying to protect her or hold her back. It wasn't like Janie to show any sign of defense, and Mystery wasn't certain how far she would go if provoked. "Don't be rude."

"Yes, Janie," her grandmother added stonily. "You shouldn't be rude to adults."

"Mom," Mystery interrupted, "I'm going to make Dad and John some coffee. Do you want to come in or not?"

"Grandpa's here?" Janie asked, surprised.

"Yes," Mystery nodded, "he's on the roof helping John."

"*He is?*"

"Yes." Mystery could hear the surprise in her daughter's voice, but Maude acted deaf to it.

"I'll pass on the coffee," Maude said. "I only came down because your father did. He insisted on helping that man on your roof."

"*John*, Mom," Mystery exasperated. "His name is *John*."

"Whatever," Maude said.

Mystery threw her arms up in the air and turned around to enter the house.

"Well," Maude sniffed, "I guess that's my cue to leave."

"Guess it is," Janie said emphatically. She picked up Bennie and waited for her grandmother to move off the porch.

"Say bye to Grandma." Janie's voiced dripped with artificial sweetness.

"Bye," Bennie said.

The sound of Bennie's high-pitched little-boy voice shocked Mystery.

"Bennie," Mystery sang, taking him from his sister. "You said 'bye!'"

"He said 'John' when we were inside earlier," Janie said flatly. Mystery noticed that as she said it, Janie looked directly at her grandmother. "I think Bennie likes him."

Bennie nodded, and Mystery added, "You do?"

Without acknowledging the moment, Maude added, "Please send your father directly home after he finishes up there."

Mystery didn't hear her as she left. Bennie had finally talked without provocation. At that point, nothing else, not even her mother's disapproval mattered.

chapter six

Liv Randall

As Liv stared out the window at the clear plastic bag stuck on Ilsa's rose bush, she wanted to cry. For as long as she could recall, she had always wanted to cry, but it was as foreign to her as rocketing to the moon. She tried to remember the last time she had managed anything more than her eyes welling up. She thought it must have been when she was a small child, because she had no memory of doing it as a teenager. Anytime one of her girlfriends would break down and bawl over a boy or a bad grade, she would observe them intently. She wouldn't say a word, she just watched as the tears fell from their ducts and stained their shirts black from their thick mascara. She wanted to touch the tears, taste them, inspect them, and understand them. She'd heard they were salty. She had even inspected her own ducts at home. She saw the little tear-shaped openings on the corner of her bottom eyelids so she knew she had ducts. She rubbed them until they hurt and water came forth. But it was only a little bit of moisture, not enough to taste. She eventually concluded that she had the ability to cry; she just didn't have the need. What was there to cry over, really, and what result would it bring? It wasn't like a teardrop could bring a boy back or change a grade.

Once, a few years back, she had confided in Jane over a cup of coffee right here in the kitchen, that her marriage was a complete failure. Jane had told her to make the best of the situation, smile when Carl walked in the door, and take the checkbook before he left for work the next day. "Men are for money. If you want a soul mate, try looking among your friends."

Back then, she trusted Jane and wanted to believe that the women of Ma Bell, whom she had come to call her friends, knew what they were talking about. But today she felt like a fool. It had been a day and a half since the PTA meeting and Jane had called twice, sweetly pleading for Liv to call her back so they could talk. It was just after five and Jane would be getting off work, so Liv figured another call was imminent. She hadn't decided yet if she would pick up the receiver or not. She had given up on telling Carl about it long ago. He was too wrapped up in whatever was going on at work to pay any attention to her.

In the kitchen, she pulled out a cast-iron skillet. Fried chicken and mashed potatoes on Fridays. She went to the cupboard to get a pot to boil potatoes, but she opened the wrong one. There were only cups in there. Her arms felt weighted and her soul seemed weak. She had to focus on her own kitchen for a minute in order to remember where the pans were. She slammed the cupboard and closed her eyes. This always happened when her emotions got muddled. She cursed the cloud in her peripheral vision. Although she had tried to ignore it, it wasn't going away. She opened her eyes and tentatively opened the cupboard next to the stove. *Pans.* She pulled out a medium-sized pan and went to the sink to fill it with water, then began scrubbing hard on a potato. Through the streaks of wet cotton outside the kitchen window, she noticed John and Peter up on the Abbotts' roof. Liv thought it was a little bold of Mystery to allow John back in plain view of the whole town after the other night.

She picked up the phone and dialed Jane's number, but before she hit the last digit, she stopped. If she called to gossip, Jane would certainly want to talk about the PTA thing. Liv hated the protocol you had to follow to get out of a scrape with your best friend. *I'm sorry. No, I'm sorry. It was just a stupid misunderstanding.* Or worse yet, *I voted for you, I swear.*

Liv placed the receiver back in its cradle and returned to scrubbing potatoes. Next to her on the counter, her list was getting splattered with water from the pan.

"Damn," she said out loud. She turned off the running water, dumped a bit out, and placed the pan on the stove. Blood pulsed in her head, so she braced her hands on the edge of the stove and waited. Why was she doing this? She looked around the quiet, empty kitchen and wondered why she was making dinner for them anyway. Taylor was god-only-knows-where in that new Mustang, and Carl, well, he was probably at the office working on "privileged information."

She didn't want to wait for the phone to ring or stay here alone in Ilsa's kitchen any longer. She had to get away. Abandoning dinner, she ducked out the back door, grabbed her cigarettes from beneath the Adirondack chair, and hurried down the walkway to her car, mindless of the wind and rain. Before backing down the driveway, she rolled down her window and let the cool wind whip in at her, the misty rain creating a web of moisture in her hair. It fluffed her curls and wisped them about her face. She grabbed the ponytail wrap that she kept on the gearshift and pulled her hair tight in it until it was snug against her scalp. Carl hated when she wore her hair like that.

Rain and wind rocked the car. She gunned it out of the driveway and skidded past Mystery's house, then stopped at the end of Carlisle Street, unsure which way to go. She didn't want to drive through Main Street and risk running into Carl. He hadn't talked to her since the other night in his office, when she failed to notice his client's presence. She had stormed in, right past Coral Smith, and hadn't even noticed her. The cloud had blocked out her peripheral vision, but she couldn't explain that to Carl when she apologized for the intrusion. He would freak out if she told him the cloud was back. She had lost it completely once, just after Taylor was born, leaving Carl to mistrust her with Taylor or anything else. When the cloud came back after he moved her to Ilsa's house, she had managed to control herself enough to hide it and triumph at making it go away. This time it was different, and something about how she was feeling now scared her.

Liv tapped a cigarette from the pack on the passenger seat. She hadn't realized she'd left her cigarettes out in plain sight like that.

What if Carl or Taylor had seen them? Right now, she couldn't think about that. She needed something to calm her nerves.

Finally, she turned toward Smith Street, on the south side of town, and into the storm. The cliff to Cemetery Ridge looked weak, cut up with small channels of water. She hadn't liked living below a cemetery and had been working with the city council for years to abandon the ridge and consecrate a new piece of land elsewhere. To date, "elsewhere" had been hard to find. She pushed harder on the gas and sped past the ridge and out of town. She didn't come this way very often. Sheep Creek Road led to the Indian reservation in Idaho, and Liv usually went the other way toward Kennedy. She was about to give up and turn around when she saw a blue flicker up ahead. It was the kind of reflection she used to see when the sun's light hit the ocean, just a sliver of color to let you know that you were close to the water. Her grandfather used to make a bet with her to see who would spy the ocean first each time he drove her to their beach house. He always let her win. She missed them both so much. She floored it and drove as fast as she could toward the reflection.

Up ahead she saw a green signpost — Miller Lane. Her heart beat faster and for a moment she allowed herself to believe that she had entered some alternate dimension and that just ahead, outside of Glendale, was now the Pacific Ocean. She moved her hands at a sharp ninety-degree angle and the Jetta jumped to the right. The washboard road of summer fallow smacked hard against the undercarriage. Liv recalled the exhilaration of driving her grandfather's dune buggy over the dunes just outside of Ocean Shores.

Her heart rate increased with the adrenalin and rain; she flicked the windshield wipers on high. The windows were fogging up from the heat of her breath, so she clicked on the defrost button too. She became aware that she could really *breathe*. It felt like the elevation was changing. She thought she could smell the scent of seaweed and oysters through the heater vents. She opened her eyes wide to try and get a better look.

She held tight to the steering wheel, her breathing fast and choppy. Finally, she crested a small rise and slammed on the brakes. The car skidded to a halt with such force that Liv's head was smacked against the driver's side window. Instantly, the cloud disappeared from her vision and Liv, gingerly inspecting the side of her head for a cut or blood, breathed deeply, relishing the sudden clarity. Her head smarted from the clout, but the skin hadn't broken. She looked to the right, searching for the ocean, praying that it would be real. Through the murky passenger's window, she could still see the expanse of blue. She opened the door, and climbed out. She slowly turned around and stared. It wasn't real. It was an illusion, a cruel mirage in the Glendale rain. It was a house. A large white farmhouse with a simple blue roof. Her shoulders slumped. How could she have been so deluded? Through the wind and rain she stared at the house, wanting to yell at it for deceiving her.

"Why? Why?" she asked out loud, thumping her fist like a gavel on the cold, wet roof of her car. But, when she looked to the house for an answer, she was dismayed. With the two blue-gabled windows on the second floor and the red double doors in the center of the long white front porch, it seemed like it was trying to respond, as if the house itself had something to say.

"Why?" she said to it again. She waited a moment, but it simply sat there in the rain, looking back at her as if it sympathized but was unable to respond. Liv blinked. She relaxed and let her eyes glaze over, taking in the full vision in a watery mix of shapes and colors. It almost looked like a human face, and as the water cascaded past her vision, everything seemed to move. She shook her head and turned away.

"Goodbye," she said uncomfortably.

As she drove back to town her one-sided conversation reverberated in her mind. *Why? Why? Goodbye.* It became a rhyme, a tune that played over and over in her head. It was sick, she knew, but she wanted to believe it. After all, it did smell like the ocean out there and the house was vacant. Something about it seemed to call to her, to want her to be there, to need her in a way that she had not been needed in a long time.

She decided to drive down Main Street on the way home. The lights were still on in Carl's office, but the curtain was drawn on the fishbowl. She giggled, feeling an increasingly wild sense of freedom from Carl, from the town, and from the tension of her existence. She hoped he would be late. The lights were on at Emily's Hair Salon as well — pedicure night. Liv had forgotten about that. It had been on the list, but it didn't matter now. None of it did. She smiled as she drove past them. They saw her; she knew they did. Now, they would really have something to talk about.

chapter seven

Dana Abbott

he rain pounded the town as Dana left the restaurant. When she was younger, Dana used to swipe gum and mints from the counter when she thought Mr. Borghese wasn't looking, but today The Trough, as the youth of Glendale liked to call it, had earned her fifteen dollars in tips that she had tucked in her bra to keep her warm. She had dreamed of her first summer after graduating from Glendale High — small bikinis, fast cars, hot guys, warm wet kisses on a beach somewhere. She hadn't thought it would be like this — having to get a job and walk home in the rain. It didn't seem fair. She cut through the alleyway between City Hall and Carl Randall's law office. The wind didn't blow quite as hard in the alley, and Dana knew exactly where Faye, the town clerk, hid her ashtray.

She crouched underneath the back stairs of City Hall and pulled out the blue and red plaid ashtray that sat just beneath the steps. There were three half smoked butts left in the tray, each with a circle of hot pink lipstick around the end. Every kid in town knew about the clerk's secret little habit, and they wouldn't tell on her for anything. No one in Glendale wanted to admit to smoking. It was a disgusting habit and it was bad for your health, but almost everyone did it, and they all knew it. *Everyone except Janie Abbott,* Dana thought. She wanted to tell Janie that trying to be "good and proper" was not going to make her acceptable in the eyes of Glendale's upper crust. They were Mystery's daughters after all. They were never going to be anything but white trash in this town, and Dana thought Janie would be much happier if she would just accept it.

Dana pulled a cigarette from her own pack and lit it, leaning against the back wall as she had seen Faye do more often than the town clerk possibly could have imagined. She stood beneath the stairs and surveyed the town from her vantage point. On State Street, she could see the living room lights on in Cord's place. He was probably waiting for her. He was always good for a beer or two, but then she would have to pay the price and make out with him for a while. Normally, it was a price well paid, but not tonight. She felt a little older and a little wiser with the tip money she'd tucked into her bra, and she didn't want his immature hands to mess that up. Besides, her mind had not been on Cord all day; it had been on Dylan Masters. She felt like robbing the bank just to get him to frisk her.

She heard a door slam on Main Street and moved back into the corner under the stairs. Carl Randall was standing outside his office talking to someone beneath an umbrella. Dana looked at her watch. It was just after eight. Carl handed the woman the umbrella, and she gave him a quick hug and a kiss on the cheek. Then she stepped off the curb and walked away down the street.

Dana hadn't noticed a car anywhere. She wanted to step out and see where the woman was going, but Carl just wouldn't leave. He turned around and seemed to scan the area as if looking for a spy lurking behind a trash can. If he only knew. After the woman was out of sight, he lingered for a moment, and then went back into his office and out of the rain. She was the same person who had been at his office last night, the one who had obviously made Liv mad. She looked familiar, but Dana couldn't place her first name. She was certain the woman was wealthy. She could see that in the jewelry she wore. Dana thought she knew everyone in Glendale by first name, but not this lady.

Dana wanted to walk right out in the wind and rain and tell Carl that Main Street was a stupid place to try and keep a secret, but she stayed put. She knew Liv well enough from watching her for so long, but she hardly ever talked to Carl. He seemed stronger than Liv, the type of guy that might shoo you away with the threat of telling your mother that you were spying. But what was that woman doing kissing Liv's husband, and what was Carl doing allowing himself to be kissed? Dana felt her cheeks redden in anger. She didn't want anyone to betray Liv. She didn't think Liv could take it. She took a last drag on her smoke, tossed it to the ground, and walked the long way around State Street toward home, the whole time contemplating if she should stop by Liv's and tell her what she had seen. She would love to be the one to save her and protect her, but what if she was wrong? What if the woman really was just a client? She really didn't want to hurt Liv in any way.

As Dana neared her house, she saw lights on at the Randalls', but she passed by without a word. Mystery might actually listen to this gossip, after what those women had put her through. Sometimes Dana liked to talk to her mother, though she wouldn't admit that out loud—especially to Mystery. The woman was a glutton for punishment, all right, but no matter how much of a bitch Dana was to her, Mystery always seemed to find a way to forgive her and move on. Dana knew that someday her attitude toward her mother—and her sister, for that matter—would come back and bite her in the ass when she least expected it, but that day had yet to come. After her first successful day as a waitress, Dana was in a positive mood and felt good about her family—even Janie. She had given Mystery enough shit about the canopy for now. Hell, with her new job she could probably even buy one herself. She might even be able to find a kind word to say to Janie if things went well enough. Some days, her family wasn't that bad.

She had just skipped over the two large puddles overflowing at the curb and had hopped onto the sidewalk as if she were joining in a new game of hopscotch when she saw them through the window. Bennie, Janie, Mystery, and the cowboy were laughing around a candlelight glow in the center of the kitchen table. Her chair was empty, but there was a place setting in front of it. She stopped in mid-jump, legs bent, ready to go again, but instead straightened up.

She couldn't believe it. Liv and her grandmother had yanked this bastard out of her mother's closet in the middle of the night, and Mystery still set the guy up in front of the kitchen window like they were all a happy family on display. She felt the cold black anger in her heart return and her loathing for her mother bubbled to the surface. Every time Dana was about to give her an inch, Mystery took a whole mile without even thinking of what that would do to the rest of the family.

Soaked to the bone, she walked into the house, slammed the door behind her, and waited. The silence from the kitchen signaled that her anger was having the desired effect. After a moment, Janie walked out into the living room. "Dinner's ready," she smiled.

Dana didn't even look at her. She stormed past her and slammed the door to her bedroom. Leave it to her mother to send a child to do her dirty work. Mystery would be knocking on the door any minute. She dropped her purse and slipped out of her sopping clothes, throwing the whole wet pile on the floor for Mystery to clean up later. If she were lucky, maybe the carpet would mold. Her cat Snowflake stared stoically at her from her bed. The animal didn't care what Dana did — smoke, fuck, it really didn't matter. She liked that cat.

Dana glared up at the blue tarp nailed to the ceiling above her bed. Mystery had washed the canopy and put it back up. Just one of her feeble attempts to buy a little peace. Dana stood up on her bed and surveyed the mesh covering. In the left corner, she could still make out the thin brown line of a water stain. Mystery probably thought that she wouldn't notice, but she did.

She hopped down from the bed and pulled on a pair of sweat pants and a V-neck sweater. She could still feel the wet wad of money bulging out of her red lace bra. She pulled it out and lifted the lid of her ballerina jewelry box to put the money in. The ballerina twirled as a delicate tune played. Dana knew that the bitch wouldn't stop until she finished that song. Her mother once proudly told her that it was "Lara's Theme" from *Dr. Zhivago*, whatever the hell that was. She grabbed the box and threw it against the wall. She'd seen Liv do that before, only in Liv's world there was always something new in its place within a few days. The ballerina broke off and lay in mid-pirouette upside down on the carpet, but the music continued until the song ran out.

It had been five minutes and not a knock at the door. She walked to it and waited. She thought about lighting one of the smokes she had stolen from the ashtray at City Hall. Mystery would smell that and come running for sure. Instead, she decided to take the opposite attack. She opened the door, walked to the kitchen, and stood in the doorway. She could see Mystery and Janie shoot warning looks at one another. This was much better.

"Dana!" Bennie yelled.

She shot him a quick smile, but didn't say a word. She felt her razor sharp tongue cutting into the roof of her mouth, but that wasn't Bennie's fault. The cowboy smiled at her with fork and knife in hand. He had a half-eaten steak on his plate. His baked potato was piled high with sour cream and chives and his wine glass was half-empty. He appeared to feel pretty much at home. The problem was that no one had asked her if he could be at home, and unfortunately for all of them, this was her house, too.

"Dana," Janie said, "if you're going to eat then sit down."

She glared at her sister. It pissed her off when Janie tried to talk to her like they were the same age. Janie was five minutes younger than she was, and it showed.

"Dana," Mystery said, "you remember John. He's staying for dinner. I tried to do the roof myself but as you can see, that won't work. John offered to help. I just wanted you to know because you might be seeing him around here for a while. He brought us some steaks as well."

"A while?" she sneered. She took her place at the table and began serving herself. She peeled half a baked potato, placed it in the middle, and began cutting it up with the knife.

"And Grandpa, too," Janie smiled.

"Yeah," John said, as if he thought his input was wanted in any way, "Mr. Abbott is sure a great help."

"*My* grandfather is helping you?"

"Yep," John said.

"So anyway, John," Janie said, changing the subject, "you were telling us about your cattle."

"Yes," he said proudly. "Well, they're a Hereford-Angus mix. Like I said, I have forty head right now, but there should be about ten more this spring, that is until we butcher."

Mystery passed Dana the gravy. Dana stared at her until she set the dish down. Mystery knew that Dana was a vegetarian. Meat was full of fat, she had told Mystery that before. Was Dana just supposed to start eating meat and gravy simply because her mom was fucking a cattle butcher?

"Babies?" Bennie asked excitedly.

"Calves," John corrected.

"When did *he* start talking?" Dana asked.

"He's been talking ever since John arrived. Isn't that weird?" Janie laughed.

"It's amazing," Mystery added. "Janie and I have spent this whole day just talking to him, and he can say anything. It's like he had the words in there the whole time and he just didn't have a reason to say anything until now."

"It's not that amazing," Dana said, chewing a bite of plain potato, "he probably thinks that John is his dad. He wouldn't know the difference."

All eyebrows rose at the table and Dana saw John wink at Mystery. Apparently, her mother had already warned him about her. John turned to Bennie.

"Do you want to come to my house and watch a calf being born?"

Bennie eagerly nodded up and down.

"Do you think that would be okay, Mystery?" John asked.

"Yes, I think so," she said.

"You would," Dana said under her breath.

"What is that supposed to mean?" Mystery said.

"Come on, Mom," Dana yelped, "he's only four years old. Do you really think he should be watching X-rated material already?"

"It's a cow, Dana," Janie interjected.

"No, it's okay," John said calmly. "Would you like to come too, Dana? There's really nothing X-rated about it."

"This from the guy hiding in the closet."

"Dana!" Mystery snapped.

The cowboy didn't say anything. He simply took another bite of his meat. Dana felt a little better. It was about time the man felt uncomfortable.

"Jesus," Janie said under her breath. "Why did you even have to come home?"

"I just got off work, which is something you obviously know nothing about." Dana sized Janie up and down in disapproval.

"Dana," Mystery said, "why don't you just go to your room?"

"Why don't you? The cowboy obviously knows the way."

"Why are you always such a bitch?" Janie asked, her voice rising.

"Janie!" Mystery yelled.

"The question is why aren't you?" retorted Dana.

"What is that supposed to mean?"

Dana stood to her feet in a challenge, but Janie stayed where she was, centered between her mother and Bennie—a trio of bonded power as usual.

"Come on, Janie! Why are you just sitting by and watching all of this shit happen right in front of your own window?"

"What shit?" Janie asked disdainfully.

Dana aimed her butter knife at the window. "Jesus, Janie, your future mother-in-law is sitting right across the street watching all of you sit here and play family like it's the most normal thing in the world. You should be embarrassed!"

"Would you both please stop cussing!" Mystery interjected.

"Stay out of it, Mystery," Dana said.

"Dana!"

John placed his utensils down. "Ladies, ladies…let's all calm down, okay?"

Dana glared at him, but Janie kept going.

"My future mother-in-law?" she asked. "What are you talking about?"

"Oh please," she said. "Everyone in town knows about you and Taylor." She tried to sound as disgusted as she felt. The thought of any man having the desire to touch her sister made her want to gag. That was as bad as this guy wanting to be with her mother. There was obviously something wrong with both of those men.

"What does everyone know about me and Taylor?"

"There's no need to keep the innocent act up in front of Mystery. She's fucked every guy in town."

"Dana!" Mystery yelled, "that is not true! Now go to your room!"

"No way," she said, pushing her chair back so hard that it tipped over. The sudden crash silenced the family, so Dana continued. "Well, *Mother*," she said calmly, "he might as well know what he's getting into before Bennie ends up getting any more hurt." She turned to John. "Mystery can only keep a man around for so long, *John*, then they can't take it anymore, and they have to leave. She did it with mine and Janie's dad, with whoever Bennie's father is, and according to Grandma, she did it with Walt Smith, too."

"That is not true!" Mystery was almost laughing now. "Why does everyone think that?"

"Well, Mystery," she said. "If the whole town thinks so, then it must be true."

"It's not," Mystery stated firmly. She turned to John. "I'm so sorry."

"Its okay," He put his hand on her shoulder and smiled at her as if nothing that Dana had just said had made any impact at all. "Dana's the one being rude. Not you."

He said it calmly and stared at her straight on as if nothing she said could affect him.

Dana held his gaze, but he didn't budge. Before any of them could say anymore, she fled from the kitchen, grabbed her wet slicker, and ran out of the house. Stopping at the curb on Carlisle Street, she saw lights blazing from the Randall house as well as every other house in sight, and she wasn't sure where to go. She could go south to her grandmother's. The crab apples on the tree in front of the Keller house would be just about ripe. She felt her mouth watering at the thought of their bitter, acrid taste. But she decided against running to her grandma. She had already eaten half of a starch-filled potato and it wasn't like she could have a shot of whiskey or a smoke with the old lady. If she could, that would be the first place she'd go.

She looked across the street at Liv's house. Liv knew about anger and rejection. Liv knew about black and white, and right and wrong. What would Liv do? God, how she wished she had a mother like Liv

Randall to guide her through life. She knew she would have been a better person then, made so many better choices. She'd probably still be a virgin, and maybe have even made homecoming princess her senior year. But, since she was an Abbott, there was no hope for her. She had known that since she was a little girl. Even her grandmother thought it, though she hadn't said it to her face. Dana took a deep breath, wiped her eyes, and headed north toward Main Street.

The storm was hitting Glendale hard. Dana thought it might be her own raging energy that spurred it on. Up ahead, she could see the yellow glow of The Watering Trough on Main Street, and she headed toward it. Her boss, Mr. Borghese, would let her in. Hell, he might even let her have a beer. After all, she was an employee. Then she saw something else. A light coming from the police station. What did she have to lose?

She walked up the steps and tapped lightly on the door. She could see Dylan through the window, sitting at his desk going over some papers. He turned, and when he saw her, he quickly opened the door to let her in.

"Hi there," the young officer said.

She sauntered in as ladylike as she could and slowly removed her raincoat. The V-neck sweater was wet despite the slicker, and sticking to her small frame. She wrapped her hands around her forearms and ran them up and down.

"Hi," she said shyly, "sorry to bother you, but I saw your light on."

"It's no problem. Are you okay? Is there some kind of emergency?"

Dana shook her head and kept rubbing her arms. "I must look a sight," she giggled.

"No," he said. "You look fine. Have a seat and tell me what the trouble is."

Dana sat on the brown leather couch while Dylan walked around to the back of the desk and poured a cup of coffee.

"Would you like some?" he asked. "I know it's late, but when you work the night shift, you tend to live on it."

"Sure."

"Cream or sugar?"

"Nope, just black please." That was how Mystery took it, so she assumed that was how all adults took it. He returned with the mug, and turned it toward her so that she could take it by the handle.

"So, what happened that has you out knocking on the police station door at nine o'clock on a night like this?"

"Oh, it's ridiculous, really."

"Well," he said kindly, "why don't you tell me and let me decide."

"It's my mother," she admitted flatly, "Mystery Abbott."

"Yes," he said, "I know who she is. And you're Dana, right?"

"Right," she smiled. "How did you know?"

"Lucky guess," he said. "How's the roof coming along?"

"Oh goodness," she said, feigning embarrassment, "you know about that?"

"There's not much in this town that I don't know about."

"Well," she said. "It's got a stupid tarp over it for now."

"Oh," he nodded.

"Well," she offered, "that's the problem. See, Mystery has some man working on the roof that I don't even know, and tonight they were all sitting at the table eating dinner like they were one big happy family."

"Oh," he said, "and that's a bad thing?"

He seemed confused. Had it been Cord, she would have rolled her eyes and turned away, but with Dylan she found the perplexity cute, almost enticing.

"Yes," she said, "it's very bad. Mystery's a tramp. She humiliates our family every time she brings a new man home."

"How old are you, Dana?" Dylan asked, leaning back in his chair. His body was exposed to her now and she wished she had the freedom to climb on top and take a ride.

"Almost eighteen." She sat up straight on the couch. "I just graduated last month."

"Then what are you worried about? You'll be out of the house soon enough, right?"

"Yes," she said taking a sip of her coffee, "but I have a little brother. What about him?"

Dylan came around the desk and sat next to her on the couch.

"That's very nice of you to worry about him," he said, "but I've met your mother. She doesn't seem like a tramp to me. Maybe she's just had a string of bad luck with men. Maybe this guy is different."

"I don't know." Dana shook her head for effect. "I don't know anything about him."

"What's his name?"

"John Spencer," she said. "He's from somewhere near Kennedy."

"Well," he said, standing to attention in front of her, "I have some connections in Kennedy, and John Spencer shouldn't be that common of a name. Would it help if I checked the guy out for you?"

"Oh, would you?" she clapped. "Without letting Mystery know?"

"Of course," he said. "If there's nothing funny about the guy we wouldn't want to scare him. And if there is, then we can deal with that together. Okay?"

Together, Dana thought. She had never felt more comfortable with a man than she did right this minute.

"Thank you, Officer Masters," she smiled.

"It's no problem," he said. "I'm always here."

"Always? Don't you ever go home?"

"This is my home," he laughed. "It's part of the cheap deal the city gets for hiring me. This is my room and board."

"Wow," Dana said, looking around. "Do you have a fridge or anything?"

"Yes. There's a little apartment in the rear of the building. It's not much. Just a bed, stove, fridge, sink, bathroom, and television. But it's free so I don't complain."

"Wow," Dana said, "I wish I could find a place like that."

"Actually, there are a few places around town. You'd be surprised. Tell you what, when you are ready to move out, I'll take you around and show you where they are."

"Really? I thought I knew everything about Glendale."

"No one knows everything about their home town, believe me," He motioned her to move toward the door. "Do you want me to give you a ride back home, Miss Abbott?"

"It's Dana, just Dana." She stared hard at the rain for a minute and thought about what it would be like to sit next to him in the police car.

She decided against it. She was warm now and she had enticed him enough for one night.

"No," she said. "I can walk. The rain will do me good." She turned, stood on her toes, and kissed the officer on the cheek, just as she had seen that woman do to Carl earlier. She got just close enough to his ear to be sensual, and just far enough away to be safe. He placed his arm on her shoulder and patted her on the back. "Thank you again, Officer Masters," she said.

"It's Dylan," he laughed, "just Dylan. Why don't you stop by tomorrow night after you get off work? I should have the information for you by then."

"You know where I work?"

"Of course," he said, pointing to the restaurant. "Like I said, not too much happens in this town that I don't know about. I'll see you tomorrow night."

As she walked back up State Street, Dana smiled at Cord's house. He had no idea that his time with her had just run out.

chapter eight

Janie Abbott

The next day was Saturday, a day previously longed for by Janie as a day of freedom and lounging about in her pj's and fuzzy slippers. Since graduation, however, Saturday had lost its appeal and become just another day of waiting and wanting. Waiting for something she did not know and wanting something she had yet to attain. The rain subsided a bit and the clouds parted, exposing an unforgiving steel-blue sky. The wind coming off Cemetery Ridge blew even colder than it had in the last few days. Janie, lured outside by the change in the weather, sat on the porch swing and listened to John and her grandfather working on the house. The side of the Abbott house was piled knee-deep with rotted black roofing, moldy newspaper, and broken 2 × 4s. Janie knew she should probably help pick up the mess, but she didn't feel like moving. Taylor had just dropped her off after taking her to Kennedy to see a movie, and all she wanted to do was snuggle up with the afghan on her front porch—by herself.

It seemed that the whole time they were in Kennedy, Taylor was talking about how lucky she was that he was taking her away. Away from her mother and *all* the men in her life, away from her trampy sister, and away from having to be responsible for Bennie. She nodded her head in agreement every time he talked about it, but she couldn't admit that the whole topic made her uncomfortable. She didn't want to hurt his feelings like that. He was so excited, but every time he talked about "how this would be best for her," she felt anger growing inside of her.

Just before leaving town, Taylor took Janie into Victoria's Secret and told her to pick out the outfit for their wedding night. A gift. That was what he called it. He was buying. She looked at a few nightgowns and even a bra and panty set. With each one she looked to him for approval, but the hungry-looking smile on his face made her nervous, as if he were sizing her up like a piece of meat. Finally, she just told him that she would surprise him, and they left. When they got home, she ran to her front porch as if they were playing some children's game and she would be safe just by touching home base. Now she felt ridiculous. Everything in her mind was screaming for her to tell Taylor that she had made a mistake by saying she would run away and marry him, but he seemed excited, so happy to be with her and only her, and she loved Taylor, right? They had been friends for so long that it didn't seem fair to hurt him like that.

Janie kicked her feet back and forth and stared across the street at the Randalls' house. *Janie Randall.* She pondered what Liv would be like as a mother-in-law. She had always been polite enough to Janie, but Janie could tell that Liv had higher expectations for her only son than to marry an Abbott girl. Even though they lived right across the street, the Abbotts epitomized the "wrong side of the tracks" to the Randalls. Janie also wondered what people in town would think of her. Would she still be Mystery Abbott's daughter, or would she move up in rank?

She leaned back against the arm of the porch swing, facing away from the road and away from the Randalls' so that she could watch the weather moving in over Cemetery Ridge. Wispy fingers of fog clawed over the banks toward the Smith house. Raindrops began to plop on the sidewalk. Janie smiled and curled up with her mother's afghan. It smelled of Downy and fresh rain. She wanted to stay right here forever.

The fog seemed to bump and move carelessly over what Janie could see of the lilac bushes and silver headstones leaving only the tallest ones at the edge exposed. The cemetery was Janie's favorite place in Glendale, night or day. That was where she and Taylor had played hide-and-seek and kick-the-can as children, eating lunches of white crackers and vanilla frosting, and drinking Cokes until they were sick to their stomachs. At the time, it had seemed obvious that they would end up together.

Taylor didn't go up there anymore, but Janie couldn't stay away. She knew most of the headstones by heart, but visited Fawn Hemmingway the most. Her headstone was carved out of pink marble, with a sleeping cherub at its base. The inscription simply said her birth and death dates: March 10, 1930, and March 12, 1945. Janie always wondered if Fawn had celebrated her birthday that year and then died in some freak accident, or if she had suffered a long and grueling illness that finally ended just after she turned fifteen. Her headstone gave no indication, no eulogy. For the past five years, Janie had faithfully visited Fawn on her birth and death days. The year that Janie turned fifteen, she made Fawn a Betty Crocker cherry chip cake. Dana had taunted her mercilessly as she left for a walk with the pastry in hand, but Janie had escaped without divulging whom the cake was for. Right now, she missed Fawn. She longed for her as she always had when she felt scared or alone. She had told Fawn about Taylor, but she hadn't told Taylor about her visits to Fawn. Now they were supposed to elope. How was she going to explain to Taylor that she didn't want to leave Glendale, and that she didn't want to leave Fawn?

A car turned west onto Carlisle Street, drawing Janie's attention away from Cemetery Ridge. It was Cord Galloway's black Chevelle. As it pulled up in front of her house, she heard Guns N' Roses blaring from the speakers, and her toes immediately started tapping out *Welcome to the Jungle.* Cord had on sunglasses and was blowing a pink bubble with his gum. He turned off the engine, stepped out, and strolled up to the porch. Janie's eyes were drawn to his body. It was so like Dana and so unlike herself, but she couldn't stop staring at him. Her sister's boyfriend was hot.

She turned her thoughts to Taylor. That was safe. Taylor had a nice body; any girl in town would tell her that. He was trim with showy muscles from working out all the time, and he had a washboard stomach that he let Janie pinch whenever she wanted to. Cord didn't look like that. He was short, and his muscles were simple. You could tell he didn't lift weights. But there were the other things that Janie couldn't stop staring at. There was the movement of his jawbone when he chewed his gum, the deepness of his brown eyes, and the fact that she had never seen jeans fit a boy so well. She wanted to tell him that he could make millions modeling his butt for Levis, but it sounded like something Dana would say. When he approached, he lifted his sunglasses to rest on his soft, brown hair, and shoved one hand in his pocket. He stood halfway down the sidewalk from the porch and smiled at Janie.

"Hi there," he said. His voice was so soft that she could hardly hear him, especially at that distance.

"Hi."

"Is Dana around?"

"She's at work."

"Oh," he said. "Do you know when she'll be back?"

"Not sure. I guess you two had a pretty late night last night?"

Janie had no idea why she was saying this to him, after all she hardly knew him, but she couldn't seem to stop herself.

"Huh?"

"Well, she ran out last night. I just figured she ran to you." *Too much information*, she said to herself.

Cord cocked his head to the side, and stared to the east. *Whoa. His profile is even better.* His jawline looked like it had been chiseled out of stone. He turned back to her and chomped down hard on his gum.

"It's Janie, right?"

"Yes." Her heart was beating so fast that she was certain if he got any closer he would see it thumping in her chest.

"Well, Janie, can I stand on the porch out of the rain?"

"Sure."

He walked slowly forward. Janie wanted to pinch herself. She didn't know what to do. *What if he wants to sit down? What if Dana comes home? What if Taylor is watching?* He leaned back against the porch wall, took his sunglasses off his head, and ran his fingers through his hair. She caught a whiff of cinnamon gum on the air and began to salivate. It smelled like Big Red.

"How's it going with the roof?"

"Fine, I guess," she said. She placed her feet on the ground to stop herself from swaying back and forth. *This isn't a swing set, Janie.*

"I asked Dana if you needed any help. I'm pretty good with roofs."

"I don't know," she said, "you'd have to ask the men up there."

"Well," he said, "Dana already told me she didn't want me to help, so I guess I'd better stay out of it."

Janie shook her head. "That's Dana for you." Without hesitating, she stepped out to the end of the porch and yelled up at the men. "Hey John, Dana's boyfriend offered to help. What do you think?"

"Sure," he said. "If it's okay with Mr. Abbott."

"That's Peter."

"I mean Peter." She heard John and her grandfather laugh in unison at John's apparent inability to stray from formally addressing his elder.

"Fine by me," Peter replied. "The more the merrier."

"Janie," John called. "We're actually about ready to break for lunch. Can you let your mom know?"

"Sure."

"Well," Cord said smiling, "I guess I have some time to kill. So what are you doing out here in the rain?"

"Oh, I don't know. Just being alone, I guess." Just then, she heard Taylor's car fire up. He pulled out of his driveway and stared hard at them. Janie felt the hairs on her arms stand to attention as if she had just been caught cheating on an exam. He didn't make eye contact with her or lift a hand to wave; he simply kept his gaze on Cord.

"Who was that, your boyfriend?"

Janie nodded. "Did you rebuild that car on your own?" she asked, hurriedly changing the subject.

"Mostly. My brothers helped, too. Do you mind if I just hang out until John needs me?"

"Okay," she said too quickly, "but Dana won't be back for a while."

"Well, I could just talk to you... if that's okay?"

Janie moved over on the porch swing and offered him a seat. There was a large space between them, but she found she liked that he was sitting on the porch with her. For a few moments, neither of them said anything, yet in no time at all they were comparing their families and histories. Janie found herself so immersed in the story of his life on the reservation in Idaho that she stopped taking furtive looks at his body and started looking him in the eyes.

"Why don't you go back?" she asked.

"Well, the land and the cabin are still ours, but my brothers have all moved on."

"What about your mom?"

"She lives on Oak Street with me. She's not much for getting out though."

"Why not?"

Cord lowered his head and smiled.

"She's got problems," he admitted.

"Problems?"

"Yeah, it's kind of embarrassing. She doesn't go out much, so my brothers and I take care of her the best we can. She's a lot older than your mom, Janie. She had me when she was in her mid-forties. I was an afterthought."

"That puts her in her early sixties, right?" Janie asked. "That's not old."

"It is when you've drunk and smoked your whole life. She's on oxygen and every kind of medication you can imagine. So my brothers and I each take her in for six months. This is my turn, so I moved her into town to be closer to the doctors."

"So what about your farm?"

"It's a ranch really, although not a working one. All the livestock is gone and I can't afford to get more. Besides, I can't work it by myself and make a living at an outside job. I just have to face facts. This country isn't set up for ranchers right now." He looked off to the east again. She was surprised. That was pretty deep for a young guy living on State Street.

"And your father?" she added cautiously.

"Dead," he said flatly. "Died in a drunk-driving accident just past the ranch when I was a kid. So it's just me, you see."

"I'm sorry," she said. "I didn't mean to pry."

"No, it's fine. I didn't mean to go off on politics."

"Well," she said, smiling sheepishly, "I'll give you a little tip. That guy you are about to start working with is a rancher."

"Yeah?"

"Yep, I guess this is your lucky day."

"You have no idea!" he laughed. "I'm really glad we had a chance to talk Janie. You're so much different than your sister." He was looking directly at her now and smiling. She liked that. She liked to hear him say her name in his soft voice. It made her name seem so feminine, so pretty. She hadn't thought of her name as pretty until she heard it from Cord Galloway's lips.

John and her grandfather descended the ladder and Peter nodded to Janie as he left for home. John walked up to the porch and leaned back on the railing. Janie had never seen men be so comfortable around her house before. For the most part, people in Glendale avoided Mystery Abbott's house for fear of the wild rumors it would cause, but these men seemed oblivious to possible scandal.

"So," John said, removing his wet glove and extending his hand, "you're Dana's boyfriend, are ya?"

"Yeah," Cord replied, "I guess. I'm Cord Galloway." He seemed to be looking to Janie for confirmation.

"Well," John chuckled, "with a girl like Dana, you'd better know for sure if you're her boyfriend or not. I'm John Spencer. Pleased to meet you and glad you want to help."

"The rancher?" Cord asked.

"Yep," he smiled, "how'd you know that?"

"Janie told me."

John looked at Janie and smiled. His big grin made him look like Gary Busey. "Well, look, Mr. Abbott, uh, I mean, Peter, said he has to be done for the day, so I guess I'm going to stop as well."

"Oh," Cord said disappointedly, "okay."

"It looks like the wind isn't going to let up." John looked out at the willow branches strewn about the ground. "You'd think that tree would have lost all its branches by now. Would you be interested in helping us tomorrow, Cord?"

"Sure. Are you sure it's okay if I help?"

"I've never turned down a volunteer yet," he laughed, clapping him on the shoulder. "Seems like there's not a lot of them in this town."

"Well, I gotta go, Cord," Janie said, standing up next to John. "I'll tell Dana you stopped by when she gets home tonight."

Cord stood and shook John's hand. "That's okay," he said, turning his head toward Janie.

"Huh? Why not?" Janie asked.

He turned around to face her directly, put his sunglasses back on the rim of his nose, and smiled, but in a way that made him appear a little sad. "Because wherever she was, she wasn't with me last night."

Janie smiled as he walked off the porch. She could have sworn she saw him wink at her from behind his sunglasses, though she told herself it was probably just a trick of the light.

chapter nine

Mystery Abbott

The temperature in Glendale had reached an all-time record low of thirty-five degrees on Saturday evening. Janie told Mystery that John would be staying for dinner. As he washed up in the bathroom, Mystery gazed out the kitchen window into the fading night and wondered again how she was going to pay him. This morning his truck had been full of insulation, black tarpaper, brown roofing shingles, and all kinds of other roofing things that looked brand new and expensive. But, when she tried to inquire about how much they cost, he simply blew her off with a kiss on the cheek and his patented line about how *they* would worry about it later.

"I have friends at Habitat for Humanity," he had explained, "and at the hardware store in Kennedy. Don't worry about it."

She didn't want to make him feel bad or unwanted after all he had done, but she couldn't rid herself of the feeling that she and the kids dangled from a long rope over a bottomless pit of financial ruin. She had always been able to hang on by a thread but feared that this time any sudden movement or change of direction would break the string. She would be solely responsible for her family falling into darkness.

Accepting John's help tested the strength of that thread, and she knew it.

Mystery tried to take her mind off it by watching Bennie play with his multicolored building blocks. He had them sorted into red, yellow, green, and blue, and one by one was stacking them in four symmetrical towers. A little plastic army guy stood beneath each tower, positioned to shoot them all down. His tongue was licking in and out of his full pouty lips, indicating his total dedication to the project. She laughed inwardly at Maude's accusation that he looked anything like Walt Smith. Walt had black hair for goodness' sake. Bennie's was blond, and there wasn't any man around with lips like her son's—those came directly from his father's family. Luckily, no one had noticed that yet. People saw what they wanted to see in children. If everyone believed that he was Walt Smith's child, they would find a way to convince themselves that Bennie's snow-white hair was darkening, or that his pudgy four-year-old tummy was similar to Walt's beer belly. She wondered what Walt would have to say about it, and prayed that the rumors hadn't reached his desk. The poor man had enough on his mind, and she didn't think he could take any more stress.

Mystery had always done her best to maintain a professional relationship with Walt. She didn't go into his office alone. If he wanted to talk to her, she asked him to come out to the counter. When Walt or any of the mechanics asked her to stay and have a beer, she politely declined. They all understood why, and they did their best to convince her that no one was going to think *that,* but she knew better and so did they. None of the wives liked her, and they definitely didn't like that she had been the only woman working with their husbands for the past five years.

However, now that everyone knew about John, she didn't feel quite as worried about it. She wasn't sure if it was pure exhaustion from dealing with her roof and her family, or the fact that she felt like she was finally hitting rock bottom and really didn't care anymore.

Earlier in the day, in an attempt to clear her head, Mystery had gone into the office. Normally, Walt was the only one who worked on Saturdays. *I like my employees to have a full weekend,* he always said. She thought it would be a good time to thank him for all he had done—including the extra pay for the days she missed last week. She also wanted to let him know that she would be back on Tuesday. If she could manage it, she would have everything fixed by the end of the day on Monday. The store was empty, so Mystery moved toward the back office beneath the hum of fluorescent lights and found Walt sitting at his desk, head in hands. He looked dejected, and the sight of this normally confident, happy man in such a state saddened her. She checked behind her for any customers and then decided that either way, she was going in. In the back of her mind, she attributed her courage to John. He had been there for her when no one else would even look in her direction, not caring what kind of gossip his actions would cause. She could at least repay his kindness by being that kind of friend to another. Walt had always treated her and her children well, in spite of what the women in town might think about her, and she wasn't about to walk out on him now.

His office smelled of peaches from the air freshener plugged into the wall. From the splattered papers on his desk, she could see that he'd been crying. As the door clicked he looked up, startled out of his apparent reverie.

"You okay, Walt?"

He wiped his cheeks and pushed a large stack of papers toward her. The top page stated "Coral Smith vs. Walt Smith." It was all Mystery needed to see. She pushed the papers back and waited for him to regain control.

"I never saw it coming," was all he could say.

Mystery heard the water turn off in the bathroom. John would be out in a minute, and here she was, lost in thought. She smacked her leg with the dishtowel and went to her bedroom to change. She had to face facts. No matter what he thought right now, John wasn't *really* here. He was temporary. She would make dinner one more time, and she would enjoy John's company for one more night. Afterward, she would thank him for the work he had done, pay him what she could, and then politely—without tears—ask him to leave.

They could go back to seeing each other in private, away from the prying eyes of her mother and neighbor, and far away from the problems in her daily life. Maybe they would still be able to be together under the cover of darkness on Mondays and Wednesdays—after she fixed the roof and the town found something else to gossip about. Yes, that was it. She would tell him later tonight.

She dressed in plain jeans, a white cotton tee-shirt, and sandals, and then stood in front of the mirror on her dresser and pulled her hair up into a ponytail. She added a simple silver chain and silver-tone studded earrings. Her mother had said that being pretty was always Mystery's problem, but Mystery just didn't see it. The reflection in the mirror seemed drab, worn-out, and used up by all her years of stress and heartache. Pretty? She hadn't seen herself that way in years. In fact, she couldn't recall the last time she had taken the time to really *see* herself at all.

She moved closer. The mirror on her dresser was a bit off-kilter from the impact of the crash, but she had managed to clean the dresser top with Old English and had placed a white doily over the middle to hold all of her make-up and jewelry. It was good enough. In fact, with the polish it looked better than it had in years. She rubbed the edge of the dresser. Sometimes it takes a disaster to make a person care for the things they normally take for granted. Mystery whispered a silent promise that she would polish it every month from now on. She had neglected it for too long, and it deserved better than that.

She studied herself in the mirror. Neglected for too long. She took a moment, pulled out the ponytail and combed her shoulder-length blonde hair until it seemed to regain a little of its luster. She placed a pewter comb up on one side behind her ear and let the rest cascade down onto her shoulders. She dabbed a little foundation under her eyes, and on her lips she added a hint of pink lipstick. She pinched her cheeks and stood back. Maybe she was pretty. Maybe a little attention was all she needed.

She was about to head for the living room when the phone rang. She ran her hands through her hair and immediately regretted pulling it from the ponytail. She knew that ring. It was her mother. She should just let the machine get it. *Why?* she thought. *Why now?* She wanted to lift a fist to the air and curse fate for all the hell that it brought her, but she knew better. Challenging fate only made things worse in the end. She lifted the receiver and sighed, "Hello?"

John came out of the bathroom just then in his gray thermal ribbed shirt and brown Carhartt jeans. He ran his hand through his tousled hair, trying to coax it into place. He looked better than ever, and she felt her stomach tighten at the sight of him. She watched as he sat down on the loveseat next to Bennie and began pulling on a pair of wool socks.

"Hello, Mystery," Maude said on the phone. "Is that man done on the roof?"

Mystery turned to the hallway and lowered her voice.

"Do you mean *John*?"

"Whatever."

Mystery rolled her eyes. Apparently her mother hadn't heard a word she had said earlier. "Well, you should know, considering that Dad is working with him. Why don't you just ask Dad?"

"I'm asking you," Maude said. "It's your roof."

"Well, he's not done yet, Mom. He's just done for the night. There's still a lot to do."

"Will he be going home for the night, then?"

"After dinner."

"Are you sure?" Maude asked in a sugar-sweet tone.

"That's none of your business," Mystery answered in the same syrupy tone.

"Mystery, the whole town knows that man was caught dead to rights in your closet. Do you really want them saying more about you? Don't you think it's best that he sleep in his *own* house?"

Mystery contemplated telling her mother that she was thirty-six years old, not seventeen, but she didn't want to tempt Maude just then, lest she soon find her mother standing face to face with John right there in her living room.

Mystery turned when she heard the couch squeak and saw John walk over to the coatrack and pull out a bag he had left there earlier. He handed it to Bennie, who grinned as if John were Santa Claus himself. Mystery watched as Bennie pulled out a brand new cowboy hat similar to John's.

"Great," Mystery whispered.

"What?"

"Huh?"

"What did you say *great* for?" Maude asked.

"I didn't realize I had," Mystery replied flatly. "Look Mom, can I call you later?"

"Mystery," she said, "do you really think allowing that man to have dinner with the children is a good idea?"

"His name is John, Mother! *John.* What the hell is with you and names anyway?"

"I don't know what you are talking about."

"Yes, you do. First, it's my name, then Bennie's, and now John's."

"Well, your name explains itself," Maude laughed.

"If you hated it so much, why on earth did you name me that?"

She glanced toward the living room, and yes, John had taken note of her demeanor on the phone, so she lowered her voice. Maude's tone became very serious, as it did every time she referenced the origin of Mystery's name. "It was your father's idea, you know that. Now please, dear, please send that man—John—home before things go any further."

"I think I owe *John* at least dinner for working on the roof."

"You've gotten three kids out of dinners like that—"

"No, I haven't," Mystery snapped.

"You know what I mean, Mystery. You can't put the kids through another boyfriend. Look at Dana, for crying out loud."

"What about Dana?"

"Why do you think Dana is the way that she is? And Janie?"

Mystery felt the hairs on her neck stand up. She could handle her mother pointing out her own faults, mainly because they were often true. However, she couldn't stand Maude saying that the kids were bad people. Dana may have been a problem, but she was still a *kid.* Her mother didn't have the right to judge her. Not yet. And Janie? What could she possibly say about Janie? "What about Janie?"

"Come on Mystery," she said. She sounded fed up. "What do you think she and Taylor do up in that tree fort all day?"

"I don't know," Mystery said, taken off guard, "play?"

"Play *house*, maybe. She does the same thing that you did with boys at your age."

"Mom," she said fighting back the tightness in her voice, "Janie's fine. I've got to go."

"Call me when this is all over," Maude said. "And I mean before to-morrow morning."

Mystery hung up the phone without another response, and walked out into the living room. Through the window, she noticed the bright sensor light in the rear of the Randall house go out. Just beneath it, barely visible through the dark and rain, she could make out Liv Randall sitting in a lounge chair facing the other direction. For a moment, Mystery thought she saw the red glow of a cigarette in Liv's hand.

John got up as she entered the room.

"What's the matter, Mystery?"

Mystery changed direction mid-step, moving toward the kitchen to gain some more time. She needed to clear her head. He followed her in, leaving Bennie to play with his new hat.

"Nothing, it was just a bad phone call," she said, her voice brittle. "I'm sorry, can I get you a cup of tea, or a beer, or something?"

"No," he said. "Why don't I get you one?"

He took her wrists gently and led her to a seat. She didn't want him to do that, to be so caring. It would only make things harder when she had to tell him to go.

"You need something," he said. "Do you have any brandy?"

"Yes, above the stove," she laughed. "What would make you ask for that? Most people don't drink the stuff."

"Well, I do." As he rummaged around in the cupboard for the bottle, Mystery pondered how nice it would be to be able to just look in there without having to stand on a step stool. "One single slug of brandy is the best thing for everything from the flu to bad moods to cold nights around a campfire."

"Is that what all the cowboys drink?" she giggled, feeling better in spite of herself.

"Nope," he said. "Most drink whiskey. Besides, I'm not a cowboy. I just raise cows."

"Why the hat and the belt buckle then?"

"The hat hides my bald head and the belt buckle holds up my fat belly." He grabbed his nonexistent belly and shook it up and down for effect. Mystery laughed, and accepted the small shot of brandy. For a while after Bennie was born, she had taken to drinking a shot of brandy at night to help her sleep. The bottle had been tucked away in the cupboard for four years now. She was surprised that it hadn't all evaporated.

"Now," he said, easing up next to her, "what was that phone call about?"

He had maneuvered his legs around her chair so that she had nowhere to go.

"Nothing," she said, looking away. "I'm fine, really."

"No, you're not." He stroked her hair. "You don't have to protect yourself from me, Mystery. That call was about me, wasn't it?"

Mystery raised her glass, and John poured her another shot. She knew that she shouldn't drink right now, she had dinner to finish and kids to feed, but the call from her mother had upset her more than she cared to admit.

"Who was it?"

"My mother."

"Oh yeah," he laughed, "Mrs. Maude Abbott. I like that one." He was shaking his head up and down and laughing through a goofy grin. For a moment, Mystery almost believed him.

"How can you say that?"

"She's feisty," he said.

"Yeah, feisty. She named me after a whore, John. She says that's why I am the way I am."

"She didn't..."

"Yep," she said seriously. "I think she might be right."

"About what?" He had reached over and was rubbing her thigh with his strong hands, but his brow was wrinkled with consternation.

"About me, about us," she said. She pointed into the living room where Bennie was pulling his hat on and off. "Look at him."

John turned his head and Mystery saw him smile as he watched her son. John sure liked him, and why not? Bennie was easy to like.

He hardly ever said a word and spent most of his day hugging anyone who walked in the door. And Bennie liked John, that was obvious. But that was also the problem. Janie was warming up to John, too. Dana wasn't, but that was no surprise. The amazing thing was that Dana's attitude didn't seem to bother John; it was more of a challenge than a threat. Those were all the reasons Mystery could think of to end this thing right now, before any more cowboy hats or belt buckles changed hands and before any more work was done on the roof.

"What about him?" John asked.

"He's starting to like you."

"I like him, too. That's actually a good thing, Mystery."

"No," she said, moving his hands away from her legs. "No, it's not." She got up and walked to the stove to put some distance between them and have a better view of Bennie. John sat back in his chair, as if ready to wait out her protests.

"Mystery," he said, "what's the matter? Was it something your mother said?"

"No," she said. "And yes. But she *is* right, John."

"Right about *what*?"

"It's just like I told you before, there was a reason that I made you park your car out back."

"I know," he said, sitting up straight. "It's because everyone in this godforsaken neighborhood has their eye on you."

"Well, that," she said calmly, "but it's also because of Bennie, and Janie, and Dana."

"What about them?" he asked. He was clearly confused.

"You wouldn't understand," she said, shaking her head. "You don't have children."

"Okay. Explain it to me."

"The problem is that I can't let them get attached to you, John."

"Why not?"

"Because it's not healthy for them and it's irresponsible of me. I'm getting their hopes up, and when you go away I will have to explain why I did that to them."

John rose and wrapped his warm hands around Mystery's bare arms. "What if I don't go away?"

"You will," she said.

"What if I don't?" he asked again. He looked down and squeezed her arms, trying to force her to return his gaze.

"You *will*," she said with a little more conviction.

"Mystery," he said, "I love you. And Bennie."

Struggling to compose herself, she challenged, "What about Janie and Dana?"

"What about them?" he asked.

His honesty always took her unawares, and, for a moment, she felt a surge of motherly protection kick in for her eldest children. "Well, they are a part of my family, too."

"Well, I hardly know them," he said, "but I'd like to get to know them better."

"Janie maybe," she hedged, "but not Dana."

"Well, that's the other thing. They are your daughters, Mystery, but they are almost eighteen. You don't have to live your life around their needs and desires anymore."

"See," she said, "that's exactly what I'm talking about. You don't have children. You don't understand."

"Yes, yes I do." Mystery could tell he was trying to hold on. "I do understand. What I'm trying to say is that none of that matters. You're worried about me going away, and I'm trying to tell you that I'm *not* going anywhere."

"Just wait," Mystery said decidedly. "Just you wait. You don't know me all that well yet. You'll go away. Everyone does."

"Are you talking about the girls' father? Or Bennie's? Is that what you mean?"

"Them, and others, too. People rarely stay together John. I don't want to put the kids through that again."

"Well, I'm not just anyone, Mystery."

She could tell she was getting him angry and it felt good. If she pushed hard enough now, she could break him and end this thing before it went any further, before he had a chance to try to fool himself into really loving her.

"I've never been in love with anyone, Mystery. I was beginning to wonder if I ever would be, but after being with you — *and your family* — I know now that I was wrong. I *am* in love. You are the strongest person I have ever met. You have put up with more crap from your mother and this town in order to protect your children, more than I ever would have. So please don't tell me what I do know and what I don't know because my instincts are usually dead on. You're the one, Mystery. You're the only one."

"You don't know that," she said quickly, twisting out of his grasp. "You don't know me, or my life. You've only seen it at night when no one else is around except you and me. Did you see that roof up there?"

"Yes," he said, crossing his arms, "I've been seeing it all day."

"Well," she continued, her voice rising, "that was no accident. That was not just one of those bad things that happen to good people. That is the kind of thing that happens to Mystery Abbott all the time. My roof falls in, my furniture breaks, my garden freezes out when my neighbor's is just fine, I get pregnant from a one-night-stand, and I lose every man I've ever slept with — not that there have been that many — once he figures all that out. So I'm going to save all of us the trouble. That is the only responsible thing I can do, and then maybe, just maybe, everyone in this town will stop pointing at me and my children, and for once say that I made a good decision!"

She pulled out her pewter hair comb and tossed it across the table.

"Mommy?"

Bennie stood in the doorway, holding his new cowboy hat in his hand just like John always did. His lip was trembling as he looked back and forth from her to John. She shook her head and scolded herself for hurting her child again. She got down on her hands and knees in front of Bennie. "It's going to be okay, honey."

Bennie looked up at John as a single tear escaped his blue eyes and rolled down his pudgy cheek. "It's okay, little buddy," John said.

Mystery felt a sudden urge to protect Bennie right this minute. He'd never seen adults fight. She wiped her eyes and smiled at her son. John came over and bent down next to Mystery. She stiffened her posture.

"There's nothing to worry about," he said. "You know how it feels when you skin your knee? How it hurts and you just want to cry?"

Bennie nodded his head.

"Well, that's how your mommy feels right now."

Mystery closed her eyes, and shook her head. "No," she whispered, "no, that's not it. Not at all."

John leaned his face into her hair and took a deep breath. "Marry me," he whispered. "Marry me, and move away from here."

She felt her anger dissolve into butterflies in her stomach and a crazy urge to laugh, but the look in his eyes said he was serious. She moved away from his tempting arms and walked over to the window, her safety zone. John stayed on bended knees next to Bennie, but followed her with his eyes for a moment before he smiling reassuringly at Bennie and placed the cowboy hat firmly on her little guy's head. Mystery marveled at him. John seemed blind to anything but her child right then. He really did love Bennie.

"Do you own your house?" she whispered with her back to him. She knew she shouldn't be asking such a personal question. She had always been thankful that finances hadn't been a part of their everyday conversations, and now she was opening the door to it. But it had been on her mind, just beneath the surface, gnawing at her, trying to force her to admit to herself and to him that she was just not in his league.

"Well, yes, I inherited it. Why? Does it matter?"

"No," she said. "It's just..." She trailed off. This was none of his business. He was just her boyfriend, for goodness' sake. A boyfriend who obviously hadn't experienced a bit of financial trouble. She was the only one of the two who had those problems, and she had brought them on herself by having three kids and no father to help raise them. She certainly wasn't about to make that his problem.

"It's just what?"

Her cheeks reddened, and her heart began to pound. She turned back around to face him, arms crossed and closed off to any more questions. "I can't leave Glendale," she said brusquely, refusing to meet his gaze. "I'm sorry John, it just won't work." She grabbed her purse off the counter. "Please tell me how much the roofing material cost," she said, pulling out her checkbook, "I can't afford to pay much more than that, I'm afraid, but I would like to reimburse you what I can."

He was silent, but she couldn't bring herself to look him in the face.

"Consider it a gift," he said firmly.

She waited, knowing that she had to be strong to get this over with as quickly as possible, but he said nothing more.

"Bennie," she heard him say finally, "I'll be back, li'l pard."

"Bye, John," he whispered solemnly.

After John left, Mystery pulled Bennie into her arms. She was doing this for him, she kept telling herself. Bennie and the girls. They had to be all that mattered.

chapter ten

Liv Randall

L iv stretched her arms out away from her body and then pulled them in tight around her. She was bobbing beneath the darkness of water. She hugged herself and spun her legs in a circular motion twirling round and round. Finally, she felt brave enough to open her eyes. She was perfectly suspended like a buoyant piece of driftwood, somewhere between the cold black sludge at the bottom and the harsh cold air above. The water was so thick that it felt like she was swimming in split pea soup, yet she moved freely, jetting back and forth, side to side, round and round like a ballerina. She opened her mouth, sucked in the salt-flavored algae, and was surprised to find she could inhale the water deeply into her lungs. It was the most natural breath she had ever taken.

Where was she? It seemed she had been here many times before. It was like a protective womb, someplace she never wanted to leave. It had to be the ocean. Where else would she feel that free? But it didn't make sense. The ocean was icy, biting, and made her feel utterly alive. This place was warm and slow, someplace she wanted to fall asleep in and never wake up. She rolled over and over in the murkiness until —*SMACK!*

Her head hit something hard. Before her, a sea of blackness emerged and blocked out the green light of the water. She pulled her head back and stared at the oak planks of her bedroom floor and the line of drool starting from her lip and ending in a puddle. *It was only a dream.* She rolled onto her back and fought the bed sheet binding her legs. The house was quiet except for the electricity humming and the ticking of Ilsa's birds-of-prey clock in the hallway. She closed her eyes and tried to sink back into the water. She held her breath and tried to pull her head under but, just like every other wonderful dream she'd had, it was an ephemeral moment and she'd be lucky if she ever got it back.

She sat up and looked at the window. The dim light of another stormy day in Glendale dawned and with it, all of her problems and fears came flooding back: Carl, Mystery, Taylor and Janie, and the betrayal by her supposed friends. She felt her body weaken at the thought of one more day in this existence.

She crumpled up the sheet, threw it aside, and took her usual place by the window. The red truck was gone this morning and Mystery was sitting on the porch swing watching Bennie play with his Tonka trucks at her feet. He had on a cowboy hat just like that man's. John what's-his-name. Mystery was clearly trying to brainwash the child. She wondered if the woman was ever going to return to work. Walt Smith was probably paying for her time off anyway. Everyone in town knew why he hired her.

She shook her head and tried to stop thinking such bad thoughts about her neighbor. She hadn't been such a gossip before becoming involved with the women of Ma Bell. Liv wished it hadn't turned out that way — that *she* hadn't turned out that way. She hadn't meant to become such a horrible gossip or such a horrible neighbor. But Mystery always seemed to ask for it, and now she was doing it again by flaunting the evidence of her newest affair right there on her front porch for everyone in Glendale to see. She didn't even have the decency, or the wisdom for that matter, to keep it a secret.

She thought of the man in Mystery's closet. He was tall, stockier than Carl, and he filled out his Wranglers perfectly. She had seen a picture of George Strait modeling Wranglers somewhere before. That was the first time she ever thought a cowboy looked nice in his jeans. This was the second. She wondered what he was doing with a woman like Mystery Abbott.

Liv tried to imagine Carl working in the rain on their roof like John had been. She pictured him in his running shorts and a Bobcats tank top contemplating which end of the hammer to begin with. She laughed and covered her mouth with her hand. Something about the motion must have caught Mystery's eye because her neighbor covered her eyebrows with her hand and peered right up at Liv's bedroom window. Liv edged behind the protective cover of Ilsa's brown velvet drapes. Liv had always hated those drapes, but right now they created a convenient barrier from her neighbors' prying eyes.

She threw the sheets and blankets into place on the bed, yanked them into a square, and shoved the edges in around all sides. Every morning. She made the bed every morning, and no matter what she did today, she would have to do it tomorrow as well. It was like the laundry, a never-ending task. Carl had never made their bed. Not once. She wondered what would happen if she died. Would the bed ever get made? Probably not. She tossed the throw pillow on the bed and watched it land cattywampus somewhere in the middle. She knew she should fix it but instead she ignored it.

She went to the closet to grab the slacks and blouse she had picked out for herself the night before, but then she changed her mind. She could hear herself beginning to grind her teeth. She tried to relax. It was the hunger. She hadn't eaten last night. Waiting for Carl to get home had made her lose her appetite. Today, it would be coffee and plain toast. That was all. And, no slacks. She opted for jeans and a sweatshirt. It wasn't like she had anywhere to go today anyway.

Finally, she went into the kitchen for a cup of coffee. The pot had been turned off hours ago and the coffee was cold. Evidently, someone had decided on eggs over easy for breakfast and the "easy" had dripped off the counter and all over the throw rug beneath the stove. That was her punishment for not getting up and cooking them breakfast. She grabbed the washcloth from the sink and was just about to clean it up when wet egg and eggshells dripped down her wrist from within the cold cloth and landed on the floor.

She threw the washcloth at the back of the sink, and watched the gooey mess ooze off the white tile backsplash. Instantly, she pictured it drying into a deep seventies-yellow right there on the tile. She would be scraping egg off the tile for a week. Not that anyone would apologize or notice.

She turned from the sink and saw an egg-smeared note on the counter next to the stove.

Jane called twice last night.
Dora called once.
Call your friends back.
I'll be late.
—Carl

She clenched her teeth again and panted for air. From beneath the sink, she snatched a paper bag and breathed deeply into it. If she passed out in here, no one would find her for hours. Considering the note, maybe even longer.

"I'll be late. Carl," she muttered angrily. She took another deep breath in the bag.

Why couldn't he just say it? Just once without her having to beg for it. Was it that hard to write, *Love* or *I love you*? She guessed that maybe it would be hard to write if you didn't love someone. She grabbed a new pack of cigarettes hidden with the cleaning supplies, and ran out to the deck. Between breaths from the paper bag, she puffed on her cigarette. She moved to the west end of the porch to stay downwind and out of Mystery's sight. Even on her own back porch, she could not find space. She always told Carl she felt like she'd had more privacy in Seattle, but he told her that was nonsense: *Liv, how could you have privacy in a big city with so many people?* The thought of their conversation irritated her. No matter what she said, he contradicted her and told her that she was being stupid. She knew that was what he thought of her, stupid and unlovable.

She took a deep drag from the cigarette, the kind that would hit the bottom of her lungs so hard that it might cause irreversible damage. Her chest constricted as the smoke moved around inside her lungs. She closed her eyes and tossed the cigarette into the wet grass, knowing full well that she should pick it up. Instead, she turned her back on it and let it smolder.

Alone. She wanted to be alone. She should just go back in and get her list done, as she had for as long as she could recall. If she just got back to it and successfully crossed off a few of the numbered items, she would feel better. Accomplishing tasks always made her feel a little better, a little more necessary, a little more like she mattered.

Once inside, however, she grabbed a raincoat and galoshes and ran back out to her car. Her hands started to shake again and fingers of darkness clawed their way in around her temples. She had to go. If she stayed here it would take hold for sure.

She quickly got in the Jetta, ripped out of the driveway, and skidded down Carlisle. She knew Mystery was watching her but she didn't care. If she didn't hurry, that cloud would get her right there in front of everyone, and then who would they be talking about on Carlisle Street? But then she remembered: Ma Bell was already talking about her.

It took her ten minutes of bouncing and slamming the undercarriage of her car on Sheep Creek Road, but she finally made it to the Miller house again. Its beauty truly did remind her of the ocean. As she stared at the farmhouse with the bright blue roof, she felt her heart rate even out.

She wanted to run to it, to be with it, but she forced herself to calmly survey the grounds. A stream had formed in the ditch alongside the driveway from the incessant rain. If it didn't stop soon there would be a flood. A lack of life was taking its toll on the house. Without people in it to open windows and breathe life into the place, it was beginning to wither away just as its owners had. Soon it would be gone too. Aging and dilapidation bugged her as much as fingernails on a chalkboard, and she wished there was someone she could reprimand for the neglect.

With exaggerated control, Liv drove up the circular drive. The house was symmetrical and she could tell from the manner in which the grounds had been laid out that it had been beautifully maintained at one time.

When she got out of the car in front of the house, the wind was blowing steadily but the rain seemed to have given up its all-out at-tack in favor of a constant drizzle. The fragrance of lilacs mingled with the light scents of algae and seagull droppings. Where those smells might be coming from, she didn't know, since there probably wasn't a seagull within miles of this place. A tire swing, freely propelled by the wind, undulated beneath the branches of a large cottonwood tree just to the north.

She made her way beyond the long white front porch to the rear of the house. The breeze blowing in from the east made her mouth water: fish, algae, and sea mist. She had heard her friends complain about smelling the pulp factory from Lewiston on days that the wind blew in from the south, but no matter how much she wanted to, she had a hard time believing that even the strongest of winds could bring the smell of the ocean to Glendale.

In the backyard, a sagging clothesline still supported three clothes-pins, and a large maple creaked in the wind. The yard was yellow and unkempt, full of fairy rings and buttonweed, and the abandoned raspberry patch next to the tool shed had grown over, drooped from neglect. By this time of the season, raspberry bushes were normally full of the ripe red fruit, but not this year. Instead the long limbs were spindly, the leaves brown at the edges. There wasn't a berry in sight.

The adjoining fields appeared to be about three football fields long and ended just at the edge of some tree-covered hills, giving her the feeling of complete seclusion. For being in the country, this place was perfect. No one to bug you, no gossip, no people you had to be nice to. Here, Liv felt as alone as she did in the city.

As she appraised the end of the yard, her heart stopped — there was the water she had dreamed about the night before! It wasn't an ocean, it was a pond. Cattails protruded from the pond's forward edge, par-tially obscuring it from view, but she was certain it was the same one. Out in the middle, a single-person canoe was tied to a little floating dock. Liv took a deep, careful breath and realized the pond was the source of the smell. It didn't seem possible, and it had been years since she had been to the ocean, but it truly did smell of fish shops and crab pots. She strode through the tall weeds in the yard and pulled the cat-tails aside to stick her hand in the water. It was warm compared to the rain, and with the algae, it did feel like split pea soup. She stifled a laugh. She wanted to jump in and swim around just as in her dream, but she knew she wouldn't be able to breath like she had while asleep.

She stared for a while longer with her hand still immersed in the water. Suddenly, she realized that her peripheral vision was restored out here. The gray cloud was nowhere to be seen. It was probably just the vast openness of the fields, but it felt good. She felt like she could breathe again, as if the air was thinner here than it was in town. The Miller house was barely three miles away from Glendale and yet it seemed like a world apart. She reluctantly pulled her hand from the water, and wiped the green slime on the wet grass.

She stood and looked around at the rest of the grounds. Next to the back porch, she noticed a small rose garden with three conspicuous gaps in it. They looked like freshly dug graves. Someone had been out here digging up the dead occupants' roses. She felt her newfound peace slipping away at the thought of someone robbing the house of its beauty. *The bastards didn't even care enough to fill in the holes.* She shook her head and walked back to her car out front. As she turned to say a final goodbye, she looked up to the porch and saw a large hole in one of the windows. It looked like a rock had been thrown through it.

"Who would do such a thing?" she murmured.

She stepped onto the porch, half expecting a woman in an apron to walk out with an apple pie in her hand and ask her to sit down for tea. Through the window, she could make out a large foyer still filled with the Millers' belongings. On the walls were several paintings, a large oval mirror, and what looked like family pictures. She wondered how anyone could leave all of that behind.

Beyond the foyer, Liv could make out the kitchen. Yellow with black trim. It even had an old boiler heater in it. Just inside the window Liv could see the latch, only inches from her hand. In seconds she could be inside. She bit her lip and looked over her shoulder. It was trespassing and her husband was a lawyer. Her chin went up. That settled it.

She turned back, gingerly reached through the broken pane, and, with a single flick of her fingers, the window was open. A rush of stale air forced its way past her like a freed prisoner, pulling the lace curtain out through the open window. The house had been closed up for too

long. She climbed through, thankful now that she had opted for jeans
and a sweatshirt, and gently pulled the curtain back inside, calming it
and returning it to its rightful place in front of the window.

Liv stood still just inside, as if fearful of disturbing a sleeping resident. Although she knew the house was vacant, she could sense some
kind of life force in it.

"Hello?" she bellowed, walking toward the long cherrywood dining
room table in the middle of the room. In the very center was a vase
of dead white roses. The attached card read, "Sorry for your loss." No
one had even bothered to throw them out. She ran her hand along the
table and closed her eyes. The place was beautiful and she felt sensual
just being in it.

The high-ceilinged kitchen was bordered all around in black ceramic tiles. Above the center island was a large brass pot hanger that
still held all of its pans. A spiderweb had formed from the hanger to
the ceiling. Liv went to the closet, opened it, and smiled. There was
the broom just where she would have left it. She took it to the island
and swatted the cobweb down. *Better.*

In the sink there was a white china coffee cup, stained brown with
the remnants of an old moldy cigarette still in the bottom. *Dora,* she
thought. Dora was the realtor in town, the only person she could think
of who would have access to this place. She had to be the one who had
left the cigarette. Liv felt like calling her and having a word with her
about it, but then Dora would know that she, Liv, had been inside the
house.

The old wood floors creaked to life as Liv walked to the stairs and
looked up at the large open landing. It was dim inside the house on
such a dreary day, so she instinctively flipped the light switch. She
was shocked to find that the power was still on. She quickly mounted
the steps and flipped the switch at the top to turn the power off.

"Hello?" she called again walking to the end of the hall. At the far
end of the hall, Liv slowly turned a white ceramic handle. With a click
and a creak the door welcomed her. It was just as she had predicted.
The master bedroom, right where she would have placed it. A four-
poster cherrywood bed leaned up against the east wall, and two large

windows faced south. Out them Liv was treated to a spectacular view of the pond and the surrounding landscape.

She opened the window and sat on the edge of the bed, mesmerized by green-gold fields surrounding the dark pond. In the center, the white canoe bobbed up and down. The whole scene was as symmetrical as the house. The rightness of it was calming to Liv. She took it all in, running her hands up and down her arms. She unconsciously touched her collarbone like Carl used to do when he'd try to seduce her. Just to the west of the house, Liv could see the sun had fought to peek through the dense clouds just enough to shine a couple of orange fingers over the surrounding mountains and poke holes in the gray of the Glendale summer. Liv smiled. The smell of the ocean was stronger in here, and as she licked her lips, for the first time in her life she tasted the salt of her own tears. She closed her eyes and wept. Finally, she had found a place that made her feel something: alive, free, and sexually awake. She couldn't quite grasp what it was yet, but she knew one thing for certain: tomorrow she was coming back. This was one thing that the women of Ma Bell would know nothing about.

chapter eleven

Dana Abbott

Dana was glad the rain had finally let up. Her new perm couldn't take much more. It was still breezy and it seemed to be getting colder instead of warmer, but there were cracks in the clouds tonight that betrayed the presence of an orange glow well after eight o'clock. Her mother used to say, "Red sky at night, sailor's delight. Red sky in morning, sailor's warning." She wouldn't tell Mystery that she liked that little quip, but it seemed to be foolproof. Maybe there was hope for this summer yet.

Her arms had goosebumps, but she was determined not to put on her sweater. It had been a month since she bought the little red tank top in preparation for this summer. At the time, she had bought it to wear for Cord. Today, it had a new purpose. She wasn't about to cover up just because someone forgot to tell Mother Nature that it was the end of June.

She had seen Dylan drive by twice while she was at work. He hadn't looked up but she knew that he was watching her. His office was only two blocks away. Now she could see the cruiser out in front, but the fading sun on the windows made it difficult to tell whether the lights in the office were on or off.

She heard the hum of a car following her as she walked home from work. It wasn't loud enough to be a truck, so it couldn't have been one of the farmers she had smiled at while pouring their coffee. They were always good for an inappropriate glance at her tush when they thought she wasn't looking. When she caught them, she'd make certain to stay bent down to get extra packets of creamer from the bottom shelf or facing the order-up window to collect plates of eggs and hash from Mr. Borghese. She could always work an extra tip out of the farmers, even the ones who only came in for coffee.

She concentrated hard to see if she could figure out what kind of car it was without looking. It sounded familiar but she couldn't place it. She felt hot eyes on her back and she didn't want to turn around and disturb them, so she continued walking at the same pace toward the police cruiser. The car continued to follow her at a safe distance, but this guy was taking a little bit longer than Dana normally allowed. She'd give him ten more seconds and then she would turn and fire off a warning glare.

Honk!

Dana jumped and turned, prepared to flip him off, when she realized that it was Cord. She sighed and remembered that she hadn't called him in a couple of days. He just wasn't a prospect. She had hoped he would get the clue and leave her alone, but he continued to drive toward her as if he was entitled to some connection to her that other men were not. She glanced ahead at the police station and could now see that the lights were definitely on. Grudgingly, she allowed that even Cord deserved an explanation.

She reluctantly waited at the curb for him. He pulled up and turned down the radio. It was Damn Yankees again. She wanted to tell him that the eighties were dead, that his music was the same crap that her mom listened to, but then she figured, why bother? It wouldn't be her problem for long. He leaned over to the passenger side and rolled down the window. She bent over and leaned in, letting her tank top fall open so that he could see her cleavage.

"Hi Dana," he said. "Why didn't you stop?"

"Didn't know it was you," she replied.

"Well, who did you think it was, your other boyfriend?"

Dana eyed him for a minute and then flashed an insincere smile.

"So what are you doing out here?" he asked.

"Nothing. Just getting off work. I thought about stopping by."

"Oh," he said.

He didn't beg her to get in, but he seemed to be contemplating the idea. Maybe it was a test. She stood there for a few moments, giving him a chance. He'd better step lightly. She didn't take much crap off men.

"Look, Cord, I'm sorry that I haven't called you. I've been pretty busy with the new job."

"Like it a lot, huh?"

"Love it."

"You must be working late," he said. "I couldn't find you last night."

"Yep, overtime."

Dylan flashed through her mind again.

"Oh yeah, how's that going?" His voice was dry and he stared straight ahead as he asked her, as if he really couldn't care less about her answer. He was going to try to punish her for not calling him. That was fine. Dana could take a little spanking if it made his ego feel better.

"It's good," she said. "You should stop in. I kind of figured that you might do that sometime this week."

"I've been in Idaho, *remember*?"

"Oh," she said recalling that he had mentioned something about that. "What have you been up to there?"

"I'm thinking about fixing up the place. Maybe buying a few cattle. What do you think about that?"

"Sounds interesting."

He snorted.

This was going to be a little more than a spanking. Well, she would allow it just long enough to make him feel like he was still in control, but not much further than that. She'd be damned if some guy that she was about to dump was going to make her feel bad for ignoring him or his stupid dream about living in the hills somewhere in Idaho.

"Can I get in?" she asked.

He hesitated a minute. She hated men who sulked. She swore that when she finally dumped him she would blame it on his attitude.

"I guess," he said finally. He was looking across the street. She didn't know what he was trying to see since all the businesses were closed. The only car in sight was Coral Smith's Cadillac parked in front of Carl Randall's office. It had taken her a while to figure out who she was, but when she did, she had wanted to personally slap Carl Randall for betraying his wife. *He's stupid*, she thought. *Bold, but stupid.*

"Well, I don't have to. I was just heading home anyway."

"Suit yourself," he said.

"What's your problem?" she snapped. It wasn't that it would matter much longer; she just wasn't about to play his game.

"Me? Nothing. I saw you walking and I thought I should let you know that I'm helping John with the roof."

"*Our* roof? I thought I told you, that is Mystery's problem, not mine."

"I'm not doing it for you."

"Well then who are you doing it for? Mystery?" she laughed.

"Why do you call your mom Mystery?"

"Because that's her name."

"Well, it's rude."

"Actually, it's none of your business. Now tell me why you are helping when I'm pretty sure I told you not to."

"Actually," he repeated, "that's none of *your* business."

"It's my house!"

"No," he shot back, "it's Mystery's house. You already said it wasn't your problem."

"Why are you doing it?" she sneered.

He continued to smile out the window away from her. "If you want the truth," he turned toward her now, "Janie asked me to help."

"Oh, that figures," Dana said.

Cord put his hand up to his mouth. It looked liked he was attempting to cover a grin. Suddenly it dawned on her. She could not believe it, but she was fairly in-tune with these kinds of emotions. She could spot desire at fifty paces, but she didn't want to believe that a guy like Cord Galloway would feel anything for a girl like Janie. "You have the hots for Janie, don't you?" Dana asked, half hoping he would laugh in her face.

Instead, Cord shook his head, and smiled out the driver's side window. He was practically glowing. The thought of Janie making it with a guy like Cord disgusted Dana, especially after she had been so close to letting him have his way with her in the car the other day. That temptation alone should have been enough to keep his mind on her — even when Dana wasn't around.

"Good luck with that one, Cord."

"Why?"

"Well, for one, she's had the same boyfriend since birth. For another, there's not a man alive, including her boyfriend, who has ever been unable to unzip those jeans."

"Maybe I'm not looking to get in her pants, Dana."

"Yeah right! That's what all men want. Although, I have to say that I've yet to hear of any man other than Taylor wanting that from Janie."

"What is it with you hating your family?"

Dana looked across the street, "I don't know," she said. "I guess it's because everyone else does."

"No they don't, Dana. You know, for twins, you two are nothing alike."

"You can say that again," Dana agreed. "So...I guess that means we're breaking up?"

"Yep." He seemed so unmoved. Dana had never had a boy break up with her. It didn't seem right. Her other boyfriends had at least put up a fight or begged for one last time. Sometimes she'd given it, other times she hadn't. Cord didn't seem to want either. He just wanted to be let go. It sparked anger she hadn't felt before.

"So that's it?" she asked. "It's just over?"

She backed away from the window and readjusted her shirt.

"Oh please, Dana," he said. "Don't act like you were just waiting around for me. It certainly wasn't me that you were with the other night."

"What are you talking about?"

"Janie told me you were out all night after you blew up at Mystery for having a man over. You certainly weren't with me."

"The little witch!"

"Don't blame her," he laughed. "You're the one who lied. Whoever he is, I hope he's worth it."

"Oh, he is," she purred, looking down the road toward the police station, "He's a cop," she challenged. She watched Cord's eyes for a reaction, but saw none.

"A little old for you isn't he?"

"Mature maybe," she said. "Not old."

"Well, be careful with that," Cord said. "You both could get in trouble. Goodbye, Dana."

As he sped off down the road, tires squeaking on the wet pavement, Dana's jaw dropped in amazement. She wasn't sure what to think. He had just left her right there on the side of the road. On Main Street. And he had left her for Janie. She let the thought of it sink in. She pictured Janie in the backseat of Cord's car, trying to figure out exactly how to make him moan the way that Dana had. Janie would need directions and a map to figure that out. She looked down the road to the police station and then back to Cord's disappearing car. It was over. She stood still to regain her bearings.

Within moments, her anger subsided and she turned her thoughts to Dylan Masters. Actually, this was okay; she would deal with Janie later. She had told Mystery that she would be out with the girls tonight. And thanks to her new status as an employed adult in the family, coupled with the fact that Mystery really didn't want her around right now, there had been no argument. By the time she reached the police station, Dana felt herself return to normal. Dylan would not turn her down.

She could see him through the slats of the blinds, sitting in the light of his desk lamp as he had been last time, going over some papers. He studied the printed pages as his muscled arm raised a coffee mug to his lips. He looked so strong. Dana felt her body tighten at the thought of being in those arms. When he glanced up and saw her through the window he got up, waving her inside. She quickly opened the door and stepped into the office.

"Hello Dana," he said professionally. He leaned back against the desk and continued to shuffle through the papers. His lips were pursed, and for a moment he looked fatherly, like he was going to accuse her of exactly what she was there to do and then quickly take her home to her mother for confession.

"Hi," she said quietly. "I just stopped by for the results on John."

His legs were spread as he leaned up against the desk and Dana could make out a slight bulge in his pants. Contrary to popular belief, Dana knew that males were not the only creatures who ogled the other sex. She wished he would just look the other way for a while so she could detail his body with her eyes.

"Well," he said, pulling the papers from his desk, "everything checks out. Aside from a parking ticket ten years ago, the guy is as clean as a whistle. Not even a credit problem."

"Oh," she said. "Well, that's great." She walked to the window and peeked through the blinds, trying to use the silence in the room to her advantage.

"Would you like a cup of coffee?" he asked, getting up and going for the pot.

"I thought you'd never ask," she replied. She sat down on the couch and pulled her shirt down to expose her breasts a bit more, just as she had done for Cord only moments ago. When he returned, she motioned him to sit down next to her. He did so reluctantly. She could tell he wasn't going to be as easy to break as other men in this town, and the thought of that excited her.

"I'm not going to bite," she said.

Dylan looked at the window and then sat up against the far side of the couch. "What are you doing this summer besides work?" He was trying to make polite conversation, something Dana was very good at with men.

"Oh, I keep myself pretty busy," she said, although she could not think of with what. She thought about what she had seen Liv do.

"I do a lot of work around the house at night, go to the pool occasionally during the day. I jog as often as I can in between."

"Wow, ambitious. What about a boyfriend?" He smiled sheepishly.

"Nope," she could honestly say, "no boyfriend. I tried dating through high school, but the boys in this town are too immature for me."

Just then, someone tapped on the door and Dylan rose to his feet. "Too bad you aren't five years older, Dana Abbott. I wouldn't hesitate to ask you out."

He took her cup of coffee and motioned her to the door. He was about to turn the doorknob when she reached up and covered his hand with hers. "What's worse, Dylan, is that you aren't five years younger. I might just have asked *you* out." She paused before letting go and stood to give him a soft peck on the cheek.

"Until tomorrow then." Without waiting for him to question what she was referring to, Dana walked out the door, right past Carl Randall who had his fist in midair, prepared to knock again. She didn't even say hello.

chapter twelve

Janie Abbott

The clouds had parted temporarily over Glendale. The sun was shining brightly this morning but the temperature was still somewhere in the fifties. Janie sat out on the porch and tracked a bumblebee as it traveled from dandelion to dandelion collecting pollen with its back legs. It wasn't moving very fast. It was just too cold out for ambition. Her mind wandered to Cord Galloway and the fact the he would be coming to help with the roof this morning. She wasn't sure where John was, and when Janie had asked, her mother had said she didn't know either. She felt a bit guilty for sitting out on the porch swing with an ulterior motive, but it was her porch.

She glanced over at Taylor's house. He was gone with his friends again. Football this time. He had called twice and asked her to come cheer him on. She hadn't called him back, and she didn't come out on the porch until after she saw his car leave. He had cruised by slowly, and she held her breath until he was down the road. She felt guilty for treating him like this, but she couldn't seem to help herself. She didn't want to be with him right now, but she didn't have the courage to tell him so.

One month from today, she and Dana would turn eighteen and

Janie could be a married woman. Thirty days was all she had left of her childhood. She wasn't going to college. She'd already told her mother that. When her mother had asked why, she simply said that college wasn't her thing. She couldn't admit to her the real issue: that even with scholarships, they couldn't afford it. Mystery wanted her to go so badly, but Janie really wouldn't need to if she married Taylor. He wanted her to stay at home, just like his mother did. He had already mapped out that plan for her.

Janie grabbed the blanket from the back of the swing and placed it around her shoulders. She was wearing jeans and a tank top, and even with the blanket she was still a little chilly. Dana came out on the porch and sat on the steps. She had a cup of steaming coffee in hand and was wearing her pink miniskirt and tank top, seemingly oblivious to the weather. Sitting above her look-at-me cleavage was a large silver cross. Janie thought that was a nice touch even though chastity was obviously not Dana's calling. As far as she knew, her sister had yet to set foot in a church. She would probably burst into flames just crossing the threshold.

"Waiting for Taylor?" Dana asked, looking across the street instead of at Janie.

"No," she replied. "He's playing football with his buddies."

"And you're not sitting on the sidelines like a good little girlfriend?"

"Nope," Janie said flatly.

"Then what are you all dressed up for?"

"I'm not. Just jeans."

"Yeah, and your nicest tank top," Dana said as she took a sip from her cup.

Janie pulled the blanket tighter around her body.

"When did you start drinking coffee?" Janie asked, changing the subject.

"Couple days ago, not that it's any of your business."

"Don't you have a job to go to?" She wanted Dana to leave before she called her out on anything Janie couldn't deny. Janie had always thought her sister could see right through her and that she couldn't lie well enough to fool Dana.

"Yes," Dana said. "That's more than I can say for you."

Janie looked away. Arguments with Dana were best avoided. Dana turned toward Janie and said, "So, are you going to tell me why you did it?"

"Did what?"

"Why you invited Cord to work on the roof with John?"

"I didn't invite him," Janie said. "He offered."

"Well, you certainly didn't stop him, did you?"

"No. Why should I? Someone has to get it done, and he said he's had experience with roofs."

"Oh, has he?" Dana arched her eyebrows in a look of mock surprise. "Looks like you know more about my boyfriend than I do."

"No, I don't," Janie snapped.

"It's okay, Janie," she said. "Don't get your panties in a bind. Or, I guess I should call them briefs, in your case."

Janie felt her cheeks turning red, signaling a *touché* to Dana. She tried to ignore both the sly grin and Dana's cold gray eyes as they bored into her.

"You want him here, don't you?" Dana accused.

"It's fine with me," Janie countered. "What's weird is that it seems like you *don't* want Cord here."

The wrinkles around Dana's eyes creased together as her eyes narrowed, and Janie felt an unfamiliar surge of triumph. If she could just maintain a level head and patient tongue, she might actually win this one.

Dana sighed dramatically. "I can't expect you to understand this, especially because you don't seem to mind your boyfriend monitoring your every move, but I don't need Cord around here watching me all the time." She turned away from Janie for a moment and gestured to the house across the street as Janie glared at her behind her back. "What's with you and Taylor anyway?" Dana asked.

Janie wasn't sure what she meant. Dana usually didn't care at all about Taylor and rarely asked about him. It was probably a trap. "I don't know," Janie said.

Dana turned and looked closely at her sister, softening the creases around her eyes.

It was the deadliest kind of trap Dana could lay, and Janie knew she was in no position to win the argument under these circumstances.

"Janie, you don't know men like I do."

"Most girls our age don't."

She could see the steel move back into her sister's eyes. "What's that supposed to mean?"

Janie hesitated. She could either go in for the kill or back off and lose the argument. She closed her eyes for a moment and decided to deviate from her tactic. "What about Taylor and me?" she asked. "Why are you asking about him now?"

"What do you see in that guy anyway?"

"Well, he's smart, he's going to be successful, and he loves me. Why?"

"You think Taylor Randall *loves* you?"

"Yes," Janie said firmly. "He loves me."

"I guess that's why he sleeps with every other girl in town then."

Janie was silent. "What do you care anyway?" she finally asked.

"I don't."

"Why do you hate me so much, Dana? What did I ever do to you?"

Dana looked off down the road as if idly weighing her options. When she looked back at Janie, she said, "Because you're Mystery's good little girl. You always have been." With that, Dana set her cup on the porch railing and pranced down the stairs. Without so much as a turn of the head, she walked away.

A coldness seemed to settle over Glendale again, and Janie shivered. Somehow she had always known that Dana felt that way. As if by simply sharing their mother's womb, Janie had taken something from her that was Dana's and Dana's alone.

A heavy black cloud had moved in to block the sun and raindrops now spattered the sidewalk. Janie was beginning to feel claustrophobic in this weather. As if on cue, the screendoor slammed against the house as a naked Bennie rushed out onto the sidewalk to catch raindrops on his tongue.

"Bennie, you get back in here." Mystery followed him out the door, ran down the steps, and swooped his little body up in her arms. He laughed and pulled away from her.

"Rain," he laughed. "I want rain!"

"Oh, Mom," Janie said, "let him have it. It's probably the first time he's ever said the word."

Mystery gently placed him down and returned to the porch to sit by her daughter.

"I suppose he should be dressed at least," Mystery said.

"He's fine, Mom. He's just a little boy."

"We will hear about this, you know," Mystery said, pointing across the street.

"So what?" Janie replied. She glared at her future mother-in-law's house and cringed at the thought of how controlled her life was about to become. Just then, two vehicles turned the corner and headed east on Carlisle Street. Her heart fluttered as she saw Cord pull up in front of the house. John trailed him in his work truck. She looked from Taylor's house to Cord's car and instantly felt guilty. What was she doing?

"Mom," she said. "I'm going to take Bennie in."

"Why? You just said keep him out."

"Well, he might catch a cold in this weather," Janie said hurriedly, taking Bennie by the hand to lead him inside. But at the sight of John getting out of his truck, the little boy struggled against her and pulled away to run and greet the men.

"Bennie!" she called.

Cord was getting out of his car too, smiling at Janie. She did her best not to make eye contact.

"You must be Cord," Mystery said as he approached. "I'm Mystery, this is Bennie, and this is John."

"Hi," Cord said, reaching out to shake Mystery's hand.

"We've already met," John said to Mystery.

"What are you doing here, John?" she asked quietly.

"Working," he said.

"Me too," Cord said.

"Actually, Cord, I don't need you today." John looked up into the rain that was now cascading off the old metal gutters at the roof's edge. "I'm not sure it's safe up there, and I don't want you to get hurt."

"Are you sure? I've been on slick roofs before."

"No thank you, son," he said, walking for the ladder. "I need to do this alone today."

"John?" Mystery probed.

"What, Mystery?" He waited a moment and then added, "I don't leave things half done."

Janie tried to gauge what had changed between her mother and John since the day before. Without another word, John climbed the roof to work beneath the black cloud above.

"Mom?" Mystery turned to her and Janie saw a gleam of tears in her mother's eyes. For a moment, it didn't even matter that Cord was standing there. "What's going on?"

"Nothing," Mystery smiled. "You just stay out here and visit with Cord awhile. I'll get Bennie some clothes."

She placed her hand on her daughter's shoulder, picked up a squirming Bennie, and went back inside.

"Is it me?" Cord asked. "It's not that bad up there."

"No," Janie said. "I don't think so. I'm not sure what's going on."

For a moment, Cord didn't say anything. He just turned and watched the rain with her. She didn't know what to say about what had just happened.

"Can you go for a drive?" he asked.

"Why?"

"I need to talk to you."

"I can't."

"Please," he implored.

Janie looked up to the roof and back at the front door. She didn't want to stay here and Dana would be at work for a while. She hesitated for another moment. "Okay," she agreed.

Ten minutes later, they were driving through the gates of the cemetery. Rain dripped from the maple trees, leaving a sticky film on the ground. The wind and rain brought forth a deep earthy smell as if the caretaker had just opened a new grave.

A few yards ahead was Fawn's gravestone. The vase of fake tulips Janie had placed there in March had fallen to the side. Normally, Janie would have stopped to right it, but not today. Fawn would have to wait.

Cord rounded the last corner and faced his Chevelle so they could look out over the town. This was the first time she had seen it from the vantage point of a car, and she was surprised to see that it looked like a nice place to bring a date.

For a moment they stared out at the town, and an uncomfortable silence settled between them.

"Nice weather, huh?" he said.

"Yeah, weird, isn't it?"

"It happens. Can't control the weather." His voice was so soothing that Janie wished he would continue talking forever. She waited, clenching her hands to relieve the nervousness she felt about being alone with him. He seemed not to notice, simply looking out the window at the passing clouds instead.

"So, what's up?" she finally asked.

"I had to see you," he said, leaning up against the car window. The rain tap-danced on the roof and water ran down the windshield blurring the outside world.

"What did Dana do now?"

"Who knows." He looked angry. Dana had that effect on many men.

"Do you mind if we get out?" In answer to Janie's request, Cord simply got out and came around to her side to open her door. Together they looked out over the bluff at the town below. Janie could see John working on the roof despite the rain, a woman on State Street rushing to pull her laundry from the clothesline, and Dana walking out of The Watering Trough. It was the hot pink miniskirt that gave her away.

"Oh great," Janie said, turning as if Dana might spot her on the bluff with Cord.

"What is it?"

"Dana," she said as she pointed her out. "She's right there, by the restaurant."

"So?"

"Doesn't it make you feel a little weird that you are standing here with your girlfriend's sister?"

He looked at her, but he didn't respond. She kicked a rock under the car.

"I suppose you want to know why I asked you here," he said.

Janie nodded and braced herself. She could tell he was angry with Dana for something, and with her luck he probably just wanted some insight. Worse yet, he probably wanted her help.

"I just wanted to see you," he breathed. "Alone."

Janie peered up at him from beneath her lashes. Half of her wanted to believe what she had just heard, and half of her wanted to slap him for thinking he could have them both at once.

"Look, I know you have a boyfriend but I have been up all night thinking about you. I can't seem to get you off my mind."

His directness was shocking.

"But you're dating my sister."

"Actually, I'm not."

"You're not? I talked to Dana this morning and she acted like you were."

"Well, I'm not. I broke it off with her yesterday, just after I talked with you."

"You hardly know me — "

"I know, I know. But for some reason, Janie, I feel like I do."

Janie put her hand to her mouth to cover the smile that was spreading unbidden across her lips. She didn't want to look too eager, too immature for that type of forward comment, but when Cord leaned in to kiss her she didn't push him away. When he pulled back slightly, his eyes were closed as if he just had a long drink of something that quenched his thirst. He opened his eyes and smiled, ran his warm lips tenderly back over hers, and breathed onto her nose and chin. His breath smelled wonderful, warm and natural, like wild sage. She wondered what her breath smelled like. She should have chewed some gum or at least taken a drink of water before letting him kiss her. She withdrew just a little.

"I have a fiancé, Cord."

He studied her for a minute but seemed undeterred by the information.

"Janie, if you tell me to, I'll back off and never see you again. But

I swear I see the same feeling in your eyes when you look at me. Don't I?"

Janie nodded reluctantly. She knew it was probably just hormones. If she were smart, she'd run home, meet Taylor in the treehouse, confess all her sins, and let him take her right then and there. But the truth was, she wasn't smart in that way. Whether she liked it or not, she was an Abbott, daughter of Mystery and sister of Dana, and their track record with men wasn't exactly impressive.

"Don't I?" he repeated.

"Yes," she murmured. "You do."

* * *

It was after noon when Janie finally returned home. The rain didn't let up as she dashed up the steps and dropped into place on the porch swing. She had agreed to dinner tomorrow night at Cord's house, although how she was going to get there without Dana or Taylor finding out was beyond her right now. She could hear Mystery hammering something inside the house, probably still working on the ceiling in her bedroom. She knew she should offer to help, but she couldn't. Not now. She needed to be alone and sort out what had just happened. Taylor's car was parked in the driveway across the street. She wondered if he had called. At least she had been smart enough to have Cord drop her at the end of Carlisle Street. She couldn't imagine what Taylor would do if he saw them together. She closed her eyes, pulled the blanket around her shoulders, and prayed that she wouldn't find out.

chapter thirteen

Mystery Abbott

On Tuesday, the pounding commenced at seven o'clock sharp. Mystery awoke with Bennie curled against her front and Janie snuggled up at the end of the couch. She rubbed the sleep from her eyes and wondered what in the hell was going on. She had been dreaming about red ink on her overdue bills again. Her head ached and she wasn't sure if it was from the pounding above or the dream. Mystery thought she had made herself perfectly clear to John that he was to be done with the roof, but then he had turned up yesterday. He was about to leave without so much as a goodbye when she had stopped him at his truck, placing her hand on his wet shoulder.

John, let's just meet on Wednesday like we used to. We can talk then. I'll be back tomorrow.

With that he had driven away, and now here he was again, proving his determination to finish. She could hear the muffled beeping of her alarm clock from her bedroom. She had intended to sleep in there, and have the kids sleep back in their rooms in order to regain some normalcy, but it hadn't happened.

She flipped the covers back, letting the cool air wash over her. Bennie shivered as the chill hit him, so Mystery scooted out the end of the couch. At some point in the night, Janie had ventured out to the couch as well and was now curled up at the far end. Mystery smiled and had a vision of her daughter at Bennie's age. Time flew so fast. She tucked the covers in around Bennie and Janie. *Warm little tacos tucked safely in their shells,* she thought. That was what she used to call them when she tucked the edges of the covers around the kids at night.

She went to her bedroom, smacked the alarm button, and then went to check on Dana. Thankfully, she was there. Mystery had been trying to give her some leeway about curfews since Dana had taken on the responsibility of holding down a job, but lately Mystery feared that with all of the stress in their lives, Dana might not come home at all. Mystery watched her sleeping daughter for a moment. Dana's face was calm and peaceful instead of creased with anger as it was during her waking hours. She wondered where she had gone wrong with Dana and if there was any way to right things. Mystery quietly pulled the door closed and made her way to the kitchen to make coffee. She needed it to clear her mind.

As she listened to the coffee machine warming up, she glanced at the clock. She had an hour before she had to be at work. Walt had continued to offer his help and to tell her to take yet another day off, but she just couldn't take him up on either offer. She wanted to be at work, away from the pull of John and the responsibilities of her home, and she wanted to be close to Walt, too. Walt had done so much for her; she couldn't abandon him now when his own life was coming apart.

As she sat at the table and listened to John pounding away, she fingered the pile of bills that had flooded her mailbox this week. She had once heard of a man who put all of his bills into a hat and pulled them out one by one as he could afford them. Then, if any bill collectors got crabby with him about them being overdue, he would threaten to take their statement out of the hat for that month. As Mystery flipped through the stack, she thought about doing just that. Ever since the kids were little she had juggled bills to keep the family afloat. With the roof project and her time off work, she feared that they wouldn't make it this time. Her last check had barely covered the groceries and her car payment. The next check was usually reserved for the remainder of the household bills and the house payment. Something would have to give.

"Morning!"

Startled, Mystery knocked her cup to the floor. Broken bits of china scattered under the table "Great," she sighed, "that's the second cup this week."

"They're ugly anyway," Dana said, reaching past her mother to pour herself a cup of coffee. Despite the cool weather, she was already dressed in Daisy Duke cutoffs and a skimpy blue tank top. Mystery suspected Dana was trying to attract attention from every man in Glendale who would give her the time of day. She just hoped the men had the decency to look the other way. Dana looked far too much like Mystery had at that age, at least for a mother's comfort level. She was the perfect lure for attracting the wrong sort of men.

"They were your great-grandmother's," Mystery said.

"How'd *you* get them, then?" Dana sneered.

Mystery took a deep breath and stepped carefully over to the closet for the broom and dustpan. She scooped the mess into the pan and sadly watched the fragments fall into the garbage can.

Janie appeared at the threshold with Bennie following her. "What happened?" she asked.

"I dropped one of Grandma's teacups."

"Again, Mom?" Janie laughed. "That's the second one this week."

Janie was still in her rumpled clothes from last night. Bennie was in his short-sleeved Thomas the Tank Engine jammies. If this weather kept up she might have to pull his bunny suit pajamas out of the winter clothes.

"Good lord," Dana said, "those cups are completely hideous. If they were mine, I'd drop them all in the garbage."

"I'll remember not to leave you any china when I die," Mystery laughed, hoping humor might divert her daughter's mood.

"Not if any of it is that ugly."

Mystery rolled her eyes and tried to swallow the anger that was already building at Dana after only a few sentences. From outside she heard the deep sound of a car pulling up in the driveway. Dana stood on tip-toes to see who it was and then scoffed, "What is *he* doing here?"

Dana's face contorted as she turned toward Janie. Mystery stopped sweeping the floor and looked back and forth between her daughters. Janie smiled at her sister and crossed her arms.

"Oh look," she said, "Cord is here."

"I see that," Dana said. "Why?"

From Dana's tone, Mystery knew that something was not right.

"He's working with John," she said. "I thought you knew that."

Mystery looked to Janie. Normally, she was as blindsided as Mystery whenever Dana chose to vent her frustrations on her, but there was something different in Janie's body language today.

"Cord is still coming to help with the roof?" Dana asked. The question was clearly not intended for Mystery. Janie said nothing, just smiled.

"If John will let him," Mystery interjected. "He said it was too dangerous yesterday. What is all of this about?"

"I asked you a question," Dana said, ignoring Mystery.

"I think Mom already answered that," Janie replied.

Mystery stood between Janie and Dana, fearing an immediate increase in volume that might carry up to the roof. She closed her eyes and willed John to keep pounding. Dana stepped forward and for a moment, Mystery thought she might pounce on her sister and take Bennie out in the process.

"Whoa," she said, arms spanned between them, feeling like the referee she had become. "What's up here? Dana, I thought you asked Cord to help."

Dana crossed her arms and stepped closer to Janie.

"Look, you two, I have to get to work. What is going on?"

"I didn't invite him, Mom. Janie did."

"Okay," she said, confused. "Well, Janie, thanks for inviting Cord to help, but you really should have cleared that with Dana first."

"Why?" Janie said, keeping her eyes fixed on her twin sister.

"Why?" Dana reiterated. "How would you like it if I asked Taylor to help without your knowledge?"

"That wouldn't bother me at all. And besides, I think you and I both know that that is not *even* the same thing."

"Oh really," she said. "Mom, can you believe this crap?"

Mystery wasn't certain what to say. On the surface, Dana seemed correct. However, both history and the fact that she was calling Mystery "Mom" right now indicated otherwise.

"It sure seems the same to me," Mystery said. "But it also seems that I'm missing something."

"It's pretty clear, Mom. For some odd reason that no one knows yet, Janie asked Cord to come over here to play carpenter without my knowledge, and you don't see that as the same thing?" Dana's voice was rising over the roofing noise. The pulse of the hammering reminded Mystery of popping microwave popcorn: everything is fine until the popping slows to every two or three seconds. Mystery called them the warning pops. She looked to the ceiling and listened. Still one pound every second or so. She had some time.

"Well, that certainly *seems* to be what's going on," Mystery said. "Janie?"

Mystery was getting a little tired of the words *seems*. She wished they would all get to the meat of the matter so she could understand what was really happening.

"Of course you'd ask her," Dana said. She flung her arms up in the air and turned away from her sister. "Don't trust me."

"Dana, wait," Mystery said, holding up her hand like a traffic cop. "Janie has a right to say her side as well. Janie, why did you invite Dana's boyfriend to work on the roof without her knowledge?"

"She never said *boyfriend*, Mother."

Mystery heard Dana huff as she turned around to face her sister once again. If Mystery were smart she would point out the inconsistencies in both of their stories, grab Bennie, and leave the two of them alone to handle it. However, as the old saying goes, curiosity got the cat, and, like it or not, when it came to the dynamics of Dana and Janie's relationship Mystery was most definitely the cat. She had no siblings and she didn't understand the pure and unfettered animosity that having one could bring forth. Thinking better of it, she turned to Dana anyway.

"Dana, is Cord your boyfriend or not?"

"Well, he was," she whined, "right up until this little tramp got her hooks into him."

"Ha!" Janie yelled. "Look who's calling who a tramp."

"Okay. Okay," Mystery said, arms raised again, "let's lower our voices." She knew that she would have an easier time controlling Janie, so she worked on her the hardest.

"Janie," she asked patiently, "does Taylor know about this?"

"Know about what?" Janie asked.

"That his innocent little girlfriend is a slut," Dana interjected.

"Shh," Mystery said, pointing to the roof. "They'll hear us."

"So what. Let them," Dana said. "Cord should know what he is getting into. That is if he hasn't already."

"Wouldn't you like to know," Janie laughed.

"Yeah," Dana said. "I'd love to." She stepped forward and challenged Mystery's boundary line. Mystery held up her hand to block her but Dana pressed in on Janie, who stayed safely beyond Mystery's arm.

There was silence in the room and Mystery noticed that the pounding had stopped. Not even a warning pop.

"Great," she said, "they heard you."

Dana smiled triumphantly, and Janie rolled her eyes. "Let 'em hear us," Dana said. "Neither of them are *my* problem." She stormed past Janie, pushing Bennie aside in her wake. He smacked his head on the wall and started to cry.

"You jerk!" Janie said, leaning down to comfort Bennie.

"Dana, get back here!" Mystery ordered, "Bennie didn't do anything to you."

"Screw you both," Dana replied. "I barely even touched him."

"Dana!" Mystery yelled. She could hear the men descending the ladder.

"It's no wonder Janie is such a little tramp. Just look at you, *Mom!*" Dana hollered back at her.

"*Tramp*?" Janie yelped, leaving no time for Mystery to defend herself. "There is no way you of all people can call me that. You've humped every guy in town."

Dana made a move toward Janie again as John and Cord entered through the front door. "Take it back," she demanded.

"You take it back," Janie said. "You're the one saying all the horrible things to *my* mother."

Mystery felt a sudden fear for Janie. She might be angry, but there was no way that she had the tools to win a fight against someone as street-smart as Dana.

"She's my mother, too," Dana said stubbornly. "And someone has to say it. She won't listen to Grandma, or Liv, or anyone else."

"She doesn't have to," Janie said.

"Well, she should," Dana said. She turned and faced Mystery. "You should be embarrassed. I'm embarrassed just to be your daughter. You should at least have the decency to keep your affairs a secret."

Mystery felt her face flush with embarrassment as she looked past Dana to the men standing just beyond. They were soaked from the rain and their hair was plastered to their heads. John held Mystery's gaze, but Cord kept his head low. He didn't look at either girl. What could Mystery say? Dana had the facts correct, just not the meaning.

Dana continued her tirade. "Did you even think about us at all as you were doing all of this? How embarrassing this might be to the rest of the family? I mean, you don't see Liv hiding men in the closet, or Grandma, or Jane Caldwell, or Dora Sievers, or any other mother. Only you, Mystery."

"You might not see it, Dana," she retorted, "but that doesn't mean it doesn't happen. Those women are no better than me, you just fail to understand that."

"Yes they are, Mystery. They haven't made a laughingstock of their families they way you have. Hell, we don't even know who Bennie's father is!"

"Dana, shut up!" Janie said, casting a worried glance at Bennie.

Dana glanced at her little brother, too, but her anger seemed to override any self-control she had.

"Fuck you, Janie."

"No," she said decisively, "fuck *you!*"

Dana was visibly shocked by her sister's sudden boldness. A tense silence hung over the kitchen.

"Fuck you!" they heard again.

They all looked down at Bennie, now standing between his two sisters. His legs were spread and his little fists were his hips like a miniature version of the Jolly Green Giant.

"What did you say?" Dana asked in surprise.

"Fuck you," he repeated. "Don't talk to Janie that way!"

He took a step toward his older sister and Mystery's heart dropped. She felt a little foolish, but said a quick prayer that Dana wouldn't hurt him for cussing at her. Dana had never intentionally harmed Bennie, but Mystery didn't really trust that she wouldn't. But just as Mystery reached out to grab him, Bennie pushed her arms aside and ran to John. John stooped down and put his arm around the little boy.

"You shouldn't say that, Bennie." John said. "That's a bad word."

"They shouldn't fight," Bennie whimpered. He turned in John's arms and then frowned fiercely at his sisters. "You shouldn't fight," he repeated more steadily.

"I know you won't believe me, Mystery, but I didn't mean to hurt him," Dana said through clenched teeth before spinning around and storming off to her room.

"I'll meet you back outside," Cord said to John. "Janie?" He extended a hand to her.

"I ... I'm coming."

Before Cord left with Janie, he gave Mystery a slow smile. There was something humble in his connection with her, as if he wanted to say that he understood. Mystery gave a wobbly smile in return. Prior to today, she'd had reservations about the boy. Although she didn't want to admit that it was true, her concern had more to do with him living in those slum houses on State Street than anything else. She knew it was wrong, but she wanted something better for her daughters.

"You okay?" John asked.

"I can't believe Bennie talked like that," she said, shaking her downturned head.

"I hate to tell you this Mystery ..." He touched her cheek to draw her eyes to his. "Bennie doesn't talk because he can't get a word in edgewise around here with you women. He needs a man around."

"That's sexist, John," she said, and brushed his hand away.

"I don't mean for it to be." He grinned down at Bennie as he continued, "It's just a lot of stress for us men to keep up with, isn't it li'l pard? Us guys got to stick together."

Bennie nodded his head as John ruffled his hair and smiled. Only then did Mystery realize that John wasn't dumping on her or judging her, he was making a joke about what just happened to make Bennie feel better. He was amazingly resilient and she wanted to believe that he always would be, but she also knew from experience that she was the only person who could shoulder this family's stress for as long as she had. She didn't have a choice about dealing with it; everyone else did.

Mystery watched Bennie curl himself around John's wet pant leg. He laid his head on John's knee and nodded up and down at her.

"I have to go to work, John."

"That's fine," he said. "We'll be here when you get back."

"Are you sure?"

He kissed her lightly on the cheek and left the room with Bennie in his arms. No matter how hard she tried, she could not get John to leave, and each day it was becoming more difficult to ask him to go.

chapter fourteen

Liv Randall

Since breaking into the Miller house, Liv felt more alive than she had in all her years in Glendale. Last night she had fallen asleep easily next to Carl, and this morning she woke at six feeling rested and ready for whatever today had to bring. And to top it all off, Carl and Taylor were both long gone by the time she'd stepped out of the shower. She poured a cup of coffee and went to the living room to relax. She couldn't recall the last time she had done that. Before, there had always been too much to do, but right now, she couldn't remember what it all was. As she kicked her feet up onto the ottoman to watch the rain cascading down the front window, she lost herself in thought of the Miller house. The master bedroom, the pond...cool breezes fluttering past her. There was no sound in her daydream, only the smell of algae.

She lifted her cup to her lips and was shocked awake by the cold coffee. She noticed a ring around the cup's inside edge, as if the coffee had been left to sit in the cup all day. But, how was that possible? She had just sat down. A shiver of fear spread through her, but she tried to ignore it. Everything was fine. She had a little bit of tunnel vision from the cloud, but other than that she felt great. There was nothing to worry about.

She returned to the kitchen for more coffee and noticed that Carl had left three notes for her on the counter before he left this morning. The first two said to call her friends back. Jane had called five times in the past two days, Dora twice, and Emily once. Ma Bell was putting "nice girl" Emily on the job to see if they could force Liv to call back. The last answering machine message from Jane simply said, "Call me." No pleading, no begging, just a direct order intended to be elusive enough to entice Liv into rushing to the phone. Well, this time Ma Bell wouldn't get their desires or fears satisfied.

The final note asked about the box of cigarettes on the counter. Were they hers or Taylor's? And if they were Taylor's, she needed to do something about it. She crumpled the notes and threw them in the trash. The egg mess from the previous day was still smacked against the backdrop of the sink and crusted over on the tile. She made a swipe at it once with a clean washcloth but it didn't do much good. After that, she threw the wet washcloth in the sink. It wasn't her mess anyway. As she grabbed her slicker from the hook by the sliding doors, the birds-of-prey clock began to tweet. She waited, counting. *Seven, eight, nine, ten, eleven.* She held her breath. It stopped. Eleven. She couldn't imagine where the time had gone. She should have had half of her list done by now, but right this minute she couldn't remember where she had left it.

It was pouring buckets as she left the house. The wind was howling, and according to the local forecast, it was only going to get worse. Liv noticed the red, white, and blue pansies that she planted every year in the same spot Ilsa had done in preparation for the Fourth of July. They were spindly and black at the edges from the frost. Ilsa's yard wouldn't be perfect this year.

She grabbed a shovel from the garage and strode to the front of the house. It didn't take her long to dig up the three best rose bushes. She was certain that if she asked, Carl could tell her what prize his aunt had won at the county fair with them. Surprisingly, someone had picked up the plastic bag that had flown over from Mystery's house.

She didn't know who had done it, but she was sure it hadn't been Carl or Taylor. With her around, neither of them lifted a finger. It had to have been one of the Abbotts, maybe even Mystery's boyfriend.

Since last leaving the Miller house, Liv had been trying to figure out how best to get information on the place. There was only one other person who knew anything about the house besides Carl, and that was Dora. Liv knew she would have to answer some questions and accept some apologies to get the information she wanted from Dora, but it would be worth it. She grabbed her keys and cigarettes from the counter and pulled the door closed behind her. Before getting in the car, she carefully placed the roses and the shovel in the trunk.

Across the street, John was again straddling the roof, with another man helping him with the repairs. Janie was sitting on the front porch swing, and gave a tentative wave as Liv drove past. Janie seemed more timid around her than usual, and it made Liv feel guilty for being so cool toward her.

As Liv turned out of Carlisle, she looked south and noticed that a large chunk of earth had given way from the bank below Cemetery Ridge. She had never liked the idea of bodies being buried six feet underground on a bank that sat at least one hundred feet above the town. She wondered what would happen if there was an earthquake, but she didn't think any of these people thought too much about it.

When she got to Main Street, she flipped a U-turn by John Deere and parked in front of Carl's office. She threw her smoke out into the rain and walked next door to Dora's. Across the street, Liv saw Betty Brown, a nurse at the local doctor's office, going through her mail as she exited the post office. Since Betty was a larger gal, Ma Bell had always referred to her as Big Betty whenever she came up in conversation. Liv called an uncharacteristic *Hello, Betty!* through the rain. Betty looked up and smiled, but when she noticed that it was Liv, she gave a half-hearted wave and returned to sorting her mail.

Liv slowed as she passed Carl's window. She could see Carl on the phone at his desk. Directly beneath him on the window was his name and title etched in gold: "Carl Randall, Attorney at Law." He thought the round window was a clever touch, but Liv thought he looked like a fish in a fishbowl. She should have knocked and waved, but then again, he should have cleaned up the egg on the counter. Avoiding the sudden urge to raise a middle finger to the window as she passed, she continued on to Dora's.

Rain dripped from her jacket, and she shook her hair like a wet dog, her ponytail slapping her cheek as she did so.

"Liv," Dora said, scooting out from behind her desk. "What are you doing here?" Dora sat down in one of the client chairs and motioned Liv to do the same. She handed Liv a couple of Kleenexes to dry her face with, but Liv motioned them away. She liked the water on her face. Dora's hair was short, pinkish-red, and flipped up in the back from curlers that she wore to bed every night. Whenever she moved or turned her head, the single curl that rounded her neck bounced around in response.

"Are you okay?" Dora gushed. "We have all been so worried about you. Jane says you won't return her calls."

"I'm fine, Dora," she said, brushing the rain from her jacket.

She took the proffered seat and noted that Dora looked remorseful. Liv knew she'd have to endure a few minutes of groveling before she could get to her real intention. She could humor Dora that long.

"I heard that the rain is supposed to let up in a couple of days," Dora said brightly.

"That's too bad," she replied. "I like the rain. It reminds me of home."

"Not me," Dora laughed. "My hair can't take much more of this."

"I guess I don't like that part," Liv conceded, although in truth she hadn't touched her hair in two days.

"Emily is making a banner living at the hairdresser's. I can't even get in for an appointment."

"Oh," Liv said. Just a few more minutes, and then she could reveal her face card. The quicker she got her answer, the quicker she could get out of town.

"Look, Liv," Dora said placing her hand on her knee, "we really are worried about you."

"We, who?"

"We," Dora repeated, surprise showing in her eyes. "Your friends."

Liv nodded, focusing on Dora instead of the cloud at her temples. "You really don't have to worry about me. I'm fine."

"Really?" Dora eyed her doubtfully. "Are you sure you don't want a Kleenex. You're squinting."

"No," Liv said, consciously relaxing her eyes. "Really. I've never felt better."

"Okay. It's just that..." Dora trailed off and then got up to close the door to her empty sitting room.

"Just what?" Liv asked.

"Well," she stammered. "It's just that you don't seem to handle these things very well."

"What things?"

"Honey," Dora continued. "You know we all worry about, well, you know."

"You all know *what*?" she snapped. Liv was beginning to lose her patience. The required small talk was taking longer than a few minutes.

"We all know what you do when you get stressed out. Husbands might be blind, but it's no secret to us girls. Hell, I had the same problem when I was younger."

"What are you talking about, Dora?" Liv pressed.

"You, and the fact that you go home and stick your finger down your throat when you're stressed out." Dora smiled through her bright red lipstick. Liv noticed a smudge of it on her front tooth. Normally, she would help her friend out by delicately pointing to the offending tooth, but she didn't have time for niceties. Her patience was gone.

"*Excuse me?*"

"Don't treat me like I'm stupid, Liv. We all know. I'm not judging you. It's just that we are all *extra* worried now, after that whole business with the PTA and all."

"Oh Dora," she said smoothly, her words dripping with sugary sweetness, "everyone makes way too much of the PTA stuff. You're right, I was upset at first, but now I'm fine. Really. It was actually quite a relief. Forget it, okay? I came here to ask you about something else."

Dora sat still for a minute and goggled at her. Liv swore she could see tears actually welling in the woman's eyes.

"Honey," Liv said. "Really, it's fine. I'm glad that you care, but I'm great. The real reason that I am here is to ask you for some history on the Miller house."

Dora frowned as she dabbed at her eyes with a tissue before getting up to resume her position behind the counter, making a superwoman-like switch from concerned friend back to realtor. "What do you want to know?"

"I just wondered about it, is all. Why is everything still there? Have there been any bites on the place? That kind of thing."

Dora was goggling at her again, eyes wide with anticipation. "Are you looking at it for personal reasons?"

"No, no," Liv said, waving her off. "Someone from Seattle is interested, that's all. It's an investment thing."

"Oh," Dora said. "Who?" Dora was drooling like a dog waiting for a treat.

"Just a friend," she lied.

"Bummer," Dora said, relaxing into the curve of her chair. "I thought it might be your brother."

"No way," Liv said firmly. "I won't let him within a hundred miles of this godforsaken town."

"Or your neighbor, huh?" Dora laughed.

Liv's face reddened at the thought of her brother with Mystery Abbott, but when she spoke again her voice was brisk. "The interested party is a friend of mine, not a family member, okay?"

"Okay, okay," Dora said. "Well, as you know, Mr. Miller died last year. His three children are the heirs, but the oldest has power of attorney. He is the only one I talk to."

"Were you friends with them?"

"I know them. We all grew up in Glendale. But the youngest, Penny, was four years ahead of me in school, so I'm not exactly friends with any of them, if that's what you mean."

"So, where are they now?"

"Penny is in California, married with three children. The Millers' middle child, Marvin, lives in Walla Walla, and the eldest, Charles, Jr., is in New York."

"And none of them want the house or its contents?"

"Nope," she said, confidently crossing her French-manicured fingers. "Not one of them. I asked Charles about it, and he said it is too *country* for them. He said that if he brought any of that stuff home his wife would divorce him. I guess the rest of the kids feel the same way. They took what they wanted when they were here last year, pictures and photo albums and stuff, and they haven't been back since."

"That's sad," Liv said.

"Yep," Dora agreed. "Is your friend interested in the contents of the house as well? That would be a huge load off my shoulders."

"Why is that?"

"The only way that I got sale over some bigwig realtor in Kennedy was if I promised to get rid of the stuff with the house."

"Didn't they like their parents or something?"

"I don't know," she said, straightening some papers on her desk. "Didn't really ask. I think it might have to do with the mother."

"What about her?" Liv asked, leaning forward conspiratorially. "What did she do, beat them or something?"

"No, nothing like that. I guess it's no big secret. Actually, as you probably know from being married to that guy next door, there can be no secrets at all in Glendale." Dora's voice became grave when she spoke of Carl. It was fairly typical of the women in Ma Bell. None of them liked men, especially men who were married to their friends. They were the ultimate bastards.

"Carl doesn't tell me anything about his law practice. He keeps his mouth shut about clients."

"Yes," she said. "I bet he does. But I'm not talking about his client. I'm talking about disclosure laws."

"Oh," Liv said, acting like she knew what Dora was talking about. "What about them?"

"Well," Dora said. "Mrs. Miller died long before you and Carl moved back to town."

Liv wanted to correct Dora and tell her that Carl was the only one who moved *back* to this town, but she decided to keep her mouth shut. None of that was important anymore. "Yes, so?" she said, goading her on.

"Well, I have to tell all potential buyers, so you might as well tell your friend and save me the trouble. Mrs. Miller was sick. She was seventy-five and had brain cancer."

"Oh, that's terrible."

"Yep," Dora said, "and though the kids tried, Mr. Miller, sweet old dear that he was, refused to put her in a nursing home or in the hospital. He took care of her himself."

"That is sweet."

"Unfortunately, it ended tragically. One morning, before Mr. Miller was even out of bed, Mrs. Miller had some kind of delusion from the cancer or the drugs, or something. Evidently she walked out back, fell in the pond, and drowned."

"Oh God," Liv said. She thought of her hand moving back and forth in the warm water of the pond. A pond where someone had drowned.

Dora had stopped talking and was looking quizzically at Liv. Liv followed her gaze and noticed that her hand was moving as if she had immersed it in the water. She pulled her hand in toward her body and smiled sheepishly.

"Yes, well," Dora nodded, "it was terrible. There was speculation that she did it on purpose, but of course there was no way to tell. After that, Mr. Miller became a recluse. He stayed pretty much on the farm until he passed away last year of a heart attack. Most people say that he never got over her death."

"Did he die at the house, too?" Liv asked.

"No. Actually, he had come into the pharmacy to get his heart pills. Isn't that ironic? He dropped right there in the aisle of the pharmacy and died."

"Wow," Liv said. "That's quite a story. I will definitely tell my friend." She got up from her chair and grabbed her raincoat.

"That's it, then?" Dora asked.

"I guess so," Liv said. "Thanks for the information. I just wanted to make sure that no one else was looking at the place right now, because I saw that someone had dug up the rose bushes out back."

"Oh, those," Dora said, coming around the desk to see her out. "No, no one is looking at the place. Hell, you're the first bite I've had. Jane wanted those, so I dug them up for her at the beginning of summer."

Liv spun around and stared at the realtor. "*You* dug them up?" she asked.

"Yes, I told you, the kids don't want anything to do with the place. At least Jane will take care of them."

"You didn't even fill in the holes," Liv said.

"Sorry, I really didn't think anyone would care. You're the first person who has been out there besides me in six months. If it will bother your friend when she comes to look, I'll make sure they are covered back up."

"It's fine," Liv said. "Dora, one other thing. Did you leave the dirty cigarette in the china cup in the kitchen, too?"

Dora cocked her head like a dog sensing trouble. Liv regretted the words right after she said them. "How would you know what was in the sink?" Dora said. She crossed her arms and quirked an eyebrow at Liv. "Olivia Randall, did you break into the house I'm trying to sell?"

"No," she said. "I saw it through the window." She quickly picked up her purse and turned to the door. "Really, Dora," she chided. "If you want my opinion, you should be more careful and more considerate of the homes you sell. How do you think Mr. Miller would feel if he knew how you treated his house?"

"I don't know, Liv," she said. "The man is dead. But it has obviously upset you, so I promise I will take care of it."

"Good," Liv added. "I'll let you know when my friend is going to be in town so you can get it done before he arrives."

"Oh, it's a *he*, is it?" Dora asked.

"Yes," Liv said as she carefully stepped through the doorway. She was beginning to feel like a blind person, as if she had to move her hands out to her sides so as not to bump into anything.

"Well, at least that explains something."

As Liv closed the door, Dora's last comment reverberated in her mind. She wasn't sure what that could possibly explain about anything. Oh well, it didn't matter. The women of Glendale could make trash out of anything. So what if Dora thought she was bringing a man to town. Let her think it. She looked up at Carl's office window as she walked by. He was leaning back in his chair still chatting away on the phone. She wished he put the same dedication into his marriage that he did into his clientele. Maybe things would have been different. He didn't even notice that his wife had just walked by. Maybe Dora's comment was just what she needed. What would Carl do if he thought she was having an affair? The thought tantalized her and gave her a new idea.

Ten minutes later, she was once again at the Miller house. The rain had mellowed to a thick drizzle. It seemed that the weather was always different out here than in town. She removed her rain hood and pulled the ponytail holder from her hair. The release seemed to allow her vision to clear a bit. The breeze tousled wisps of damp hair, tickling her neck and face. She pulled the shovel and burlap bags from the trunk of the Jetta and planted the white roses in the holes. When she finished, her hands were completely covered with wet earth. She placed her fingers together as if she were washing up in the cool soil. The dirt was revitalizing. Dora would know who had done it for sure. She would call Jane, and Jane would call Emma, and so on down the line. If Liv was making the place nice for her "potential buyer," he must be someone important.

Before leaving, she visited the pond. Raindrops escaped down her cheeks like cold sweat. She took a deep breath. It really did smell of the Pacific out here. She sat at the edge of the pond, wiped her hands on the grass, and lit a smoke. What she could see of the sun through swift-moving cloud breaks was fading fast behind Cemetery Ridge, highlighting the few east-facing headstones that stood like sentinels over the town. This was the place where Mrs. Miller had ended her life here on earth. The green pond was smooth as glass now. She pondered how long the ripples had lasted when the old woman dropped in. Once they were gone, so was she. The rain had stopped and the breeze was slight inside the bowl of the mountains. Glendale was a world away out here. She heard frogs croaking in the cattails, oblivious to the horror that had once taken place within the borders of these waters. She thought it was strange how easily things were forgotten by earthly creatures. Hardly anyone knew about Mr. and Mrs. Miller.

Their lives had been reduced to a side note that Dora was forced to tell potential buyers.

She took a deep breath, stuck her hands in the murky water to wash the dirt off, and then felt strangely compelled to suck the liquid from her fingers. Out here, it was just her and her ocean.

chapter fifteen

Dana Abbott

t he rain drove the citizens of Glendale indoors, and Dana had to move fast to keep up with the influx of customers at The Trough. Not even the farmers wanted to be outside anymore, and no one seemed to want to leave the comfort of the restaurant.

She had told Mr. Borghese that she would work a double shift if he ever needed her to. After all, she really had nowhere else to go. She couldn't stand to see her mother and John at home, even though she thought she sensed a bit of much-needed apprehension in John. Mystery, however, seemed too comfortable, too cared for. And as for Janie, well, she wanted to avoid seeing her sister altogether. It wasn't that she was mad at Janie about Cord—she wasn't. She was avoiding her because Janie was right, and it was getting harder and harder for Dana to avoid admitting that. The only time she didn't feel like a stranger in her own home was late at night when she'd perch on her window ledge and watch Liv. But lately something was changing with Liv, too. Instead of cleaning her house well into the morning hours, Liv was beginning to sleep. Last night she had even gone to bed around the same time as Carl, which was something Dana hadn't witnessed in years. Dana didn't know what to do with herself. There she was, wide awake, and Liv had gone to sleep. Even watching Liv was starting to make Dana uncomfortable.

Dylan had driven by twice during her last four-hour shift, but he hadn't looked up. By six thirty the farmers had finally gone home, but there were still three kids at the counter and one family in a booth. The kids were slowly licking their strawberry ice cream cones from bottom to top, in no hurry to go out into the driving rain. The family was waiting for their young daughter, who refused to eat the cooked carrots that accompanied her meatloaf. The father had tried everything from slathering them with butter to dipping them in the gravy, but the little brown-haired girl with chipmunk cheeks refused to budge. Dana just about lost it when she heard the mother say, "We're not leaving here until you finish those carrots." She thought about forgoing her tip and booting the whole lot of them right out the front door, but instead she walked to the back to remove her apron. Mr. Borghese was busy mopping the floor. He turned around and smiled at her.

"They won't leave," she hissed.

He peered out the windowless opening of the serving counter, and then turned back to her. "Give them five minutes," he said with a wink.

Dana shook her head at the patience of her boss and walked over to the family at the table. The carrots had been separated into two piles on the little girl's plate.

"Whatcha doin'?" Dana asked her.

There was no movement from the child.

"Autumn," said the mother, "when an adult addresses you, you answer them."

Dana ignored her and said, "Autumn, what don't you like about the carrots?"

"They're cold, and they have gravy on them."

"Autumn," said the dad, "you said you wanted gravy on them."

"I said I *like* gravy," she complained. "I didn't say I wanted it all over my stupid carrots!"

"Well, the cold part is easy enough to fix, but the gravy I can't do anything about," Dana said, also ignoring the father. "So what do you say we make a deal so that you and I can both go home?"

"What deal?" Autumn asked. Neither her attitude nor her gaze had shifted.

"I will warm up the carrots and give you a free cookie, but only if you finish those carrots in three minutes."

"Okay," Autumn grumbled.

"Thank you," the mother said to Dana.

"I didn't do it for you," Dana said under her breath, taking the plate and hurrying back to the kitchen.

Within ten minutes, the girl had her promised cookie and the family was getting their coats. On the table was a nice fat ten-dollar tip from the father. When she went to clean up the mother's plate Dana noticed a whole pile of carrots hidden under the uneaten dinner roll.

"Come on, boys," Mr. Borghese called from the kitchen. "Time's up." When the boys left their money at the counter, Dana saw one of them swipe a pack of gum from the register. She was about to say something to Mr. Borghese, but he placed his finger to his lips.

"That's what it's there for, honey," he smiled.

Since her first day of work, Dana could not get over his kindness. Mr. Borghese was thick around the middle, bald on top, and he sported a white apron painted with everything from ketchup and mustard to milkshakes and hamburger grease, but even so, she wished all men were like him.

Dana had just begun cleaning up the ice-cream drips left by the boys when the bells on the door chimed. This could *not* be happening. She didn't care who it was; she wasn't about to serve another person. She turned around to announce that they were closed, only to find that it was Dylan standing at the counter. She strolled over and stood tall behind the register.

"We close at seven, officer."

"I know," he said with a nervous laugh, his eyes scanning the empty tables and booths. Dana liked that he seemed more vulnerable here in her territory than when they were in the police station together.

"But for a man of the law, I guess we can spare something," she teased.

"I was just thinking about a cup of coffee..."

"Sure," she said, "coming right up."

"No," he whispered.

"No?" She lowered her eyes, fighting back a grin.

"I meant with you," he whispered. "Can you meet me at my place? I'll leave the back door open."

"Sure. Give me ten minutes?"

"Okay then."

Mr. Borghese was peeking through the serving window now. "Hi, Dylan," he said. "What brings you out?"

"Oh, it's darn cold out there, and I was just going to get a cup of coffee, but Dana said you had already cleaned the pot."

"Oh, that's no problem. It only takes a minute to make more."

"No," he said, holding both hands up in front of him, "it's no big deal. It was just an impulse. I really don't need the stuff at night. I'll make sure to stop in earlier next time." He smiled cautiously at Dana as he turned and, then hastily opened the door.

"Bye, Dylan," Mr. Borghese called out.

"See ya," he said. "Bye, Dana."

Moments later, Dana approached the rear of the police station as instructed. Her heart beat like crazy at the thought that Dylan wanted her alone and in secret. She was so excited she could hardly breathe as she stepped in the back door. The studio apartment was larger than Dana had expected. To the left were a bed, nightstand, and dresser with a candle burning on top. To the right was a small kitchen with a café-style round dining table and two high-backed white chairs. Dylan walked in from the front office. He had removed his police uniform in favor of nylon jogging pants and a gray sweatshirt. She could hardly take the look of him as a civilian in clothes clearly intended for relaxation. He had two cups of coffee in his hands and placed each on the table.

"Hi," she said. "What's up?"

"Coffee?" he offered. He still looked so stern, almost as if someone had died and he had been sent to break it to her, but she knew that wasn't it. She accepted the coffee and sat across from him at the table.

"I thought it was too late for you to drink coffee," she said playfully.

He smiled back at her and sat down in the other chair.

"Officer Masters," she said, "what's going on here?"

"I don't know," he said. "And I told you to call me Dylan." He was visibly nervous about something. He leaned back in the chair until its front legs came off the ground, and ran his hand through his short brown hair. "I don't know," he said again. "I don't know what I'm doing."

"With what, Officer...Dylan." She reached over and placed her hand on his knee.

He stared at her hand but didn't remove it. Dana gave him a reassuring squeeze.

"I don't know why I asked you to come over here. You're seventeen and I'm twenty-five. And worst of all, I'm an officer of the law. Do you know what we do to men like me?"

"What men like you?" she asked. "I'll be eighteen in a month, and it's not like we've done anything wrong."

"I have," he said. "I can't stop thinking about you, Dana."

She bit hard on her cheek to suppress her smile. He put his hand on top of hers and gently pulled her close to him. She looked into his eyes and whispered that it was okay.

"Tell me to stop," he murmured.

"No," she breathed.

He kissed her neck and slid his hand up the back of her shirt.

"Tell me to stop," he said again.

She smiled and said nothing. She leaned her head back and moved closer to him, trapping him against the back of the chair. Her body tingled as he ran his tongue down her neck. Finally, his hand slid up her leg and found its way underneath her miniskirt, but then he stopped and pulled it away. In the low light, she could see the surprise in his eyes.

"I was hoping you would stop by work tonight," she said.

She stood up and removed her skirt, keeping her eyes on his. She lifted her shirt and removed her bra, exposing her naked body to him. His heated gaze roamed over her for a moment before he picked her up and carried her to the bed. There, he held her arms above her head and studied her body. He seemed too rigid, so methodical, so unlike anyone she had been with before. She could tell from his expression that he was angry with himself for giving in, and she liked that. He ran his hand down her side and caressed the small curves of her body.

His hands were so large that when he gripped her sides and pulled her squarely down beneath him, they covered her whole abdomen. Dana moaned as she felt his penis touch her.

"Only once," he said tightly, "never again."

"Sure," she agreed, "only once."

She covered her mouth with the back of her hand and tried not to make any noise, but as he moved inside her, she couldn't help it. The intensity of the situation brought tears to her eyes and she gasped, unable to contain her breath or her voice. Dylan placed a light hand over her mouth, and thrust himself inside her. He kissed her on the forehead and moved his mouth down her cheek to hers. She felt her body contract involuntarily. It had never felt like this before. Her mind raced like she was spinning round and round on a carnival ride. She knew that she was being loud but she couldn't help it. She grabbed onto Dylan and pulled him harder to her in an attempt to sustain the feeling, but it was diminishing. Just as it was over, Dylan let go of her mouth and repeatedly thrust his body hard against her until he finally collapsed on top of her. She turned her head to the side and smiled between pants of air. She had been with four boys, and none of them had done what Dylan Masters had just done to her.

"Oh my god," he said, rolling off of her.

"Yeah," Dana said, smiling to herself.

"I am so dead."

"No you're not," she said, rolling over and snuggling up to his side. His body was warm and solid. He was so much older than her and yet she felt as if they were made to do this with each other. For the first time, Dana found what she had been seeking. Dylan was a man — passionate, forceful, and determined to elicit as much pleasure from her body as needed to satisfy his obvious hunger. She could do that for him. Whether he knew it now or not, they were meant to be together, and she was going to do everything possible to make sure that happened.

chapter sixteen

Janie Abbott

hivers ran up and down Janie's arms when she knocked on the door of Cord's house, partly from knowing that Cord was only feet away from her, partly because of what she was about to do, and partly because of the cold rain that fell in sheets beyond the protection of the porch. She finger-combed her hair, knowing that by the time it dried, her curls would be frizzy and tangled. What a sight she would be. She turned around, facing away from his door, rubbing her hands together and stomping her feet to stay warm. Mystery had actually pulled their winter clothes back out from storage in the front closet. Janie had been reluctant to take her gloves but now she was thankful that she had them. This summer was not fair.

In the fading light she scanned Cemetery Ridge. Through the fog, the statues and monuments resembled an incoming garrison on the hill. She hadn't been back to Fawn's grave to pick up the vase of tulips. She felt a bit guilty, but for the first time in five years, she had no desire to go to the cemetery.

She wished Cord would hurry up and answer the door. They had planned to meet for a late dinner after Cord and John were done for the evening, in hopes that most of the gossips would be in by that time. While Dana was probably still at work, Taylor could be just about anywhere. Janie had avoided him successfully since their trip to Kennedy, but he would find her sooner or later. He always did. She would have to break it off with him — she knew that — but she just wasn't up for it yet. Standing here on the porch, she was afraid for herself and afraid for Cord. Taylor Randall was not going to take lightly that she was breaking up with him for another guy.

She scanned to the north one more time before knocking again, and this time ringing the bell. She heard footsteps approaching the door. Her heart began to pound harder. Finally, the door opened and Cord stood in front of her in his stocking feet, Levis, and blue faded tee-shirt. Her back was freezing, exposed to the elements and the eyes of Glendale, but her front was immediately warmed in his presence. She smelled spaghetti sauce with lots of oregano, and the low hum of a bass guitar. It seemed warm and peaceful inside.

"H-hi," she stammered.

"Hi. I'm glad you came. Come in." He ushered her in and took her gloves and jacket. Dana probably would have worn something slinky and inviting to reveal her true intentions, but Janie was so nervous that she had gone for comfort. She had on brown boots, a faded pair of button-fly jeans, and a crew-neck black tee-shirt. She had reluctantly added a blue windbreaker just before she left. It felt like protection, though she wasn't sure what from. She'd thought maybe it would buy her time if Cord tried to undress her, but now she felt silly and not at all sexy or enticing.

"It's freezing out there," she said.

"I know. Weird, isn't it?"

"Yes. I don't think it has ever been this cold in June."

"You don't have to," he said, "but feel free to take your shoes off and kick back on the couch while I finish dinner."

Janie hesitantly removed her boots. That eliminated her option of running out the door in a hurry, but she decided to take the chance. She wished she could get her emotions straight. She wanted him, and then she was afraid to want him. Maybe she wasn't ready for this yet. Cord walked into the open kitchen and left her to find her own way further into his apartment.

"I've never been in one of these houses," she said. "I've always wanted to see inside."

"Feel free to have a look around. They may not look like much on the outside anymore, but the woodwork in here is fantastic."

Three waist-high windows ran the length of the outside wall up the staircase to where Janie assumed must be the bedrooms—his and his mother's. In the center of each window was a different colored stained-glass tulip. The walls and ceiling were cream-colored in every room, including the hall, and boasted pitched ceilings lined with thick black beams. Framing the oak door were two long skinny windows of the same stained glass tulips.

"I can't believe that these windows haven't been broken."

"I know," he agreed. "Even with all the people who have gone through here since the houses were changed into apartments, somehow the glass has escaped damage. Amazing, huh?"

He was leaning over the bar smiling at her, and she felt herself blush. She walked the length of the entrance hallway. The walls were adorned with simple black and white pencil sketches of animals in dark picture frames.

"Who drew these?" she asked.

"My mom. She used to draw them when we lived in Idaho. When I was little she'd sell them at art stands alongside the road for a little money."

"They're really great. Where is your mother?"

"She's with my brother," he said. "When I told her that you were coming over, she offered to leave."

"She didn't have to."

"That's what I said."

"So, it's just us then?"

"Just us," he said. "I hope that's okay."

"F-fine," she stammered.

Cord came from behind the bar that separated the kitchen from the living room and handed her a glass of red wine. He put his hand on her shoulder.

"Relax," he said. "It's only dinner."

"I know." Janie tried to sound confident, but her voice caught when she said it.

He went back to the kitchen and retrieved a large bowl of spaghetti, a wicker basket of sliced garlic bread, and a small salad. He had previously set the coffee table and motioned her to sit on the pillow he had placed on the floor just opposite him. She sat and took a sip of the wine while he dished her up. She had never had a man serve her before. She found it not only sweet, but sensual as well that he presumed it okay to fill her plate. When she ate with Taylor she usually had to get his plate as well as her own.

"Bon appétit," he said, raising his glass to her. She returned the gesture and dug in heartily, as he had done. After only a few bites, she felt herself relax. "I guess I haven't eaten today," she said. "After what happened this morning with Dana, I just couldn't bring myself to eat much."

"Good, because I made enough for ten people. I like to cook when I'm nervous."

She blushed again at the thought of him being nervous. It hadn't occurred to her that Cord Galloway might get scared. "Well, we'll make a great pair then," she laughed. "I like to eat when I'm nervous."

He lifted his glass and toasted again.

"Where did you get the wine?"

"A present from my mother," he said. "For us."

"She hasn't even met me. Did you happen to tell her that I was only seventeen?"

"I told her," he smiled, "but age has always been something of a relative term for my mother. It must be the Indian in her. She goes by maturity, not age. And I told her all about you."

"You did?"

"Then there's the other thing."

"What other thing?"

"Well," he continued, "remember what I told you? She is an alcoholic so she always gives me *alcohol* for a present." He laughed and Janie joined in. Nothing about his family seemed to bother him or embarrass him. Facts were facts. The good and the bad. He was so unlike the people of Glendale.

Just then, something hit the picture window in the living room. Janie jumped as another muffled thump came from the side of the house. Her hand shook as she set her drink down. It was Taylor. She knew it. Who else would be throwing rocks at Cord's house? Cord was getting ready to head for the door when she stopped him.

"No," Janie said. "Please don't open it."

Janie stood and walked to the side of the picture window, careful not to be seen. Through the water streaking down the glass, they could see Taylor leaning against the driver's door of his car, looking back at them. His arms were folded and his legs crossed, as if he was signaling his willingness to wait them out. It was freezing out there and Janie noticed that although he was wearing no more than a muscle shirt and shorts, he didn't even seem to be shivering. Cord went for the door again, and again Janie tried to stop him. She didn't want to see them duke it out right there on State Street.

"Janie," he said, "that guy is throwing rocks at my window. I'm going out there."

"No. Please, Cord."

"Give me one good reason why not?"

This was the first time she had seen Cord be a tough guy, and she didn't like it. "Why *not*?" she repeated. "Why does it matter if you go out there or not? That's just what he wants."

"Because I know guys like Taylor. Hell, my brothers and I used to be just like him when we were younger. He's a pompous SOB who thinks he can intimidate people to get what he wants. It might work on you, but it certainly won't work on me."

"I know. I know," she said. "It's just…"

"It's just what, Janie?"

"It's just that I feel guilty."

"Why?"

"Because I was so scared that I haven't told him about you yet."

Cord raised his brow and waited.

"Well, now is as good a time as any. Let's go out and tell him together. I'm not afraid of him."

Janie ducked her head and walked back to the coffee table, hoping that he would follow. He didn't. He stood like a guard at the window. She took a long drink of her wine. She had never had wine before. It was bitter and sharp as she choked it down, feeling his eyes on her back as she drank.

Cord seemed to relax and refocus on her. "Janie, just how long have you been afraid of Taylor Randall?"

Janie spun around and faced Cord, ready to deny the question. She opened her mouth to defend her lifelong friend, then closed it again as the question reverberated in her mind. *How long have you been afraid of him?*

"Honestly," she said in a small voice. "I don't know." The guilt of the betrayal weighed on her and tears stung her eyes. Things between her and Taylor would never be the same if she continued this.

"Janie," Cord said, leaving his post at the window and walking to her. "I'm sorry, I really am. It just isn't right for you to be afraid of him, that's all."

"I know," she cried out.

"Then what happened?" Cord rested his hand on her shoulder.

"It wasn't what happened. It was more something that he said. It's stupid really."

"What was it?"

She looked up at him and flashed a nervous grin. "He said it would be best for me if I married him because then I wouldn't end up destitute and alone like my mother."

Cord thought about that for a minute.

"Stupid, huh?" she said anxiously.

"I don't know. Do you think you'll end up destitute and alone if you *don't* marry him?"

"No...I don't know. Before the Randalls moved here, I felt like a low-life in this town. Mystery Abbott's daughter. Then Taylor and I became friends, and for a while it seemed like everything was going fine. My family had even been invited to a few barbecues at the Randalls'. Then Mom got pregnant with Bennie, and once again the Abbotts were the talk of the town—except me. I was Taylor's girl. To everyone else, I was better than my mom and Dana." Janie pointed to her chest. "I was the exception."

"There is nothing wrong with you or your family, Janie," Cord said bluntly. "There is something wrong with the rest of them. Other people aren't like this, you know."

"But what if they're right?" Janie asked sincerely. "What if I am making the same mistakes that Mom made? Mom has always followed her heart instead of her head, and look where that has gotten her?"

"That got her you and Dana and Bennie. And John. Doesn't seem all that bad to me, and it certainly doesn't seem destitute or alone."

Janie moved back to the window and peeked out at Taylor, careful to stay in the shadow of the blinds. He reached inside the driver's side window, and honked the horn. She stepped back quickly and turned to Cord.

"I don't know what to do," she admitted.

"Look, it's pretty easy. Do you love him?"

"I don't know. I don't want to hurt him."

"Not wanting to hurt someone is not love."

"I don't love him like he thinks I do," Janie admitted.

"Well, that's it then."

"What's it?"

"Janie," he said. "You and Taylor have been friends for how long?"

"Years," she said.

"If you haven't grown to love him in that amount of time, I don't think any marriage license is going to change that. Do you?"

Her head spun with the realization that Cord was right. She didn't love Taylor, and marrying him wasn't going to change that.

"No," she said. Then more confidently, "No, it's not."

Silence hung between them as she watched Taylor out the window. Finally, he threw his hands up in the air and got back into his car. He didn't leave, though, and that scared Janie the most.

"Janie," Cord said softly. "How about going away for a little while?"

"What did you —? Away?"

"Tomorrow," he said. "Would you go away with me tomorrow?" He was smiling that crooked grin that made her heart race.

"Where?"

"To Idaho. To my family's house. I want you to see it."

She should say no. She shouldn't go away with him. She hardly knew him, and she had a fiancé to deal with. "I don't know, Cord," she said hesitantly.

"It would only be one night."

One night. Her heart began to race at the thought of it. Until now, she had only spent one night out of Glendale, and that was with her friend Robin when they went away to her parents' cabin for the weekend. No. It would be totally irresponsible. She couldn't just up and leave everything and everyone like that.

"What about the roof?" she asked.

"I'll tell John I can't make it until the next day. We're almost done and he's been so focused, he hasn't really needed me anyway."

"I don't know," she said again.

"Please," he said, smiling as he reached out to her. "No Taylor, no Dana. Just you and me."

No Taylor, no Dana. Just her and Cord far away in a safe place where no one in this town could judge her for it. She thought of all the times she had made the "right" choices. All the nights she made sure to be on her own porch by eight o'clock so that Liv Randall wouldn't label her a harlot like she had her mother and her sister. She had been proud of her choices up to this point, but here with Cord she didn't feel like she had to worry about rumors that might cause the problems she had always feared.

Why not? After all, she had graduated. She was almost eighteen, and right now she wanted to be with Cord more than anything. Maybe it would be nothing. Maybe she would go away with him and find out that she missed Taylor. Or maybe not, but she had to know before she let this go on any longer.

"Okay," she agreed. "I think I'd like that." They ignored Taylor for the rest of dinner, thankful that he didn't throw any more rocks, but uncertain as to why he wouldn't leave. Late at night, under the cover of the moon, Janie and Cord walked out the back door and up to Carlisle Street. Janie didn't know how long Taylor waited. She didn't want to know.

chapter seventeen

Mystery Abbott

Mystery looked out at the rain on Carlisle Street. The two mud puddles at the end of her driveway rippled in the yellow glow of the streetlamp. The puddles had been there in the spring for as long as she could remember, but rarely this late into June. As a child, she had fantasized that what she called "muddles" were really lakes with tons of fish and algae just beneath the surface. She remembered jumping over these very puddles so as not to disturb the fish when she left her parents' house on Oak and walked downtown to buy forbidden licorice or bubble gum with her allowance. There was a small one at the top, which fed into a larger puddle just beyond the driveway, toward the road. The town maintenance man, Harry Lind, filled them with a thick coat of gravel every year but each spring they returned, leaving deep impressions in the asphalt. So many children had outgrown those puddles, Dana and Janie among them, and now Bennie.

Mystery's thoughts drifted. It had been a long day at work. Walt seemed to be holding up well, and had even remembered to put his blankets away before work this morning. His normal busy spirit seemed to be returning, and he said he had Mystery to thank for that.

He had requested that she keep the divorce a secret for now. Coral wasn't ready to tell the family, and considering that Melinda was her sister-in-law and one of the biggest gossips in town, Walt had to agree. The people of Glendale would be all abuzz soon enough. Unfortunately, the horrid weather was forcing farmers into John Deere for parts they normally would put off buying until after harvest, and Mystery was afraid that if Walt kept sleeping in his office, he wouldn't be able to keep the secret for long.

The wind picked up sharply, and the black and yellow water lapped at the banks of the puddles as she heard John murmuring the end of the bedtime story he'd been reading to Bennie. Bennie had begged him to stay for dinner, so he did, and then Bennie had pleaded for a bedtime story, so he read him one. After spending an evening with them, minus the girls, John had seemed to relax. He had even grinned at her before Bennie dragged him off to his room.

Inside the walls of her own home, it all seemed so easy. There was a loving man who had eyes only for her and her children. Right this minute he was sitting on the edge of Bennie's bed reading Beatrix Potter even after he had spent the day fighting wind and rain to make sure that they had a roof over their heads. The roof was almost complete. Cord had helped all day, giving Mystery's father a much-needed reprieve, but Cord had told John he would not be able to help tomorrow. John said that was fine, he only had a little bit left to do anyway.

So, unless something changed, Mystery surmised that she and John would stop seeing each other on a daily basis. A part of her wanted to believe he would want this forever. He said that he did, but so had the girls' father, and she hadn't seen *him* since the girls were a few years old. And then there was Bennie's father. Even after almost five years, she still smiled when she thought of him. But he, too, had only been around a couple of times since their child was born.

John had been quieter than usual tonight, and his eyes had seemed to follow her as she prepared dinner. All evening she had felt as though he had something to say. Something she wasn't certain she was ready to hear.

The streetlamp shook as the wind slammed against it, breaking her reverie. She decided she had better get the oil lamps ready just in case, and turned away from the window.

"Oh, shit!" she yelped. "You scared the crap out of me."

"Sorry," John said as he silently padded in from the kitchen. "Bennie just fell asleep. Are you okay?"

"I'm fine," she said, edging past him into the hallway. "He didn't ask for me?"

"Nope." John sounded so proud, and Mystery knew she should be thankful. Bennie still wasn't happy that he had to sleep in his and Janie's room instead of hers, and she had been in no mood to fight with him this evening. She grabbed two lamps and the box of matches from the hall closet and skirted him again on her way back to the kitchen.

After placing the lamps on the table, she slumped into a chair and pulled her legs up into her oversized shirt. What a sight she must be. She was wearing her favorite gray sweatpants that had a streak of pink down the leg from when she had painted Dana's room. Her shirt was a man's Mariners tee-shirt that buttoned down the front. She had once thought it was all she had of Bennie's father. She had planned on saving it for Bennie, but one night, late on the bills and with no money for food, she had pulled it out and cut the sleeves off in a fit of rage at the man who left her with nothing but more debt and more shame. After she had done it, Bennie toddled into the room, bottle in hand. That was all she needed to realize what the man had really left her with. After that, she forced herself to wear it and accept it. She put her chin on her knees and sighed as she wrapped herself deep in the shirt's folds just as John came in and sat down next to her.

"What's wrong, Mystery?"

"Nothing," she lied. "It's just that he usually wants me to tuck him in."

"Well, he was pretty tired."

"The lights are going to go out," she said. As if on cue, the lights flickered. "See?" She twisted up the wick on the oil lamp and lit it. Blue-orange fire shot up along the line of the wick. Mystery turned the lamp down until it was nothing more than a soft yellow glow, and then she carefully replaced the glass chimney.

"I light these even when the power doesn't go out," she said. She turned the base carefully, watching the oil slosh back and forth inside the clear glass. "It humbles me somehow. I like to think I could survive without anything, even electricity."

"You do," John said. "You're amazing, Mystery."

"No, I'm not," she said with an ironic smile. He was so naïve and it made her envious. How would he know about surviving without anything? He hadn't had to lie awake at night plotting how he could scrape together three dollars for a gallon of milk so that his kids could go to school with the illusion that everything was okay. He hadn't had to sit at the kitchen table and sort which bills could be paid and which would have to wait. Nor had he ever had to break out the oil lamps for his children to do their homework by because he had put off paying the electric bill a little too long.

He placed his hand supportively on her knee and held her gaze in the glow of the lamp. Just then, as predicted, the lights failed. Out of habit, Mystery looked across the street to be certain that the failure was not hers alone.

"Mystery," he said. "What is wrong?"

Not that she expected him to understand it, but she decided to be straight with him. An arrow through his heart was the least vicious thing she could do to make this ending clean and neat.

"Bennie doesn't even want me to tuck him in anymore. He wants you."

"So?" he said. "I thought that was a good thing."

"I don't know, John. He's getting too used to you."

"I hope that is a good thing as well."

"I wish the girls would come home," she said. "It's pouring out there and it's so cold. What do you guess it is? Maybe twenty-five, thirty degrees at the most?"

"It's at least thirty-five. I'm sure that they are fine. They're practically adults."

"I was practically an adult at their age too," she scoffed, "and look where that got me."

"I'm sure they're safe."

"Safe in whose bed?"

"Mystery, just because they're late doesn't mean they're out screwing around." He crossed his arms and waited. She had been avoiding eye contact with him all night, but curiosity got the better of her and she looked up at him, a question in her eyes.

"You're doing it again," he said pointedly.

"Doing what?"

"Sounding like Maude."

"Like *Maude*?"

"You heard me," he wasn't raising his voice, but he was stern. "You're going to punish Bennie for not begging to have you tuck him in instead of me, when the kid was so bone-tired that he fell asleep before I even finished the first chapter, and now the girls have to suffer for something that they probably haven't even done."

"Well, you didn't say that Bennie fell asleep that soon!"

"Oh, please," he snapped. "Now this is my fault?"

"No, I didn't say that."

She felt a sense of accomplishment growing along with his ire. She wanted to hold onto that and drive him so far out of her house and her life that he wouldn't be able to find his way back, wouldn't be able to hurt any of them by leaving. But at the same time, she wanted something else entirely. She could see herself running into his arms and saying, *You're right, you're right. I'm sorry. I was wrong.*

But she had done that many times before. She had tried to make it work with men. She had tried to admit when she had gone too far or when she was just plain wrong, and look where that had gotten her. Nowhere but alone. In solitude she was safe from ridicule, safe from pointing fingers, and safe from pain. John slammed his hand down on the table, shaking the oil lamp.

"I've tried Mystery," he said. "I've really tried. I know that things haven't been easy for you. I know you hate how your family makes you feel and what people in this town say about you. You blame yourself for getting pregnant twice and for not being married the second time. You can go right on blaming yourself, your children, and the men who left you — even the choices that you've made — but I will be goddamned if I will sit here and let you blame me. I love you. Hell, I even want to marry you and be Bennie's father and try to be a father to the girls, but I'm not going to take the shit from you like you take from your mother. I won't do it!" John grabbed his hat from the back of the chair and stood. "Well, I'm going. I have cattle to feed before bed. I'll be back in the morning to finish the job."

"Don't bother," she said.

"Unlike some people, I finish what I start."

"What in the hell is that supposed to mean?"

"You have all night alone in your bed to figure it out." He seemed about to walk right out, but something stopped him. For a moment, Mystery hoped that he would turn around, take her in his arms, and force her to love him so that she had no choice and no way out. She held her breath as he reached into his back pocket and turned back toward her.

"Here," he said, throwing a folded piece of white paper on the table. "I have been waiting all day to give you this, so you might as well have it. Although now I'm not sure what good it will do."

With that, he stormed out in the rain. Mystery sat still at the table, concentrating on the blue light of the fire in the lamp as he revved up his truck and sped out of the driveway. She took a deep breath; the silence was broken only by the tick of the clock on the wall and the patter of rain on her new roof.

She unfolded the heavily creased paper. It looked like it had been read and refolded more than a few times, and there was a greasy thumbprint in the upper left-hand corner. The words appeared to have been copied in a cut-and-paste format from the computer.

Rev 17:5 And upon her forehead was a name written, Mystery, Babylon The Great, The Mother Of Harlots And Abominations Of The Earth. 6. And I saw the woman drunken with the blood of the saints, and with the blood of the martyrs of Jesus: and when I saw her, I wondered with great admiration.

Rev 7:18 And the woman which thou sawest is that great city, which reigneth over the Kings of the Earth.

Then in his own hand John had added:

Your mother is wrong, Mystery. You're not named after a whore. You're named after a great city.

Love ~ John.

Mystery reread the note. She clutched the paper to her chest and cried. Here she was yelling at John, telling him about her fate, and then he goes and hands her this. She wiped her eyes with her shirt and flattened the paper down on the table to reread it. Her mother had said she was named after a whore. Mystery hadn't really questioned it or researched it. She had been too busy surviving the knowledge that she was doomed to failure in love because of her name.

Sometimes the nature of the name just takes over, Maude had said. *'Dana' is a strong name and 'Janie' and 'Bennie' are sweet because they have feminine endings.* What kind of crap was that? Maude Abbott had controlled Mystery with comments like that ever since she could recall, and now she was doing it to the kids. To top it all off, Mystery was pushing John away as well, to protect him from the fate her mother said she was doomed to. She thought of all the times she had felt bad about herself, had felt unworthy, had done her best to make people see something more in her than being a "whore." And it was all rubbish. She folded the letter, went to her room, and laid down on the bed. Mystery Abbott had just about had enough.

chapter eighteen

Liv Randall

The next morning Liv looked through her rain-blurred kitchen window at the new brown shingles adorning Mystery's roof. It was almost done, and Liv felt a little disappointed. She had enjoyed watching the men work. Yesterday, as she drove home from the Miller house, she had seen John kneeling on the roof pounding in nails, and she actually thought about stopping by to see if Mystery needed anything. That is what a good neighbor would do, and she hadn't even properly introduced herself to Mystery's boyfriend yet. Had her neighbor been anyone other than Mystery, Liv would have gone into full Good Samaritan mode long ago, baking food, offering shelter, organizing Ma Bell into hosting a fundraiser, and coaxing every business in town to donate time and money to help. Yet, all she had done so far was manage a weak wave or two as she drove by.

She scowled at the clock. She was supposed to be at a quilting meeting in an hour, and it was her turn to bring dessert. She should probably go — after all, she had run out of the PTA meeting without a word to any of her friends — but she couldn't stop thinking about the Millers' pond. She ran her hands through the warm dishwater in the sink, and then reached up and turned the nozzle hard to the right. The rush of cold water was initially shocking, but she got used to it quickly. If she thought about it just the right way, it was even somewhat invigorating. She tried to recall who it was that took cold showers every day. Katherine Hepburn? Liv decided she would give it a try. She finished washing the dishes and was drying her icy hands on the towel when Taylor entered the kitchen, still in his pajamas from the night before.

"Good morning," she said.

He grunted something in her general direction and grabbed a box of cereal out of the cupboard.

"Would you like anything else?" she asked. "I can fix you some eggs."

"Mom, if I wanted eggs, I would say so."

"Okay." She paused before adding in a too-bright voice. "What's wrong with you this morning?"

"Nothing."

She rehung the towel and started to load a box at the foot of the sink. She hoped Taylor would continue to ignore her long enough that she could get everything she needed without arousing his curiosity. Inside the box she placed a bottle of wine and two wine glasses, Windex, an old cloth diaper of Taylor's, Endust, dish soap, an apple blossom candle, and some matches. She took the box to the door and added it to the four empty boxes she had put there the night before. She figured Carl would have tripped over them while getting his running shoes this morning, but he hadn't said a word.

"Late night with Janie?" she asked, attempting to make light conversation.

"Hardly," he grumbled.

"Oh? Are you two having problems? I haven't seen her around here lately."

"Like you would care, Mother," he snapped. "You're the reason that she doesn't like to come around."

"Excuse me? I have always been respectful to Janie."

"Well, you certainly haven't been nice to her mother, and Janie knows that."

She hated to admit it, but he was right. She hadn't been very nice to Mystery. She didn't know that it had made Janie feel unwelcome, though, or that Taylor would even care. Janie and her mother were nothing alike. She didn't see how one had anything to do with the other. Liv hadn't given it much thought until now, but she actually liked Janie. The girl had always been polite and courteous whenever she came over, and on many occasions Janie had gone so far as to wash her and Taylor's dishes when they finished eating. Liv had wanted to tell Janie to run screaming the other way instead of ending up in a life of servitude to her son, but she hadn't done so. Janie seemed to center Taylor, to ground him somehow. He had always treated women with about the same regard as his father had, but with Janie he was different. It really seemed to matter to him what she thought.

Liv wanted to apologize to Taylor for making Janie feel unwelcome, but she could see in his furrowed brow that it would only instigate more animosity. Whatever his problems with his girlfriend were, they were none of her business. She grabbed the boxes and her coat and walked to the door.

"Where are you going?" he asked.

"Out."

"Out where?"

"Why? Do you need me to do something for you?"

"No," he said. "You've just been gone a lot lately."

"Well, I have stuff to do," she said. "Oh yeah, a letter came for you yesterday from Evergreen. If it's about tuition, leave it on the counter for your father, okay?"

"Whatever," he said.

With that she walked out the door, feeling lucky to have escaped without a laundry list of errands she would need to do for him. She hadn't seemed to mind before. No matter what his attitude or needs, Liv had always enjoyed doing whatever he wanted, but today she only wanted out.

She took a deep breath hoping to suck the water droplets out of the air and into her lungs. She had been surviving in dry country for too long. The descending chunk of earth on the bank just below Cemetery Ridge had slid over halfway down to the yard behind Coral Smith's house. Maybe, if Liv were lucky, it would keep moving like the Blob and swallow her and the Jetta whole. Tufts of green grass still rode on the top of the disengaged land, as if by distancing itself from the cemetery it would have a better shot at staying alive. She wanted to tell it that the closer it got to Glendale the less of a chance it had.

She headed the back way out of town on Smith Boulevard to get a better look at the slide on the bank. It was beautiful: large and destructive. The rain beat hard upon it and she hoped she would witness the landslide, but it failed to move as she passed. Up ahead was the high school. She had walked through those double doors so many times that they seemed more familiar to her than the front door at home. Jane's and Emily's cars were parked right out in front. They didn't even have enough respect for her to try and hide their treachery.

She pushed hard on the gas, ready to leave black marks on the pavement, until she caught a glimpse of Carl's car snuggled up in the trees behind the ball field. Liv turned on her wipers to get a better look. School had been out for almost a month now and Carl wasn't one for volunteering anyway — that was Liv's job. So what would Carl be doing here? She pulled in behind the school and waited, forcing her eyes to fight through the fog that seemed to be moving closer and closer around her vision with every stressful event.

His car looked abandoned. She slowly drove around the football field, trying to avoid the water-filled potholes in the parking area.

When she got within yards of the car, she stopped. A flash of color had caught her eye in the overgrowth of lilacs. She rolled down her window and squinted to see between the branches. There, in a small clearing, Carl and a woman in a yellow jogging suit were standing just inches apart underneath a black umbrella he was holding. His other hand rested on her arm and he appeared to be pleading with her about something. She had her head in her hands, her shoulders shaking as she sobbed. Finally, she looked up, nodded slowly, and threw her arms around him. He let the umbrella fall and returned the hug. Together, in a single embrace, they were exposed to the rain, and neither of them seemed to care.

Liv put her hand on her heart and stared at them. She didn't want to see this, but she couldn't help it. It was like watching a car wreck. She couldn't believe it. Carl was hiding beneath a thicket of lilacs in the rain comforting Coral Smith. Jane had told her about Carl and Coral's heated affair in high school. They had gone to every prom

together, every Sadie Hawkins, every Homecoming dance. She told Liv
about how they had been inseparable from their freshman through
senior years. Liv knew about Coral, of course. Carl told her that they
had dated off and on, but it was a high school crush, nothing more,
and, as she recalled him saying, it was probably less. When they grew
up, they found they had nothing in common.

"I don't even remember that girl now," he had told her after hearing
what Jane had said.

Liv had believed him. And why not? She had dated the same guy
for a few years in high school, and there was no way that she wanted
to be with him now. Those things happen to everyone, and then everyone grows up. Liv tried to recall ever seeing Carl and Coral saying
more than a friendly hello to each other in the time she had lived in
Glendale. It just didn't add up. But there was the time in the office the
other day, and now here they were again, the king and queen of the
prom, standing behind the football field of their alma mater hugging
in the freezing rain.

She shook her head and slammed the Jetta into reverse, spinning
her tires and roaring out of the parking lot. It was no secret that Carl
hadn't been happy with Liv since they had moved to Glendale. She
wasn't like these women. Before they moved here, Liv had been a bank
teller. She was well on her way to becoming a branch manager when
Aunt Ilsa died and left them the little house on Carlisle Street. Taylor
had been thriving at school. They all projected a future for him in his
grandfather's law office.

She was certain she had told Carl then that she didn't think she
could live in Glendale. She had been there once, and once was enough.
To her it was a town full of women who had no life, no hope, no education past Glendale High, and, as far as she could see, no aspirations
beyond that. Liv remembered the look on Carl's face the day they
finally moved in. She hadn't believed in auras, but that day she
swore she saw beams of colored light—reds, yellows, magentas, and
greens—radiating from him when he accepted the key from the realtor, whom she came to learn was his old classmate Dora Sievers. He
was home and this home had nothing to do with Liv. He was arrogant,

giddy, and overflowing with exhilaration at finally being reunited with his past.

After seeing him today, Liv realized that there may have been more to his past in Glendale than he had divulged.

She pressed on the accelerator. Out of the corner of her eye, she saw the black cloud begin to move like liquid around her. If she didn't hurry she was going to pass out. She felt a single warm tear on her cheek. She blinked her eyes for more, but there were none. She concentrated on the tear to keep her focused through the driving rain.

As she rounded the last corner to Charles Miller's house, she could finally see the whole building from foundation to rooftop. The cloud lingered in her peripheral vision, taunting her with a possible comeback, but she no longer had the sensation that she was going to pass out.

The house looked so solid and strong. It seemed to be waiting to hold her, to protect her just like Carl was holding and protecting his mistress.

Out back she could see the pond. Her foot on the accelerator felt weightless, almost lifeless, and it did not move to the brake. She thought about ramming her car into the middle of the pond so that the cold murky water would wash over her. She pictured herself sitting in the driver's seat as the car slowly filled with water until it was all over.

She let her foot off the gas and waited for the appendage to decide what to do. Her foot was in charge now. It could either save itself or come down to the bottom of the pond with her. Just before the edge of the pond, her foot moved to the brake and slammed hard. It might be too late. She looked over the dash to see the outcome of the decision it had made. The car came sliding to a stop. Mud spun out from beneath the Jetta. She opened the door and looked down at the front tire. It rested just over the bank. One or two inches further and it would have plunged in for sure. She liked the precision of it. Not too far, but just close enough.

She stepped out into the mud and rain, slammed the door, and left the car right where it sat, aimed at the pond. She grabbed the boxes from the trunk, and ran to the back door. The last time she was here she had left it unlocked so that she wouldn't have to keep climbing in and out the window. She was thankful for that now. Her breath was coming in short spasms, but she was certain that once she got inside, the house would calm her.

She entered through the rear mudroom and walked straight into the kitchen unaware that she was leaving muddy footprints on the floor. She laid her car keys on the counter, just as she did at home, and opened the window over the sink that faced the pond. A cold breeze, unlike the harsh wind in Glendale, blew in through the curtains. It smelled of the ocean again, and her heart was instantly calmed. When she opened her eyes, the cloud had released its grip on her. She was safe yet acutely aware of the wind flowing through her blouse, feathering her skin. She thought about taking off her shirt to allow the wind to caress her, something Carl hadn't done in a long time, but she stopped herself. Right now, she had work to do.

At the bottom of the stairs she absentmindedly stepped out of her shoes. As she carried the boxes up, a picture hanging askew on the wall caught her attention. It was a black and white photo of a man dressed in army fatigues and a woman in a simple light dress suit standing in front of city hall. The woman had a pillbox hat over her curly black hair and a bouquet of flowers in her hands. The man had one arm wrapped around her tiny waist and the other straight down at his side. Someone had doctored the old picture on a computer so that the flowers were colored in with pink and the diamond on the woman's hand was illuminated with a fake sparkle. Below the picture was an inscription: *Happy 50th Anniversary, Claire. Your love, Charles.* Liv straightened the photo.

"Yeah, right," she whispered. "Don't believe him, Claire. He's probably having an affair with some gal at the bank."

She picked up her things and walked the rest of the way up the stairs. No. That wasn't fair. The Millers didn't live in Glendale. He had loved her. Liv felt it in her heart when she went into that bedroom. He really had loved her, yet their children wanted nothing. She didn't get it. They didn't even want an enhanced photo of their parents' wedding. Is that what Taylor was going to do to her after all she had given him? She had spent countless hours preparing scrapbooks commemorating his life, and making sure that he had the best of everything. His bedroom was filled with solid oak furniture that she had had custom-made for him when they lived in Seattle. He always had a new pair of Nike's. For his twelfth birthday, she had forced Carl to buy him his first Rolex watch. He had baseball cards inscribed by every Seattle Mariner and a football signed by Steve Largent. Since birth, Liv had given Taylor everything a boy could ever want, and now what? Sometime next month he was just going to go off to college and leave all of his stuff behind like it didn't even matter.

She passed the Miller kids' rooms on her way to the master bedroom, where she put down the boxes and opened the wooden shutters on the windows. The view of the pond and surrounding fields gave Liv the same peace and serenity that looking out over the ocean gave her. Something about the sway of the wheat fields made her begin to believe that it really was the Pacific Ocean. It was here at this house that she felt weightless, like she could just open her arms and freefall from the window, then glide like a bird over the land. She closed her eyes. Her heart ached at the thought of jumping, at the thought of leaving them behind. But then she pictured them: Carl and his slut, Taylor, and all the women who were ousting her at the PTA meeting. As far as she was concerned, they could all go straight to hell. She was here, alone, surrounded by her private little ocean breeze, and she was going to make something happen that none of them expected.

She took an ashtray and a black marker out of the moving box. She lit a cigarette and set it in the ashtray on the window ledge. The breeze blew the smoke back into the room, but she didn't mind. It could be a little smoky in here and it wouldn't affect anyone but her. However, unlike Dora who left the cigarette in the sink, she would be sure to clean it up. She took a long drag of the cigarette, uncapped the marker, and set three moving boxes side by side. On each she wrote a name: Penny, Marvin, and Charles, Jr. Then she carefully sorted their dead parents' belongings for them.

She cleaned out the closets and made three piles of clothes. In Penny's box she placed her mother's wedding dress and an apron that she had taken from the closet downstairs. She also added the contents of a forgotten jewelry box she had found tucked on a shelf in Penny's closet. In Marvin's she added two of his father's black jackets and a photo of him and his father fishing that she had seen on the landing. The inscription on the bottom read, "Marvin's first fish. Avery, Idaho. 1965." In Charles Jr.'s box she placed his father's watch, which she found in the back of the nightstand, his slippers, which were still at the base of the bed, and the photo of his parents' anniversary, taken from the stairway wall.

It took her three hours from start to finish, collecting and redistributing Charles and Claire's belongings to their children for them, but by the time she was done the Millers had something to remember their parents by. They might simply look through it and throw it all out, but at least they would have to think of their parents a year after they were gone. She took each box to the appropriate child's bedroom and then walked back to the hallway for the last box. On top of the contents was an unopened package of blank note cards. Each card showed a picture of a child at the beach trying to make a sandcastle that was being swept away in the breeze. Inside the cards, she wrote a little inscription to each of them: *We created this life and these memories for you and for your children, not so they could be sold to the highest bidder. Love, Mom and Dad.*

She placed a box in each room and taped the cards to each of their doors. Then she retrieved the fourth box from the hallway and went back into the master bedroom, where she unpacked a large white comforter and matching pillowcases, light purple sheer lace curtains, and a matching afghan. From the bottom of the box, she pulled out the white satin nightgown, bathrobe, and a pair of satin ballet slippers that she had worn the night of her wedding. She hadn't taken these mementos out of her hope chest since she and Carl had returned from their honeymoon. She had no idea what she was saving them for until now. Below that was a small amber-colored bottle that Dr. Viego had given to her last year when she told him that she was having trouble sleeping. She fanned out the nightgown on the bed and placed the slippers on the wood floor just beneath them. Then, she hung the bathrobe on the hook behind the door, sat the pills on the bedside table, cleaned up her mess, and sat at the window to finish another cigarette. At the base of the stairs she found her shoes, clay drying around the edges. She didn't recall taking them off, but it didn't seem to matter. Things that used to bother her didn't seem so important anymore. The house didn't care that she had tracked mud in. It understood her. It didn't blame her, and for that she would be eternally grateful.

"I'll be back," she said aloud as she pulled the back door closed behind her. She got the feeling that she shouldn't let go, that the house wanted her to stay. She reached up with her free hand and patted the glass window of the door.

"I'll be back," she said again. "I promise." Then she leaned in and gave the cool window a soft kiss, leaving a ring of lipstick on the glass. The lips looked so real, so inviting. She couldn't wait to return.

It took Dana hours to get ready. Bennie pounded on the bathroom door, and Mystery yelled down the hallway, but Dana refused to open the door until she was done. Mystery didn't seem to understand the need for order and beauty, and Dana honestly didn't get what Cowboy John even saw in her mother. Mystery was over thirty, she had three kids, she rarely wore makeup, and her clothes were completely out of style.

Dana pushed up her bra and pulled her shirt a bit lower to expose her round bosom, then dabbed a little perfume just between her breasts. She studied herself in the full-length mirror. Though it was still freezing outside, she had on short white denim cut-offs, a tight pink tank top, brown sandals, and a pink coral ankle bracelet. At the last minute, she added large hoop earrings and arranged her hair up in a pink scrunchie. She checked out her butt one more time. She liked it. Who wouldn't? She had given up eating all day yesterday just to be certain not to add any unwanted pounds today. Her butt looked smaller than ever in these shorts. She ran her hands down the curves of her behind and thought about how she was going to feel in less than a half hour. Dylan had taken a chance and called her at home earlier in the day. She practically had to wrestle Janie for the phone.

"What time do you go to work?"

"I have to be there at four o'clock."

"Can you meet me at three?"

"Again?" she laughed. "I thought you said it was only one time."

"Just meet me, okay?"

She felt her body heat up at the thought of him wanting her. "Sure. Where?"

"Behind the football field, in the lilac trees."

Dana practically melted into the floor at the suggestion. Everyone in town knew what meeting out behind the football field meant.

She added three layers of deodorant and reluctantly stepped away from the mirror. As she left the bathroom, tripping over Bennie on his way to the toilet, she noticed Janie packing a small overnight bag in her bedroom. She had all of her clothes out on the bed in separate piles, as if she were doing laundry, and one bag that was already packed to the brim.

Today Dana felt bad for the way she had always treated Janie. She should just come clean and tell her that she could have Cord. Why not? Dana certainly didn't want him, and she'd love to see the look on that snobby Taylor Randall's face when Janie dumped him. That alone would be worth conceding to her. But she knew that it wouldn't happen. Her voice would betray her as it always did when she opened her mouth to talk to Janie. Her tone always came out snippy. It was a bad habit, one she might not be able to break.

"Whatcha doin'?" Dana asked.

Janie jumped when she saw her sister in the doorway, and then quickly glanced back at her bed as if Dana had just caught her in the room with a boy. "Nothing," she said. "I'm...I'm going to Robin's for the night."

"Wow," Dana said, "you two must have big plans with all those clothes." She could hear the sarcasm in her voice, even though she wasn't trying to be that way.

"No," Janie replied as she busied herself with the clothes. "Not really."

"So which one are you sneaking out to meet? Taylor or Cord?" Dana was attempting to make a joke, but she knew the moment that she said it that it hadn't come out that way.

Janie fumbled with a pair of socks and her face turned a telltale shade of crimson.

"Neither."

"Can't decide, huh?" Dana felt her compassion for Janie turning to resentment. She had no idea why it happened, but it always did. Maybe it was Janie's unkempt hair or her complete lack of make-up.

"Can't decide about what?" Janie asked.

"To make it with the good boy, or do it with the bad boy."

"Dana, please." Something in Janie's tone of voice made Dana pause. Janie seemed almost remorseful. She wanted to ask Janie what she meant, but she hated getting into a deep conversation with her. The one thing Dana hated more than anything was having a bonded connection with her sister. People assumed that because they were twins they were close. Dana hated birthdays and Christmas because everyone bought them matching outfits and toys. Other people didn't see them as individuals, but Dana did. She and Janie were nothing alike. They were *fraternal* twins. No one in Glendale seemed to understand that fraternal meant different.

"You know it's true. Everyone else might think that you're this good little girl who is going to save herself for Taylor Randall, but I know you, Janie. The only reason you want Cord is because he was my boyfriend. Well, you know what? You can have him. But let me warn you little sister, he wasn't that good."

By the look on Janie's face, Dana could see that she had made her point. Now it was just a matter of how long she should stand in the doorway to drive it home. Janie resumed folding her socks. "Dana," she said calmly, "for what it's worth, I'm really, really sorry."

Dana crossed her arms and stalked away before the situation got anymore out of hand. Though she tried to push her sister's voice from her mind, it replayed like a broken record as she walked to meet Dylan. *For what it's worth, I'm really, really sorry.*

Janie was sorry? For dating a guy that Dana didn't like in the first place? That was what Dana *really, really* hated about Janie. If Janie were a smart woman she would be able to see that, but she wasn't smart. She was stupid and she was weak. She thought of everyone but herself, and that was why Dana hated being her twin.

Dana looked up ahead from beneath her umbrella. She was freezing but she couldn't let it show just yet. Deep in the thicket of lilacs, just out of sight, Dana could see Dylan's car. He had brought the plain cruiser this time, the Caprice that bore no lights, simply the words "Glendale Police" on each door. When she reached it, the car was empty. She felt stupid peering into an empty police car. What if he was watching her?

"Psst," she heard, "over here."

She looked in the general direction of the voice, and saw Dylan looking at her over his shoulder, just zipping his blue pants after relieving himself. She froze in place, struck by the feeling that she had been here before and seen this exact image, except that it wasn't Dylan; it was Todd after the football game when she was just fourteen. She felt dirty and naked and she swore that she could still feel the raspberry bramble slicing into her lower back. She tried to force the vision away so that Dylan wouldn't pick up on her discomfort. She plastered on a smile and sauntered in his direction.

He finished readjusting his gun belt as he waited for her to approach. He stayed hidden safely within the green lilac leaves. The purple and white flowers had long since wilted from the cool weather. Her body warmed at the knowledge of what he was covering up by zipping his pants. She remembered how intense, almost painful, it was when she had sex with Dylan. Nothing had ever made her feel so aware of her body, and she wanted it again. Small drops of rain fell from the overburdened leaves and landed on her tank top as she closed the umbrella.

"Aren't you freezing?" he asked.

"No," she said, opening her arms, "I like it."

Dylan looked toward the town as if monitoring the scene for unwanted voyeurs. He was obviously nervous about being out here with her. "Well," he said, "you do look great." His eyes wandered up and down her body drinking her in. Even at this temperature, the tank top seemed too much now. She wanted to rip it off, take off her shorts, and lay naked with him on the wet leaves until he made her moan over and over again. Dylan could replace the horrid memory of that night here with Todd, she just knew he could. She stepped closer to him but he failed to take the hint.

"What did you want to see me about?"

He paused for a minute, staring at the gray town. "We can't do this, Dana."

"Do what? Stand in the rain by the football field?"

"You know what I mean. We can't see each other anymore."

"Okay," she laughed, reaching for his belt. "Blindfold me then and I'll do the same to you, Officer Dylan."

"Dana, I'm serious. I could lose my job. I'd get run out of town, or worse yet, I'd probably go to jail."

"No you won't. I'm sure you know that the legal age for sexual consent in Washington is sixteen. I checked. And, since I'll be eighteen next month, you have nothing to worry about."

He turned back toward the town and Dana followed his gaze. She wanted to tell him to screw the legal system. People did it in other countries and it was perfectly acceptable. Hell, it was probably even okay in Nevada.

"So you're eight years older than me, big deal," she said.

"It's a big deal in the eyes of the law and in the eyes of the community."

"I'm not going to tell, if that is what you're worried about."

"No," he said, "I'm not worried about that. It's just—well, it's just wrong, that's all. I made a mistake the other night. It was crazy, it was rash, and I wish I could take it all back."

Dana folded her arms and stood still. The cold was beginning to penetrate. *He wished that he could take it back?*

He turned and faced her in the silence. She looked him in the eye and tried to control her anger toward him. Mistake or not, she wasn't ready for this to be over. She had to make him see reason, just as she had the other night. She placed her hands on his rib cage and slowly moved them down until they came to rest on his hipbones. "I understand," she said. "Really, I do. I don't want you to lose your job or get in any trouble, but please, please don't say it was a mistake. I know you enjoyed yourself. I could feel it. You liked it just as much as I did. Maybe even more."

"Really?" He was smiling now, and Dana could see that his eyes were focused on her and not the town.

"Maybe we could just sit in your car and talk out of the rain?"

"Sure," he said.

She led the way to the police car and he dutifully followed. When they got inside, Dana rubbed her hands up and down her arms.

"I thought you weren't cold," he said, removing his jacket and handing it to her.

Only three more pieces of clothing, she thought. *This was easier than playing strip poker.*

"Dylan," she said, placing her hand on his thigh, "I'm sorry about the other night, too. Really I am. I just got carried away."

"I know," he said, "and believe me, if you were older, I'd love to get carried away with you again."

Bingo!

"Dylan," she said slyly. "I'll go, and we can pretend this never happened if you want to."

He nodded his head in reluctant agreement. Dana moved over into the middle of the seat and let his coat fall away from her.

"Only if you kiss me one more time."

"No," he said, "I can't. If I do, there's no telling what I might do to you."

Dana leaned within inches of his face, and breathed her warm breath onto his lips. He leaned back ever so slightly so she arched her body on the seat, and sat up on her knees. He had nowhere to go. He closed his eyes and mouth in a feeble attempt to block her out, but it was no use. She traced his lips with hers, barely touching him with the tip of her tongue as she carefully unzipped his slacks. She felt resistance in his body. She knew that this was difficult for him, so she took it slow. Finally, she had her hand all the way inside his boxers. She swore that he was even more excited than he had been the other night.

"Dana, no," he said, grabbing her hand.

But she stayed put, kissing softly behind his ear, whispering "it's okay" and "shh" while gently caressing his warm flesh. She reached down with her free hand and gently moved his hand up her shirt, guiding him exactly where she wanted him to go. He moved his body as far toward her as he could and then finally, of his own volition, placed both hands on her hips and eased her back on the seat. It was a little crowded in the car and her leg was pushed uncomfortably up against the steering wheel. He wouldn't even look at her as her pulled her shorts off. As he entered her, she cried out at the sharp pain that ripped through her. He was no longer being gentle.

"I didn't want to do this," he said.

"Yes, you did," she tried to softly counter, but her words were choked off as he pushed himself harder into her. She hit her head up against the passenger side door. The switch in emotion was so overwhelming that it pulled Dana from her fantasy and almost ruined the pleasure of it. He grabbed hard on her breast and bit down on her shoulder.

"Dylan," she said. "Stop!"

But the words must have seemed more wanting than fearful because he moved harder and harder into her. She tried to push him off, but her hands ended up compressed between their two chests. "Dylan," she said. "Slow down." He didn't seem to hear her. She could hardly breathe beneath him. Before she even had time to enjoy herself, he raised his head like a wolf about to howl and released himself into her. She was unable to react with the weight of him on top of her. When he was done, he rolled off her and sat up in the driver's seat with his pants halfway down below his knees. He ran his hands through his hair, panting hard, and stared blankly out the window. Dana moved her legs to sit as well, still trying to figure out what had happened. She wondered if it had been good for him. She had always wanted a man to please himself by taking what he really wanted. Dylan had done exactly that, but it left her feeling a bit different than she imagined it would. Jaded, was the only term that came to mind.

"Dana," he said, turning to her, "I'm sorry. Really I am."

She turned her head and looked at him, wondering the whole time if he had drawn blood on her shoulder. The pain of it enraged her. This was not how she had planned it. "I'm stopping by tonight," she said coolly.

"Tonight? No. You can't —"

"You owe me." She sat up, pulled on her shorts, and then angled the rearview mirror toward her so she could survey her shoulder. There was a deep red bite mark just above the collarbone. She smirked at the memento of unbridled passion that he had left on her skin. He even pierced the skin. He leaned in to look at the mark, but she covered it up. She took a moment to straighten her hair, ignoring his pleas to be understanding, see reason. When she was done, she looked over at him and placed her hand on his mouth. Before he could say any more, she leaned over and kissed him. There was no response, but she didn't care. He owed her now and he knew it.

"Leave the back door open again," she said. "I'll be there just after nine."

chapter twenty

Janie Abbott

J anie waited until she saw Taylor leave to play football with his buddies. She held her breath until he passed her house. He stared but didn't stop. When he was safely out of sight, she left a message on his phone. She was going to the lake with Robin for the night.

"Meet me at the treehouse at five o'clock tomorrow. Bye." She had decided to tell him the truth but not until after tonight.

She told her mom the same story. She'd be back before eleven the next day. Her mother's unquestioning trust left a lump of guilt in Janie's throat. She made small talk about the roof in order to ease her shame, but all Mystery said was that John should be finished anytime. Her mother looked sad, but Janie was too nervous to ask why, so she quickly said that Cord would be back tomorrow to help John. It seemed a dead giveaway, but, once again, Mystery didn't question her.

Janie met Cord out of sight at the end of the street. She said nothing as she slid in next to him on the front seat, and they drove out of town. Up ahead of the school, the police cruiser was rumbling toward them.

"You okay?" he asked.

"Yeah, of course," she responded, but didn't quite meet his eyes. She had brought along an overnight bag and placed it in between them on the seat. She had packed and repacked it three times and now it seemed more like luggage than an overnight bag.

"Wanna put it in the back seat?"

"No, it's fine."

She said it too quickly, she knew that, but she wanted it close to her. Not because she wanted it between her and Cord, but because it was all she had from her house. A sudden bout of homesickness gripped her. As a child, she was the only kid she knew who had a hard time going away from her family overnight. Sometimes, she feared what might happen to them while she was gone. How her grandmother might hurt her mother, how her neighbors would monitor them. In her presence, everyone seemed more careful, their normally razor-sharp tongues and laser-like gazes suppressed and shielded; but regardless of how they tried to hide it, she'd seen what they did when they thought she was too young to notice. All kids do.

She kept her eyes focused on the road as they left Glendale behind them. In reality, there wasn't a single soul who knew where she was, so if anything happened while she was away, she would have no way of knowing. Up ahead she could see another car approaching. Since when had so many people used this road? It seemed that the whole town had come out to witness her lie.

"Oh no," Janie said ducking down into the seat, but she was too late to hide from Liv Randall. But instead of glaring at Janie as she had expected, Liv seemed oblivious to anyone else on the road.

"Why are you hiding?" Cord asked. "Who was it?"

"Taylor's mom."

"I don't think she saw you," he said. "She didn't even look over at us."

Janie said nothing, just sat back up in her seat. As they passed the entrance to the cemetery, she discovered what real guilt felt like. True betrayal cuts like the thorns of a rose, a simple slice that leaves a deep agonizing pain to remind you of something you should not be doing. She might have fooled Mystery, and possibly even Taylor, but not Fawn. Though Janie wasn't a religious person, she believed in spirits, and she knew she couldn't fool Fawn. Her hand tightened around the door handle. She wondered how Dana lied like this all the time. It was exhausting. Cord reached over the bag and put his arm around her.

"You sure you're okay?"

"Sure," she said, flashing him a shaky smile.

Cord squeezed her shoulder in silent commiseration.

Janie had not been any further on this road than to Charles Miller's house for the reception after his wife died. She didn't know the Miller's well, but her grandmother insisted that the whole family attend to show their respect. She had figured that the road just came out to a highway or a town eventually. Four or five miles out of Glendale the brown dirt turned to orange rock, giving the road an orange sherbet look. It wound up and up, deep into a thick wood she hadn't seen before. There was a mountain out this way with driveways jutting off to secret homes deep into the woods. Most of the driveways were chained off with "No Trespassing" or "Enter at your own risk!" signs. She tried to look down the evergreen-lined drives for a glimpse of a house but she couldn't catch one. They had been driving for at least a half hour without any conversation between them. Janie knew she should say something. Last night they had no problem making conversation about their planned overnighter, but in the light of day the guilt of what she was doing overwhelmed her thoughts, and she was finding it hard to think of anything meaningful to say.

"Who lives up here?" she asked.

"Oh, some of them are people who work in Glendale, others go to cities further south, some are loggers, and others might be hiding out from the law. I don't really know. Everyone just keeps to themselves." He looked out the driver's side window at the expanse of trees around him. He seemed to be searching for something. "Rumor has it that a famous writer lives up here somewhere."

"Who's that?"

"Hell, for all I know it could be Stephen King," he said, smiling. "Like I said, people keep to themselves. If he wanted people to know where he lived, he wouldn't be living here. He'd be living in New York or somewhere like that."

Cord popped in a CD. Def Leopard.

"You sure like the eighties, don't you?" Janie laughed.

Cord didn't say anything, just grinned and began beating out "Let's Get Rocked" on the steering wheel. They wound up into the mountains for a while longer, and just when it seemed they were about to crest the hill and start down the other side, Cord flipped on his blinker and turned left. He stopped in front of a chain-link fence and got out to open the gate. Janie stayed in her seat, one hand on the doorknob, the other on her overnight bag.

"Are you okay?" he asked again as he slid back into the car. She hadn't realized that her body language suggested she was planning a quick escape.

"Yeah," she said, releasing her hands. "I'm just a little nervous."

He leaned back in his seat and asked quietly, "Where exactly do you think I'm taking you?"

"I'm not sure," she giggled, attempting to be lighthearted.

He turned toward her, put one leg up on the bench seat, and let his arm drape over the back. "You don't trust me, then?"

"Of course I do," she replied hurriedly. "Why wouldn't I trust you?"

"Why *would* you trust me?" He gave a comical leer.

She smiled back but didn't know what to say. He was right. She didn't know if she should trust him or not. She wanted him to take her away so that she could experience him alone, but she wanted the safety of others around them as well.

"Remember what I was telling you in the cemetery the other day?"

She shook her head, and assumed the same relaxed position that he had taken.

"This is my home," he said. "I want to share it with you."

She thought about what Dana said earlier about him not being worth it.

"Did you sleep with Dana?"

"Why — ? No."

"She said that you did."

"Figures. Look, Janie. I wish I had seen you first, really I do. And, I am sorry for dating your sister, but I don't regret it."

"You don't?"

"No, it led me to you. I see that clearly now and I have no regrets. I hope you can see it that way too."

He turned back in his seat and drove through the gate. The narrow driveway curved down through a dense thicket of pines until it opened onto a wide expanse of green lawn surrounded by a wooden fence. In the center of the clearing sat a picture-book log cabin with a rock fireplace on the left-hand outside wall. In the front yard, an apple tree filled with pink blossoms hung over an ornate white metal bench. Janie could see herself sitting on the bench reading a book while eating a freshly plucked apple.

As Cord removed a cooler and a couple of grocery sacks from the car, Janie walked the perimeter of the yard. Past the rock fireplace the backyard opened onto an old garden and raspberry patch. The garden was completely overgrown with buttonweed and morning glory. Around the other side, a black prefab pond was half filled with murky water, and in the middle a bullfrog sat perched on what was left of the lily pads.

She heard the trunk lid close, and Cord called out, "Come on, I'll show you the inside."

The cabin was made mainly of logs and plaster, with an open-beamed ceiling that peaked over the living room and the open kitchen. A couch and coffee table were arranged in front of the stone fireplace, and two lanterns sat ready on the mantle. In the kitchen was a small wooden table with two chairs, a butcher block cutting table made out of an old stump, and a pump-handle faucet that siphoned water from the well into a porcelain sink.

In the back were two bedrooms. One bedroom had been for his mother, he said. It had a double four-poster bed and an unadorned nightstand. The sight of the bed made Janie fold her arms across her chest and run her hands comfortingly up and down her shoulders. *It's okay. He didn't say we were sleeping in there.*

The other bedroom had been for the five boys. On two walls were matching wooden bunk beds that had been carved by Cord's father and eldest brother, and on another wall was a single bed built much later when Cord was born. Each room had a washbasin and coat hooks. There were no closets, no bathroom, no storage of any kind. Janie felt like she had gone back in time a hundred years. Everything was so basic, only there if it was truly necessary. What appealed to her most was the lack of any plastic in the cabin. Everything here was hand-crafted and built to last.

"I'll get a fire going in a minute," he said as he walked her back to the kitchen. "It's always colder on the mountain than it is in the valley."

Janie said nothing; she just stood in the kitchen and waited. She wasn't sure where to begin or what he wanted her to do. It would be dark outside within a half hour, and then they would be in the house alone together. He walked around the wooden bar that partitioned the living room from the kitchen and put his arm around her.

"You're thinking about me and Dana still, aren't you?"

"No," she said too quickly. When she looked up at him, his eyes were gentle on hers and she felt silly for being so uncomfortable when they were alone. After all, he wasn't Taylor. He wasn't pushy or grabby. With Cord, she felt better in his presence than away from it.

"Just stay close to me tonight, if that's okay?" she asked.

"Okay," he said. "I'm with you." He kissed the top of her head again and smiled.

"I'm just a little nervous. I've told lies I never dreamed of telling, I've left home, and I'm staying the night with a boy somewhere far away from Glendale."

"Look," he said, "I'm really glad that you're here, but I can take you back anytime. I don't expect anything from you."

"I know," she said. She raised up and kissed him on the lips. Here in his cabin she felt grown up. Dana always told her that she was just a baby, so much younger than her twin sister, even though they were only minutes apart. But something in what Dana said was right, Janie realized. She was just a baby. She hadn't dated any other boy but Taylor. She had never had sex. She hadn't even traveled outside of Washington before. She felt herself shrinking in his arms. Cord was older than her. He had probably had sex with lots of girls. Who was she to compete in that league? She was Janie Abbott, not Dana Abbott.

From behind his back, he pulled out a small package that had been hastily wrapped in a paper bag and tied with a blue ribbon. There was a small tag on the ribbon that simply said *Janie*.

"What is this?"

"Open it," he smiled.

She took the package out and untied the ribbon. Inside was a small heart pendant on a silver chain.

Janie's heart jumped. She placed her arms around him and said thank you.

"I love you," he whispered in her ear.

She held on a little longer, shocked by his admission. *Love? He loved her?*

"How do you know that you love me?" she whispered back.

"I just do," he said. He moved out of the embrace and looked into her eyes again. "I've dated other girls, and every time I've found myself looking out into the future for the next one. The next one who would make me feel that spark of excitement that seemed to fade with the last one. With you, I'm not looking any further."

She stood back and surveyed him. "You hardly know me, Cord."

"I know. And there are a thousand reasons that anyone could give that would make what I say a lie, but I don't care. None of them can change the way I feel."

The thought of love made her nervous. She had been trying so hard to dissect her feelings for Taylor that she had come to think she might never know what true love felt like. She hadn't had many positive examples in real life. With her grandparents it seemed so ritualistic — as if they had to love each other simply because they had agreed to do that years ago. What Dana deemed "love" seemed to come from a physical connection, if at all. It had only been recently that Janie had caught a glimpse of true love, and it was in the eyes of her mother and John when they thought she wasn't looking. She had never seen the lines on her mother's face soften so beautifully nor had she ever seen her purely and genuinely smile. She realized that she wanted that not only for her mother, but also for herself.

She reached down for Cord's hand and pulled him slowly to the back room before she had a chance to change her mind. It was part wanting him and part wanting it to be over with. She was tired of thinking about doing what was right. She had done that for seventeen years. This was her time and it was her choice, and not Taylor, nor Mystery, nor Dana, nor anyone else was going to guilt her into doing it their way. She wanted Cord. If she kept thinking of it that way, it was simple.

"Are you sure?" he whispered. "Please don't feel that just because—"

"Shh," she put her finger to her lips and began removing her clothes. By the time they were done undressing she could just make out his form in the moonlight. His pale peach-colored skin was luminescent. He really was beautiful. Dana's image flashed before Janie's eyes. She was in the shadows of the room, smirking at them. Janie shook her head to erase the image. Dana wasn't in the room with them. She couldn't see the warmth in Cord's eyes as Janie sat down on the bed and guided him on top of her. She was nervous. She didn't know if she was doing this right or not. Maybe she was supposed to be on top. For an instant, she felt the weight of Taylor pinning her down. She closed her eyes and tried to block out the vision.

Cord propped himself up on his elbows, waited for her to open her eyes again, and then looked deeply into them. She feared that he was reading her thoughts.

"You're beautiful," he said.

"No, I'm not." She turned away from his gaze.

"No," he whispered, "it's true. I've never seen anything so amazing in my life." Cord leaned down and kissed her neck. She opened her eyes and looked about the room. Nothing. The corners were empty. There was no one here to judge her but him.

They made love slowly for so long that the moon was high in the star-speckled sky before they finally parted. For Janie, it was more than just a learning experience, as she feared it would have been with Taylor. With Cord, it seemed that both her body and mind knew what she was to do. It took her forever to fall asleep in his arms, and it was only then, in the earliest hours of dawn, that she realized there was more than one place on earth where she could feel completely at home.

chapter twenty-one

Mystery Abbott

Wednesday night was the night John normally stayed over. Janie was gone and Dana would not be home until well after midnight. When Mystery got home from work John had just finished taping and mudding the Sheetrock in her bedroom. She thanked him in her usual manner by offering dinner. He stayed, but most of the conversation was between John and Bennie. She thought about thanking him for the letter, but she felt so foolish for the way she had treated him, and so exhausted from their conversations about the negative aspects of her life, that she hadn't found a moment to bring it up. After dinner he grabbed his coat and hat and headed out for the night. There was no mention of the fact that this was their "normal" night together. She thought he would protest leaving as he had before, but he didn't.

Mystery spent the rest of the evening washing and drying her bedding, vacuuming the floor, and hanging as many clothes in her closet as possible while Bennie played quietly in the living room. As she placed her undergarments and socks in a box next to her shoes, she paused a moment then stepped in, closed the door, and listened in the darkness. She could hear Bennie humming his ABCs, and the occasional creak of the house from the wind. What must John have felt like when she shoved him in the closet that night? She could only imagine what he thought as her mother and Liv were sniffing him out.

There's a man in here; I can smell him!

Mystery emerged from the closet and stifled a laugh. It had seemed so horrifying the other night, but with a little distance, Maude's accusation was kind of funny.

Bennie fell asleep amongst his Legos in the living room around ten, and Mystery continued to tinker in the silence until midnight. She was surprised at how much she had accomplished in two hours. Without the usual daily distractions of work and family, her house was spotless. She was getting sleepy and she couldn't think of anything else to do to keep her busy. With Bennie now tucked into his bed, and Dana yet to arrive home, Mystery accepted that very soon this was how life was going to be. She took the time to brush her teeth and wash her face, something she felt too burned out to do most nights, and then she finally gave up and went to bed.

At three in the morning, she woke with a start as wind slammed against the house. She jolted from her bed and immediately checked the ceiling. It was fine. It was just the wind. Nothing more.

She tossed and turned all night, fighting the urge to call John and tell him that she was wrong and stupid and sorry. She had read his note more times than she could remember. Her mother had called three times after John went home the previous evening, and all three times Mystery deleted the message.

"Call Grandma," Bennie said, but she did not.

Sometime before her alarm was set to go off, Mystery woke to hammering again. She opened her eyes and focused on the ceiling. The light fixture in the center of the room shook in response to each thump. Mystery fought the blankets that were twisted around her ankles, straightened her pajama pants, ran a hand through her hair, and headed for the living room window. John's truck was parked nearly sideways in the driveway. Mystery grabbed her sweater from the coatrack and stepped sockless into her shoes before walking out onto the porch and into the cold.

Thump! Thump! Thump-thump-thump!

Mystery turned in the wind and rain and spotted John perched like a pigeon on her roof pounding nails into the asphalt shingles.

"John!" she bellowed through the rain. "What are you doing?"

He placed his hammer in his lap and frowned down at her. The new shingles gleamed in the rain, and Mystery feared that they might be slick. John reached behind himself and retrieved a flask. He looked at her, raised it high in a silent toast, tipped it back, and guzzled the contents. Mystery looked over at Liv's house and then back at John.

"John," she said again, "what are you doing?"

"Finishing *your* roof," he called back.

She was about to say something else but was stopped by the noise of the hammer. In an obvious effort to block out any conversation, John grabbed shingle after shingle and pounded as fast as he could. Mystery knew there was no way he was getting those nails in straight.

"John!" she called again.

No response. Mystery shivered and looked down at herself in her soaked pajamas. Any minute now Liv would be at her window monitoring the situation for Ma Bell.

"Fine!" she yelled. "Stay up there until you fall off."

She went back inside and checked the clock on the wall. Five o'clock. She had to be to work by eight. She went to Dana's room and peeked in. Dana was sprawled on her bed, her covers askew on the floor. The thumping had yet to wake her or that lazy spoiled cat. Dana must have had a late night. Mystery closed her door and walked to the back of the house to Bennie and Janie's room. Bennie was curled on one side in Janie's double bed. His little legs barely made it halfway down the mattress and his blankets were tucked perfectly around his little frame. He didn't look as if he had moved all night. She closed the door in a futile attempt to muffle the pounding above and tiptoed to the kitchen to make coffee.

For the life of her she couldn't figure out why John seemed so angry, or why he was drinking like that. Last night had been relatively uneventful. She wanted to make him stop, but she didn't want to stand out there all morning and attract the rest of the gossipers. She loaded the coffeepot with double scoops. It was the only concession she allowed herself when she went to the grocery store. There were some things that she could live without: new pantyhose, makeup, she'd even go without breakfast if she had to, but she would not go without good, strong coffee. It was the only thing that gave her enough energy to get three kids and herself out the door every morning. She decided that despite everything, she should offer him a cup in hope that it would lure him down from the slick roof.

She wished the coffeepot would finish. She looked away from it to heed the adage about a watched pot, but it still seemed like it was taking forever. The rain was making it impossible to see out. It looked like the windows were steamed up from a good day of canning, but Mystery knew that if this rain didn't stop soon, there would be none of that. She had already lost her tomatoes to the frost, and the peas weren't faring much better. June rains were important to the farmers, but it was getting to the point where enough was enough. It had been raining on and off all summer and according to the latest forecast, it wasn't going to let up for at least another week. She turned from the window and glared at the coffeepot.

"Finish!" she said.

The coffeepot gurgled its response. Just then, a sleepy Bennie wandered into the kitchen. He wobbled over to her and lifted his arms. She picked him up and he cradled his head against her neck.

She cuddled him back. Her strength, her rock. For Bennie she could do anything. If she could muster the will to end things with John, it would be best for Bennie. Just ask her mother or Liv, or anyone else in Glendale for that matter. It was bad enough that he didn't have his father. It would be worse to get his hopes up for a replacement and then disappoint him. He was already too attached to John.

"Did you sleep well?" she asked as she filled two cups.

He nodded his head and then brought his fist up to rub the sleep from his eyes.

"Good dreams?"

He nodded again and then pulled back to look at her.

"What did you dream about?"

"John," he said through a yawn.

"Oh."

Bennie looked around the kitchen and then tucked his plump little hands in between their tummies for warmth.

"Where's John?" he asked.

Mystery laughed at his amazing ease with words now. She pointed to the roof and gently set him on a chair.

"I'm going to take him some coffee. Wanna go?"

Bennie hopped down and walked beside her to the door. She put his coat on over his jammies, and reached for his shoes.

"No," he said.

"Honey, it's cold out there. You have to wear shoes if you want to come out."

Bennie pushed his shoes aside and walked behind the coatrack. There, hidden in the back was a brand new pair of brown and black cowboy boots, just the right size for Bennie's feet.

Bennie took them out, sat down, and expertly put the boots on.

"When did you get those?"

"John gave them to me when he put me to bed and read me a story. Yike 'em?"

It was a long sentence for him and she had to bite her lip to avoid pinching his cheeks and telling him that she "yoved 'em."

"Yes," she said. "They're great."

Bennie clomped past her and opened the door. She watched him as he sauntered out in his zip-up bunny jammies and his new cowboy boots. He seemed so much bigger than he ever had. Before, she had always thought of him as her baby, but that image was starting to fade with his growing independence. She knew she should be happy that he had finally found his voice, but in her gut she felt the pain of longing for something she would always miss.

The wind had picked up a little and lifted the curls on his head as he walked down the steps and turned to summon John. Mystery stayed in the shadows under the roof of the porch.

"John!" he called.

"Well, hey there li'l buddy," he drawled. "Did I wake you?"

"Yes," Bennie called back proudly.

"Well good. All good ranchers are up 'fore the sun comes up."

"I'm up," Bennie said. "Can I he'p?" He started for the ladder.

"No, Bennie," Mystery said sternly, stepping out onto the sidewalk to stop him.

"I wanna he'p!" he yelled, struggling to free himself from her.

"Not today, li'l pard," John yelled. "It's too dangerous for li'l cow-pokes like yourself."

His overuse of the word li'l worried Mystery. She wished he would come down from the roof.

"Why don't you come down for a cup of coffee," Mystery said.

He swayed a little as he looked down at Mystery. "Not today. Got a lot of work to do if I'm going to finish this and be gone by tonight." She noted his emphasis on the last words, but what could she say?

"*Please*, Mommy," Bennie begged. With that he kicked a little leg in the air to accent his cowboy boots.

"Nice boots," John said.

"T'ank you."

"You're welcome."

"Thank you for the boots, John," Mystery said, "but you shouldn't have."

"I didn't do it for you," he said tipping the brim of his hat at Bennie. He looked up in the air and then closed his eyes, letting the rain fall on his face. "On second thought, I guess I'll have a — whoa, shit — "

"Mommy!"

John had leaned back too far, tilted to one side and slid down the roof on his belly. Somehow, he managed not to fall to the ground, but he had missed the ladder by at least a foot and was dangling precariously off the edge of the roof, hanging onto nothing but the rotted gutter.

"John! Hang on, I'll get the ladder!" Mystery yelled.

Mystery yanked the ladder through the muck that lay beneath the gutter. John swung his legs back and forth until his foot made contact with a rung. He reached a wet hand over, grabbed the opposite side of the ladder, and heaved his body onto it. He descended with exagger-ated care. When he was all the way down, he still held onto the ladder, as if to thank it for rescuing him.

"John," she said, reaching for him, "are you okay?"

"Like you care," he said. He ignored her hand and ruffled Bennie's hair as if nothing had happened, but she could hear him breathing heavily as he walked by.

"Wanna have coffee with me?" John asked.

Mystery was about to answer when she realized that he was still talking to Bennie.

"Sure!"

John wrapped his arm around Bennie and swaggered up the stairs, but he almost seemed to be holding onto Bennie for support. Mystery rushed past him as they ascended. His face was a pasty white and his eyes were completely red.

"I think I better get the whole pot," she said.

"Yeah, you do that," he replied, "an' bring an extra cup for my li'l pard' here, would ya?"

John slumped down on the porch swing, and gave a ragged laugh as it lurched back and forth. Bennie joined in, completely oblivious to the intensity of the situation.

"Bennie," Mystery said, "why don't you come with me?"

"Nope," he said. "I'm staying with John." He squeezed in next to John and giggled up at her. John flashed Mystery a challenging smile.

"I'll be right back," she said.

By the time she returned, John had already downed his cup and was ready for more. As she poured him another, he reached into his pocket, pulled out the flask, and added a liberal amount to the brew.

"John," she said, "what's in that?"

He looked at the flask in mock confusion. He turned it around and pretended to read it but both sides were unmarked. He pushed it in her direction. "Don't know," he snorted, "why'n't you try it an' find out."

"No thanks," she said. "Bennie, please go inside and get dressed."

"Uh-uh," he said.

"Bennie," she warned.

"Go on," John said. "Do 's your mother says. I'll be here when you get back."

"Promise?"

John squinted up at Mystery. "Promise," he said. "An' *I* always keep my promises."

As the screen door closed behind Bennie, John began weaving slightly from side to side.

"John, what do you think you're doing?"

"Minute ago I was fixin' your roof. Now I'm drinkin' coffee."

"Coffee and what else?"

He raised the flask again as if to toast her, then, slurring a bit added, "I already said, I dunno."

"Where'd you get it?"

"Bar in Kennedy. I's there until the lady kicked me out at two, an' then I've been drivin' around ever since."

"You can't work on the roof. You're drunk. Did you even make it home to feed the cows last night?"

"Now, you sound just like my wife," he said, wagging a finger at her.

"Well, I'm not your wife," she said.

His expression hardened and he looked at her as straight on as he could. "I'm getting the roof done today."

"No, you're not."

"Yes, I am," he said, as his chin went up a notch.

"Why?"

He failed to respond immediately, but his expression was cold as ice. Mystery tried to find the slightest bit of love and compassion in his eyes but saw only stubbornness and anger.

"I already told you that, too," he said. "I always finish what I start."

"Well then finish it tomorrow — when you're sober."

"No." He stood up, wavered a bit, downed the rest of his coffee, and stomped off to climb the ladder. On the third wrung he missed and came crashing down again. Mystery ran over to steady him, and he grabbed onto her arm. For the first time in two days she felt the warmth of his body next to hers, and even in his drunken, ornery state, she wanted to lean in and pull him close to her as she had done so many times in the past.

"Okay, John, okay," she said. "You can finish the roof today. But you have to promise to come in and sleep it off for a while. I won't let you kill yourself with Bennie watching."

John leaned heavily against her, breathing hard as she helped him climb the stairs to the porch. She felt awash with guilt for the pain she had caused him. She just wanted to get him inside and into a warm, dry bed so he could sober up and feel better. *If there's anyone watching,* she thought, *let them watch.*

When she finally got him to her room, he collapsed on the bed, docilely letting her remove his wet clothes until he was in nothing more than his tee-shirt, underwear, and socks. Bennie watched from the doorway and she smiled at him.

"John's not feeling the best, honey. You go and play while he sleeps, okay?"

As she pulled the covers back and tucked him in, he clung to her forearm.

"Wish I always had a li'l gal like you to care for me. Never met a woman who has so much love to give an' yet chooses not to give it."

Mystery gently pulled away when he turned his head to sleep. The picture in her bedroom seemed so complete with him there that she left the door partway open so she could watch him while she got ready for work.

chapter twenty-two

Liv Randall

L iv sipped her hot coffee and watched out the window as
Mystery helped John into the house. A week ago, she would have
picked the phone right up and given Jane a play-by-play of the
whole event, but not anymore. Today, she didn't want Jane's negativity
to interrupt her surveillance of her neighbor and the cowboy. She was
especially drawn to how close Mystery held John as they ascended the
stairs.

From what Liv had gathered prior to cutting her friends out of her
life, Mystery and John had been seeing each other for less than six
months. Six months, and yet watching them together, it seemed as
though they had been a couple forever. John easily wrapped his arm
around Mystery's shoulder and leaned his head down into the crook
of her neck. Mystery placed one arm firmly around his waist, while
the other supported his chest. There wasn't even a glimmer of light
between their two bodies as they mounted the steps.

Before moving to Glendale, Liv was sure she and Carl had touched
each other like that. She recalled long nights of making love with the
window open so they could hear the waves crashing against the shore
near the little cottage at Ocean Shores. She remembered looking at

Carl constantly, thinking about how lucky she was to have such a handsome and successful husband.

Last night she laid perfectly still for an hour next to Carl's warm body with a similar lack of space between his back and her side. It was a final test on Liv's part to see if there was anything left between them, but he didn't turn to her. She had cleared her throat at ten thirty and turned to face him at ten forty-five, stomach to back. That was what she had done in the past to clue him in that she wanted to have sex, but these days he didn't seem interested. A disapproving grunt was the only reaction her touch had elicited.

"Good morning!" Carl strode in from the living room, dressed in his jogging suit and carrying his work suit on a hanger. Without so much as a kiss, he walked to the coffeepot and drained the last cup. She contemplated offering up a kiss of her own but then recalled his lack of response to her affections last night, and remembered that she had decided it truly was over.

"Morning," she said. "Taylor up?"

Carl looked around as if searching for Taylor in the shadows of their kitchen. "Doesn't look like it. It's summertime, you know." He flashed her a comical smirk in obvious satisfaction with his sarcastic remark.

"You talked to him about those cigarettes, right?"

Liv raised her eyebrows but ignored the comment.

"Going jogging again?"

"Yes," he said.

"Well I hope you break a sweat this time." She dumped her coffee in the sink.

"Hmm," was all he said, as if he hadn't even heard her. He picked up the paper and started reading it as he poured milk on the cereal she had set out for him.

Watching Mystery's house through her kitchen window, with the rain finally starting to abate, Liv wanted so badly to know what they were doing in there.

"Actually, on second thought, I hope you don't." Behind her, she heard Carl at the table finishing up the rest of his cereal and coffee but not acknowledging her statement. She silently catalogued each movement as he stood, grabbed his suit, and padded over to the door for his shoes. Liv craned her neck around to fume about the mess she knew she'd see on the table and huffed out of the room. The thought of cleaning up after him galled her, but having to initiate a courtesy farewell might make her slap him, and he definitely wasn't worth that.

In their bedroom, Liv lit into the organizational task she had started after last night's failed attempt to entice Carl. She yanked open the middle drawer and began pulling out her spring sweaters and stuffing them into a box.

"Well, maybe you wouldn't be so tired and unable to have sex with your wife if you didn't have so many extracurricular activities during the day," she scoffed.

"What did you say?"

Liv spun around and saw Carl standing in the doorway of the bedroom. It took her a moment to realize that her comment had been out loud. She turned and opened her top drawer, busying herself to buy some time.

"Were you talking about me?"

"Pardon me?" she asked.

"You heard me, Liv. Were you talking about me?"

"No," she said, and then decided to take another tactic. "And, so what if I was? It's not like you'd care." She pulled all the clothes out of the next drawer without even sorting them and crammed them into the box. When she was done, she slammed that drawer and continued down. Carl stepped in from the doorway. She was having a hard time seeing him as the blackness encroached once more. Either he was going to have to leave or she was. She grabbed the box and barged past him, elbowing him into the hallway wall. Getting out of there was like coming up out of water for a breath of air. She exhaled deeply and made a dash for the brightness of the kitchen. She set the box down by the door and started rapidly folding the contents. She didn't know why. She didn't really have to fold them, but she wasn't ready to leave without all of her clothes, and she had to do something.

Carl now stood in the kitchen doorway just as he had in the bedroom. She could barely make him out with the absence of peripheral vision, but he seemed to be studying her. Liv tried to picture what a man like John would have done had Mystery stormed out of the room.

She couldn't believe that she was thinking about that, comparing her twenty-year relationship with her husband to the six-month fling her neighbor was having next door. Nonetheless, she continued to ponder the question. She just knew John would have walked over, taken her in his arms, and forced her to tell him what was wrong. Charles Miller would have done the same thing, she was certain of it.

She finally looked up at Carl, skinny from all of his jogging or whatever else he was doing, and she wanted to vomit. After the last visit to the Miller house, she had managed to keep a full meal of salad and iced tea down. After being back here for one night, her stomach felt way too full again. "What do you want, Carl?" she finally asked.

"I have about five minutes," he said, noting his Rolex. "Would you like to explain yourself?"

She brushed past him again, going back to the bedroom without answering him. *Five minutes,* she fumed silently as her gaze skittered around the room. Five minutes was all he had for her to explain that she had no idea who he was, who she was, or what the hell she was still doing here. She was packing boxes of her own clothes in front of his eyes and he didn't even stop to ask her why. He followed her back into the bedroom like a trained dog and that ticked her off even more.

"Liv," he said calmly, "what did you mean by *extracurricular activities?*"

She managed to focus on the dresser, then yanked opened the last drawer, hands trembling, to stuff its contents in the box: shorts, skorts, pedal pushers. It really didn't matter any more. She felt the adrenaline coursing through her body. "Why don't you tell me?" Liv retorted.

"I would, if I knew what in the hell you were talking about." She slammed the drawer and went for the closet: skirts she had bought specifically for the PTA meetings, Calvin Klein slim fits, straight-legged pants for barbecues, Wrangler shirts. Things she wouldn't have been caught dead wearing in her old life. Before Carl had brought her here, she wore lacy tank tops and tight-fitting polyester jackets with short, smart-looking skirts and high heels—heels you could wear in the rain but definitely not the snow.

"Are you changing your wardrobe again?"

"*My wardrobe?*" Her voiced squeaked in outrage. Could he really be this stupid?

"You're cleaning out your drawers. Are you changing your wardrobe again?"

"Yeah," she smirked, "that's what I'm doing. What else would I be doing?"

"Who really knows with you, Liv," he fired back.

"What is that supposed to mean?"

"It just means that Taylor and I think that you have been acting strangely lately."

"Oh you and Taylor think that, do you?"

"Yes, we do," he said.

"Did you two have a midnight powwow about the crazy person you both have to live with or something?"

"Something like that," he nodded. "Look, Liv, you're never home, and when you are, you are secretly packing stuff in and out of the house. You're pissed off at me about god knows what, you are leaving things undone that would normally drive you insane not to complete, like the dishes and the laundry. Your friends call and you don't call them back. Melinda called for you again last night, and we keep having to make excuses for you."

"Well, don't!" she snapped. "They're not my friends anyway. For all I know, you probably hired them to take me under their wing when we moved here."

"What the hell kind of nonsense is that?"

Liv marched over and stood right in front of Carl, her face within inches of his. "Look, Carl," she said, "none of this was my idea. These are your friends, this is your town, and this is Ilsa's damn house. I was just brought along for the ride."

"Are you serious?" he asked. "I'm sure you don't remember through the fog of sleeping pills and antidepressants, but we made this decision together, Liv, and it is *our* house."

"Oh no we didn't," she ground out. "And just to set the record straight, the sleeping pills are because I can't sleep in this stupid quiet little town of yours, and I was only on antidepressants one time in my life,

206 — Amy Warwick

for post-partum depression after giving birth to *your* son — nothing more!"

"Who the hell has ever heard of not being able to sleep because a town is too quiet?"

"Lots of people," she said. "People who live in the city. People like me!"

Just then they heard a rustle from the hallway. Taylor came walking out of his room in his tank top and boxers. "What's going on?"

"Nothing," Liv said. "Just go back to sleep."

"Jesus Christ, Liv, it's not like he's still five years old." Carl turned to Taylor. "Your mother and I are having a fight," he said.

"No kidding. About what?"

"It's nothing for you to worry about, Taylor," Liv said.

"Yes it is," Carl corrected her. "He lives here, too. I was asking your mother what has been going on with her lately."

"Oh. Did you get an answer?"

"No, not yet," Carl continued. "Maybe you can talk some sense into her. She was talking about some extracurricular activities that I have going on, or something like that, and so I merely pointed out that she is the one who's never at home, and then she flipped out and started packing boxes."

Taylor looked at the boxes and then back to his father. "What are the boxes for?"

"Beats me," he said. "You'd have to ask her."

"Unbelievable," Liv said. "You two are having a conversation as if I'm not even in the room."

"Well," Taylor said, "then why are you packing?"

He didn't have a shred of concern in his voice. He sounded just like Carl, so matter-of-fact and logical. Liv turned back to the boxes and continued filling them. "And for another thing, Mr. Lawyer," she said. "You should get your facts straight when you are telling a story to a disinterested party. I was packing the boxes *before* the conversation happened."

"Well, whatever," Taylor said. "So what, are you moving out or just going shopping?"

Liv finished folding the lid on the last box and walked past them both, ignoring the question. They followed her down the hallway and into the kitchen.

"So, which is it, Liv?" Carl said. "I'm really late, so I need you to tell me if you are just pissed off and you'll be over it tonight, so that I can leave and give you your space, or if this is a serious issue."

"Serious issue?" she asked. "Give me my space? What the hell is it that you think of me?"

"I think I know you pretty well. You've had these tantrums before. However, for the sake of our son's education, I can't lose this client if you are just pissed. The way I see it, it's pretty cut and dried."

"When have you ever lost clients because of me?"

"After Taylor was born and you got depressed."

"So what? A lot of women have post-partum depression. And it wasn't like you were there."

"You don't even remember, Liv. I was there. I am always there—"

"No you weren't," Liv interrupted as calmly as she could. "My grandmother was there with me. Not you!"

"Whatever, Liv," he said, throwing his arms up in the air. Carl turned to Taylor, and Taylor nodded his head.

"I don't give a fuck if you lose every client in this town," she shrieked.

"Yikes," Taylor said, and moved to the cupboard to get a bowl of cereal.

"Is that your plan?" Carl asked. "Do you think that if I lose every one of my clients then we can just up and move back to where you were begging me to take you away from in the first place? Is that it?"

"You know what, Carl," she said, reigning herself in to mimic his irritating composure. "For a lawyer, your memory really sucks. Of course that's what you lawyers are best at, isn't it? You twist and turn the truth just like a piece of Play-Doh until eventually it becomes whatever you want it to be, and you believe it, too."

"I didn't twist anything," he said flatly. "You've been ranting and raving about being better than this town for so long I don't even think you know what the truth is anymore."

"Well, let me remind you," she said. "The truth is that *you* wanted to move here, not me, and certainly not Taylor. You didn't even tell me about our move until after you signed the papers!"

"I had to sign the papers in order to inherit the house. That didn't mean we had to move here."

"Don't bring me into this," Taylor said, calmly pouring his milk as if this was a normal morning in the Randall house. "I like it here."

"Well, you didn't," Liv said. "You wanted to stay with your friends at your old school. You wanted to stay on the coast just as much as I did. But not your father; he didn't care what we wanted. I gave up my job, my friends, my family, everything. And for what? So your father could run back home as the successful lawyer and sit in that godforsaken fishbowl window day in and day out waving as all the girls from *high school* walk by."

"I'm outta here," Taylor said taking his bowl and leaving the room. "Good luck, Dad."

When he left the room, Liv and Carl stood silent for a moment. "It wasn't that way, Liv," Carl said, unruffled. "You hated working and being away from Taylor. You hated the traffic and the smog and the rain. You said it's what made you depressed and that maybe the dry climate over here would help you to feel happier."

"That's not true," Liv practically cried. It couldn't have been. Her mind was beginning to cloud over as Carl twisted the truth to his advantage. "I never said that. When did I say that exactly?"

He placed his head in his right hand and rubbed his temples. "Look, I'm not going to have a fight over semantics while fighting another battle with you at the same time. I can't nail down a time and date from five years back. You know perfectly well what I mean."

"Oh, do I? Well, why don't you enlighten me?"

"You've made friends here, Liv. You've run the PTA ever since Taylor was in junior high school. You started a quilting bee. You have the stupid Ma Bell with your little girlfriends. Hell, the people in this town love you more than they love me."

"My little girlfriends," she mimicked. "Are we in high school again?"

"Whatever," he said again, shaking his head. "Look Liv, you know you have made a life here, and that was nothing I forced upon you. You've been just as happy here as Taylor and I have."

"No Carl," she said, looking him dead in the eyes. "No, I haven't. *You've* been happy here. You just chose to look the other way because you were either too busy or too scared to see what was going on right in front of you."

"Oh, yeah? And what was that?" His voice was expressionless and he was looking at the floor now, as if he didn't really want to take part in this conversation anymore but was being forced to.

"That you were losing your wife."

She expected that to hit him like a hammer on the head, but it didn't. He simply looked up and said quietly, "How come this is the first I have heard of it?"

"The first?" She gave a bitter laugh. "The first? Oh, please."

"Liv, you've never told me that there was a problem."

"I shouldn't have to."

"So what, are you leaving me or something?"

"Why?" she asked. "Does it matter?"

"Of course it matters," he said grudgingly. "But I'm not going to try and force you to stay anymore."

"Carl," she said, "you don't love me, you don't touch me, you haven't even tried to have sex with me in almost two months."

"Oh, is that what this is about again? Me not telling you that I love you?"

"Yes!" she yelled in frustration.

"Fine. It's not like I don't have other things on my mind you know, but whatever. I'll tell you I love you. You'd think after twenty-odd years of marriage you would know that."

"It's only been nineteen!"

"Okay, nineteen." He looked down at his watch and walked to the door. "Look, we can have this discussion later. I'm late now. I have to go." With that he grabbed his suit and shoes and opened the door to leave.

"Fuck off, Carl," she snarled. "Those are the last words I have to say to you."

"Somehow I doubt that."

After Carl was gone, Liv noticed Taylor standing in the doorway, cereal bowl in hand. "I'm sorry you had to hear that." After a brief pause, she added tightly, "I'm also sorry if I ever did anything that would make Janie feel unwelcome here."

"Yeah, well it's a little late now." He didn't look up at her, he simply shoveled the last of his cereal into his mouth, put his bowl on the table, and left.

She reached under the sink and grabbed the paper bag to breathe into again, then changed her mind. *Let it take me,* she thought, *right here, right now. How would they feel then?*

The cloud swirled as she slowly dropped the bag, and suddenly picked up the phone. Her call was answered on the first ring.

"Jane," she said in a monotone. "I just wanted you to know that I wish you luck as the new PTA president."

"Thanks, Liv," Jane replied with surprise. "I'm so glad you called. And for what it's worth, I just want you to know that I let that snooty little bitch Jolene have it after you left. We all did."

For what it's worth, Liv thought. She wondered how many times she, herself, had made that statement after the fact.

"Liv?" Jane said into the silence on the phone line.

"Yes?"

"So, are you okay, then? I mean with everything? You know we are all here for you if you need us."

I don't need anything anymore, she thought. She had just given her the green light for screwing her over by becoming the PTA president. She didn't think anyone would know about the house yet. "I'm fine," she said. "I just told you. No hard feelings."

"Look, I know it's none of my business, but you are one of my best friends, and if we women don't stick together, our husbands will be out screwing every woman in the county."

"Screwing every woman in the county? What are you talking about?"

"Liv," she laughed, "it's happened to all of us. My husband with Joni from the bank. Melinda's husband with some woman in Butte,

Montana, years ago. It happens in every marriage. We just don't think it's right that everyone knows but you."

"Seems like you gals have been talking a lot lately." Liv carried the phone with her to the window in the bedroom and once again spied on the Abbotts. The swing on Mystery's porch moved carelessly in the breeze. There was a warm glow coming from her kitchen. She wondered if Mystery was baking something.

"Liv? Are you still there?"

"I'm listening. You're talking about Carl?"

"Yes, honey," she said. "That is exactly what I'm talking about. There are ways we can handle it, you know. We've done it before."

"Ways?" she questioned vaguely.

"Yes, ways," she said. "Remember Joni? The one I just told you about?"

"Yes..."

"She didn't just move away, you know."

"She didn't..."

"Hell no," Jane giggled, then trailed off awkwardly when Liv didn't respond. "Liv, are you okay?"

"Fine," she breathed. "What about Joni at the bank?"

"Let's just say Ma Bell asked her to leave."

"Oh. How come I didn't know about this?"

Jane hesitated. "We wanted to include you, really we did. But there is that little fact that you are married to the only lawyer in town. You understand, right?"

Liv gave an aggrieved sigh into the phone. "Oh yes, I understand..."

"So," Jane said, "do you want us to help?"

"Hmm? Help with what?"

"Come on, Liv. Do you want us to encourage Coral to leave town? Melinda would just love to help."

"But she's her sister-in-law," Liv protested half-heartedly.

"All the better reason to boot her ass out of town," Jane laughed.

"What do you do, tie her up in a gunnysack and drop her at the nearest train station or something?"

"No," Jane laughed, "nothing like that. It's more to do with the

212 — Amy Warwick

power of persuasion. She wouldn't want to be our enemy. Really, she wouldn't."

"I imagine you're right," Liv said distantly, as she continued to look at Mystery's house. "But no. No, thank you. I think I'd like to handle this on my own."

"Okay then. But just remember that we are only a phone call away."

"Mmm hmm."

"Hey, before I go, can you tell me if there is any new action with your slut neighbor?"

Liv looked back out the window at the quiet little house with the yellow highlighted kitchen window. "No," she smiled. "No action at all."

chapter twenty-three

Dana Abbott

ana finally emerged for breakfast as Mystery was closing her bedroom door and leaving for work. With the rain lightening up, Dana had opted for a short black tennis skirt and a light blue tank top with a white sweater over the top. She felt elated and free, unencumbered by Mystery's choices and Janie's pull on her as a twin. Being a member of the Abbott family, she never felt quite like her own person, but today something felt different. Choosing Officer Dylan—such a pillar of the community—had freed her from her future in Glendale's lower echelon, and elevated her to the status of policeman's girlfriend. *How about the police chief's wife?* she mused.

"Morning, Dana," Mystery said.

"Hey, where's Janie?"

"She stayed at Robin's last night. I think she said they are going to the lake today."

"In this weather? It's freezing out there."

"I guess. Look, your grandmother is going to babysit Bennie this morning, but I really need you to take care of him this afternoon."

"I can't," she said brightly. "I have a job, remember?"

"Oh crap, that's right."

"As a matter of fact, I'm working a double today, so I'd better get down there."

"See ya tonight, then," Mystery replied.

"I'll be late," Dana called over her shoulder as she made a dash for the door.

"Have a good day."

"You too," Dana said. She didn't feel any animosity toward her mother this morning. She had other things on her mind. She felt energized on her walk to work. There was no wind to speak of, but the chill in the air was invigorating. Even in this morning's cold, Glendale seemed like the most perfect place on the planet. With Dylan Masters close by, Dana couldn't imagine being anywhere else.

The town was alive for a Wednesday morning, with three cars buzzing past one another on Main Street, and four or five pedestrians actually having to wait to cross the street. She guessed that people were out taking care of business while the rain was at bay. Dana thought it was a shame to see so many people donning coats and sweatshirts on a day when she herself was so warm. She was certain that if anyone got close enough they would feel the heat radiating from within her. As she passed the restaurant and waved at Mr. Borghese, he pointed playfully to his watch and gave her a single finger to indicate she had one hour before she had to be at work. She smiled back and gave him a double thumbs-up.

Carl Randall was standing outside his office talking to Coral Smith. Dana made a point to walk by and say hello. Carl fidgeted with his keys in the pocket of his pressed pants. He kept biting down on his lip and his well-shaved face flexed with tension. He didn't return Dana's greeting; instead, he remained focused on Coral, nodding his head in agreement with whatever she was saying. Coral gave Carl a hug and a kiss on the cheek then put her sunglasses on despite the gray skies, looked around them for a moment, and quickly walked in the other direction.

"Hi," Dana said again.

"Oh, Dana, good morning," he replied. He still looked stern and his usual politically friendly smile was absent.

"You have some lipstick on your cheek," Dana pointed out.

"Oh, thanks," he said, awkwardly rubbing his cheek with his thumb. He quickly turned and marched back into his office. Dana turned back and saw Coral go into the bank; she didn't like the woman and she wanted to follow her in there and tell her that. Carl was Liv's husband, and Coral had no right snooping around trying to entice him. Especially right now when Liv obviously needed him the most. Dana understood that now too—the need for a man to hold you even when you're hard to hold, to love you even when you're not easy to love.

She was contemplating whether or not she should go confront Coral when she saw Taylor moving straight at her. Now how was she going to get to the police station before her shift started? Taylor looked pissed. Though her sweet sister didn't know it, the boy had a temper. She had seen it flare up one time when he came to the house to find Janie. When Mystery told him that she wasn't home, he had pushed right past her and into Janie's room to look for her. He was so angry when he didn't find her there that he had glowered at them on his way out, slamming the door behind him without a word of explanation. Later he acted as if it hadn't happened, but Dana did not forget the look on his face. She told Janie that night that Taylor was obsessed. As was typical of her naïve little sister, she hadn't believed Dana. She had said that Taylor wouldn't hurt a flea. She was right about that; he wouldn't—in front of Janie, that is—but Dana knew a little more about men than her sister. That boy was trouble.

"We need to talk," he said. He grabbed her by the elbow and steered her back in the direction from which she had just come, past Carl's office and behind city hall. He let go of her arm and paced back and forth in the damp grass, seething silently. She couldn't see what her sister saw in him. Right now he looked like a spoiled little jerk. She really didn't have time to hear about his problems with Janie. She only had forty-five minutes before she had to be at work, and if she didn't go now, she would have to wait for almost twelve hours before she could be with Dylan again. She decided to give Taylor five minutes. That would be enough time to finish a smoke and make her way to the police station without arousing much suspicion.

She pulled a cigarette from the last pack she'd had Cord buy for her. She doubted she'd be getting cigarettes from Idaho anymore, but it didn't matter. She'd be eighteen in a month and then she could buy them on her own. Or maybe she would quit. After all, Dylan didn't smoke. She sat down on the top of the picnic table and lit the cigarette. Taylor stood in front of her and opened his hand for one.

"The wonder boy smokes?"

"So what?" he said. "So does your sister."

"Yeah, right."

Taylor rolled his eyes and lifted the smoke to his mouth to emphasize his point. Dana *really* didn't like him. He was a prep, just perfect for Janie. His bleach-blond hair was matted down in the middle with gel and was sticking straight up in the front. Dana figured that he had more product on his hair than she ever had on her own. Everything on him was Nike white and blue. His jacket, warm-up pants, and tennis shoes all matched perfectly. He looked like he was ready for a tennis match.

He was completely unimpressive. He was the type of boy that wanted to be a badass just as long as he had mommy and daddy's bank account to protect him. She wasn't surprised that he thought he was cool enough to smoke, but she was surprised that he allowed Janie to do it. Smoking wasn't a very ladylike thing for Taylor Randall's girlfriend to do.

"So, what do you want, Taylor? I have to be to work soon."

"Where were you last night?"

Dana stopped halfway through inhaling the smoke and quickly blew it from her lungs. "Why?"

"I just wanted to know if you were with your boyfriend, that's all."

She snubbed out her half-smoked cigarette in the ashtray on the picnic table. It was now nine fifteen. Dana hoped that this wasn't going to take very much longer. "Why do you ask?"

With a sideways glance at her, Taylor rolled his cigarette on the edge of the ashtray next to her leg, sharpening the cherry into a fine red point. He seemed to be holding something back, wanting to savor some secret. Dana suddenly wondered if he knew about her and Dylan. She didn't really care if it came out in public about them, but Dylan did. He was the cop in town and she was underage. For his sake, she was going to stay calm instead of telling this little bastard off.

"Did you know that you are supposed to be my sister-in-law?" he offered.

"No," Dana laughed. "How do you figure?"

She wasn't sure where this was going, but he didn't seem to know about Cord and Janie.

"I'll tell you a secret, Dana," he said between puffs, "I'm not going to Evergreen like my parents have planned."

"Congratulations." She leaned back on one hand in order to put some space between her and Taylor and smoked with the other. It really didn't matter if the boy rocketed to the moon and back as long as she could get out of here without him blowing her cover.

"I'm going to travel the country," he smiled broadly, pointing his cigarette at her. "I'm taking off and Janie is going with me. Do you know where our first stop is going to be?"

"Disneyland," she jested. Her bare legs were beginning to shiver in the cold.

"No. Las Vegas. Janie has agreed to leave Glendale and marry me."

"Okay, I'm surprised," Dana said cautiously. "But what does that have to do with me and my boyfriend?"

"Just answer the question," he said calmly. "Were you, or were you not, with him last night?"

"Are we talking about Cord?"

"Why, who else are you fucking this week?" There was a twisted look in his eyes, as if he hoped she really would admit there was someone else.

"Screw you, Taylor," she said. "I don't have to tell you a thing."

Taylor slammed his hands down on either side of her bare legs. She could feel the heat of the cigarette next to her thigh. He was leaning halfway over it and glowering directly in her face. Dana sat up, risking the burn, and matched his stance.

"I'm not Janie," she said. "I'm not just going to roll over and take your shit like she does. So, if you have something to say to me, just say it."

Dana pushed him to the side and got up. Her arms may have trembled, but honestly, he had no idea who he was messing with. If Taylor Randall so much as touched her, all she would have to do is tell Dylan and he would throw his ass in jail. She couldn't tell Taylor that, though.

"Fine," he said. "Just tell me where Janie was last night, Dana?"

She turned back to see him cracking his knuckles. Dana wanted to laugh. The girls in this town pined away at night over Taylor Randall, and all the while, he pined away for Janie Abbott.

"Mystery said she went to Robin's." It was freezing out and yet Dana could see sweat form on Taylor's brow as he resumed pacing.

"Well, that's what she told me, too. But I think it was a lie," he said, through clenched teeth. "You see, Janie has been acting a little weird lately. She didn't return two of my phone calls and she's always going off on walks without me."

"Taylor, what do you want from me?" she huffed. "I've about run out of time for this."

"Do you know that Janie and I haven't slept together?"

He was pacing back and forth in front of the table, not looking at Dana. He seemed to be lost in his own little angry world, and prudish Janie was the center of his attention.

"Well, I kind of figured that," she laughed. "Janie's a wedding night kind of girl."

"Yeah, she told me that also. I've been trying to get her to sleep with me for almost three years now, and she still says she wants to wait. I've been more patient than any other man would ever be because I thought it would be worth it."

"Oh, I don't know if it will be worth it or not," she shrugged, "but it's just *great* that you two have waited for each other."

"I didn't say *I* was a virgin, Dana," he snapped. "I've had other girl-friends. You know that. It's just that I always knew that I would end up with Janie."

"Well, sounds like you're going to, *brother*." She stifled a laugh.

"I thought so, too," he said. He was cocking his head back and forth from side to side and Dana could hear cracking in his neck. She wanted to tell him to calm down, he wasn't prepping for a boxing match, but he continued on, "I thought so until last night. See, I thought it was you that I saw, but it was actually Janie."

"How the hell could you get us mixed up? We're twins, but thank God we look nothing alike."

"It was dark," he explained. "I saw her at Cord's so at first I just assumed it was you. I was going to stop and ask where Janie was, when I figured out it wasn't you on the steps of his house — it was Janie. By the time I got out of the car to confront her it was too late, he already had her in the house. So I threw a couple of rocks at the window until she finally had to look out through the blinds." He continued pacing back and forth, his energy level making Dana exceedingly uncomfortable. "They didn't come out though. I think Cord was afraid or something because I waited out front for well over an hour, and he never showed. I bet they snuck out the back door."

As he rounded the table, Taylor snagged another smoke from the pack and continued on. Normally, Dana would just mock Taylor with a well-timed finger down her throat when he started talking about Janie, but this time she listened. It was making Dana both nervous and curious at the same time.

"So I called Robin this morning, and guess what? Their answering machine says that they'll be out of town for two weeks. Now how is Janie coming back from the lake with them today if they are going to be gone for that long?"

"Maybe they are bringing her back or something."

"Jesus, Dana, you're sounding as naïve as your sister. I think Cord is trying to seduce her into giving it up to him first."

"So she did choose the bad boy," Dana laughed.

He didn't seem to hear her as he prattled on.

"I swear to God that if he forced himself on her I will kill him."

"Now wait a minute," Dana interjected. "I know Cord; he wouldn't — "

"Maybe. Maybe not. But I have waited for three years to be with her, and I will be damned if some lowlife is going to take it from me."

"Jesus Christ, Taylor, you act like taking her virginity is some prize you're going to put on your mantle."

"It is," he scowled. "She'd better goddamn well be a virgin when I marry her or I swear to God I will kill that guy."

She didn't like the look in Taylor's eyes. "Lighten up. I'm sure Janie didn't sleep with him. Why don't you just ask her? There's probably some logical explanation. In the meantime, I have to get to work."

"Doesn't it bother you at all that your boyfriend might being banging your sister at the same time he's giving it to you?"

"Look," she said, tossing him another cigarette and ignoring the question. "Stop by work tonight if you need to talk, but at least let her explain herself first."

"Fine," he agreed. "She left me a message to meet her at the tree-house when she gets back. I'll give her one chance. She's worth that much."

As Dana walked away, shivers prickled up and down her arms. Glendale's weather seemed about to take a turn for the worse.

chapter twenty-four

Janie Abbott

As Janie climbed the ladder to the fort, she had no idea what she was going to say to Taylor. She was almost late and her nerves were even more on edge because she had to pick up Bennie from her grandmother unexpectedly. Dana and her mother had to work. She couldn't help being a little resentful. Knowing that she could always be counted on was making her feel a bit used. As if sensing her impatience, Bennie screamed and kicked all the way into the house when she mistakenly said that she was going to the treehouse to meet Taylor.

"I wanna go too!"

"Not this time." Janie sat him down a bit too forcefully on the couch and he began to wail.

Luckily, John wandered out from the bedroom and talked Bennie into helping him load up all the old roofing next to the house. Janie didn't ask what he was doing sleeping in her mom's bedroom in the middle of the day; she didn't have time, and she had her own problems to deal with.

As she rushed to the treehouse, she was relieved to find that Taylor had not arrived yet. Normally in the summertime, she came out daily to prop open the little wooden window so they wouldn't boil to death if they camped out at night, but today that wasn't necessary. After the precipitation ceased, a cold biting wind blew into town and Janie was thankful that her mother had placed their sweatshirts out and within easy reach.

Taylor arrived ten minutes after five. He always made a point of being late. Janie used to think it was because he had so many more commitments than she did, but today it made her nervous. She wanted this over with.

She was sitting in the beanbag chair with her back against the wall, wringing her hands to stay warm, when Taylor climbed through the trapdoor. He pulled the footstool up in front of the floor hatch and sat down, blocking her only way out. He fished two cigarettes out of his pocket and angled one toward her. She waved it off, saying no thanks. She wasn't going to smoke anymore.

Taylor placed the cigarettes on the table and moved over onto the beanbag next to her. Without hesitating, he placed his arm around her shoulders and used his hand to pull her head down into the crook of his neck.

"There," he cooed. "That's better."

Janie felt cold and rigid, like she was cheating on Cord. She was sure Taylor would sense the tension soon and that would be her cue to explain everything to him.

"I miss you," he said.

"I'm right here," she replied.

"Only one week until we leave."

"L-leave?" she stammered, uncertain what to say.

"Yes. For Vegas."

She knew she should move away from him and get it over with, but she was suddenly petrified. She still didn't want to hurt him and was unsure of what might happen if she did. Cord was still at his place with his mother, after all. He had said he would arrive within an hour, but it seemed like a lifetime.

"Have you told anyone?" he asked.

"No," she replied shakily, "have you?"

"Nope, it's our little secret." He closed his fingers around Janie's wrists and pulled her up onto her knees to face him. He maintained his hold on her wrists as he leaned forward and kissed her lightly on the lips. She was still as stone at first, and then tried to pull away but Taylor quickly moved and laid her underneath him. He smiled as he placed his hand on her waist and began to work his way beneath her sweatshirt. She was breathing rapidly now as she gently tried to push his hand down, but he took it the wrong way and went to work on removing her pants. She pulled her lips from his and turned her head to the side.

"No, Taylor. Please stop."

"No, honey," he whispered, shaking his head. "After all, we're almost married. I don't want to wait any longer. I've waited for you long enough."

She grabbed his wrist and pulled as hard as she could, but he resisted with all his strength. Her heart began to beat faster and for the first time she felt real fear in his presence. She remembered Dana warning her about his temper. She thought she had always trusted him, but today she realized that somewhere in the back of her mind she had *never* trusted him. It was always fear that led her to do what he wanted, not trust.

"Taylor!" she yelled. "Get off!" She pushed hard on his chest but he continued to kiss her, forcing his body down on hers and working harder at removing her pants. What the hell was he doing? She thought about screaming, but who would hear her? By the time Cord arrived it would be over. She hit Taylor in the back and bit him in the neck but he persisted. Within minutes, he had her pants down to her knees and was working hard on his own. When he finally got his down far enough, he stopped moving and pinned her arms above her head. She stopped squirming and met his gaze. He didn't blink as he looked into her eyes, and that was when she realized, after all of her years of knowing Taylor, that he had planned this. It was the same routine that they had gone through for years in the treehouse, only this time he was not going to take no for an answer.

"Taylor," she asked softly, "what are you doing?"

His leer unnerved her, but he didn't make any further moves. He held fast to her wrists when she tried to move them. "Janie, stop squirming and I won't hold your wrists so tight."

She relaxed and he did release his grip, but when she tried to move, he squeezed again and shook his head disapprovingly at her. "If you answer one question, I'll let go of your wrists."

"Get off me, Taylor. Please. You are hurting me."

"Answer my question first." He smiled at her as if they were playing spin-the-bottle or truth-or-dare and he was just about to win.

"Fine," Janie simpered. She tried desperately to ignore the feel of his penis next to her thigh.

"Are you still a virgin?" he asked.

"*What*? What is with you and that damn question?"

He pushed against her midsection reminding her of what he was capable of, and repeated the question.

"Taylor, don't. Please."

He wrapped one hand around her wrists and placed the other one beneath her thigh.

"I don't want to have to do this, Janie," he said matter-of-factly. "And if you answer my question, I won't."

He leaned down and gently kissed her on the lips, but his eyes glittered all the while. "Tell me, sweet Janie," he cajoled. "I have to know."

She decided to try another tactic and call his bluff. A small part of her wanted to believe that he was playing, he was just taking the game a little farther this time to see if she would give in. After all, he had tried to have sex with her many times before and she had always been able to get him to stop. "Taylor, please get off of me. We need to talk."

"No," he laughed, "talk to me like this."

"I can't, you're hurting me." He remained on top of her, but loosened his grip on her wrists.

"Okay," he said, "now talk."

"Taylor," she said diplomatically, "you are my best friend and I don't want to hurt you."

"Then don't. You're confused right now, Janie. That's all. I don't want you to make a mistake that we will both regret."

She searched the beautiful eyes she had known for so many years, hoping to see the deep blue that was warm and inviting when she pleased him instead of the icy blue when he didn't get his way. A tear escaped her and slid down her cheek. She forced herself to look at Taylor as she delivered the news.

"I don't want to go to Vegas, and I don't want to marry you." She said it as softly as she could, but he didn't take it any better that way than if she would have screamed it in his face. She could see red in his eyes now and the tendons in his neck began to bulge. Even though it was freezing outside, it was getting hot in the fort. Droplets of sweat formed on his brow, and one dropped smack in her eye. She wriggled around again, but this time he tightened his grip around her wrists.

"I waited for three years for you," he said, his voice becoming hoarse with anger. "Three fucking years."

"You didn't wait for me, Taylor." She spoke almost apologetically as she had learned to do every time she had denied him in the past. "You had a different girlfriend every week. Don't act like you didn't sleep with them."

"They meant nothing to me, Janie," he said defensively. "You know that. Those girls were just to get me by until you had sex with me. You knew that then and you know it now. It's not like it really bothered you."

She was tired of his game playing, tired of countering his accusations with contrition and white lies meant to placate him, and even more tired of constantly having to coddle him in order to get him to hear what she had to say. It was time for the bold truth, no matter what the cost.

"Taylor! I didn't want to have sex with you then any more than I want to have sex with you now. Okay, do you get that now? I'm sorry, Taylor. I just don't. So please, just let me go."

He held fast to her wrist and grabbed her thigh.

"But you want to have sex with Cord, right?"

"Taylor, stop it! Don't do this."

"That's it, isn't it?"

"Let me up and I promise I'll tell you everything."

"Promise, huh? A promise is what marriage is, Janie!" He spat the words at her. "A promise is what we had, and I know that if we have sex you'll see that you should keep that promise."

"Taylor," she cried, as she thrashed under him, "please don't, you're hurting me."

"Just hold still, Janie, and when we are done you will see that this is really what you've wanted all along."

She couldn't believe that he was doing this. She strained against his grip on her wrists. He was trying hard to part her legs and hold her wrists at the same time. He was larger than her and much stronger, and Janie knew that eventually her strength would give out and then Taylor would get his way. Her life flashed before her, and all she could see was Taylor haunting her. She would become his victim, and it would leave a mark on her that she would have to deal with for the rest of her life. She didn't want that. She didn't want Taylor Randall to be with her forever. She continued to fight against him, determined not to let him win.

Just then she heard a rattle behind her and Taylor let go of her wrists long enough to partially turn around. Janie pushed him off of her and reached down for her pants, quickly pulling them up. There was a shadow poking through the trapdoor but through her tears and the dusky light, Janie couldn't make out who it was.

"Get the fuck out of here!" Taylor yelled at the intruder.

"Janie," she heard, "are you okay?"

It was a man's voice, but she couldn't place it. For all she knew it could have been Charles Manson coming through that door, but she didn't care. "No," she choked out, "please get me out of here." She tried to get to her feet, but Taylor held his hand up to block her exit.

"Look, mister," he said with all of the conviction of a boy who felt he could tell anyone what to do, "I don't know what you are thinking coming in here, but you are interrupting my fiancée and me, so get the hell out."

"I'm not your fiancée," she cried, "now move."

Janie swatted his hand away and crawled toward the hatch, but Taylor grabbed her shoulders before she could leave and looked her in the eye.

"Janie," he pleaded, "don't do this. Don't make a mistake that you and I are both going to regret."

"I think you heard the lady," the voice said. It was John. Janie scrambled toward the door and was about to climb down behind him, when she stopped and turned around. Taylor had come for an answer and something in her was not going to leave without giving him one.

"Just so you know, it was already too late, Taylor. I gave what you were waiting for to someone else." She was shaking so hard she could hardly descend the ladder. John waited just away from the tree and lowered his head as she turned toward him. From above she could hear a pounding on the floor.

"Janie, are you okay?" John drew her to him and she buried her face in his jacket.

"I'm f-fine," she said, looking up and swiping at the tears on her cheeks. "Nothing happened, okay? He, he just scared me, that's all."

"Janie, Janie," he crooned, rubbing his hands up and down her back as if attempting to warm her. "Stop. Don't protect him."

"I'm not," she said, attempting to sound composed. "It's just that you stopped it. You know? So, nothing happened."

"Okay, Janie," he nodded. "Let's talk about it later. Right now, let's get you home. Then I am going to deal with Taylor."

He placed his arm lightly around her and led her to the porch. He sat her down on the swing and wrapped the quilt around her. When she found her voice again she said, "John, you aren't going to say anything, are you? I mean to Cord?"

John held up his hand to silence her. "First off," he said, "men aren't as stupid as you think they are. Well, most men. You didn't do anything wrong. If anyone should be embarrassed it's that little bastard who's still hiding out in the treehouse. Second, you're a big girl, Janie. You can handle this yourself. But if you need to talk, you know where I'm at, okay?"

She nodded her head. "And you won't tell Mom?" she whispered.

John ran his hand through his hair and contemplated the question. "Well, that's a tough one. I can't really lie to your mother, Janie."

"John, please," she pleaded, "you don't understand. Mom has enough on her mind." She let the blanket fall and examined her wrists, rubbing the swollen red marks around them. "She has enough on her mind," she whispered again.

John sat next to Janie and examined the marks. For the first time, Janie felt like breaking down and crying right here in front of this man she hardly knew. She didn't know if it was okay, or even if it was proper, but when she felt her body heave into a single large sob, he put his free arm around her and cuddled her in his arms just like she imagined that a father would. It wasn't fair, and Janie knew it was just an illusion. There had been men before who had tried to fill the father-figure role—her grandfather, Carl, and even Walt on a number of occasions—but in reality, none of them were anything like a father. They were friends, and now here she was at almost eighteen, leaning on this man as if he were the real thing.

"Okay," he soothed, "I won't tell Mystery. But I want you to know, I've never lied to a woman, not even my own mother, and neither should you. I think you should tell her."

"But why—"

"Because she's your mother," he said.

Out of the corner of her eye, Janie saw Taylor walk to his house. He turned to them both and glared. Janie felt her skin turn cold as his blue eyes bored through her. John watched him as he walked across the street. He whispered to Janie that it was okay, it was over, but Janie knew for certain that it wasn't even close to being over for Taylor Randall.

chapter twenty-five

Mystery Abbott

Mystery tried to be casual when she got home from work that evening. It was later than usual, but she had stayed after work to talk to Walt. She knew that if anyone saw her car there after hours there would be hell to pay, but she swallowed her fear for his sake. He was doing better, and for that he thanked her.

You're a true friend, he'd said as she left the room that had now become part office, part apartment. *I learned from the best,* she'd replied as she fluffed the pillow on his couch. *John Spencer is about the best friend a person could ask for.*

She hadn't expected John to be there when she got home, but when she rounded the corner and saw both his and Cord's vehicles parked in front of the house, she had a sudden sense of peace. Both men seemed like such a part of their lives now that she almost dreaded seeing the roof get done. As she approached the house she said hi to them both, but only Cord responded.

John would be gone tonight if she didn't do something to change it. She offered to make them some coffee, but John declined and resumed hammering before she could get in another word.

She had received her weekly paycheck today. Though Walt had

been kind enough to pay her for the whole week plus a two-hundred-dollar bonus that he claimed he owed her from the previous Christmas, it wouldn't be enough to pay her normal bills and cover the roof repair. If she skimped on groceries and paid half the mortgage, she could probably manage it, but they would really have to skimp. She could buy Janie and Bennie off with Top Ramen or macaroni and cheese. Luckily, Dana usually ate at work these days, and if she did eat at home, it was mostly just cottage cheese or pretzels. Those were cheap enough. For herself, it would be another few weeks of Wheaties or Cheerios.

She pulled out her recipe box and gathered the ingredients for wheat bread. That was at least something homemade. She could throw together a little chicken soup from the stock in the freezer and she would have it made for another night at least. She hoped John would stay for dinner. She had yet to figure out a way to thank him for the letter about her name, and she thought dinner might help. Bennie had been playing blocks in the living room, but when he heard the mixer rev up, he came running to help. She wasn't in the mood for an assistant tonight. She told him so, but he scooted a chair over to the counter anyway.

"I can he'p!" He smiled, sticking his hand in the dough.

"You're going to get sick," she said. "There's raw eggs in that. Now why don't you go find Janie."

"Don't wanna. She's in the bathroom cryin', and I don't yike Janie cryin'."

"Crying?" she asked quizzically. "Are you sure, honey?"

Bennie nodded. She pulled the beaters from the dough and washed her hands.

"How long as Janie been crying?" she asked, quickly wiping her hands on a towel.

He shrugged and said, "Since her and John got home."

"Where were they?"

"Treehouse."

The beaters clanked as Mystery dropped them in the sink. *In the treehouse,* she thought. *John and Janie?* Bennie reached around her and swiped one, then he ran off into the living room. She should stop him, she knew that, but she couldn't believe what she was thinking. *John?* It would be just like her to pick a man that ended up being—well, someone bad. Her mother and the rest of the town would have a field day with this. They had warned her about that treehouse but she hadn't listened, and now her daughter could be suffering for it.

She washed her hands under the warm water for a long time, trying to reason out what Bennie had said. It didn't make sense, but innocent children don't lie. She carefully covered the mound of dough with a damp towel, and slowly placed the bowl in the oven as if any sudden movement might kill the rise. Then she summoned her courage and walked outside. It was getting dark. They would be down soon, but this couldn't wait.

Cord spied her as she walked out of the house and, reading the emotion on her face, nudged John. The pounding stopped, and for a moment the whole town seemed quiet. John straddled the peak of the roof and waved his hammer nonchalantly. Bennie wandered out onto the porch and sat in the swing licking the last of the dough from the beater. His nose had a thick glob of dough on it.

"What is it?" John asked.

"What's going on with Janie?"

John glanced over at Cord and then back at her. "Why?"

"Is there anything you need to tell me?"

John looked uncomfortably back at Cord and shrugged his shoulders. "No," he said.

"No," she repeated.

"No."

"Is she okay?" Cord asked. He was already shifting to climb down the ladder when John stopped him with a brief shake of his head and a calming hand on Cord's arm.

"Mystery," John said, "maybe you should go back in there and ask your daughter what's wrong."

"I'm asking you first."

"Well don't. Ask Janie."

"Fine. I will." She stomped back into the house and slammed the door, hoping that the reverberation would knock him right off the roof and onto his thick skull. She took a few deep breaths and slowed her pace on the way to the bathroom. Bennie dodged in front of her and pounded on the door.

"Janie, Mommy wants you to come outta there." Janie didn't say a word.

"Shush. Go away now, Bennie," Mystery urged.

"I'm gettin' Janie," he said, hitting the door again.

"No," she chided. "You had your chance to get her for me when I asked you to earlier. Now go find something else to do."

"No," he frowned, looking up at her, "I want Janie."

"Bennie," she said firmly, and, raising her voice even further, added, "go to your room right now!" Mystery rarely lost her cool with Bennie. Until recently, the child hardly said a word, and his defiance now was shocking. "Go!" she said again. She closed her mouth into a firm line and pointed.

"Okaaaay," he stomped off with a huff.

She knocked on the door and quietly called Janie's name. No response. In all of their teenage years, Mystery had spent countless nights trying to coax Dana out of the bathroom, mostly because Dana couldn't stand leaving her image at the mirror, but she hadn't once had to pry Janie out. "Janie," she said, "if you don't answer me, I'm going to get my key for this lock."

"Just leave me alone, please."

A deep sob came from beyond the door and Mystery's heart sank.

"Janie, honey, please open the door. Whatever it is, you can tell me." There was no response for a moment, and then the lock clicked. The door opened and steam rolled out of the bathroom. Janie stood there wrapped in a large purple towel, wet blond curls clinging to her shoulders, her eyes red and puffy.

"Janie," she said slowly, as her throat constricted with worry, "what's going on? Bennie told me something happened with John."

Bright red veins accented Janie's deep blue eyes. She gave Mystery a quizzical look.

"Janie, what happened in the treehouse?"

Janie retreated into the steamy bathroom where she started crying again. Mystery thought about running back outside and forcing John to tell her what had happened, but she didn't want to leave Janie alone.

Mystery eased into the bathroom and brushed a wet curl off Janie's shoulder, but her daughter pulled away. "I'm so sorry," Mystery said.

Janie turned around, eyes lit with anger. "He promised."

"Who?"

"I hate men. I'm glad you didn't get married again."

"Me, too," she said, "consider him gone."

"Gone? What—no," Janie said, her shoulders slumping as a sigh escaped her lips. "He told me to tell you anyway."

"Tell me what, Janie?" Mystery was practically crying with confusion.

Janie took a deep breath and sat down on the edge of the tub. The steam had cleared. Bennie peeked around the corner and asked in a dramatic whisper, "Janie, you okay?"

Janie gave him a trembly smile, and then covered her face with her hands as her shoulders shook with silent sobs.

Mystery reassured him with a hug, then said, "She's fine, honey. You go on back to your room and Janie will be there in a while, okay?"

"It's *our* room," Bennie insisted but did as he was told.

With Bennie gone, Mystery sat down next to Janie and placed a hand on her daughter's leg, nervous that she might push her away.

"Janie," she said, "you can tell me anything. Now, please tell me what happened."

"Something bad," Janie choked out.

"With John?"

Janie appeared bewildered and then laughed through her tears. "God, Mom—no. John hasn't done anything wrong. What would make you think that?"

I don't know, she wanted to say, *my mother always telling me I make stupid choices*... Mystery heaved an obvious sigh of relief and pushed her own feelings aside for the moment. Janie managed a weak laugh and Mystery joined in hoping to lighten the mood. "Then who? Cord?"

"No...and yes."

"Did something happen between the two of you?"

There was the slightest hint of a genuine smile behind Janie's teary eyes. "Well, yes..."

"Oh. I see," Mystery said as she patted Janie's knee. "Is that all?"

"Is that *all*?" Janie repeated.

"Well, no," she stammered. "I didn't mean *all* like it was nothing."

Janie abruptly stood up, and Mystery's hand fell away from her. A moment ago Mystery felt Janie had relaxed enough to talk, but now she thought Janie was slipping away. With Dana it had been easy. She hadn't told Mystery when she started having sex; Mystery had just known it when Dana started sneaking in late at night and taking long hot baths before bed — a dead giveaway.

"Oh, Mom, what am I going to do?" Janie put her head in her hands again and gave in to the flood of tears.

That was when Mystery noticed her wrists.

"Janie, what happened?" She stood up and gently took Janie hands in hers, turning them over. "Who did this to you?"

Janie pulled her hands way. "I thought John told you."

"Told me what?"

"That Taylor tried to rape me!"

"Oh my god!" Shock, confusion, and rage welled up inside Mystery in rapid sequence. "I-I thought this was about Cord," Mystery said.

"It *is* about Cord, Mom. *And* Taylor!"

"I'm so confused ... "

"Well, let me clear it up for you." Then, as if to herself, she added, "Yes, that's what John said I should do." She took a deep breath and everything tumbled out. "Taylor tried to rape me in the treehouse — the one we built together and stayed the night in together so many times. I hated staying the night there with him. Did you know that? He always wanted me to have sex with him. Every time I stayed in that damned treehouse, I had to fight him off. Well, since I wouldn't give in to him, he decided to just take what he thought was his. His! Like I'm a piece of property or something."

Janie seemed to muster some kind of strength from the confession. She shook her head and Mystery glimpsed the slightest hint of a smile on her face. "You know what the funny thing is? He thought he was taking my virginity. My virginity, Mom! Can you believe that?"

"Um, yes? No?"

"No," she said calmly, "I lied to you Mom."

"Okay," Mystery said, trying to keep up with Janie's scattered explanation. "About what?"

"I didn't stay the night at Robin's. Robin's not even in town. I stayed the night with Cord up on Sheep Creek Road in Idaho."

"Oh," Mystery said, a little dazed. "Sheep Creek Road?"

"In Idaho," she said again. "At his family's house. We stayed the night together. We slept in the same bed. I know that's not right, but we did."

Mystery knew that there was something more she should be saying in response, but the overload of information had deadened the shock of Janie's deception. "Wait...you spent the night with Cord and then that little bastard Taylor raped you?"

"Well, he tried anyway," Janie said. "John must have heard me while he and Bennie were cleaning up the roofing junk because he stopped him. He stopped Taylor. Can you believe it? And I thought John told you, but he didn't."

"No," Mystery said quietly, "he didn't."

"But now I don't know what to do, Mom." She sagged back down onto the edge of the tub, the frenetic energy of a moment ago used up.

"Do you want to press charges? I can call Officer Masters if you want and have Taylor arrested."

Janie raked her hands through her wet hair and shook her head. "No, I don't want to press charges." Her insistence reminded Mystery of the time that Janie had gotten her first pair of roller skates when she was six. She had fallen down so many times that her knees were bloodied all the way through her jeans. When Mystery had tried to apply the bandages Janie pushed them away, and stood back up on her wobbly legs, stating, "I just don't know *why* I can't roller skate." Janie was the strongest person that Mystery had ever known. If anyone could get through this without carrying it as baggage, Janie Abbott could.

"No charges, Mom," Janie said with a dismissive wave of her hand, then let the words rush forth. "I'm not talking about Taylor now. He didn't succeed in getting what he wanted. Pressing charges would only make him feel like he had scared me enough to control me. I just keep thinking about Cord. Should I tell him? I'm afraid he won't understand. I couldn't face him when he got here. He came into the house, but John shooed him back out, saying they needed to get the roof done, I guess because John knew I had been crying or something. I don't know."

Mystery wedged herself in next to her daughter and put her arm around her, pausing for a moment in an effort to find the right words. Up on the roof the pounding continued. John was taking out his anger at her with a hammer and nails.

"Janie," Mystery said tenderly, "you didn't do anything wrong, honey. And if Cord loves you he will understand."

"That's what John said."

"You two sure had a long conversation about this."

Janie nodded in agreement. "He's a kind man, Mom."

"Yes, he is. And I'm glad he was there for you today, but I still think we should press charges against Taylor. What if he tries this again, with you or with someone else?"

"No," Janie stated firmly. "I understand what you mean, but I am not taking this to the law. I am done with him and his family. My childhood with Taylor Randall is over Mom, and I refuse to spend any of my adulthood reliving in a courtroom what happened for ten minutes in that godforsaken treehouse with Taylor Randall. This might not be the way you or anyone else would handle it, but it is right for me."

Mystery paused, ready to argue her point again. Taylor Randall should not be allowed to get away with this, but when she looked in Janie's eyes, she realized that it was not her choice. Like it or not, Janie was an adult now.

"Well then, there is one thing we can do right now."

"What's that?"

"Get dressed and meet me outside." Mystery's eyes glittered as she pointed overhead, nearly drowned out by a staccato burst of pounding. "If men can take their aggression out with tools, so can we. Let's get rid of that damn treehouse."

"Seriously?" Janie laughed.

"You said it yourself: your childhood is over. Let's destroy that piece-of-crap treehouse."

Mystery was nearly out of the room when Janie called her back. "Mom? Thank you."

"Oh, honey, you're welcome. Smashing that sucker will feel good."

"No, not just for this. I mean for everything. I know life hasn't been easy on you, but you always have a way of protecting us when times get tough. I just wanted you to know that it matters."

Mystery placed her hand over her heart, unable to say a word. She couldn't. Her voice had caught in her throat and tears welled in her eyes. Everything she had done had mattered to someone even when she thought no one had noticed.

With renewed purpose, Mystery strode out to the porch and called up to John.

"Can't hear you!" he yelled back.

The cold wind blew through her shirt and hair as she cupped her hands around her mouth to shout, "I need a hammer and a crowbar."

"What for? Gonna bash my truck window in for something else I didn't do?"

"No," she called, "it's for Janie."

"Huh?" Cord interrupted, "what's going on now?"

"You two just stay on the roof," Mystery instructed. "Luckily for you, this is about someone else."

John smiled down at her for the first time in a long time, and she felt a rush of energy. He pointed his hammer at the back of the truck and then, grinning, told Cord to get back to work. She retrieved the tools just as Janie came out onto the porch. She saw her daughter cringe as she looked over at the Randalls' house, so she handed her the crowbar with a comic leer and a flourish. They walked arm in arm to the tree-house, like a team. Mystery thought about women being considered the weaker sex and she almost laughed out loud. John had said that Mystery was the strongest person *he* had ever known, and she was beginning to believe it. She had seen that strength in her daughter, too. She felt John and Cord watching them as they approached the old willow tree.

"Destroy it," Mystery told Janie. "The treehouse is on our property, not his. Destroy it."

Janie hesitated, then slowly climbed the ladder alone and looked around at the inside of the fort that she and Taylor had shared for the last five years. Mystery waited patiently at the bottom of the tree. In a moment, she saw the crowbar emerge with a crunch through the north-facing wall of the fort. Mystery began to clap and from the rooftop, John joined in. She turned to see John yell, *Go, Janie!* while a confused but supportive Cord began to clap as well.

Mystery looked in every direction she could see in Glendale. Northwest to the Randalls, south to her parents, and east and west to all the neighbors who loved to sit behind their windows and watch her and her family. Today she hoped that all eyes were on the Abbott house on Carlisle Street.

chapter twenty-six

Liv Randall

It took Liv until almost six to finish baking the cherry pie and gather her remaining clothes. Carl hadn't called. That was okay, she reasoned, since it would make things easier anyway. As the day progressed, the black cloud had hung just at the outskirts of her vision. She needed to stay focused if she was going to make it through.

At times, she had wanted to forgive him. If she looked at it the right way, she could see the hand of fate stepping in. Carl shouldn't have married her in the first place. She was an ocean girl, a mermaid who fell in love with city life. He was a small-town boy who loved fishing and could spend hours drinking beer at neighborhood barbecues. She pined for the blustery, sandy beaches of the Pacific Ocean, while he loved hunting for bait frogs on the banks of the Glendale River. They had nothing in common, while he and Coral had everything in common. Liv's nineteen-year marriage to Carl couldn't compare to the childhood memories and connections he had with Coral. At one point, she found herself starting to cry, starting to feel. The black cloud became fluid; it moved and danced, threatening her with a complete takeover. Carl would say she was crazy, but she knew better.

Taylor walked in, slammed the door, and then repeated the process at his bedroom. Liv decided to make an attempt at peace with her son, but when she tapped on his door he told her to go away. She sighed, knowing she would not be forgiven for ruining his relationship with the Abbott girl. She would have to make amends with Janie, and maybe, just maybe, it could be her last gift of love for her son.

She scooped up the box for Dana, stacked the pie on top of it, and fought the cold wind on her way over to her neighbors' house. The biting chill in the air was getting worse, and she wondered where the rain had gone. If she didn't know better, she would swear that it was February. Her small frame shook under the load and the fear of rejection, but really, what more did she have to lose? Moreover, something told her that though she definitely deserved it, Mystery Abbott would not reject her.

John was on the roof again with the other young man. She smiled up at them and they waved their hammers in response. As she climbed the porch stairs, she caught a glimpse around back of broken wood piled next to Mystery's garage and a gaping hole where the treehouse used to be. All that was left of it was the wood-planked floor.

Bennie answered her knock. He really was a darling little boy. With his blond hair and bright red lips he looked so much like Taylor when he was younger, before Taylor's hair and his attitude toward her had darkened. He had a half-eaten chocolate chip cookie in one hand and the remainder smeared on his face. His hair was unkempt and the knees of his Buster Browns were stained with dirt and grass. He looked like the most perfectly happy little boy, so much like Taylor at that age, always dirty and smiling. She tried to recall exactly when her son's smile for her had faded.

"Is your mom here?" she asked.

"She's in the kitchen," he said. "Whatcha want?"

"Wow, Bennie," she smiled. "I've never heard you talk."

"John makes me," he said gnawing off a bite of the cookie. "Cowboys hafta talk."

"Sounds like good advice," she agreed. She felt a little stronger in the child's presence. He was so direct. He didn't glare at her or cower from her; he simply held an unedited conversation. She liked that. "Can I talk to your mommy? I came to bring her something," she said.

"Why? You don't yike her."

"Of course I do," Liv said in surprise.

"No, ya don't," he said. "You don't yike her. Everybody says so."

Tears welled up in her eyes again. They had been so hard to produce before, but now she was having a hard time holding them back. How stupid could she have been? Just because he didn't talk didn't mean that he was deaf or blind. "Bennie, I...I brought your mommy this pie to say I'm sorry."

"Okay," he grinned. "I'll get her. Mommy!"

She prayed she would be as easily forgiven by Mystery. Within a moment, Mystery appeared, dishtowel in hand, clearly taken aback by Liv's presence at her door.

"I'm sorry," Liv said. "I didn't mean to interrupt."

Mystery glanced at the box and the pie and then down at Bennie. She bent to wipe his mouth, but he pushed the towel away.

"She's sorry, Mommy," he said. "And she gots pie."

"I think you've had enough sweets, little man," she said. "Why don't you go play?" Bennie scooted off before he had to endure another mouth cleaning from the wet towel.

"Hello, Liv. What can I do for you?" she asked, but did not immediately invite her in.

Liv was nervous. She hoped that Mystery couldn't see the dark cloud Liv carried with her. "I brought you a pie." She gestured toward the pie with her chin, but Mystery made no move to take it.

"Thank you," she said. "But what is it for?"

"Mystery, can we talk?"

Mystery looked back into the house as if there were other people in the room. "What, you mean in here?"

"If that's okay. I brought some things for Dana and I thought we could talk over dessert." Liv shifted the box a little and the pie slid forward. Mystery dropped the hand towel just in time to catch the pie before it splattered on the hardwood floor. She laughed, and Liv felt the tension ease a bit. "I'm so sorry," Liv said.

"No problem," Mystery laughed, "I guess now that the pie is in the house you'd better come in, too."

Liv followed her into the kitchen, trying to not gawk at the home that was so different from her own. The simple decor was pleasing. "The house looks good since the other night."

Liv bit her lip. Everything she said sounded so judgmental, but she didn't mean for it to. Mystery responded with a tentative smile. "It's been a lot of work, but we managed."

Liv sat down at the table while Mystery silently gathered plates and silverware. The pounding above continued. Bennie jumped up in the chair next to Liv's and stared at her. Liv smiled at him but wasn't certain what she was supposed to do or say.

"Bennie," Mystery said, playfully smacking him with the towel, "staring isn't nice. Go see Janie or something."

"Oh," Liv said, "is Janie here? How about Dana?"

"Just Janie. Dana's at work." Mystery handed Liv a silver pie server. Liv carefully cut the pie and placed a piece on each of their plates. Despite the lingering tension, Mystery's kitchen was warm and inviting, and Liv found herself relaxing even though she knew she didn't have a right to.

"It's a great looking pie," Mystery offered, "I didn't think that you baked."

Liv felt the jab in the comment and swallowed hard on her first bite. "Oh, I do occasionally," she said.

"Liv," Mystery said calmly, placing her fork down before even trying a bite, "I don't mean to be rude, but what are you doing here? Does this have anything to do with Janie?"

"Nothing," she said, "nothing with Janie, really." She could see that Mystery didn't trust her. She didn't know why she had thought a pie would change that. It had seemed like such a Glendale thing to do to make peace.

"So, then why are you here?"

"Well, I know that you could probably care less, but it appears that Carl is having an affair."

Mystery placed a finger to her lips, cut another piece of the pie, and instructed Bennie to take it to Janie. Liv had forgotten that the little boy was listening. After he left, she told Mystery that she was sorry.

"It's okay, I just really don't want to explain the word *affair* later."

"I'm sorry, it's just, well—"

"You think it's with me, don't you?"

"No," Liv laughed. She felt oddly detached from the situation, as if she were talking about someone else's husband. "No, Mystery, I know it's not you."

"So, again, why are you here?" Mystery asked quietly.

To Liv's surprise, Mystery's tone wasn't objectionable or hostile. She seemed sincere.

"I don't know, really," Liv laughed again. "It just seems like such a funny thing. Carl having an affair."

"Well, are you sure that he's having an affair? I don't know him very well, but it just doesn't seem like Carl."

"That's what I said when I first heard, but people have seen it."

"You don't have to tell me who it is," Mystery said, "but if you don't mind me asking, what exactly have people seen?"

"They've seen them together at his office before and after hours, and I saw them together once there, too."

"Maybe he is just handling a case for this person."

"I don't think so." Liv shook her head. "After hours with the blinds closed? And, I know it's true because the woman is Coral Smith, his high school sweetheart."

"Oh," Mystery said biting her lip. "Coral Smith. Have you asked Carl about it?"

"No," she said. Why should she ask him? He'd just lie anyway.

The light fixture above the table shuddered with the pounding. "They're supposed to be done any minute now," Mystery sighed.

"It looks like they're doing a nice job. Who's the kid with him?"

"That's Cord. Janie's..." she stopped herself. "He's a friend of the girls. So, who is giving you all of this information about your husband anyway?"

"Lots of women in town," she said.

"Lots of women like Melinda and Jane?"

Liv looked awkwardly at her pie and shoved a cherry off to the side. It seemed funny to be embarrassed about having friends like Melinda and Jane, but in Mystery's house they suddenly seemed like trash.

"Look, Liv, I know they are your friends, but those women see a lot of things that aren't real."

"Really?"

"Really," Mystery said. "Look, I'm not as stupid as you and your friends seem to think I am. I know what you've said about me. I know what *all* of you have said."

"You do?" Liv asked sheepishly.

"Of course. Just because it's said in a circle of *your* friends doesn't mean it stays there. It gets back to my mother, who loves to tell me all about it. Worse yet, it gets back to my daughters. And contrary to what you seem to believe, not even half of it is true."

"I know," Liv agreed. "Look, Mystery, you probably won't believe me, but I've hated Glendale ever since I came to visit, long before moving here. I hated the gossips, the liars, and the cheaters. Before I moved here I was a different woman. I swore I would not become like any of them. It didn't seem to bug Carl. 'It's just small-town gossip,' he would say. I stayed out of it for a long time. I didn't have any friends or any social life. I listened to what they said but I didn't join in; I didn't fit in with that crowd. Not until that night."

Mystery abruptly stood to start tea and while doing so peeked out the doorway to check for Bennie.

"You know what I'm talking about, right?" Liv said.

Mystery nodded without looking at her. Liv could see her retreating, and she wanted to stop her. She wasn't here to blame her neighbor or point fingers. She had done that long enough.

"I didn't know you knew," Mystery said quietly. "Did he tell you?"

"No," she said. "He's never breathed a word. Even when I called him on it, he wouldn't budge. Either way, I knew. Now all I want to know is why you kept it a secret after you became pregnant with Bennie. I mean, hell, the man is rich! He could have provided for Bennie for the rest of his life. Why did you just let it go without so much as a fight?"

Mystery fumbled with the tea bags, obviously ill at ease. This wasn't going how Liv had hoped. She wasn't here to interrogate Mystery about the past, and yet, that's exactly what she sounded like. Mystery peeked out into the living room again, watching for her son.

"Mystery," she said, "it's okay. I'm not trying to accuse you of anything or hurt you in any way. I promise I won't tell Bennie or anyone else, but I need to know if I've been right all of these years or not."

Mystery looked at her dead on. "Then why do you want to know, if you aren't going to tell anyone?" she said. "It's none of your business."

"I know..."

"No, you don't know. I know you think I'm a terrible parent. You've already made that very clear, but if you think for one minute that you have any right to my little boy, I'll tell you right now that you don't."

"No," Liv said quickly, desperate to contain the situation. "No, that's not why I came over. I swear."

"Then why?"

Liv rose, and walked to the high window above the kitchen sink. The day was slipping away. This was her last chance, and she knew it. Her last chance for truth and her last chance for closure. She squared her shoulders and faced Mystery.

"Because I'm leaving, Mystery," she said.

"Leaving? Where?"

"Away," she said. "I can't take it anymore—this town, these people, or my marriage."

Mystery was silent for a moment. Liv watched as she swallowed hard and idly stirred her tea.

"It's true," Mystery said at last. "It's all true. Your brother is Bennie's father. I don't know what you want to do with that, but now you know. It was a fling. I admit it, I had one." She raised her head and addressed Liv directly, her resolve strengthening with every word. "One. But that doesn't mean I've had any others. Not with Walt Smith. Not with anyone. John is the first man I've been with since your brother."

Liv held still for a minute and contemplated the broken piece of pie on her plate. The thought of eating it made her feel nauseous.

"Mystery," Liv said steadily, "I owe you the truth as well. Patrick liked you from the moment he saw you, when he came for those visits after Carl moved us here. He was the one who made me invite you to one of Carl's damn barbecues. He was with you all night, feeding the gossips. I didn't understand the women's reservations about you, and I didn't want to, but then I saw him slip in your back door in the middle of the night. I was mad at him. I was mad at you. Jane and Dora kept calling me after that, pressing me for information, warning me to keep him away from you. I didn't know what to believe."

Liv again looked off through the window at the gray skies beyond. She felt like she was presenting a dissertation about the rise and fall of her tenure in Glendale society, and she was coming to the climax.

"But that's how gossip works, isn't it? It preys on lonely victims who want so desperately to be part of the group. People like me, I guess. After that night I felt for the first time that I had something to offer to the conversation among the women in Glendale."

Mystery's expression was inscrutable but Liv withstood it without flinching.

"Wow," Mystery said at last.

"I'm sorry you had to suffer all this time," Liv continued, "but have you thought about telling him?"

"Who? Patrick? He knows about Bennie."

"*He knows?*"

"He's known since just after Bennie was born. He and Bennie have met. Bennie knows him only as 'Patrick' for now. Someday, when he is older…we agreed to tell him, but until then we want it to be a secret. We both agree that shipping him back and forth would be a bad idea, but if Bennie knew about it, he would want to go."

Liv struggled to recall the last time she had talked to her brother. They weren't close, but she couldn't believe he had kept that big of a secret from her for this long. For being the biggest gossip in town, she really knew nothing about the truth.

"Liv, I told you what you wanted to know. Now I am going to ask you not to tell anyone. Do you think you can do that?"

Liv was silent for a minute and then turned back to Mystery. "I promise," she said crossing her heart like a child. "I'll take it to the grave. I think you're crazy, though. He's making a mint now."

"He's helped in the past, and he'd help again if I asked him to."

"Wow," was all that Liv could muster.

The pounding from above stopped.

"They must be done up there." Mystery wasn't smiling as she looked up at the ceiling.

"He seems like a good man, Mystery," Liv offered.

Mystery nodded and attempted a small smile. "He is a good man."

"You should consider yourself lucky. He should, too." She hugged herself as if against a sudden chill. "Thank you for letting me say I'm sorry."

"I'm glad you came over. I'm sorry to hear that you are leaving, Liv."

"Yeah, me too," she said. "I thought I could make Carl love me by being who he wanted. But, it didn't work that way. There's always the house, the meetings, and Taylor and Carl demanding things. There's nothing in it for me, just for me. Do you know what I mean?"

"Let me ask you something Liv," Mystery said. "How long has it been since the world had to stop, lie down, and wait just for you?"

Liv thought for a moment and smiled. "Not since I had a job in Seattle."

"That's too long."

"I know," Liv said. Tears brimmed under her eyelids again. She wanted to embrace them and let them fall down her cheeks, but not yet. She turned away from Mystery and pointed to the box in the corner of the kitchen. "Those are for Dana."

"Dana?" Mystery said.

"Did you know that she watches me at night?"

"She *does*? No, I didn't know."

"Yes," she nodded. "I stay up cleaning so that I can be alone without Carl and Taylor constantly demanding something, and Dana stays up watching me. She doesn't know that I'm aware of her but I have been for years. At first, it bugged me. I felt like she was invading my space, my time. Then, after a while I came to like it. No one knew but us."

Mystery shook her head and busied herself in topping off their already full teacups.

"I know it's none of my business, but she's too skinny, Mystery." She stopped herself. This new attempt at peace was still a bit foreign to her tongue. "Don't get me wrong. I'm not saying that's anyone's fault, but I was her age once, and that was when I got started."

"Got started doing what?"

"Well, with her slight build and her...um...need to get a man's approval, I would bet you money that she is making herself throw up."

Mystery sighed and acknowledged her fears. "I hope you're wrong, Liv."

"Me too. Look, I brought my clothes for her. I am giving them to her.

And there's a note in there, Mystery. It's nothing really. It's just something to say that I'm sorry for not being a good neighbor or a good friend." *A note to tell her that the person she idealizes is a fake, a fraud, a nothing at all.* "Maybe it will stop her, maybe it won't. I don't know." Liv gave a quick half-smile and sipped at her tea.

Janie walked into the kitchen just then and stopped short as she saw Liv at the table. "Oh," she said. "Mom?"

Janie looked nervous, and Liv regretted every bit of pain she had caused her son and this girl. With a brittle smile and a deep breath, she put down her tea and reminded herself that she could rest soon.

"It's okay, Janie," Mystery said, moving to her daughter's side. Liv noted how naturally she placed her arm around Janie's shoulders without asking. "She came over to bring some stuff for Dana and to talk to me, that's all."

Liv pushed in her chair and then unceremoniously dumped her piece of pie in the garbage under the sink. That done, she faced Janie and said, "I owe you an apology."

"For what?" Janie looked to her mother in confusion. Liv could not believe what an incredible bitch she had become since moving to Glendale. She had actually made a child—her son's girlfriend, no less—afraid of her.

"I'm sorry for making you uncomfortable in my home, Janie." She knew the girl had every right to hate her but this was her only chance to change the future for her son. "Taylor loves you," she said. "I want you to know that no matter what I've done to make things uncomfortable for you and him, he has always loved you."

Janie shook her head and Liv could see shock and something else mixed with the tears in her eyes. Mystery kept her arm firmly around her daughter's shoulder.

"I hope that whatever I have done, it doesn't come between you and Taylor."

"No," Janie said coldly, "nothing *you* have done would."

"Okay," she said, holding a hand up. "Okay—"

The creak of the kitchen door interrupted her as John and Cord walked into the room, both wearing exhaustion and surprise on their faces. Liv took their arrival as her cue to leave.

"I'll be going now. I'll leave the pie for you," she said to Mystery, "and keep the plate. It was Carl's Aunt Ilsa's pie plate. I couldn't care less if he ever gets it back."

She gave a brusque wave to the others, then silently accepted Mystery's offer to walk her out to the porch.

Out of earshot of the group, Mystery wished her good luck.

"Thank you," she said, and meant it. "I think everything will be okay now."

As Liv crossed the yard to her house, she heard a deep rumble. For a moment she thought it was thunder, but out of the corner of her eye, she saw it. Had she not come to visit Mystery, she might have missed the large section of earth as it cascaded down the canyon wall below Cemetery Ridge. Not everything in Glendale was as stable as the townspeople wanted it to be.

In Ilsa's house, Liv picked up the list by the kitchen sink and crossed off item number two: Mystery Abbott.

Dana knocked again, harder this time. She had knocked twice already, but figured that he probably couldn't hear her with the wind howling between the police station and the John Deere dealership. A thick frost had formed on the doorstep and Dana had to be careful not to slip in her sandals and get all dirty before she got inside. Finally, she heard his footsteps approaching from down the hall. She cocked her head toward the door. He didn't seem to be moving as fast as she would have if their roles were reversed. She ran her hand over her chest. Her white tank top was pressed tight against her bust and her silver cross necklace rested just between her breasts. She was absolutely freezing.

She stamped her cold feet and surveyed the streets behind her as she waited. She was okay with people seeing her at his apartment, but he wasn't, so she had to respect his request for discretion. It was just after ten. State Street was deserted, everyone driven inside by the dark and the rain. She could see the glow from yellow kitchen lights and silver-blue television sets but nothing more. No movement. No action. No one else with any ambitions except herself and the new cop in town. She was happy not to be a slug like the rest of them. A man like Dylan gave a girl like her something to work hard for, and eventually, if she played her cards right, they would all know it.

When he finally opened the door, he initially focused just where she had intended him to. She pushed out her chest to give him a better angle, but he quickly looked away. He was wearing a pair of gray sweats and a black ribbed tank top. In his left hand was a half-eaten leg of chicken — at least that explained the delay — but he didn't usher her in as he had done the time before.

"Dana," he said, "what are you doing here?" He glanced past her for any onlookers and wiped his mouth with the back of his hand.

"There's no one watching. I made sure," she smiled. "I just wanted to drop by and see what you were up to." She stubbornly avoided rubbing her cold arms.

He looked past her again. "Look, Dana, we didn't agree on tonight. I mean, what if someone sees — "

"Someone like who? In this weather and at this time of night? Not likely, Dylan."

"Well, it's not safe to just stand out there. You might as well come in." He stepped back and allowed her inside.

With the door closed behind her, Dana stood still for a moment, unsure what to do next. Dylan walked off down the hall without asking her to follow. Last night when she dropped by, he had lifted her up in his arms the moment she was in the door and rushed her to the bed. Twice he had told her *not again*, and twice he couldn't help himself when he got her alone. What was the difference now? She looked down at her clothes to see if they were the problem. She looked fine. Her pants were trim, her shirt taut. Maybe it was the jeans? It was the first time she had worn jeans around him. Did they make her look fat? She'd never wear them again. It was just that it was Friday at work and it was freezing outside. Mr. Borghese said they should dress casually on Fridays. It made the customers feel more relaxed as they went into the weekend.

In the kitchen she rubbed up against his back and said, "Well, I have an hour or so..."

"Dana," he said, wiping chicken grease from his lips with a paper towel, "I don't know..." He pulled away from her to drop the bare chicken leg and greasy paper towel into the garbage can beside the breakfast bar. Dana followed him even those few steps. Last night, as moonlight streamed through the window, they had sat naked while they nibbled leisurely on cold turkey sandwiches. He'd even let her have a sip of his beer. After that, he had picked her up like his bride and carried her back to his bed where he made love to her one more time before she walked out into the cold to go home. Again he had told her that that would be the last time, but again she hadn't believed him. Tonight she wasn't certain if she was even welcome.

"Dylan?"

"Look, Dana, we need to talk. Sit down." He patted one of the barstools, the one she had straddled last night. She sat down and dropped her bag next to her.

She wanted to say, *What's the problem? Just get to the point so that I can get you beyond it, and we can make love again.* However, she knew that she had to stay calm. Managing men required patience. "Talk about what?" she asked in her most receptive tone.

He leaned on the corner of the breakfast bar next to her stool. "I just can't have you walking up to the back door at all hours of the night."

"Well, that's where you told me to come," she said.

"I know. I know. But not every night. I mean jeez, anyone could see you."

"I've always been careful," she said. "No one has ever seen me. And that's what we agreed on."

"I know," he repeated. "But I already told you how dangerous this is for me."

"Well, it won't be next month."

He tipped his head to the side and studied her for what seemed to her an interminable amount of time, and then finally shook his head and gave her a cockeyed grin. "No," he laughed. "You turning eighteen isn't going to change that."

"Why not?"

"Dana," he said again. He was starting to sound more like a father than a lover. She felt her cheeks heating up; her patience had limits. She wasn't going to allow him to treat her like a stupid child.

"You're worried because it would be too soon? People would figure it out. I just meant in a few months. Maybe then, if people began to see us together in public, you know, every once in a while, then it wouldn't be such a shock to them."

He stood up from the counter and walked around the kitchen. He was turning circles now. Pacing. Running his hands through his hair.

"Dylan," she said, "what is it?"

He came back to her and took her hands in his. His large hands enveloped hers. He was warm, and, for a moment, she became excited at the thought of his hands wrapping around her ribcage.

"Look, don't get mad," he said cautiously. "This isn't my fault. But you're seventeen, and I'm almost thirty."

"You're twenty-five," she corrected coolly.

"Yes," he said. "That's eight years older than you. *Eight years.*"

"In a month it will be seven years," she said sweetly. "*Seven years.*"

"Not in the eyes of Glendale," he said.

She stood up and turned from him like a spoiled child. "So what?" she said. "Who cares?"

"I do," he said firmly.

She turned back toward him and folded her arms. Standing up she knew that he could survey all of her now from head to foot. It wouldn't take long. It hadn't the other day at the school and it hadn't last night either. His resistance would soften; it would just take time. She stepped closer to him and turned out the light. Only the fluorescent bulb of his desk lamp illuminated the room. It wasn't candlelight, but it would do. She eased around behind him and wrapped her arms around his midsection. She ran her arms down his shirt and slid her hands inside his sweatpants. She was careful not to touch what she just knew he really wanted her to touch. She simply worked around it, fingers tickling his inner thighs and intertwining in his thick, coarse hair. She sensed his warmth in the center growing as she moved her hands around on his body. She could still feel his resistance, but he didn't pull away. She knew that she had to be careful. He was definitely weakening, but not quite enough yet to guarantee a win.

"Dana, I can't. I really can't."

"Yes, you can," she whispered. "Just one more time."

"Just one more time?"

She stood on her tiptoes and whispered it again into his ear. "Just one more time and we never have to do it again." She felt herself getting more excited as she enticed him. It was so drastic, so final, and it turned her on more than she had ever known. She hoped that it was the same for him. If she had to, she'd say it to him every time they were together, and she'd force them both to believe it — until the next time. He turned around in her arms, his chest touching hers as she moved her fingers closer to his center. He sucked in a ragged breath. Finally, she gave him his reward and wrapped both of her hands around his penis. He leaned his head back and released a soft moan.

"You promise?" he asked. "This will be the last time?"

"I promise," she lied. He leaned down to kiss her hard on her lips. He ran his hands up and down her arms, caressing her, brushing the sides of her breasts, and then he placed his hands on her shoulders and pressed her down to her knees beneath him on the kitchen floor. If it hadn't been for the fridge behind her she might have fallen over as he pushed himself into her mouth. In his excitement, he grabbed her by the back of the head and forced himself farther and farther into her mouth. She tried to pull back and stop him. This wasn't the way she had planned it. Tears stung her eyes, but within a few seconds he was done. He stayed motionless for a moment, forcing her to swallow him down. It was warm and bitter, but she knew the effort would please him. Finally, he released her and staggered backward. She stood up awkwardly, knees aching as she rose from the floor. She carefully wiped her mouth and turned to him. He sat down in the chair and released a pent-up breath.

"That was incredible."

"Yeah," she said, "it was." She put her arms around him, wanting him to hold her. He circled one arm around her back and patted her.

"Sorry," he said. "I guess that wasn't the best for you."

"No, no. It was great, really."

"Really?"

She looked him squarely in the eye. "Yeah, but now you owe me again."

"Owe you?" he asked. "I thought you said this was our last time."

Dana leaned down and snatched her purse off the kitchen floor, then marched off down the hall to the back door. "We didn't have sex," she said over her shoulder. "You owe me *again*."

He caught up with her at the door. "Dana," he said grabbing her by the wrist, "do you want me to return the favor right now?"

"Nope," she said. "I'll let you know when you can pay up."

"Uh-uh," he said flatly, "it's now or never."

She crossed her arms and glared at him. "You just had me suck your dick and then you have the nerve to tell me it's over?"

"This could cost me my job. I can't."

"No, it won't," she said flatly. She had had just about enough of Dylan thinking that he was calling the shots.

"I'm sorry," he said. "I really am. It just wouldn't work between us. You know that. It's not possible. It's not safe." He grasped her chin and forced her to pay attention. "Promise me that you won't tell anyone."

She was paying attention all right, weighing her options. She could run away crying like a child, or stay and fight for what she wanted like an adult.

"You need to listen to me, Dana."

"I won't say anything, *Officer* Dylan," she said. "But, when you change your mind, and you will, you know where to find me." With that, Dana left. She waited for her eyes to adjust to the streetlights before leaving the security of the staircase. He didn't really want this to end, she knew that. It was a game with him. One that she knew her years of experience with men had trained her for.

She stepped off the stairs and into the dark night. Only then did her self-satisfied smile fade. Across the street, just in front of Cord's house, was a Mustang with its engine running. Taylor Randall was crouched in the driver's seat, his baseball cap was pulled down as if to cover his gaze, but Dana knew that he was watching her. She looked back at the closed door of Dylan's apartment. She had nowhere to go but past Taylor on State Street and up to Carlisle.

The cold drove through her clothes and made her skin prickle with fear. She felt Taylor's eyes on her as she passed him, and it made the chill in the air even worse. She could tell from the look in his face that the talk with Janie had not gone well. At first, she thought she would be glad to see Taylor Randall get dumped, but now she could see that his anger could have unforeseen consequences. She was going to avoid talking to him at all costs.

He let her pass by without saying anything. She finally took a breath when she came to Carlisle Street. Up ahead, she spotted the pool of light in the Randalls' backyard. Liv stood as if in the spotlight wearing a long flowing skirt with a simple pink tank top. To Dana she looked like the perfect vision of an angel. Smoke swirled from the cigarette in her hand, and tonight she seemed completely unconcerned that someone might see her. Her clothes ruffled in the wind, but she seemed somehow unaffected by the chill air blowing off the ridge.

Dana knew Taylor had been following her down the road. She hugged herself to ward off the chill wind and her prickling nerves. She had to warn Liv that he might see her smoking. If ever there was a time that they should commiserate about their nighttime habits, this was it.

Dana strolled onto the Randalls' back deck and sat down in the Adirondack chair as if she was about to have a heart to heart with her own mother. She wondered what it would feel like to do that with Mystery. For a moment, she felt like she was betraying her.

"Bad night?' Liv asked.

"The worst."

"There's a smoke under the chair."

Dana hesitated.

"Go on," Liv pointed. "We both know that you smoke as much as I do."

"Thanks," Dana said. She felt around for a moment before her fingers landed on the cold cardboard box.

"So, what happened?"

"Men," Dana said, lighting the cigarette from the lighter in the box.

Liv laughed and faced away from Dana to take another puff. "Someone told me once to always smile, and it will make you feel better."

"I'll have to try that," Dana said, blowing the smoke out and rolling her eyes.

"Don't bother," Liv laughed, "it doesn't work."

"Well what does?"

Liv tilted her face up at the pearl-shaped moon that appeared to be keeping an eye on them from behind the drifting clouds. She closed her eyes, stood still a moment and said, "I know you watch me at night."

Dana felt her cheeks turn red. She said nothing but inhaled deeply from her cigarette. Liv seemed to be focused on somewhere far away. There was an odd glaze over her eyes, and if she didn't know better, Dana would think that Liv had been smoking something other than cigarettes.

When Liv focused on Dana again, her eyes looked dead calm. "You shouldn't do that either," Liv said.

"Sorry."

"You might learn habits that you'll regret."

"I might learn some that I won't."

"Not likely," Liv said tossing her cigarette into the wet grass. "I visited your mom today."

"That doesn't sound good."

"I left some things for you with her."

"For me?"

"Yes," she said. "Some clothes that don't fit me anymore. I seem to be gaining a bit of weight lately."

"Don't worry," Dana said. "You'll lose it."

Smoke circled around Liv's face when she turned around. To Dana she was breathtakingly beautiful. "No," Liv smiled. "I'm done with making myself lose weight. And for the record, I hope that you are too. You're much too pretty to be sticking your finger down your throat."

Dana felt a stab in her chest, as if Liv was completely severing herself from Dana. She felt like she was being punished for daring to love someone. Tonight was not the night for loyalty and commitment.

"Well," Dana said, standing up hurriedly to control her emotions, "I'll think about it. I actually just came by to warn you that Taylor was just a little ways behind me on State Street, in case you didn't want him to see you smoking."

"Thanks," Liv said, "But I'm giving that up too."

"Okay," she sighed, tossing her cigarette in the grass just as Liv had. "Well, goodnight then."

Before she could leave, Liv touched Dana's wrist. Liv's small hand was freezing, and Dana still thought it odd that she was not shivering. She seemed unaffected by the drop in temperature.

"Dana, your mother is a good person. She loves you and Janie very much. You should know that." With that she gave Dana a hug, something Dana had not let her own mother do since she was a little girl. Dana froze for a moment, then wrapped her arms tight around Liv and breathed deeply of her lavender-scented hair. She was even more beautiful up close, and Dana could not understand for a moment why Carl would want to hold anyone else. She was on the verge of telling her so when they saw Taylor's headlights turning onto Carlisle Street.

"I should go," Dana said.

"Take care of yourself," Liv said.

"You, too."

chapter twenty-eight

Janie Abbott

anie's hand was freezing as it dangled over the edge of her bed, but she was too sluggish to pull it back in. She tried to open her eyes, but they were weighted with sleep as well. It had to be morning because she could hear Bennie racing cars through the kitchen. She knew that she should get up and help her mother with him, but her body was heavy with fatigue. She pulled her hand back just under the edge of the quilt her grandmother had made for her thirteenth birthday. She had been dreaming about Cord, and she wasn't ready to let go of that warm feeling just yet.

It didn't take her long to fall into another dream of her and Cord making love in the cabin, but this time they were not alone. A girl floated just below the ceiling, watching them. She had long, wavy blond hair and a perfectly white complexion with full pink lips and round rosy cheeks. She wore a white knee-length dress and bobby socks that came just above her ankles with black-strap tap shoes. The outfit looked just like the one her friend Robin had worn to her first communion in second grade. It was almost too perfect.

"Who are you?" Janie asked.

Fawn.

Janie's heart raced with excitement and a twinge of guilt. She wanted to tell her about Cord and what had happened with Taylor, but time seemed to be slipping away. Fawn seemed to sense her trepidation because she shook her head and smiled down at Janie.

You're fine, Janie. Fawn looked toward the window as if something had distracted her. When she looked back at Janie, her face was creased with concern. She pointed to the window, and then faded into the early-morning shadows.

"No," Janie called, "don't go yet."

But Fawn was gone. When Janie looked to where Fawn had pointed she saw a man peering in, tapping lightly on the window with a hammer. The man's face was obscured by some reflection and Janie wasn't certain who it was. *Crack!* The hammer rapped against the window, and Janie watched as the crack in the glass slowly opened wide to allow the intruder access.

"No!" she shrieked. She and Cord rolled over as one and stared at the person floating through the opening. It was Taylor. He was coming at them with a hammer.

"No!"

"Janie. Janie, wake up!" Someone was shaking her. She tried to shake her own head to fight the arms of sleep that were wrapped so solidly around her body but she couldn't seem to get out of there.

Taylor was at the edge of the bed now. She wished Fawn would come back and protect them from him. He was staring at their naked bodies and screaming something at them that she could not hear. Taylor brought the hammer up, and Cord raised his hands over their heads. Janie cringed in fear of the impact. Time stood still as Taylor slowly lowered the hammer and extended his hand to her. She flinched away from it, turning back to Cord, but he had looked the other way. She didn't understand why Cord had turned away from her. She had trusted him. She still trusted him. She wasn't conscious of taking Taylor's hand until he pulled her to her feet. The sheets were wrapped around her like a toga, but she twisted back toward Cord.

"No, Cord!" she cried. "Please don't leave me."

"Janie," she heard, as if from far away. "Please wake up! Janie what is wrong with you?"

The voice sounded like her mother. But her mother wasn't at the cabin. Her mother was at home.

"Janie. Janie, talk to me, please."

"Okay," she mumbled. "Okay... I can't seem to wake up..."

"Janie! Now!"

Janie felt her head snapping back and forth but she didn't think she was doing it voluntarily. What more did the voice want? She had answered her and told her that she couldn't wake up. If she would just give her another minute she might be able—

"Janie! Damn it, wake up or I'm going to call 911!"

"Okay," she said, concentrating on her eyes. They wouldn't open no matter what she did. She worked on the left one and could see a sliver of light. She raised her eyebrows and forced her lids to part. In the light, she could see her mother sitting on the edge of her bed. Her arms were outstretched, moving something. She could see some dark movements out of the corner of her eyes, moving back and forth.

"Janie!"

"Mom?"

"Oh, thank God! Are you okay?"

Janie finally opened her eyes and looked around the room. Cord was standing next to her bed holding tight to Bennie who was crying into his shoulder. She sat up and looked at the window. Nothing. No man with a hammer, no cracks.

"Mom? Cord..." She reached out her hand to Cord. The solid warmth of his touch sent a shock of electricity up her arm and she felt herself fully awaken.

Bennie clambered out of Cord's arms and snuggled up with his sister on the bed. She stroked his wet cheek and told him to hush as he sobbed onto her tee-shirt.

"It's okay," she said. Her voice cracked and her body felt weak. "Mom? What happened?"

"I don't know," she said. "Cord stopped by to see you, but since you were sleeping he decided to help me pick up the rest of the roofing.

We both heard a scream and came running, but you wouldn't wake up. I shook you and shook you, but you wouldn't come to."

She looked from Cord to her mother. Mystery's face was white, and Janie could see tears on her lashes.

"Are you okay, Janie?" Cord asked.

"Yes," she said. "I was dreaming about…" She peered up at her mother. She didn't know if she should say it in front of her. Should she tell her mother that she was dreaming of the first night that she had ever made love?

"About what?" he asked.

"About the other night," she said. "The other night in the cabin."

Cord smiled, a touch of crimson on his cheeks.

"I'll go," Mystery said.

"No, Mom," she said. "It's okay. Maybe you'll understand it better than I do." She retold the dream in a G-rated version for the sake of her brother. No one moved while she spoke, but sadness settled in Cord's eyes. His hands squeezed tighter around hers as she told him about how he had left her too.

"I wouldn't do that, you know," he said. "I wouldn't just let you go."

She smiled tenderly at him and asked her mother. "Mom," she said, "what does it all mean?"

"Well, I'm no dream reader or fortune teller, but I can tell you that I have had many cryptic bad dreams over the years. I think that it just means you are scared. You are obviously scared of Taylor. But I think you might be a bit scared of Cord, too."

Mystery stood to let Cord sit next to Janie. With him next to her now, her mother seemed small and very much alone. Janie relaxed back against the pillow and observed her mother highlighted in the gray morning light. Mystery shifted uncomfortably back and forth on her feet and rubbed her arms up and down.

"Mom, where's John?"

"He's gone." She nodded her head firmly as if to give the statement an air of finality.

"Gone? Gone where?"

She lifted a hand and batted away an escaping tear before Bennie could see it. "Gone," she said. "Just gone. The roof is done. Cord and I finished picking up the last of the mess outside. Everything is back to normal. You know?"

Janie sat up on her bed and leaned back against her pillows. She felt like she had been drugged. *Gone? He seemed like he wanted to be here. He came to dinner and gave Bennie a cowboy hat, and there was that day in the treehouse. The treehouse. That's it.* She looked up at her mother, wide-eyed.

"Was it because of what happened with me?" she asked.

Cord looked confused, but he didn't interrupt her for an explanation. Somehow in the morning light, after talking with her mother as John had suggested, she wasn't afraid anymore.

"No," Mystery said. "Of course not."

"Then why?"

"Why what?" Bennie asked.

Mystery and Janie both smiled down at the little boy whose sweet blond head rested comfortably on his sister's chest. "Bennie," Mystery said as she made quick eye contact with Cord, "why don't you go get a cookie from the cookie jar."

"One fo' Janie too?"

"Come on little buddy," Cord said, swooping him into the air. "I'll even help you get some milk."

After Bennie and Cord bounced out on the errand, Mystery turned away from Janie and looked out the frosty window.

"Mom, what happened with John?"

"Honey, it just wouldn't have worked out, that's all. It was better to end it now before we got anyone's hopes up. Least of all you kids. So last night after everything was done, John packed up his truck and left."

Janie walked to the window and stood by her mother. She could feel the cold emanating from the single-paned window. "Least of all us *kids*?"

Mystery nodded, her eyes glistening with tears again. Another stray one had found its way over the dam of her lower eyelid. She swatted at it as if it were a loose hair.

"Mom," Janie said, placing her arm protectively around her shoulder, "I've got news for you. For one, Dana and I are hardly kids, and for another, you already got someone's hopes up." Mystery looked at her quizzically. "Bennie, Mom. He adores John."

Mystery raised a backward hand to her trembling lips. She seemed shaky and Janie saw how years of struggle had taken their toll on her mother. Her hair, once bright and glossy with blond highlights had dulled to a light brown with hints of silver. Her eyes bore the lines from too many nights of worry, and the small wrinkles at the sides of her lips pointed downward. Too many frowns and not enough smiles. Janie wasn't sure if her mother looked good for her age or not, but she knew she didn't look happy, and that she suddenly looked older. Janie's heart wilted with the weight of her mother's sadness.

"Mom," she said slowly. "We aren't going to be here forever, you know."

"I know," Mystery said.

"So, why are you pushing John away?"

"I'm not pushing him away," she explained. Her voice was shaky as she spoke, and Janie wondered how many nights her mother had wanted to cry but had managed to hold it together for her children.

"There will be time for me, Janie. Later, when you all are grown and my *horrid* decisions stop affecting you."

"Mom," Janie said softly, "turn around." Mystery slowly turned from the frosty window and looked at her. "For the longest time I heard what people had to say about us, what Grandma insinuated when she thought I wasn't listening, how the other women in this town looked at all of us as if we were tramps, how you lived in fear our whole lives of having people judge us for being your daughters."

"I know," Mystery sniveled. "And I am so sorry for that."

"No," Janie smiled. "You shouldn't be sorry. Those are their issues, not ours. Not mine, not John's, not Cord's or Bennie's, not even Dana's when you get right down to it."

Mystery struggled against her tears and nodded.

"You always told me as a little child not to care what anyone thought. Well, you shouldn't either. I don't know about you, Mom, but I don't think we are all that bad."

"No?" Mystery asked.

"No," Janie replied. "Am I that bad?"

"No, no," Mystery said, turning the tables just as Janie had hoped that she would. "You are perfect, all three of you are. It's just like I told your grandma, Dana may have her problems, but she's still a kid."

"And, we owe it all to you, Mom. Not anyone else. There was no dad here, and Grandma certainly didn't help. Your decisions are what made us who were are now, so if we are okay, then you must not have made such terrible decisions. Am I right?"

Mystery paused and contemplated what Janie had just said. Janie could tell that she still had not completely convinced her that it was time to take her own life in her hands without considering what everyone else would think.

"Mom," she said without pausing to think, "I'm moving out."

"Moving?" Mystery cried. "No. You can't move out yet."

"Yes, I can. I graduated. I'll be eighteen next month, and it is time for you to realize that the life you want is not going to just wait for you until every perfect little piece of the puzzle falls into place. I am moving out. That is one less person for you to consider."

"That's not the problem, Janie. And besides, where would you go?"

Janie raised her eyebrows and looked through her window to the fallen ledge below the cemetery. She hoped that Fawn's grave had been spared, but she realized as well that if it hadn't, that would have to be the caretaker's problem and not her own.

"With Cord," she smiled. She could not believe that she was telling her mother this without even consulting Cord, but she felt that she had to in order to get her mother to see how quickly life was passing her by.

"What about college?"

"I'm going," she said. "Just like we always planned, just not from here. I hear they have a nice college in Lewiston. Maybe I'll go there."

Mystery placed her arms around her daughter and finally let the tears flow. Janie prayed that Mystery would see the truth about the life she had made for them. A life filled with doors that didn't need to be locked; freedom to be whoever they wanted to be without judgment, ridicule, or fear of disappointing her; nights of kick-the-can and hide-and-seek in a cemetery that not a child in Glendale feared. This was the life that Mystery had signed on for when she bought the little house on Carlisle Street despite her mother's protest. She had suffered the slings and arrows of a gossipy town in order to allow her children to grow up in Glendale, and for that Janie would forever be grateful. For the longest time Janie had thought that if she became a Randall that would make her a better person, someone well thought of and respected in Glendale, but now she knew the truth. She was an Abbott, Mystery Abbott's daughter, and nothing made her prouder than that.

chapter twenty-nine

Mystery Abbott

W ind from the ridge tore at the shingles of the new roof, but as she left for work through a mist of tears, Mystery had faith that it would hold. John had told her the truth. He always finished what he started, and the man did quality work. She spent the remainder of the day in the back room, silently doing billing. Walt, as if sensing her need to be alone, tended to the customers. At one point she heard him say, *That is none of your goddamned business.* When Mystery looked out, she spotted Melinda walking briskly away from the counter.

As Mystery nibbled on a peanut butter and jelly sandwich in the break room during lunch, she heard the bell above the door clank open.

"John," Walt said. "It's been a long time." Mystery placed her sandwich down and scurried out front, but it was only John Baynor from BC Farms coming into to pick up the filters he had ordered for his combine.

"Mystery," he said, tipping his hat in her direction. "I told you, Walt, the only reason I shop here is because you have such a pretty cashier behind the counter. I'm not coming back if your ugly mug is the one that is going to wait on me."

Walt laughed and Mystery smiled, trying not to let him see the disappointment in her eyes that he was he and not John Spencer at the counter. She returned to the lunchroom, threw her sandwich in the trash, and got back to the billing. An hour later, Walt sent her home for the day. She didn't argue.

As she hurried the two blocks home, she shivered beneath the towering gray cloud that had settled over Glendale. It churned internally and appeared to be morphing into a dirty-white-looking menace. It looked ominous, like the precursor to a tornado. Tornadoes had been known to touch down in Eastern Washington, contrary to popular belief. The most serious one had happened about ten years back. It ripped the cylindrical roof off a grain silo and hurled it into the side of a barn over a hundred yards away.

After Mystery jetted inside her house, she immediately went to the kitchen and turned on the radio. Today's weather forecast called for "lower thirties tonight and upper forties tomorrow, increasing wind and precipitation." *This summer is a crop-killer*, she thought. What the rain hadn't already sprouted, the frost would kill or the wind would stomp down. It didn't look like there would be much of a harvest this year at all—for the farmers or for her. She hadn't bothered pulling weeds out of her garden in days, but this morning she had finally taken the time to place a misting sprinkler in the middle of it to try and stop the frost, just in case. There would most likely be nothing in the garden this fall to can or freeze, so she might not be able to put anything up for the winter. The thought saddened her, but her family would survive. They always did.

Mystery heard Cord and Janie in her room packing her things. Bennie was giggling as he jumped up and down on Janie's bed, saying, "It's mine. It's mine!"

It seemed almost surreal to Mystery that her little girl was leaving home. Just like that, after one conversation, she was packing up and moving out. With a boy, no less. Even though Mystery had known the girls would one day leave the nest, she had been certain it would be Dana, not Janie, who would go first. Dana hadn't even mentioned moving out yet.

Mystery still didn't want Janie to go, but perhaps her daughter was right. She was an adult, and maybe it was time. Janie laughed at something that Cord said and the beautiful sound of her happiness reverberated in the kitchen. That too, would be gone soon and then Mystery and Bennie would be left alone.

As she watched the sky darken she thought of Liv, now going her own way, and Melinda, still bent on causing problems. Walt hadn't told her whatever it was that she'd wanted to hear, and Mystery wished for a moment that she had been the one at the counter today.

"Prepare for the worst, tonight," the weatherman cautioned from the radio. "This is going to be one doozy of a summer storm."

Mystery reached up on the shelf above the stove and grabbed the brandy. *It was time*, she thought as she recalled John's words: *One single slug of brandy is the best thing for everything from the flu to bad moods to cold nights around a campfire.*

She hoped it was good for courage as well. Mystery took a glass of brandy into her bedroom and closed the door. Her hands shook as she dialed the first number. She took a quick sip of liquid courage and swallowed hard as it burned its way down her throat. The wind pounded so intensely against the house that there was static on the phone lines. Only five years ago, Glendale had still used party lines. The phone company swore that the static would go away with the new system, but on nights when the wind blew this hard, the static returned with a vengeance.

Mystery wasn't sure if she wanted the call to be answered or not. Fate would decide. As the phone rang on the other end, she looked up at her newly repaired bedroom ceiling and thought about the strong new roof beyond it. She felt guilty about not paying John and Cord for their hard work, but both had refused to take a dime.

The *brrr* in her ear cut off in mid-ring, and a female voice came on the line. "Hello?"

"Is this Melinda?" Mystery asked.

"Yes," she answered. "Who's calling?"

"Hi, Melinda, it's Mystery Abbott. How *are* you?" she said shakily, emphasizing the last sentence as if they were old friends who hadn't spoken in a decade.

"Fine," Melinda said cautiously. "How are you?"

"Great, just great. Look, I just wanted to call and fill you in on what's been going on over here. I know you've been dying to know." She was trying to sound like a member of Ma Bell; she figured she'd deliver the gossip better if she pictured herself as one of the gossipers.

Mystery had just enough air in her lungs to get it all out before her voice broke and gave away her nervousness. She put her hand over the receiver as she sucked in a deep breath and waited for a response.

"Is this some kind of joke? Did my brother say something to you?"

"No, it's no joke. It's just that I know you've been trying to find out exactly what's going on with that handsome man on my roof, so I thought I'd save you the trouble of sleuthing and tell you myself."

"The trouble of what?"

"Sleuthing," Mystery repeated with a smile. "You know, detective work."

"I know what sleuthing is," she said sharply, "but why do you think that is what I'm doing?"

"Oh please, Melinda, we're both adults here. Ma Bell, right? We both know you want to know. What can it hurt if you get the information directly from me rather than someone else?"

"Okay, I'll play along..."

"Well," Mystery began, "first of all, his name is John Spencer. He has a cattle ranch up north near Kennedy, and we have been dating for about six months now. And, yes, Liv Randall did find him in my closet after I let him stay over. That part is true. However, the reason he was in there was because I didn't want the whole town to speculate and pass judgment on who I was dating. You can understand, right?"

"Sure, I guess." Melinda's reluctant responses barely slowed the rapid-fire stream of words coming from Mystery.

"Well, the best laid plans, so to speak. We got caught. Who knew that the roof was going to cave in? Anyway, to make a long story short, he volunteered to fix my roof for me. Well, actually he wanted me to sell the place and move in with him, but I was so worried about what everyone here might say, I told him no. That was when he volunteered to fix my roof. Are you getting all of this so far?"

"I guess, but who is the other boy?"

"There was no *other* boy," she said. "They're both men. The other *man's* name is Cord Galloway. He's Janie's boyfriend. Great guy. He volunteered, too."

"I thought Janie was dating Taylor."

"See that is what gossip will get you. Janie's not dating Taylor anymore."

"She's not?"

Mystery heard the excitement in Melinda's voice at this nugget of information, and she felt her own blood pump harder in her veins. For a moment, Mystery understood the thrill these women got from gossip. Information really was power.

"Nope. Janie's dating Cord Galloway, who is, as I said, a great guy."

"So what about you and John?" Her voice sounded excited as if she was grateful to Mystery for giving her the information that she needed for Ma Bell.

"Oh, yes, let's get back on track, shall we? Well, as I said, I was so worried about what everyone would say that I told him I wouldn't move in with him."

"That's too bad." Melinda's fake sympathy was well practiced but completely transparent. "Sounds like a nice guy."

"Oh, how sweet of you to be concerned. He *is* a nice guy."

"Well, maybe you should reconsider then."

Mystery cocked her head to the side and smiled. "Ya think?" she said with all the zest of a teenager revved up on Mountain Dew.

"Well, sure," Melinda agreed, her voice carrying an edge softened by self-deprecating humor. "I mean, you said he's a great guy, right? It's not like you'll find one of those in Glendale."

"Hmm...well, I'll think about it," she said smoothly, breathing a little easier now. "Thanks for the advice."

"You're welcome, I think."

"Do you want me to call you back when I decide?"

"It's up to you, Mystery," she laughed. "I've no doubt you have the nerve for it."

"I'd better," Mystery said. "Otherwise, it could get so screwed up during that telephone game you play with your girlfriends that I might end up pregnant with alien triplets. Will you let the other gals know for me?"

"Sure," Melinda laughed again, "I'll do that."

"Except for Liv," Mystery added, "you don't have to tell her. She already knows." *Gotcha*, she thought.

"*Really?*"

"Really. Bye, bye now." With that, she hung up, almost giddy with relief. What had she done? Was she crazy? She walked to the window, the phone cord dragging behind her like a loyal puppy, and promptly dialed the next number before her senses returned.

"Hello?"

"Hi, Mom."

"Yes?"

"It's me, Mystery," she said. "I just got off the phone with Melinda."

"About Walt?"

"Walt?" Mystery said, caught off guard by the question. "What about Walt?"

"Oh please," her mother said. "You're not really going to play that game with me, are you?"

"What game?"

"You have been sleeping with Walt at the office!" she spat into the phone. "Melinda saw you taking blankets in, and Walt has been sleeping at the office ever since. How many times do I have to tell you this is a small town, Mystery? Everyone sees everything!"

"You would think if they saw *everything* that they would get their facts straight." Mystery retorted. "And that includes you, Mother."

"Well, I never!"

"You never what?" Mystery snapped.

"I've never said anything that wasn't true about you to anyone."

"Yes, you have," Mystery said. "You might not have known it was a lie, but you've said stuff just the same. You've gossiped about my supposed affair with Walt Smith. Which, as I have told you, never happened. Walt is my boss and, I'm proud to say, my friend. But that's all."

"Are you *sure* that is all, Mystery?"

"Yes. You've also gossiped about Bennie, and I'm sure you've talked to people about John. So let me clear things up for you. For one thing, I love John, and, if he'll forgive me for being such a ridiculous, closed-minded woman, I'll try and get him back. For another thing, Bennie's father is Liv's brother, Patrick. You remember him, the doctor from Seattle? I told Liv about it this morning. She knows everything, and now so do you. And finally, you should reread that Bible of yours. Mystery was another name for the ancient city of Babylon, and I'm sure Dad knew that when he insisted on naming me after my grandmother. But you told me that I was named after a whore. Were you talking about the Bible, Mother, or were you talking about Grandma?"

There was silence on the other line and Mystery's jaw dropped. "You *were* talking about Grandma, weren't you?"

Again, static-infused silence.

"Mother," she said, "does Dad know that?"

"You are just like them, Mystery," she said. "Those Abbott women. They were all beautiful and they got whatever they wanted, whenever they wanted it. Your grandmother always made me feel inferior to the rest of the family because I was not as attractive as they were. They hated your father for marrying me, and then you...you ended up being just like them."

"If you think I am as beautiful as Grandma was, well then, yes I am just like 'those Abbott women.' And thank God for it. Thank God I'm not like you, bitter and so mean-spirited that you'll even gossip about Bennie, your grandson."

"Mystery Abbott," she snapped, "this time you have gone too far."

"It's funny, Mom, even Liv didn't say that to me. You know what she said?"

"Well, I —"

"She said she'd keep what I told her about Bennie a secret until her dying day, and yet she's been my worst enemy, Mother. My worst enemy was nicer to me than my own mother. How does that make you feel?"

"Like I know you better than she does." Mystery knew the self-satisfied expression that usually accompanied her mother's vicious behavior, and she could almost see it through the phone line.

"Nice, Mom, real nice. Well, this time you are the one who has gone too far. You've gone too far with Bennie by treating him like he is a bastard. You've gone too far with Janie. She couldn't care less if she ever sees you again after the way you treated Bennie on the porch the other day. You've gone too far with John. He wants me to take Bennie and move to his ranch with him just to get the hell away from you. And finally, if that weren't enough, you've gone too far with me. I'm not a bad person because the girls' father left. I'm not a bad person for choosing to keep Bennie's father a secret from people like you. Patrick didn't want a child, and I didn't want to see Bennie shipped back and forth between here and Seattle for the rest of his life. And I'm not a bad person for loving one other man in my life who has given me everything when you have given me nothing."

"One other man, Mystery? Please."

Mystery's mouth dropped. Her mother had not heard a word that she had said and yet Mystery had listened to everything her mother had said to her and about her for her whole life.

"Contrary to the rumors you've heard about your own daughter from others in this town, there have been no other men, Mother. That's the last time I'm going to tell you that."

"I'm coming down there —"

"Don't," Mystery said cutting her off. "Until you can treat me like a daughter and treat your grandkids with some respect, you are not welcome in my house anymore."

With that, she slammed the phone into the cradle and sat back down on her bed. The hair on her arms was standing straight up. She took deep breaths to steady herself before making her last call. She grabbed the snifter off the dresser and gulped down the last of the brandy. Then she dialed the final number.

She pleaded with whatever greater being might be out there to help—God, Mother Nature, The Fates—whomever she had any pull with. They hadn't always been against her. Every once in awhile they were on her side. Like the time the wind blew her mother's skirt up when she was reprimanding her outside The Watering Trough for slurping her spaghetti noodles in front of "everyone in Glendale society." She was thankful to them for three days after that. They had also been on her side the night she had Bennie. She had never seen such wisdom in the eyes of a baby. She had never felt such undying love or devotion, not even for the girls. It was something about him being hers and only hers. Alone in the hospital that night, she had convinced herself there was no father, there was only her. Just her, the girls, and their little miracle, Bennie.

On the third ring he picked up. "Hello?"

She forced herself to loosen her white-knuckle grip on the phone. "Hi," she said softly.

"Hi."

There was silence for a moment, but she had heard the question in his voice, and she wasn't sure what to say. She knew this was her chance to give as openly and unselfishly as he had always done for her, but she was afraid. There was still a chance of rejection. He had seen her insecurities and her anger. He had seen her act just like her mother. It was possible that he'd had enough.

"Mystery?"

"Y-yes." Her voice broke as she replied.

"What is it?"

She took a deep breath and forced her fears aside. "I just wanted to tell you that I told off my mother and the rest of this town."

"Well," John said. "Good for you. Do I need to come protect you?"

"No," she laughed. "And I also called to say I'm sorry. I needed to get that out."

"Okay," he said. "I'm sorry, too."

"No," she countered, nervously wrapping the phone cord around her free hand. "I'm the one who is really sorry. You were right. I was acting like my mother. I hate to admit that, but I was. And I'm sorry for something else. I haven't been completely honest with you. I do love you and I do want to marry you, but I don't think you know what that will bring."

"Such as?"

"I'm in debt, John," she admitted. "Big debt. I always have been, for a number of reasons. There is hardly any equity in this house. I have no money in my savings. Hell, I still owe money on my car and it's eight years old."

John started to laugh, but stopped himself. "Sorry, I know this isn't funny, and I don't mean to hurt your feelings, but *that* is what you are worried about?"

"Yes," she said truthfully, "how can I not worry about that? You want to marry me and take on the role of parent to Bennie and the girls, but there would be a lot more to take on than just that."

There was silence for a moment and despite the suddenly clear phone line, Mystery's thoughts were pinging around in her head disrupting the clarity she had been trying to hold on to in order to get through this much-needed purging. She didn't want to seem apologetic for who she was or why she was in the position she was in. If this was her new start, she was going to be honest. He was going to know it all so that there would be nothing else to hide.

"So let me get this straight," he said. "You will marry me, or you won't?"

"Huh?" Mystery shook her head as if to clear her thoughts.

"Does that mean you will marry me or you won't?"

"Haven't you heard a word I said? I've got nothing, John. Nothing but a deep pile of debt to bring to this marriage. Is that what you want?"

"I want *you*, and I want Bennie and the girls. We can sit down and figure out the financial implications of it later, but that doesn't change the fact that I want to marry you."

Mystery felt eighteen years of shouldering the weight alone lift with John's last sentence. He didn't care. He didn't even seem all that scared or shocked by her admission. Her failures weren't going to cost her the man she loved. He wanted her, not for money, nor fame, nor beauty. He simply wanted her, and that knowledge broke through every emotional wall she had erected. Her shoulders heaved with a noisy sob, and she collapsed on the bed, uncertain that she'd ever be able to stop crying.

"Mystery, honey, is that a yes?"

"Yes!"

"Thank God," she heard him whisper. "I'm on my way."

chapter thirty

Liv Abbott

iv stared blankly at Mystery's house. It was Friday night. The end of the workweek for everyone in Glendale, and if Liv could get all of her stuff done it would be the end of her work as well. There was a light layer of frost at the edge of her living room window. She didn't understand it and tried to reason that it was something else, dirt or just a thick layer of rain. It was the middle of summer, after all.

Carl and Taylor had refused to look at her or speak to her since their fight yesterday. That was okay. If she stayed busy she could keep the pain at bay long enough to get out of the house. She looked at her watch. Just after five. They wouldn't be home for another hour, if they came home at all. She hoped they wouldn't. Their physical presence might ruin all of her plans. Maybe. She wasn't sure, really. It wasn't like it mattered anymore. This was her decision. She didn't need or want their blessings for it.

There was no noise in the house as she wandered from room to room, finishing her chores. She washed the dishes used to make the pie for Mystery. She even put them away instead of letting them air dry in the dish rack like she usually did. She scrubbed the toilets one more time. After all, Carl and Taylor wouldn't have a clue how, and there might be guests arriving in a few days. The last thing she needed was for people in Glendale to say that she had been a bad housekeeper. She made Taylor's bed and even placed his teddy bear from childhood on the pillow. In its arms she laid an envelope.

It had taken her a long time to write a letter to Taylor—she hardly knew him anymore—but then she pictured Bennie, sweet and innocent, and the words flowed easily. She told him that she loved him. She wished him the best with Janie or whomever he chose in life. She was sorry she had failed him where Janie was concerned. She took a long last look before she closed the door. How could a kid be unhappy here? He had everything.

In their bedroom, she pulled back the covers on Carl's side of the bed, leaving her side untouched to indicate that she would no longer sleep in this bed. She supposed that they had had a good enough marriage. They were merely separate entities instead of a single soul like her grandparents had been. Like she was certain that Mystery and John would be. She was sorry that she had gotten in the way of Carl's dreams, and that he had missed his opportunity with Coral. *Don't wait any longer,* she had written to him, *not everyone has a shot at true love.* On his pillow, she laid the second envelope and left without a backward glance. This was his room now. Not hers. Not anymore.

Back in the kitchen she scratched numbers three and four off her list. She almost threw it away, but changed her mind. They should know about all that she had done for them every day. Liv hated things that were incomplete or misunderstood, and, if she took the clues away, there was a chance Carl and Taylor would be unable to piece it all together.

She took one last look around the living room. Framed pictures of Taylor adorned every wall. On the sideboard were photos of Carl and Ilsa. One of them in front of her prize rose bushes, then again at his high school graduation, and one taken with Ilsa at Taylor's birth. In the hallway were their family pictures. The three of them when Taylor was born, many of Taylor throughout school, and one of Carl and Liv on their wedding day. They both looked so happy and it surprised Liv how much could *not* be read by a single photograph. Anyone could smile, but that didn't make them happy. She pulled the photo from the wall, along with all of the other photos of her in the hallway and placed them in a box just inside Taylor's door. She hoped he would want them as he got older, but she didn't want them visible when Coral arrived. If she was going to live here, this was going to be her house, and Liv didn't want her to share it with a ghost as she had done.

She thought of all that she had done for them. She wondered if it was worth it. Maybe if she had bagged all the cleaning and prepping in favor of laying down next to them to watch a movie at night, or actually sitting through a meal, things would have been different. But, it was too late to go back now. Carl was gone and Taylor had graduated. She had done what she thought Carl and Taylor wanted, what she thought was her job as mother of the valedictorian and wife of the town lawyer, but it had left them with nothing but mutual resentment and heartache.

She walked to Ilsa's rocker, the one Carl had said was now hers when they moved in. She left one last envelope. It simply said *Bennie*.

As she drove to the Miller house, she acknowledged the black cloud in her peripheral vision. Soon, she told it. Soon.

She parked in her usual spot beside the rose bushes. They loved the rain and somehow seemed to be withstanding the bitter cold enough to have sprouted a few new buds. She wondered if the heat of summer would reach Glendale in time to save them. The wind tousled her hair free from its clip and swept deep inside her sweater as she stepped out of the car, but she didn't feel it. She straightened her sweater and wondered if Dana had gotten the clothes yet, or the letter. Maybe she could have a positive effect on at least one life.

Liv reached in and pulled the last box from the car. Although it was only six o'clock, the churning black sky above made it seem much later. The car had a full tank of gas, and the keys were in the ignition. If Dora drove by tonight, she'd be certain to think Liv was having an affair with the mystery buyer from Seattle. *The women of Glendale*, she thought. She had been right about them all along. Right about all but one.

She closed the kitchen door, shutting out the wind to preserve the stillness and comfort of the Miller house. She looked up at the ceiling and said hello. "I'm back... finally."

She unpacked the box onto the counter, and smiled over the contents. Cheesecake, a bottle of Merlot, and some bubble bath. It would be a nice way to end the day. She wished that she had taken the time to do this more often. She popped the cork on the wine and retrieved a glass from the cupboard.

Through the window she saw the canoe smack against the dock. She watched the wind push ripples across the surface of the little pond and thought she had never seen anything so beautiful. The water appeared thick and inviting. A tear escaped her eye as she drank in the beauty of the Miller property. She could understand why Mr. and Mrs. Miller had never wanted to leave. This house felt more like her home than Ilsa's house in Glendale ever had.

She turned back to the cheesecake, cut herself a big slice, and inhaled so deeply she could taste it. Thick, rich cheesecake with loads of fresh huckleberries. She had wanted this for years, but she had not allowed herself to indulge. She'd seen it too many times. That's how the women in Glendale got started down the path to obesity. They just let themselves go. They'd allow themselves just one more cookie or one more slice of pie at the PTA meetings, and then joke with their friends about it as if they had never done it before. She'd watched their waists increase by four sizes since she'd moved to Glendale, while she stayed as skinny as ever. They'd ask her how she did it, and she'd tell them she was just careful about her diet and got plenty of exercise. They always smiled and nodded, as if unsure of what that meant. But they knew. She knew that they knew what she was doing, but no one had the nerve to say a thing until Dora confronted her about it the other day. She took a big bite of the cheesecake and moaned in bliss. She should have just joined in. She might have been happier.

Liv retrieved a serving tray from the sideboard in the dining room and placed the cheesecake, wine bottle, glass, and bubble bath on it, and then made her way upstairs. She knew she should shut the lights off as she went, but then there wouldn't be a trail. In the bathroom, she turned on the tap and let the bath fill halfway, adding bubble bath liberally to the stream of warm water. She set the wine and cheese-cake down beside the clawfoot bathtub, then removed her clothes, folded them carefully, and placed them on the washstand before stepping into the froth of bubbles. She felt a tickle in her throat from the overwhelming sweetness. She couldn't recall the last time she had eaten anything richer than those cookies at the PTA meeting. They were nothing compared to the divine goodness of cheesecake. Everything was done. She could relax now. She savored her cake and leaned back in the bubbles. She thought about just falling asleep in the tub for hours. There was no rush now.

Visions of Taylor and Carl drifted in and out of her head. She had wanted to hold Taylor one last time, but after he rebuffed her in favor of his father during their fight the other day, Liv knew there was no point in trying. She had lost him. She thought of the teddy bear he had clung to as a child, waiting on his pillow for him with a letter. She remembered the night that they had forgotten that bear at her grandmother's house after a long visit to the ocean. Grandma had promised to mail it back the next day, but that hadn't stopped Taylor's wailing. He had cried so hard that he threw up all over his bedroom floor. Carl had told her to just close the door and let him cry it out, but she'd refused. She hated Carl for that. Her child was aching. She had finally convinced him to stop crying by promising to drive to a store and get him a new teddy bear. He had calmed down and within minutes was fast asleep. Carl had told her to forget it, but she had gone to buy a new bear anyway. What kind of a mother would she be if she didn't keep her promise? Taylor had clung to the new bear for two days. Carl hadn't said a word other than pointing out that coddling the boy when things didn't go his way was a mistake. When the old bear arrived, it was history. Taylor had told it that a new bear had taken its place.

Liv was glad her grandparents weren't here to see her son now. Or her, for that matter. She was certain neither of them had turned out like her grandparents would have expected.

Another solitary tear traced a path down Liv's cheek toward the warm water below. She made no move to wipe it away as she opened her eyes and sat up in the tub. Reveries were not safe. The heat of the water and the half-glass of wine were making her woozy. She sensed the black cloud wrapping its tentacles around her temples again. She always knew that the cloud would win in the end, and she felt relief at not having to fight it anymore. She didn't know if it was a real thing or some figment of her imagination. She assumed the latter, but it had been with her so long it was almost an extension of her body. She had fought it in the past — now she welcomed it.

She climbed out of the bathtub, toweled herself dry, and walked through the house naked, something she never would have done in her own home. In the master bedroom, she lit a candelabra and lay down on the large bed. She looked around the room awash in the soft yellow glow of candlelight, shadows flickering in concert with the flame. The coved ceiling seemed to wrap around her, as if to cradle her in its seafoam-colored arms. She reached up and imagined she was touching the ceiling, caressing it. Her thoughts drifted as her arms waved above her. She drew them down and hugged herself around the shoulders.

She imagined that the house was alive around her now, thanking her for breathing life back into it, but she wanted more than its acceptance and gratitude. She arched her back and kissed the very air around her, her body awakened from the strange sensuality of the moment. She reached her hand down between her thighs, touched herself with cool fingertips, and moaned softly in anticipation. She had wanted this for days. Carl had rejected her, but she knew that the house would not.

"Thank you," she gasped aloud, satisfied at last. She relaxed into a dreamlike state for some time, mesmerized by candlelight on the ceiling. She felt herself sinking into its watery green depths. When she resurfaced, it was to the objective reality of the mattress beneath her, the ceiling above. The sky outside had darkened considerably and Liv swore she could hear thunder rolling in from the south. She dressed in the white satin nightgown and slipped her feet into the satin ballet slippers. On the nightstand was the amber pill container with the original twenty pills prescribed by her doctor. She had almost taken one on the night she had filled the prescription, but then had changed her mind. He had instructed her to take them only in case of an emergency. Not sleeping didn't seem like an emergency to her then, but wanting to sleep forever certainly was.

She poured the twenty small red pills into her hand and popped them into her mouth. It took a full glass of wine to get them all down. She reclined on the bed and finished the bottle of wine. *What a perfect room*, she thought, surrounded by the Miller's personal possessions. She wondered what Carl would have done if she had just thrown out all the crap his aunt had left them when she died. But perhaps his way was better than the Miller kids'. At least Carl wanted his family's things. Unfortunately, he hadn't created any room for hers. But it didn't matter now. She was feeling relaxed. The pills were already having their desired effect.

She got up from the bed, leaving the candles burning, and unhurriedly traced her steps back down the stairs and out of the house. She had no idea what time it was, not that it mattered anymore. The smell of algae was on the wind again. She walked to the edge of the pond and stood still at its bank. The temperature had dropped precipitously, and it had begun to drizzle, but Liv could feel none of it. The water looked like ink in the moonlight, not at all like her beloved ocean, and Liv endured a moment of doubt.

She felt increasingly woozy and she almost fell down as the pills gradually took effect. Taylor's sweet baby face crossed her memory one more time, and she asked herself again where it was that she had lost him along the way. Why didn't the bond between mother and child hold fast forever? She had given him space. She had given him freedom. She had done everything he ever asked of her. Yet, somewhere along the way, they had lost each other.

Her knees buckled, and she struggled to keep her eyes open. The cloud nearly blocked out her vision now. She focused all energy on her satin ballet slippers, moving one foot in front of the other. The smell of the ocean was getting stronger now. She begged the wind and the water to fill her nostrils and her senses so that she could be lost in them forever. Eyes closed now, she plunged into the pond, just as she had imagined Mrs. Miller doing. The water was warmer than the outside air. Strange that she could feel its warmth. She opened her eyes in the blackness just as she had in her dream. There was nothing. Sinking now, she opened her mouth and inhaled. She didn't cough or sputter. She remembered what people said about all humans breathing liquid until birth. It wasn't that bad, really, and it smelled and tasted just like the ocean.

Dana had finished her shift at The Watering Trough just after nine o'clock, and Dylan had not driven by, not even once. She had walked past the police station on her way home, but the lights were off and his car was nowhere to be seen. Taylor, on the other hand, had driven by the restaurant four times, and each time he had stared her down as he passed. She hurried up State Street and did not stop moving until she reached her sidewalk. Up ahead she could barely make out Dylan's police car behind Walt and Coral Smith's house. In the dusk she could see Dylan and the town maintenance men placing orange cones and yellow caution tape in front of the cliff. Coral was standing on the back porch watching them. If this weather kept up, the whole bank would probably come down and destroy the beautiful home.

Before entering the safety zone of her house, Dana had peered over her shoulder into the glow of the streetlight. Yes, he was still there. He had followed her home again. She didn't know why Taylor was following her, but because he kept a bit of a distance, she ignored him. She really didn't want to talk to him about what he had witnessed last night at Dylan's apartment. She gave him a dramatic wave as she reached the door.

The lights were ablaze in the house, in contrast to the dark, storm-cloud–filled sky. On her walk home, she planned to head straight for a long hot bath to soak away the bone-deep chill and give her time to consider what to do next about Dylan. But when she opened the door, she stopped dead in her tracks. She couldn't believe it. There, seated around the coffee table, playing Yahtzee, were the four people she least wanted to see tonight. Bennie lay curled up on the couch under a thick Indian afghan while Janie, Cord, John, and Mystery sat cross-legged on the floor next to him. Dana took a deep breath and tried to remember what Liv had said about her mother, but seeing her there, surrounded by the comfort of a family that didn't include her, made Dana sick. No matter what she did, nothing was going to help her feel any better about them tonight. She slammed the door behind her. Bennie stirred and John put his hand up and rubbed his little shoulder. Dana turned her back to them to remove her jacket. She couldn't face them head on for fear she might give away how left out she felt.

"Hi, Dana," Mystery said, "we've been waiting for you."

"Really?" Dana said, still with her back to their judgmental eyes. "What for? It looks like you have plenty of players."

"Dana—"

"What!" she snapped at Janie. With her familiar anger returning, she spun on her heel to face them.

Janie stood and approached her with a shy smile. "Guess what?" She sounded more cheerful than Dana was willing to allow. "Cord and I—"

"Please," she interrupted again, placing her hand up in front of her sister's face, "don't tell me anymore. The thought of it makes me want to vomit."

"The thought of what?" Janie asked.

Dana said nothing, just crossed her arms and silently dared her sister to continue. She didn't know why she was yelling at Janie, but as usual, she couldn't seem to stop. The thought of immature little goody two-shoes assuming that she'd be interested in her so-called love life really irritated her.

"Dana," Janie said, stronger than Dana had ever heard her speak to her, "I just wanted to tell you that I am moving."

"Moving?" she sneered in Cord's direction. "Where? To State Street?"

"No," Janie said, "to Idaho. Cord and I are going to try and rebuild his family ranch while I go to college. I just thought you might want to know."

"Why? Are you pregnant or something?"

"No," Janie replied steadily despite the blush heating her cheeks. "But what would that have to do with it?"

"I just can't imagine you leaving Mom and Bennie, that's all. I know how wrapped up in her apron strings you are."

Mystery and John shared a look as Mystery stood up and moved to Dana's side. She placed her arm on Dana's shoulder and looked her sincerely in the eye. Dana rolled her shoulder back and looked away. Mystery knew how much Dana hated being touched by her. Did she think she could get away with it simply because there were witnesses around? Mystery pulled her arm back in retreat, just as she had every other time. Maybe this time it would be a lesson learned. But no, Mystery held her ground. "Dana, we are going to be moving, too."

"*We*? We who?"

"Well, me," she said, looking back at the others, "and Bennie. We are moving in with John up by Kennedy. And, you are welcome, as well. That is, if you want."

"You're doing *what*?" It wasn't like her mother to make decisions without running them by Dana. That was an understanding Dana had worked for years to forge between them. Mystery had always done whatever she and Janie wanted, and anytime the woman made a decision, good or bad, Dana knew she had the power to make her mother change it to suit her needs.

"And no one thought about asking me about this?"

"Well," Mystery said simply, "no."

"No?" This one was going to be a little harder than before. Mystery seemed to think that if she had an entourage behind her, it would be easier to get her daughter to submit.

"Well, we are almost eighteen, Dana," Janie interjected sarcastically.

Dana ignored her. She would deal with her later, if she felt like

288 ~ Amy Warwick

it. For right now, she wanted to work on the weakest link in their family — Mystery.

With arms akimbo, she challenged her mother, "So, what, are you getting married or something?"

"That is the plan, yes."

"Nice," she said, crossing her arms in defiance. "Real nice. Have you told Grandma?"

"Yes," Mystery said. "*And Grandpa.*"

"And what did she say?"

"She wasn't happy about it." Mystery looked back at John and smiled. "But Dad was pleased." There was an unmistakable twinkle in her eyes. It pissed Dana off even more.

"And you think that's funny?" Dana said.

"I do," Janie quipped.

"Stay out of this, Janie. If I wanted a child's opinion I'd wake up Bennie."

"Hey," Cord said, standing to his feet.

"Hey, nothing." Dana spat back. "You aren't a part of this family. You couldn't have me so you went after my little sister. It may have been convenient, Cord, but it doesn't give you a say in anything."

"Dana," Mystery interrupted. "I don't think it's funny that your grandmother chooses not to be happy. But I can't change her opinion, either. And as for Cord, he does have a say now."

"I can only imagine what my friends — hell, the whole town — will have to say about this."

"Who cares what they will say?" Mystery said.

Dana noted some new conviction in her mother. She took a step toward her. "I do," she said, pointing at her chest. "I care. And you should, too. Haven't things been bad enough without you taking my little brother and shacking up with some man we don't even know in some house we've never been to?"

"I'm sorry that I didn't consult you," Mystery said quietly. "Really I am. But honey, it isn't really your decision. You are a grown woman now."

"Fine," she said, "I guess if I'm not wanted here, then I'll leave."

"Dana," Mystery said, reaching for her again, "I didn't say you weren't wanted. Please don't storm out of here. Come back to —"

"To what?" she asked, brushing Mystery's hand off a second time.

"This is no longer my home." With that, Dana grabbed her coat and headed back out into the cold, slamming the door behind her. She paused on the front porch and gazed out on the dark windy night once more. She didn't know where she could go. Dylan's was not an option, and she didn't want to go to her grandmother's. What she really wanted was a beer. As she stepped off the porch, she saw the lights of Taylor's Mustang across the street. Taylor was still in the driver's seat, crouched and peering beneath his baseball cap as if he were a spy. She sauntered over and tapped on the window. He straightened up and readjusted his hat into the preppy straightforward fashion that made him look like all of the other boys in Glendale.

"Got a beer?" she asked.

"Got a smoke?" he responded. At her answering grin, he leaned over and opened the passenger's door.

She walked around the other side and slid in. She could only hope that Janie was at the window watching them. Taylor twisted the cap off a Bud Light and handed it to her. She lit another cigarette and passed it over.

"Is it okay to smoke in here?"

"It's my car, isn't it?" He started the engine and idled for a moment.

"Where are we going?" She didn't really care, but it made for conversation.

"Don't know," he said. "I've just been sitting here watching your house."

"For what?"

"Don't know," he said again, inhaling deeply from his smoke.

"Well, can we go somewhere else for a while? I don't want to sit here and watch them. How about the football field?"

Taylor wagged his beer at her and smiled. "What if the *cop* is out?"

She shook her head and smiled back. Finally, someone who understood her. "He's not," she laughed. "He's working on the landslide below the cemetery."

Taylor saluted her with his beer, popped the car into gear, and slammed the pedal to the floor. The tires squealed as he spun down Carlisle Street toward the school. Dana turned just in time to see the curtain drop in the front window of the Abbott house.

When they reached the field, Taylor parked the car in the middle of the empty lot leaving his lights to shine out onto the fifty-yard line. Dana swallowed the last swig of her beer and signaled for another. She was beginning to feel a buzz, but not quickly enough. He opened two more and passed one to her. She tipped it back and guzzled as much as she could without belching it back up.

"It's cold out," she coughed, tapping the passenger window with her beer bottle.

"Yeah, too friggin' cold for summertime. What is *that*?" Taylor pointed at the trees. They were moving and swaying with an incoming front of something white that was blocking out the trees and shielding streetlights from their view.

"I don't know," Dana said. "Fog?"

"I don't think it's fog," he countered as he rolled down his window and stuck his head out. "Nope, definitely not fog."

"Then what the hell is it?" Dana started to roll down her window as well.

"It's snow," he said without a hint of enthusiasm. "It's fucking snow."

"Snow?" she asked doubtfully. "It's almost July. How in the world can it be snowing?"

"Don't know," he said. "That's Glendale for you."

They watched as the whiteness danced through the beams of their headlights and moved toward them. Dana braced herself by placing her hands squarely on the door and the dashboard as if the impact was about to rock the car and sweep it away from the ground. The wind hit the car, shaking it only slightly, and snowflakes swirled around them, melting as they landed on metal still warm from the engine. Dana stuck her hand out into the chilly air. The wind glided through her fingers and snowflakes melted on her skin. "Holy shit," she laughed. "It really is snow."

"That's what I said, isn't it, baby?" His contemptuous expression belied his flippant words.

"I'm not your baby, and you know what, Taylor?" she said, feeling loose now. "With an attitude like that, I have no idea how you ever got my sister in the first place." She pulled her hand back in and rolled up the window.

Taylor's face twisted into a humorless grin and he cranked the heat.

"I've never talked that way to Janie," he said. He took a long satisfied drag of his cigarette before continuing. "I always liked the way sweet little Janie looked at me when I was nice to her. It was like it really mattered. Like she really appreciated it. It didn't matter what anyone else ever said about me, true or untrue. To Janie I was a saint."

"A liar," Dana said.

"But a *saint*," he countered. "So, did they do it?"

"Who?"

"Cord and Janie," he said. "Did he get to fuck her?"

"I don't know," she said, looking out through the windshield. Taylor flipped on the wipers and Dana was surprised to see that the football field was almost completely covered by a blanket of snow. "I didn't ask." Out of the corner of her eye, she saw Taylor's hand tighten around his bottle. He tilted it back, finished it off, and downed half of another one.

"I almost had her you know," he said.

"Really?" Dana said in a voice laced with doubt. She pulled her knees to her chest and wrapped her arms around her legs, resting her chin on her knees as she pointedly avoided giving him the reaction he seemed to crave.

"Yep, in the treehouse. I almost had her, and then that John guy came in and stopped us."

She turned her face toward him, eyebrows raised. "Are you lying to me, Taylor? When was this?"

"Yesterday."

"So, she probably *was* fucking you both," Dana said with a strangled laugh, then tipped her beer up to her lips.

"Nope." Taylor shook his head. "Not by choice. But five more minutes and I would have had her."

"Jesus, Taylor, you raped her?" Shock outweighed her two and a half bottles of beer, and reality hit with harsh clarity.

"Nah. I was going to have *sex* with her," he clarified. "It was for her own good. I told her that. I know that if we had just done it once, she wouldn't have wanted anyone else. I was just trying to save her the trouble of a mistake."

"Wow," Dana said weakly. She studied Taylor's face by the dashboard lights and saw the cold stare of hatred in his eyes. Janie hadn't said anything to her about this. An unexpected and unfamiliar surge of protectiveness washed over her at the thought of Janie trapped in the treehouse with Taylor.

"Wow is right," he replied smugly. "So what about you? I've spilled the beans; now it's your turn."

She hesitated a moment and then said, "Maybe we should go home, Taylor. This snow is really piling up."

"Jesus, Dana, you act like you've never seen snow before. There is barely more than a quarter inch out there."

"I've never seen it in the summer," she said. "And you don't have snow tires on."

"Never needed them," he replied arrogantly. "All good country boys know how to handle themselves in the snow — without snow tires. Now give it up."

"Give what up?" She sneered.

"Don't try and fuck with me, Dana. You're not my type." He laughed at his own joke and then continued, his smirk firmly in place. "About you and Officer Masters. How long have you been doing him?"

"Not long," she conceded after a few moments, "a week, that's all."

After Dylan's rejection of her in his apartment last night, Dana felt no need to protect him any longer.

"So you hopped right off of Cord and right onto a nightstick. Damn. I wish your sister were as loose as you. I might have gotten somewhere in all these years."

"I'm not loose, Taylor," she said.

"Yes, you are." He popped another beer and passed it to her, though she had yet to finish the one she held.

"Give me a smoke," he said. She set the full bottle on the floor and braced it with her feet, then pulled two smokes from the pack and handed him one. "You're practically a hooker, Dana. You just don't get paid for it."

"Fuck you, Taylor. I am not."

"Shut up and drink your beer," he replied. "It's not like I'm judging you. I don't know why you girls think that being a slut is such a bad thing. Hell, I've thought about trying you out myself a few times. Did you know that I watched Todd Evans do you?"

She said nothing, but her stricken expression seemed to please him.

"Yep," he said, he flipped on the wipers again and pointed at the windshield toward the lilacs. "In the trees up there past the football field. Me and two other guys. He told us to go up there and hide. We watched the whole thing."

Dana held her cigarette to her mouth to hide her trembling lips. She recalled how Todd had put his hand over her mouth as she screamed from the pain of it. It was awful. She had sat in the bathtub for two hours that night, bleeding and bargaining with God to take the pain away if she promised never to do it again.

"That's one of my favorite memories of you," he jeered. "We tried to get Todd to do it again but he wouldn't. He said it was too embarrassing or some shit like that."

The snow had blanketed the trees now and the football field was almost completely white. Taylor lifted another bottle in her direction, but she declined. Her head was already spinning and the beer had soured in her stomach.

"Janie's moving," she said, needing to regain control of the conversation.

"Moving? Where?"

"Her and Cord," Dana said, smiling. "They just told me tonight. They're moving to his ranch in Idaho."

Taylor took another drag and turned to her, his expression fierce. "To Idaho?"

"Yep. They're moving in together."

Taylor dropped his head back against the seat and from there tried to blow smoke out the cracked-open window. The cigarette dangled precariously from his hand and his head was lolling back and forth. Dana wanted to grab it from him and throw it out the window, but she was afraid of what would happen if she reached over him.

"Taylor, maybe we should go home. What if your parents are looking for you," Dana suggested. "They probably wouldn't want you out driving in the snow."

"My parents? Doubt it," He scoffed. "They don't do anything together. My dad is busy and my mom is an overbearing nosy bitch."

"That's terrible, Taylor. Your mom doesn't deserve that."

"Ha! I've never heard *that* one before." Taylor crowed. "How can you feel sorry for her? She's the snobby lady in town who talks shit about your family." He gave an emphatic belch.

Dana stared him down for a moment, taking her time before answering. "I watch her, you know. I probably know more about your mom than you do."

"What do you mean, you watch her?"

"Yeah, at night," she said turning toward him in the seat. "I watch her stay up all night when you go to bed. She scrubs the floors, washes the windows, and folds *your* laundry. Then she goes out on the back porch and has a cigarette and a glass of wine. Just before sun-up, she goes back to bed."

"That's creepy." He was starting to slur his words now and hiccupped involuntarily. He giggled and spittle dripped from his lips and landed on his chin. He swiped at it smearing it on his cheek, and almost dropped his cigarette in the process. "You're obsessed with my mother."

"Well, you're obsessed with my sister."

"Yeah, but your s-sister's hot."

He seemed to be having a little trouble with his esses, but he tipped the bottle back anyway.

"You know what, Taylor?" she said, sitting higher up in the seat, and tossing out her cigarette, "so is your mother."

"That's sick," he said, "there's nothing hot about her. Even my father is doing someone else. He doesn't think I know about it, but I do. He's boning that Coral S-Smith up the street."

Taylor turned to her in the seat and grinned. He blinked repeatedly attempting to widen his bloodshot eyes, and he could not stop giggling, although at what Dana could not imagine. She looked at the beer on the floor and decided not to drink anymore. Taylor had drunk enough for both of them.

"He really is cheating on your mom?"

"Yep. So what? You know what they say. 'Women are like buses. Just wait, there's one around every corner.'"

"Very funny. You're the one who's sick, you know that? Really sick."

Taylor moved toward her, grabbed her arm, and pulled her to him. She instantly regretted what she had just said.

"I'm not sick," he spat. "You women are."

He smiled and pulled her closer, and then just when she was about to shove him away, he pushed her back against the seat and peered over her into the snowy scene beyond. The smoke from his cigarette deflected off the glass and hung in the air, capturing the beam of headlights as a car rounded the southern corner of Smith Boulevard. Someone was coming, and at this hour, it just had to be someone looking for them. Dana folded her hands in a silent prayer. Taylor sat up higher in his seat and squinted at the window. On any other night Dana figured she would have enjoyed this weather anomaly by watching Liv through the veil of snowflakes from her window ledge, but because of her temper and animosity toward her own family, she was now here with a very drunk Taylor Randall instead of at home. And, ironically, home was now the only place Dana wanted to be.

"Who is it?" she asked.

"Prick who stole my girlfriend."

Dana sat up in the seat and peered into the darkness. Cord's car was slowly rounding the corner toward the football field.

"I'm leaving," she said, reaching for the door handle. "I don't want to be in the middle of some drunken fight."

Taylor's fingers were like a vise on her upper arm. "Wait," he whispered as if they might hear him, "there's someone in the passenger seat. It's Janie. Sweet li'l Janie is coming back to me and she doesn't even know it."

"Taylor, don't," she said, trying to shake him off, her adrenalin kicking in now. "Let it go. They're not worth it."

"No fucking way." He dropped Dana's arm, slammed the car into gear, and sped out after Cord and Janie.

The car fishtailed in the snow, and Dana knew there was no way she could jump out now. She leaned back in the seat and braced her feet on the floor, tipping her beer in the process. She didn't want to catch up with them and watch Taylor get into a fight with Cord. Moreover, Janie would see her as an accomplice, and with her track record of disdain toward her sister, Dana would have no way to deny it. Cord sped away through the slush when he spotted Taylor closing in behind them, showing no signs of slowing down.

Dana clutched the armrest and hollered, "Taylor, this is crazy!

You're drunk and it's snowing. You don't have snow tires on this thing, and you're not thinking clearly. You aren't going to get her back this way."

Cord and Janie sped off down Sheep Creek Road with Taylor only half a car length behind. Taylor swerved down both lanes of the gravel road in an attempt to pass and cut them off. Flying bits of gravel and snow obscured Dana's view of the taillights ahead of them. Cord was doing a banner job of keeping them in the lead. He had told her he was a good driver. She prayed that he hadn't been exaggerating.

"Taylor, please slow down!"

"Shut the fuck up," he said, without even looking at her. With only one hand on the wheel, he took a long slug of his beer, tossed the empty in the backseat, and flipped on the radio. He looked over at her now with a wild grin. "Yahoo!" he yelled.

Seatbelts! Dana tried to reach over Taylor and grab his seatbelt, but he pushed her back into her seat.

"Jesus Christ, Taylor," she cried. "You're gonna die if you don't put your seatbelt on!"

"Only if we wreck, baby! Only if we wreck."

"And we're going to if you keep going like this. You're drunk!"

"I drive better when I'm drunk," he laughed crazily.

Unable to change his mind, she grabbed her own seatbelt and struggled to get it clasped as they rounded another corner and crested a hill, still tight on Cord's tail. Dana had rarely been on this road, so she had no idea where the turns were. The blowing snow made it seem like they were flying even faster than they were.

Up ahead, she could just make out the lights of a house. She hadn't known anyone lived out here at the old Miller place anymore. She sat up higher in her seat, praying that Cord would stop there and make a stand. If there were people home, she and Janie would be safe and maybe, just maybe, they could talk some reason into Taylor. The house was close now. Light glowed in an upstairs window. She closed her eyes tight and willed Cord and Janie to pull over. She focused all her energy on Janie. They were twins after all, and though she'd hadn't tried it with Janie, she'd heard that some twins could connect like that.

Tell Cord to turn, Janie. Turn!

"What are you muttering?" Taylor barked, no longer laughing. He had leaned in close to the steering wheel and was whipping it back and forth, causing the car to fishtail. His baseball cap had been knocked out of place, and his face was alight with something wild.

Dana suddenly understood that he was oblivious to the danger he was placing them in.

"Nothing," she said shakily. She hadn't realized she was talking out loud. She opened her eyes and watched as Cord and Janie rounded the last corner and sped past the driveway.

"No!" she cried out.

"No what, bitch?"

Ignoring him, she swiped her hand across the side window to clear condensation caused by her panicked breathing. Just before the lights dropped out of sight, Dana spotted Liv's Jetta parked next to the Miller house.

J anie had been reluctant to go, but Cord had insisted they follow Taylor after they saw him spin out in front of their house
with Dana in the front seat.

"That boy is not *right*, Janie," Cord said, as they climbed into his
Chevelle. "After what happened with you in the treehouse, we have to
go after them."

John had offered to go as well, but in the end he and Mystery decided to stay with Bennie on the grounds that Cord and Janie would
only talk to Dana and try to convince her to come home.

As they entered the parking area of the football field, awed by the
swirling summer snow, Janie feared that this would be the worst place
for an encounter. The roads were slick and there was no one around to
help should things turn ugly with Dana and Taylor.

Cord pulled in slowly behind Taylor's car, the Chevelle skidding
slightly as it came to a stop.

"This is insane, Cord."

She was referring to both the weather and the fact that they were
about to get out and confront the two angriest people Janie knew, but
before either of them could decide how best to handle this, Taylor
backed up sharply, practically running into Cord's car.

"What in the hell?" Cord yelled, jamming the Chevelle into reverse. His tires spun as he flipped around. Suddenly Taylor was right behind them bumper to bumper and Cord was forced back out onto the road.

"Holy crap, Janie," he said breathlessly. "This guy is really nuts."

Janie gripped the side of the vinyl seat with her hand and held tight as Cord turned onto Sheep Creek Road.

"What are you doing?" she cried. "Where are you going?"

"I know this road better than he does, Janie." His voice was steady again, in control. "I can lose him out here."

The snowflakes became thick and heavy in the headlight beams as they rushed toward Cord and Janie. The orange sherbet-colored road that Janie had liked so much the last time they were out here was now completely white. Janie swore there was an inch of snow already accumulated on the road, but at the speed they were going it was hard to judge correctly.

This craziness was spinning out of control: Dana storming out, the weird snowstorm, and now Taylor following them like a maniac. Just hours earlier, she and Cord had been laughing with Bennie as they excitedly packed her things, and now it seemed like it might all come to a horrible end. She craned her neck around the inside edge of the headrest and watched the Mustang sling back and forth on the road behind them. Taylor didn't know this road, she was sure of it. She couldn't think of any reason he'd have come out here on this stretch of winding gravel road. Most people in Glendale took the paved roads to Kennedy or anywhere else.

"Cord, they're gaining on us!" she cried. "Why are they following us like this? It's crazy!"

She knew why; she just didn't want to believe it. Dana's long-ago warning about Taylor flashed in her mind. *He's dangerous, Janie.* But despite the horrid scene in the treehouse, part of her had been unable to accept that her childhood friend wanted to hurt her, really *hurt* her. Until now.

Cord reached over and squeezed her shoulder, gently urging her back around in her seat. He yanked hard on her seatbelt to make sure it was secured, all the while keeping his eyes on the road ahead and in the rearview mirror. With steady hands and controlled motions, he swerved back and forth to keep Taylor from passing.

Janie eyed Cord in amazement. He looked so calm.

Just then, a memory of Taylor's angry face in the treehouse flashed before her. He'd had that look in his eyes again, the one that said, *You are mine, Janie Abbott, and there isn't anything you or anyone else can do about it.*

She'd let her own fears overcome her worry about Dana.

"I'm scared, Cord. I —"

"Janie," he interrupted calmly, "I'm a good driver and I know these roads better than anyone, but that guy back there is not safe. The faster we go to outrun him, the more danger he and Dana will be in. Wet Idaho roads are no place for drunk Washington drivers, or any other drivers for that matter."

In the dim light she could see the muscles in his cheek flexing as he spoke the last words. "I'm sorry," she said. "I forgot about your father. Was it on this road?"

"Yeah," he nodded, "just the other side of the ranch. You haven't been there because I don't go that way. He was rounding the last corner before our turn when someone came straight at him. They both had been drinking, and there's a drop-off on the other side of the road. There's a little guardrail but not much else to hold them back. Neither of them had a chance."

Cord's words were spoken with quiet fortitude and no self-pity. He knew this road like no other could or should.

Janie looked back at the headlights swerving behind them, way too close for comfort. "Can you lose them?"

"I think so. We'll go to the ranch and then turn around. Just please stay facing forward in your seat. I want to keep you safe from my flying elbows," he teased with a sideways glance.

He was right; she knew that. And, she knew she could trust him to keep her safe. There wasn't a soul alive who could hurt her when she was with him. She sat back in the seat and held tight to that comforting thought.

"How much longer?'

"Ten minutes or so," he said. "I don't want to scare you, but when I get within a few miles of the ranch, I'm going to go faster to lose him. That's the only chance we have at the moment. It would be dangerous to stop and deal with him in the middle of this road."

"No, please, I don't want you to do that. Don't stop out here. I'm so scared, Cord."

"Me too, Janie. Me too."

A few miles later Cord began to speed up. Janie started to turn around and Cord gently reminded her to stay put. She felt the rear end of the Chevelle begin to squirm. She peeked over at the speedometer. Fifty miles per hour and climbing. In the side mirror she could see that Taylor was heading at them in a straight line now, perhaps trying to compensate for the lost distance. In the Mustang's shadowy interior, she could just make out Dana's head bobbing from side to side. She wondered if she was laughing with excitement or simply hanging on for dear life. Taylor was dead center in the road.

"He has a new Mustang. I think he's gaining on us," Janie worried.

"And we have a Chevelle," said Cord, slapping the dashboard. "It's older, but it's heavier and safer in the snow."

They rounded what Cord said was the last turn. With the wind there was a bit of a snowdrift in the road. Janie just could not believe that this was happening in the summertime, but she felt the car lift and glide over the top of it.

"Holy cow," Cord said as they came down on the other side. "I have never seen anything like this." Janie waited out the tense minutes by counting her heartbeats. Finally, she saw the reflectors of a driveway. "Is that it?"

"Yep," he said. Disregarding his previous warning, she grabbed the back of the vinyl seat and pulled herself around to watch. He didn't stop her this time.

"Tell me if you see them," he said.

"Won't they see our tire tracks?"

"I hope not," Cord said. "Like you said, he's probably drunk, it's dark, and he's in a hurry. And he doesn't know this road like I do. But if he does see the tracks, I will finally have my chance to deal with him. Be ready to hop out and open the gate, okay?"

With that, he killed the headlights and turned sharply to the left. The whole back end slid out from behind them and Janie was certain that they were going to flip a full circle and end up aimed right at the other car. When they came to a stop, Janie fumbled with the latch of her seatbelt before jumping out to open the gate. The wind had picked up and the snow was driving fiercely to the west. Her hands were freezing as she popped the gate free and swung it open, pushing a small mound of snow out of the drive. There had to be at least two inches on the ground up here already. Cord sped through the opening and cut the engine as Janie reattached the gate. He hopped out and stood with her in the deep brush just as Taylor's lights came into view.

"His tires are spinning now," Cord said, listening intently. "He'll stop and then he'll be stuck. That would be the best thing for them."

"And then?"

"Then we get back in the car, drive past them, and wave." He cocked a grin and added, "A good walk in the cold should sober them both up."

Janie smiled too. That was what she liked about Cord. He wasn't afraid of anything, but he wasn't mean about it, and his confidence gave her strength. As the car sped past, Janie and Cord instinctively crouched down in the tall brush.

"Where will they go?" Janie's teeth were chattering from both cold and fear.

"The road goes into a town in about thirty miles," he said. "But I'm guessing he'll turn around before that."

"Let's get back in the car. I'm freezing," she said, slipping her hand into his and leading the way.

Cord followed her to help her in. As he was just about to close the door, he stopped and looked past the car to the road, an odd expression on his face.

"What is it?" she asked.

"Oh, no..."

"Cord, what—" Before she could finish her sentence she heard it. At first, it sounded like a bear lumbering through the brush, limbs breaking, branches thrashing about. It got louder and louder, until it sounded like a freight train speeding down the hill just beyond them. Janie clutched at Cord's arm and pleaded for him to get in, but he didn't move. He stood stock-still, facing toward the noise. Unnerved by his lack of response, Janie followed the line of his gaze. The echoing sound of trees cracking and glass shattering allayed any fear she had about a bear, but a new horror took its place.

"The bank..." he whispered, as if to himself. Then, more forcefully,

"Get in. Hurry." He pushed her arm back inside the car, slammed the door, and quickly rounded the front end to slide in on his side. He skidded backward out of the drive but drove slowly once they turned onto the road, watching for the inevitable break in the brush and trees. Janie rolled down the window to listen, but the engine noise drowned out all other sounds. She stuck her head out and was met by an onslaught of snowflakes.

They turned the last corner and came to an abrupt stop as the trees parted and gave way to a bare area with a deep expanse of wood just beyond. The snow had let up, just a few flakes falling now, and moonlight filtered through passing clouds. On any other night, Janie would have found this the most romantic spot.

Cord stepped out and jogged to the edge of the road. It was silent now. The flimsy metal guardrail that had once spanned the ravine rim had been severed and splayed wide open. His hand went up to his mouth and then through his hair. Janie was trembling all over as she got out and joined him at the edge. About fifty feet down, caught precariously between the trunks of two pine trees, Taylor's car had come to a stop. Exhaust churned from the tailpipe, flashers blinked wildly, and the rear tires still spun as if trying to find the road.

"Oh my god," Janie cried, clutching at his sleeve, "we have to help them!"

Cord ran back to the Chevelle and grabbed a rope out of the trunk. After tying one end of it to what was left of the guardrail, he said, "It's not steep, but it's a long way down, and it's going to be very slick. Janie, you need to go get help."

"No," she said, wringing her hands, "I'm not leaving you."

"Janie, I can't pull them out by myself. You need to go get —"

Just then, the screaming began. "Oh god, Taylor! Help! Somebody help!"

Cord and Janie wheeled around and strained to see into the wreckage beneath them.

"Taylor! Wake up, Taylor!"

"Dana!" Janie yelled. "Dana, we're here!"

"Help! Janie, please don't leave us," Dana yelled, then "Taylor, no...oh pleasepleaseplease..."

Janie tried to clamber over the guardrail, frantic to get to Dana, but Cord grabbed her arm and held her back. "Cord, it's Dana! I've got to—"

"I know," he said. Janie tried again to move toward her sister, but Cord held firm and looked her square in the eye. "Janie, I'll get her. I promise. Just go get help. You can't get her out of there, but I might be able to."

"Not with Taylor down there!" she protested. "He'll kill you."

"Damn it, Janie," he said through gritted teeth, "he's not going to kill me. Just do what I told you to do, or they both might die!"

Cord's eyes reflected the moonlight, and Janie could see the conviction in them. She slumped against him for just a second before pulling away. He was right. Dana was still screaming hysterically for Taylor to wake up, and she knew Cord had to go down to them. He wrapped the rope around himself, knotted it securely, and began to make his way down the embankment.

"Janie," he paused and looked up to her, his voice softening. "I love you. Please be careful."

She calmed a bit with his words, but the thought of getting behind the wheel and leaving all three of them turned her inside out. How would she explain this to her mom? To Bennie? What if Dana died while she was gone? What if Taylor was already dead?

"Janie," he said again. "I love you, honey. Now *go*."

"Okay...I love you too," she murmured, as he disappeared into the moonlit ravine.

The snow was already melting as she backtracked toward Glendale. Between her trembling and the slick roads, she could barely go twenty miles per hour. Their tire marks were still visible on the curves and corners, weaving in and out of the unmarked lanes with every twist and turn.

"We should have stopped..." she whispered brokenly.

The moon shone brightly now, and up ahead she caught a glimpse of a blue roofline. She thought it must be the Miller house. A glow of light came through the trees as she got closer, but she assumed it was just a security light, since she knew the house was unoccupied. She had been so preoccupied by Taylor chasing them that she hadn't even noticed the house on their way out of town. She was about to speed past when she spied Liv Randall's red Jetta parked out back.

"Liv!" she said in relief, "Liv is here."

Janie wondered why Taylor's mom would be out here. This house had been on the market forever. She slammed on the brakes and turned sharply to the left, bouncing over snow-covered bumps until she practically rammed into Liv's car. As she got out of the car, she realized that the snow had stopped. She raced toward the back door and took the stairs two at a time, kicking snow off their slick surfaces as she went.

"Liv!" she hollered, teeth chattering audibly as she pounded on the back door. "Liv, it's Janie. Please open up."

She waited, breathing heavily. She tried to see in through the lace curtains of the frost-covered glass in the door. The yellow kitchen looked warm and brightly lit, as if the owner had just gotten up for a midnight snack. The dining room was in shadows just beyond. She didn't see Liv anywhere. She pounded again.

"Liv, for goodness' sake, I know you're in there. Please, open the door!"

Nothing. Janie leaned back and surveyed the second story of the house. Through the middle window, she made out a faint glow of light. She dashed down the steps, scooped up a handful of wet pebbles from the driveway, and hurled them at the window. They smacked the glass and fell back to the ground.

"Olivia Randall!"

Still nothing. Janie could hear the seconds ticking away in her brain. Cord must have made it to the car by now. He wouldn't be able to get them both out by himself. *Oh, Dana, please be all right.* As if she were still standing on the brink of the ravine, Dana's screams rang in her ears. She closed her eyes and said a fervent prayer, hoping that her twin would hear it in her heart. *It's okay, Dana, It's going to be okay. I swear to God if you survive, I'll never fight with you again. Never.*

She swallowed hard, knowing that was not a decision she alone could make, since she couldn't remember ever having picked a fight with her sister. Dana would have to make that choice, and then maybe, just maybe, they could find a way to be sisters.

Her swift prayer completed, she swung around, thinking she'd check Liv's car and then circle the house to try the other door. But before she reached the car, she stopped cold in her tracks. She brushed stray hairs from her eyes to try and get a better look, fear clouding her vision as much as the snow had earlier. She suddenly felt very, very alone.

"Liv, no..." she whispered in horror, stifling a scream with her hand, her face chalk-white. There, face down in the pond, blond hair floating around her head and wearing a white satin gown that made her look like an angel, was what appeared to be the thin body of Olivia Randall.

chapter thirty-three

Mystery Abbott)

From the phone booth next to Glendale High School, Janie placed an urgent call at eleven thirty on Friday night, setting into motion a chain of events that would change lives forever. Minus quarters, Janie could only call 911 before choosing to drive back to the crash site instead of rushing home to inform her mother.

When the call came through, a few people knew about it within minutes—Dylan Masters, on-duty for the police department; Walt Smith and Frank Ingram, on-call for the Volunteer Fire Department; and Coral Smith, who had been up listening to Walt's home scanner, monitoring the landslide situation at the base of Cemetery Ridge. Just after Coral heard the emergency services call, and saw the police car spin around and shoot out the end of their road, she placed a reluctant call to Mystery Abbott.

Mystery dropped her cup as Coral's unfamiliar voice delivered the news. One possible fatality and two injuries. Something about the Miller Place, Sheep Creek Road, and that the call had come from Janie, so they knew that she was fine.

"Coral," Mystery pleaded. "Dana? What are they saying about Dana?"

"The radio isn't saying," she said carefully. "They don't even know who's involved yet. Dispatch didn't give names, only that the call came from Janie Abbott and that they were out on Sheep Creek Road. I'm sorry to call you like this. I know it's not my place. I just thought you should know."

Mystery sighed heavily, torn between closing the line on the only source of information that she had, and rushing out Sheep Creek Road to witness God knew what. John had joined her at the phone midway between the living room and the kitchen, watching her reactions intently as he scooped up the fragments of yet another broken cup. She closed her eyes as if to shut out the fear, whimpering softly as she fought to think clearly.

"Do you want me to go with you?" she heard Coral ask.

Mystery was taken aback. She had rarely spoken to Coral Smith since working for Walt, mostly because she knew that as Melinda's sister-in-law, Coral would be privy to information from Ma Bell. Assumed guilt by association. She now realized how wrong she had been. Mystery looked over at John, who was setting the cup pieces carefully in the sink as if Mystery might be able to mend it with glue. It would never be fixed. *This can't be fixed.*

"No," Mystery's voice caught as she answered, "but thank you so much for offering."

She hung up the phone, shaking her head against the anguish of what lay ahead and the fragmented thoughts of what she might have done to prevent it, but it was no use. *Shouldn't have forced Dana into accepting John... shouldn't have been so blunt about moving and the marriage... always listened to Janie instead —*

"Don't." She looked up at John, who was already getting their coats. He must have read the look on her face and put it all together from Mystery's end of the phone conversation.

"This is not your fault, Mystery. Dana is an adult, and she is probably fine. Call your mother to sit with Bennie, and we will go together."

"My mother? But —"

"Mystery, please call your mother." As if to reinforce the urgency of the situation, the noon siren, normally revered as a signal for the lunch hour, wailed a nighttime call to the townspeople that something bad was happening to one of their neighbors.

Peter and Maude Abbott were at the door within minutes, although it felt like a lifetime had passed since Mystery's shaky hand set down the phone. Maude looked small and scared without the bevy of onlookers that been there the other night. As Maude sat next to Bennie, she looked up at Mystery with a weak smile before adjusting the afghan around Bennie's little shoulders. It was the first time Mystery had seen contrition in her mother's eyes, and she was struck anew by the truth of her thoughts after her roof had caved in: *Sometimes it takes a disaster to make a person care for the things they normally take for granted.*

As Mystery and John neared the Miller place, Dylan flagged them down at the driveway. Beyond the cop car blocking access to the property, Mystery saw Liv's Jetta, Carl's car, and an unidentified van parked in a semicircle around what she recalled to be a pond out back. By the van was a stretcher on which was something long and black. *Oh my god, it's a body bag.* Mystery pressed a hand to her trembling lips. It was Liv.

In any other jurisdiction Dylan probably would have been fired for releasing that information to non-family members, but something in his hollow eyes and the way he grasped her hand when she rolled down the passenger window told Mystery that he was either a very compassionate policeman or there was something of a personal stake in this.

"This appears to be a suicide, Ms. Abbott, but the car wreck is just over the border in Idaho. Not far, but I'm sorry I can't be there for your family." He looked back to the scene, lit only by the repeated strobe on his police car and the car lights below. Carl Randall had either sat down or fallen by the edge of the pond.

"I have to go," he said sadly. "As far as I know, Dana is okay."

As if an afterthought, he added, "I really hope she is, Ms. Abbott. Please tell her that when you see her."

Mystery nodded her head. *Please tell her that when you see her.* She hadn't realized Officer Masters knew Dana that well. She rode in stark silence as John drove the rest of the way up the long and winding road, her hands clasped rigidly in her lap, worrying about what she would find up ahead and reliving her last visit with Liv in her kitchen. *She gave Dana her clothes. She said that she was leaving for good.* Maybe Mystery should have listened more, but she couldn't. Or she wouldn't. Liv had worked for years to scratch away at Mystery's life, then tried so hard to make amends yesterday, but sometimes the wounds of abuse need time to really heal.

By the time they reached the scene of the accident, the Idaho State Sheriff's Department had blocked off the road. There was an ambulance snugged as far up to the guardrail as possible, its lights dark; only those of the squad car flashed their warning. The lack of paramedics bustling about in the scene scared Mystery, and she reached over to squeeze John's hand as their car came to a stop. She could see Cord giving a verbal report to the cop. He was looking toward the torn guardrail, his arms crossed around him, now pointing, then wiping his eyes. Mystery jumped out of the car before John could even get around to her side. She counted her paces until she got to Cord. When he saw her, he fell into her arms as if the sight of a friend had broken through the control he'd been struggling to maintain.

"Oh god," was all she could say before words failed her.

As if sensing her fear, Cord pulled back. It wasn't Dana. It was Taylor. Dana had been taken to the hospital. She had minor cuts, a possible broken arm, a gash on her forehead from hitting the dash, and she was scared as hell, but otherwise she would be fine. Janie accompanied her to the hospital.

"They were holding hands, Ms. Abbott," Cord said, choking back tears. "Dana and Janie were holding hands."

* * *

The next day, after bringing Dana home from the hospital, Mystery drank a strong cup of coffee on her porch as Bennie played unawares with his Tonka trucks at the far end. She tried to focus on her son, but her attention kept wandering to the Randall house. Cars were flooding in and out as Ma Bell mobilized to support Liv's husband. By nine o'clock that morning Mystery had seen them haul in two casserole dishes, numerous tins of what she assumed to be cookies, three salads, a vegetable tray, and more than a few Crockpots of food. Mystery wanted to go over, but she felt it would be too much. After all, her daughter had lived. What could she say to Carl?

Melinda and Jane had each placed a call to Mystery's house by ten o'clock to see if Dana had arrived home and to advise that they would be starting a fund on Monday at the bank to assist with any expenses that might come up as a result of her injuries, and that if there was anything else the Abbott family needed, to please let them know.

Not long after all the women had taken up residency in their deceased friend's house, Mystery saw Carl slowly walking over to her house with an envelope in hand. It was for Bennie, and Carl, in his confusion, had inadvertently opened it. Liv had left everything in her personal bank account to her nephew. As Carl watched Bennie play innocently with his trucks, he quietly said that he hadn't known Bennie was Patrick's child, but that looking at him more closely, he could now see the resemblance.

"Liv thought I was having an affair with Coral Smith," he said tonelessly. He looked dejected, his shoulders drooping and his hands in his pockets. His bloodshot eyes and the dark circles beneath them bore testament to his grief. "I didn't know that either. If only she would have said something, I would have told her that it wasn't true. I was just helping Coral with her divorce, and she didn't want the women in that stupid gossip chain finding out about it."

He shuddered with a deep breath, as if even remembering to breathe was a chore. Over Carl's shoulder, Mystery saw John come to the screen door then politely retreat into the shadows as she stood to hug Carl. Five days ago she couldn't have imagined herself standing on her front porch hugging Liv's husband for all to see, but now she understood that it didn't matter what other people thought. What mattered was how you treated your neighbor — *regardless* of what others thought.

"I hope Dana's okay," he said, his words dissolving into sobs as he dropped his head onto her shoulder.

Mystery choked on her words, salty tears burning her eyes.

"Oh, Carl," she said. "I'm so sorry. So sorry about Liv and Taylor."

He nodded and clung tighter to Mystery.

"You have always been a good neighbor," he said, pulling back and bravely looking her in the eyes. "I'm sorry we weren't better to you in return." He hugged her again and turned to leave. In the Randalls' window, Mystery could see the women of Ma Bell watching her and awaiting Carl's return.

Three days later, the sun shone steadily for the first time in months, and seasonable temperatures were forecast for the remainder of the summer. On Cemetery Ridge, high above the town, city employees erected orange caution fencing around the broken cliff's edge in preparation for the whole of Glendale to converge upon the saturated ground.

In the middle of the cemetery, two oak coffins sat side by side, perched temporarily above the earth. It was the closest that Olivia and Taylor Randall had been in years.

* * *

One Year Later

As Mystery Spencer placed the red rose on Liv Randall's grave, she shivered at the thought that the sod now covered the ground so evenly, so completely, that it appeared as if the grave had been there for a decade.

Janie had called her the day before and asked to meet her in the cemetery. She wanted to meet there every year, she said.

Carl had moved away a few months after Liv and Taylor died. The women of Ma Bell tried everything they could to keep him in Glendale, but to no avail. They even tried to set him up with Coral Smith like they thought he truly wanted, but it didn't work. Mystery didn't know where he ended up. Janie told her that with Carl now gone, it was up to them to honor their deceased neighbors. With every passing day, Mystery's children made her prouder of being their mother.

Mystery had called Dana to join them, but she was in summer

session at the University of Washington and could not get away. After the car wreck, something serious took hold of Dana, and by that fall she was enrolled in a school as far away from Glendale as she could get. She was majoring in hotel/restaurant management, and Mystery knew she would be great. She suspected that, like Carl Randall, Dana would not return to Glendale to live.

Out of the corner of her eye, Mystery caught sight of her mother walking alone up the road to Cemetery Ridge, moving toward them with a bouquet of flowers in hand. When Maude reached the graves, she stood silently next to Mystery and Janie. Maude hadn't actually said she was sorry for everything she had done to hurt her daughter, but over time, Mystery had begun to forgive her anyway. Forgiveness, Mystery decided, was another one of her long unrecognized strong suits, and something she was determined to be proud of. Mystery didn't know if Janie had called her grandmother or if Maude had come on her own, but they both waited respectfully as Maude pulled two white narcissus flowers from the bouquet, knelt, and placed them on the graves. Then she stood, hugged Mystery, and handed the remainder of the flowers to her. For Mystery, that was apology enough.

the end

photograph by Greg Hahner

About the Author

Amy Warwick lives on the beautiful rolling hills of the Palouse with her husband Waverly and their five children. She is currently at work on her next novel. For more information on Amy's writing, please visit amywarwick.com.

Printed in the United States
217307BV00002B/2/P

9 780615 268934